Divine Legacy Series, Book 4:

Chains Broken

C.J. Peterson

Texas Sisters Press, LLC

This book is dedicated to my loving husband and dear family who love and support me.

You all mean more to me than you will ever know.

Thank you! I love you!

This book, and series, is dedicated to my Dad, Gene Mann, who passed prior to this last book being published. He was a strong man of God, and left a tremendous divine legacy not only my generation, but also into the next generation as well. When he arrived in Heaven to our Lord and Savior, I have no doubt he heard the words we all long to hear,

"Well done, thy good and faithful servant."

A portion of the proceeds of this series will go to Airborne Angel Cadets of Texas – a non-profit group of hardworking volunteers who send care packages to our soldiers overseas. You can find them at: http://www.airborneangelcadets.com

To learn more about C.J. Peterson, you can find her online at:

http://cjpetersonwrites.com/

'While the stories are fiction, the journey is real!'

<u>Summary</u>

The final book in the Divine Legacy Series, **Chains Broken**, follows the A.N.G.E.L.s as they continue on their journey. There will be a wedding, Christmas, and New Year's celebrations, which should bring about a fresh start…but will it?

Kit's battle is coming to a head. Can she overcome what is trying to lay hold, or will she succumb like her mother? Have the issues of anger been worked out within the team? Who will win the battle for the Outback? What about the other box? Do the A.N.G.E.L.s have a lead on it?

These questions and more will be answered as this exciting series wraps up. Chains will be broken, and hearts and lives will be connected in *Chains Broken*. (Book 4 of the *Divine Legacy Series*.)

1 Peter 5:8 *"Be alert and of sober mind. Your enemy the devil prowls around like a roaring lion looking for someone to devour."*

John 8:32 *"Then you will know the truth, and the truth will set you free."*

Table of Contents

Prologue
Chained Hearts

"Okay, love, we need to go. Caleb, Pete, and Leah are at the truck," Nico said, leaning down, kissing Kit on the top of her head. Kit was still in their bed at Serenity Wells Station in Queensland, Australia.

"I know you need to go. I'm just exhausted. Please pass on my condolences to the others."

"I will," Nico said, sitting on the side of the bed. "Willow, Kendra, and the kids will be staying here while we're gone. I know they're loud, but I really want you to have people here."

She smiled weakly. "Thank you. I appreciate that."

Nico ran his hand over her hair. When he did, he came back with a handful of it. "What in the world?"

"I've been losing my hair lately," she confessed.

"Oh, Kit," he said, shaking his head. "I can't leave you like this."

"You have to. You need closure. Please do it for me."

"I don't –"

"Please," she said, taking his hand. "For me?"

"Fine," he said on a sigh. "It's against my better judgment."

"Nico, you are my one and only. I need you to do this. I can't be there, but you can. The kids may need you. You need this too. He was your friend."

"Right-oh." He relented. "Please eat while we're gone?"

"I will do my best."

"Willow will go with you to your appointments. Go easy on her, eh?"

She smiled."I will."

Leaning down, he kissed her lips. "I love you. Your name may be Kit, but you will always be my Katie."

"And, you will always be my Nick," Kit said with a wink.

When they said their former names, both had memories from their time in the United States flash through their minds.

"I'll hold onto those memories until I see you again," Kit promised.

"As will I," Nico said, and left for Reno.

*   *   *

After spending the night in the hotel in Alice Springs, Australia, the group boarded a plane, bringing Ethan, Charlie, and Kat with them for Danny's memorial service. As they exited the terminal in Reno, Nevada, Jon and Josh greeted everyone with a hug. As soon as they approached Angel, they gave her a light hug, but it was obvious by their reaction, they were less than thrilled to see her.

As the group waited for their luggage, Angel asked Josh and Jon to talk off to the side. "Look guys," Angel started, "it doesn't take Jon's gift to know that you are both furious with me."

"We're not the only one," Jon mentioned, crossing his arms. "What you did caused major loss, serious, permanent damage, and a lot of injuries and stress."

"Trust me. I know," Angel said, not fighting it. "God and I have wrestled about this for weeks. The archangel and I have gone rounds over the last few weeks about what went on. While I can't change the past, I *can* change the future. I'm sorry for causing so much damage and devastation. I know I have a *lot* of apologizing to do when we arrive at the Haven."

"You really have no idea." Josh shook his head. "While we would never leave you behind, you did that to us by taking off without us."

"The main emotions flying around are: anger, resentment, fury, frustration, depression, betrayal, anxiety, and worry," Jon said. "You have some major apologizing to do. This won't blow over anytime soon."

"This is a burden I must bear on my own. God and I are fine. While I can't make things right with everyone, I *can* prove that I've changed."

"Well, you'll have to bear your soul before we even attempt to bridge that," Josh pointed out.

Angel asked, "What do you mean?"

"You *are* going to speak at Danny's funeral tomorrow. You will have to face all the A.N.G.E.L.s currently at the Haven as you do so. You will have your first chance to show remorse tomorrow morning at eleven," Josh explained, crossing his arms as well. "And every person there had better feel it. Danny gave his life, and Derek is now in a wheelchair because of your actions." Getting in her face, he quietly but sternly said, "You *will* understand just how much damage you have inflicted. Every time you look at Derek, I want you to remember that *you* caused his injuries."

"Liliya could have been taken by Cassius without me jumping in!" Angel defended herself.

When she went to take a step back, she ran into Jon. "You will *not* run from *this* one."

"What do you mean I can't run from this?" Angel demanded.

"Growing up, you ran while Jesse and I cleaned up your messes," Jon said. "You caused major damage to the new teams. The remaining team members have been at the Haven for weeks. They have not missed any of the stories floating around."

"What do you mean?" she asked, pale.

"They know," Josh simply said.

"Really?"

"Did you *honestly* think this would be kept quiet?" Josh shook his head, frustrated. "You basically caused an international incident – A.N.G.E.L. style."

*   *   *

As a couple older A.N.G.E.L.s from Ireland and Scotland played *Amazing Grace* on the bagpipes, Josh stood next to the table, and Ethan, Kat, Charlie, Nico, Caleb, and Leah walked over and picked up the flag. As they properly folded it, and the song continued, the rest of the A.N.G.E.L.s stood at attention and saluted. Once they finished folding the flag, the six folding, stood at attention as well, with Charlie holding the flag until the last note was played.

Once finished, the group stood at ease. Charlie then went to hand the flag to Josh, but he shook his head no. When Charlie insisted, with both of them holding it, Josh explained, "He was your best friend. This flag belongs to you. You were with him when he went home. You held him in your arms as he passed from this world to be with the Lord. The honor of keeping this flag goes to you. We all agree that you will hold it in the same honor and high regard that you held Danny. It would be *our* honor if you would accept this flag on behalf of all the A.N.G.E.L.s." Letting the flag go, leaving it in Charlie's arms, Josh's heart broke at seeing Charlie openly weeping as he hugged the flag to his chest. Hugging Charlie, through his own tears, Josh said, "He was a good, Godly man, and a brother. A man we were all proud to know."

"Thank you," Charlie whispered, before returning to the others, who had already rejoined the group once the song completed.

Josh wiped the tears before he spoke, addressing the crowd. He started by quoting Revelation 21:4, "'*And God shall wipe away all tears from their eyes, and there shall be no more death, neither sorrow, nor crying, neither shall there be any more pain: for the former things are passed away.*' While Danny Hawk was a legend among the A.N.G.E.L.s, he was my friend, my mentor, and like a member of the family to us. Along with the other Australian A.N.G.E.L.s, he trained my siblings and me since we were little. We also recently lost the Colonel. Now, the pair are watching us, cheering us on together until we can see them again in Heaven. They have joined the other Saints to encourage us daily. What else is there to say about Danny Hawk that hasn't already been said? He cared about people. He cared about their hearts and souls. As the leader of the Australian A.N.G.E.L.s, this brought about a deeper responsibility not only to those on the missions he was on, but also on those who served under him as well. He led with courage and wisdom. He and the Colonel were given many assignments over the years, but none was as important as the one to find the A.N.G.E.L.s of this world, and get the teams started again. They did this with discernment, clear thinking, and by being continuously focusing on God. They had the foresight not only to get the teams going in their generation, but also to begin to train the next generation as well. This was their time, and they used it to the best of their ability for the Lord. It's now our time, and our opportunity to carry on the legacy granted to us by these beloved men. Danny never let an opportunity pass to share some sort of insight or pearl of wisdom as he trained us. Some of his lessons were painful," Josh said, rubbing his chin as he remembered his first challenger/aggressor game. "Some of his lessons saved me from future pain and misery. *All* of his lessons, though, were practical and sound. What I'm trying to say," Josh said, hoping they understood his heart, "is despite the moments in time where we don't get along, we are all united with God as the center. He is our main focus, and Danny, as well as the Colonel, believed that. I believe that, as do all of you here. Whether we're connected personally, or in the Spirit, the Lord binds us. As an A.N.G.E.L., and a brother and sister in Christ, we are never alone in this world. When the older generation passed the legacy on to us, I'm sure they were terrified," he said, and some of the older A.N.G.E.L.s snickered. "Trusting such an important mission to rookies must have been their worst nightmare, but they trusted in the Lord's timing. While they didn't pass it onto us lightly, they *did* do it with confidence in the faith we have in the Lord our God and one another. We are all joined together with one purpose. Let's prove to them, and to God, that they made the right decision. Let's join together, hearts united, to continue the divine legacy that was passed down to us."

16

Chapter 1
Chains That Bind

Deep in the heart of the Outback, an Aboriginal, Daku, was gathering herbs for the village. He looked up to see someone walking in the distance. Cocking his head to the side, he waited for the figure to come closer. Wide-eyed, he suddenly realized it was Pastor Allen. Dropping the herbs, he ran up to him and threw his arms around him in a hug. "Pastor Allen! I'm so grateful you are okay! Angel said you were lost."

"Oh no." Allen chuckled. "As you can see, I'm perfectly fine."

"Come. We must show you to Chief and the elders," Daku said, dragging him by his hand to the village, excitedly talking a mile a minute.

When they arrived, the clan greeted them with the same confusion Daku experienced. Chief pulled him into his house to speak with him, along with two other elders and Daku. The entire conversation was in Aboriginal, as Chief said, "I do not understand. Please tell us what happened to you? Angel –"

"I am aware what Angel said," Allen snapped. Seeing the stunned look on their faces, Allen breathed out a slow breath to compose himself. Calmer, he continued, "Angel's a sad, misguided young lady. She has some mental issues that she needs to sort out."

"She is one of the A.N.G.E.L.s," Daku said. "The Lord would not have placed her on the team if she was unstable."

Allen huffed. "There's a reason why she was demoted."

"Pastor Allen," Chief started as his countenance shifted, realizing something was not right, "You expect us to believe you over Angel? While I love you, and am grateful for all you have done for our clan, I am having difficulty accepting what Angel said to be false. Both Angel *and* the archangel stated you were lost. They said you did the unforgivable sin. How do we know for sure what you are telling us is the truth?"

Allen's eyes flashed pure black before returning to his natural brown. When it happened, everyone in the room looked at him stunned for a moment. Taking a step back, they were all immediately on high alert.

"You are to leave…*now*," Chief said sharply, resting his hand on his knife, as the other elders pulled theirs from their sheaths. Chief hoped the show of force would make it so he would not have to use his knife. He did not relish the idea of taking a life…even the life of someone from the other side. "You are not welcome here anymore."

"I will not leave. I will go where I please," Allen hissed. "I also *need* to be here. This is my assignment."

"What do you mean this is your assignment?" Daku asked.

Pulling a knife from the sheath on his hip, Allen quickly slashed the Chief's throat, down across his mid-torso, and then finished by slashing his stomach. Without another word, he ran from the house.

Everyone watched in horror as the Chief dropped to the ground. With his clothes coated in blood, the Chief fell to his side. He tried to speak, but it only came out as a gurgle. They knelt on the floor around him, so he knew he was not alone. There was absolutely nothing they could do, while they were forced to watch as he died right in front of them.

Running outside, Daku saw Allen in the distance running at full speed, out into the vast expanse of the Outback. Returning to the house, Daku asked, "What do we do now?"

"We get to Serenity Wells Station as quickly as possible," insisted one of the elders. "We must get our families there for the safety of all of us. The Sullivan's will take care of us and help us. They will help us get in contact with the A.N.G.E.L.s. I am afraid without them, we will not survive."

*   *   *

Together, the A.N.G.E.L.s had a time of food and fellowship in a celebration of life for Danny Hawk. They enjoyed a time of reminiscing of days past, along with stories of Danny. Afterward, those who didn't live at the Haven returned to their hotels in Reno, Nevada for the night. Most would be taking off in the morning for their respective countries. The remaining A.N.G.E.L.s would take off later the next night or the following morning.

In the meantime, the new A.N.G.E.L.s, along with the current and retired who lived at the Haven, gathered in the living room at around ten that night.

Jesse walked in just as the meeting started. He needed to finish painting Danny Hawk's name on the boulder before he could join them. When he came in, he sat down next to Jacob, and looked up at Jon, Josh, and Rachel, who were in the front of the room. "Did I miss anything?" Jesse whispered as he tucked his bag of paints under his seat in the back row.

"No. They just started," Jacob whispered back.

"First of all, I would like to say welcome to those who are new. Thank you for joining us," Rachel started. Her Australian accent was still thick, especially since they returned from Australia recently. "I'm sorry you found us the way you did. Losing an A.N.G.E.L. is not an easy thing, but losing a founding one makes it that much more difficult. In speaking with all of you, I have a good idea of what areas we need to work on. I am grateful that each of you has a firm foundational training. We need to sharpen your skills. We also need to set up the cyber cave for the new recruits, along with an area for those who will work on documents. And, we need to meet as separate teams to get to know one another better."

Taking a deep breath, Rachel slowly let it out before she started again. "Guys," she said, sitting on a stool, "these last few months have been both a disaster and a success." When people started to object, Rachel held up her hand to quiet them. She continued once they settled, "Yes, things went disastrously wrong, but we came together and used all of our gifts collectively to get everything sorted. I'm proud of the way we came together. God handpicked each of us before we were even a thought. I am excited to see where He takes us from here. In the meantime, Josh, Jesse, and I will be heading back to Australia for my sister's wedding. We are excited to have some precious time with our family, as well as celebrating Chrissie and the wedding."

Hanif Nassor, a new recruit from Egypt, raised his hand. When Rachel nodded toward him, Hanif asked, "Chrissie?"

"Christmas," Rachel corrected. Hanif just nodded in understanding, so Rachel went on, "Now, while we're gone, Jon will be the one in charge. When we return, I expect us to be fully up and running, and training to be in progress. There are people who need us. We need to be ready as soon as we get word from God, the archangel, or from one of those whose gift is visions or dreams." Taking another moment, she said, "I feel the need to warn you to work fast but accurately. Accuracy is more important than speed. Your speed will increase with time. There is a storm brewing, and I think it will happen sooner than later. There are forces at work that are about to collide, and I'm afraid it's going to form a perfect storm."

"What do you mean?" Josh, Rachel's brother, asked, surprised by the revelation. This was not among the points they discussed prior to the meeting.

"Y'all need to hang on," Joe explained, his southern drawl in full swing. "I warned Rachel just before we started that things are fixin' to go even more south than they went this last time."

"What is this go south?" Katia asked. While her Russian accent was heavy, her English improved daily. Still struggling with the slang from time to time, she had to ask for clarification. "What does this mean? Go south to where?"

Rachel explained, "It means that things are about to go really bad, so we need to hang on. Remember, when the storm hits to keep your eyes on the Lord. He *will* pull us through. When we're not sure where to turn, keep looking up. God *will* protect our hearts and souls."

"Is this a spiritual battle or a literal one?" asked Isaac Braham, one of the new A.N.G.E.L.s from Jordan.

Rachel regrettably said, "Both."

*   *   *

As Nico, Leah, and Caleb entered Serenity Wells Station, near Queensland, Australia, all of the station hands warmly greeted them. They were happy to have them back from Danny's memorial service in the States.

"When are the others coming?" Kit asked, hugging Nico.

"Hopefully tomorrow or the next day," he said, moving slower, and with less energy than normal. This trip weighed heavily on his soul. "We got the earliest flight available, so I could get back to you. How are ya doin', Darlin'?"

"Had better days, but I've had worse as well." Giving him another hug, she said, "I'm just grateful you're home."

"Me too. So, what did I miss?" He looped his arm around her waist as they made their way through the crowd to the main house.

"My chemo appointment went as well as to be expected," Kit said.

They walked into the living room and sat down on the couch, just as the phone rang in the kitchen. Willow, who was finishing the preparations for dinner, called out, "I got it!"

After a brief moment, Willow ran into the living room, eyes wide, one of her hands clenching the phone as if it were a lifeline. "Where's Pete?"

Nico snapped to attention. "Why? What happened?"

"Daku is on the phone. Something bad happened."

"He's outside. Radio for him to get in here. I've got the phone," Nico ordered. Leaving Kit in the living room, he grabbed the phone from Willow on the way to the kitchen. Once out of earshot from Kit, Nico asked, "Daku, this is Nico Sullivan. What's going on, mate?"

"Sir, it is Pastor Allen."

"What *about* him?"

"I saw him in the bush and brought him back to the clan…to Chief."

"You did *what*?" Nico asked, wide-eyed. "He's not human anymore!"

"I figured that out after it was too late. He killed Chief before we could get him back out of the village. I am sorry!" Daku said, panic and fear evident in his voice. "I did not know!"

"Breathe," Nico said, as Pete ran into the kitchen with Willow. Nico put the phone on speaker for them to hear. "You had no idea Allen wasn't normal. Is everyone else okay?"

"We are all at a hotel in Alice Springs. We are many, but few. We could not stay in the village. They now know where the village is located. We feared for our safety."

"Stay there," Nico said. "When we get there, I'll take care of the bill an' bring all of you here. We'll have to double-up until we can figure this out."

"Thank you!" Daku said, relieved. "It is my fault. I should have known. They warned us that Pastor Allen was bad, but he seemed normal. And now –"

"It'll be okay. We'll be there as soon as possible. Just give me the information."

After getting the hotel information, Nico hung up.

"Why are they in a hotel in Alice?" Pete asked. "I only got that they were all there. Why did they abandon the village?"

"I'm sorry, but Chief is dead. Allen killed him."

Pale, Pete asked, "Allen? As in…" His voice faded as Nico nodded. Pete gulped. "That means they know where the clan is located."

"Yes. That's why they're coming here. I need you to grab six station hands you trust, and we'll each take a truck to get all of them." Giving him a quick hug, Nico said to Pete, "I'm really sorry, brother. We'll take care of them. They're family. I'm sorry you lost your father-in-law. I know you respected an' loved him."

"I need to tell Victoria," Pete said before a thought suddenly hit him. "We need to get ahold of Charlie. He's next in line for Chief. Victoria and Grace were Chief's older daughters, but Charlie is the Chief's only son." Wiping the few tears that escaped, he said, "I have some calling to do, but we need to get to them."

"You go tell Victoria, and I'll call Charlie. Grab the station hands you want to take. Make sure Jarrah and Barwon are among them. They're our strongest."

"Okay. Meet back here in ten?" Pete asked, checking his watch. When Nico nodded, Pete ran out the back door.

"They're all coming here?" Willow asked. "Where are we going to put them?"

"Clean out some of the stables. Put the horses in the paddock. It's not ideal, but the station hands and the men can sleep on cots in the barn until we can get this sorted. The women and children will go in the bunkhouse."

"Okay. I'll tell Caleb," she said, and left.

Nico picked up the phone and dialed the Haven.

*   *   *

Hearing the computer go off in the basement, Cori whispered to Kai that she would get it. She and Charm, her seeing-eye-dog, quietly headed to the basement. She left as Rachel excitedly talked about the upcoming celebrations in Australia with some of the group. Other conversations around the room were regarding training, places to go in the area, and the excitement of getting started.

"This is the Haven," Cori said into the microphone with her Irish accent.

"Cori, this is Nico. Is Charlie still there?"

"No. He's already at his hotel in Reno. He takes off early in the morning. Why? Is something wrong?"

"His father was murdered…by Allen."

"*What?*" Cori asked, stunned. "As in…"

"Yes."

"Is everyone else okay?"

"The entire clan has abandoned the village. They are all in Alice Springs. We're on our way to get them as soon as I'm off with you. Pete's telling his wife, the Chief's daughter, right now. This means Charlie is the new Chief."

"*And* it means the crew needs to get over there. I'll alert Rachel, Josh, and Jon. The meeting is just finishing up. What time is it there?"

"Three-thirty in the afternoon," Nico said looking at his watch.

"I'll let you know as soon as we get the reservations as to what time the rest of the team will be there. Hopefully we can work our magic and get everyone else on the same flight, or close enough that they land around the same time."

"Thanks, Cori," Nico said, and hung up.

As soon as Cori came back upstairs, Rachel noticed the look of concern on Cori's face. Everyone stopped talking, and looked up at Cori.

"We have a problem," Cori announced.

"No, no, no, no." Rachel shook her head. "My twin sister is getting married in a few days. Go on back to your cyber cave, jingle bells. I can't *not* be there. I promised."

"Double negative usage, there, little sister," Josh joked with her.

She huffed as she crossed her arms. "I don't care! I promised her that I would be there. It would not only ruin her wedding, but Christmas as well."

Cori sighed as she crossed her arms. "Oh, you'll be there all right."

"What do you mean?" Rachel asked, standing. "What happened? Is something wrong at the station?"

"Does anyone know how to get ahold of Charlie?" Cori asked.

"I can," Josh said. "I'll just call the hotel. Why?"

"That was Nico. Allen found the village and killed the Chief," she explained.

Gasps were heard throughout the room.

"Uh, that means Charlie's the new Chief," Josh said in understanding.

"The entire clan is in Alice Springs right now," Cori continued. "Nico and company are going to get them and take them back to the station."

"Where will they put them?" Casey asked, imagining what Kit must be thinking.

"Doesn't matter." Rachel shook her head. "Serenity Springs will find room. I reckon the other side thinks by taking out the Chief the village will go down. They didn't count on the fact that Charlie is one of the A.N.G.E.L.s. That means the village is now under the full protection of the A.N.G.EL.s. That also means we *all* need to go to Australia."

"Why?" Jon asked.

"Two reasons: first, as I stated, they are under our protection, and are in trouble; second, that paints a bigger target on our sister's wedding. Everyone will be in one place."

"How are we all going to get there? And where will we stay?" Angel asked. "They sound like they already have their hands full. Are you sure we should *all* go?"

"Both teams, minus the IT people will be going," Rachel insisted. "Everyone else stay here. If we need you, we'll call. Cori, Kai, can you guys do your thing while we pack?"

"Yes, ma'am," Cori said.

"Sure thing," Kai said, getting off the floor.

"While you're at it, shift mine, Josh's, and Jesse's tickets, so we're together."

"We'll see what we can do," Cori said. With that, they headed to the basement. As they did, the other IT people grabbed their computers and headed downstairs as well. Even if they weren't on the main computer, they could still help.

"Dad, Derek, Jerrod, we love you, but you need to stay here," Jon said to the guys in the front row.

"I'll stay too," Val said. "I'm still in a cast."

"Only for a few more weeks, my friend," Jesse said, resting his hand on Val's shoulder. "We know you'll be with us in spirit and in heart."

"Without a doubt," Val agreed.

"He needs to come with us," Rachel insisted.

"What? What do you mean?" Jon asked. "While he *is* on our team, he's compromised."

"He can hobble around on his crutches," Rachel explained. "He needs to be there in case we run into medical issues. He and Pete can work together to keep things going in case something catastrophic happens. He can also learn more about medicinal herbs from Pete. He doesn't have to be fully mobile to do that."

"This is true," Josh said, considering it. "What do ya say, Val?"

"Yeah. I'll go," Val agreed. "I'm staying on the station, though, right? While being downgraded to crutches makes me a bit more mobile, it doesn't give me full clearance, if you know what I mean."

"Yeah," Rachel said. "We don't want you anymore damaged than you are right now."

Val nodded, as he said, "Agreed."

"Go pack a bag, folks," Jon said, looking around the room. "Looks like we'll have to put training on hold. We have a job already."

"Yes, sir," was heard throughout the room as people dispersed.

When they were gone, Rachel turned to Josh, Jon, and Jesse, and said, "We're going to have to train while we're there. While the others set up the wedding, Jon, you need to pull our guys aside and find out *exactly* where they are in their levels of training. I have an idea of where they are by talking to them, but we can't plan if we're not one-hundred-percent certain."

"Consider it done," Jon agreed.

"Good. Let's go pack, guys. We've got three stations, along with an entire village to protect," Rachel said. "This means protecting Serenity Wells, along with Koala Pass Station and Akoonah Station. We have our work cut out for us."

Chapter 2
Bound By Chains

While she enjoyed the brief moments of being home, continuously flying from Australia to America and back again was getting old. Rachel felt like she spent more time on an airplane than she wanted to lately. While this was an important and already planned trip, she hoped this portion of the job would slow down at some point. Just when she thought they would get a moment to breathe, things would flip around and end up in disaster once again.

When they landed, three of the station hands, Adoni, Iluka, and Jarli, picked them up, separating them within the three trucks. "So glad you are home," Adoni said, as he drove the crew cab truck that had Rachel, Jesse, Isaac, Delaney, and Joe in it. "I have t' say, it is getting a bit crowded, though. Akoonah an' Koala Pass have adopted some of the crew in order to lessen the load."

"Where are we staying?" Rachel asked.

"Is that a trick question? Serenity is your home. You are all staying at Serenity Wells. That was never in doubt."

"Good. While I love everyone at the other two stations, if we're going to be here, I want to be home."

"Precisely! Now, there are some here who I do not know."

"Oh! So sorry!" Rachel apologized. "Adoni, you know Jesse and Joe, right?"

"Right. Welcome back, mates," he said, nodding toward Jesse, who was in the front with Rachel, and to Joe, who was in the backseat with Delaney and Isaac.

Jesse smiled. "Thanks!"

"Yeah. Thanks! Glad to be back. This is a beautiful country!" Joe added.

Adoni beamed in delight. "Appreciate that."

"This is Delaney. We picked her up in Ireland," Rachel continued. "She was with us last time we were here, when we went in and out via Alice Springs."

"Right," Adoni said in understanding.

"Pleasure to meet you," Delaney said, sticking her hand out from the back seat.

When Adoni shook her hand, Rachel added, with a grin, "She and Joe are together."

"*Together*...together?" Adoni asked, surprised.

"Yes, sir!" Joe grinned, with his arm around Delaney.

"Good onya, mate!" Adoni said, happy for him.

"Thank you."

"And, this is also one of our very new ones, Isaac. We got him from Jordan," Rachel introduced him.

"Glad to meet you," Isaac said, shaking Adoni's hand.

"Pleasure," Adoni said, nodding his greeting in response after shaking his hand, while focused on the road in front of him. "Now, when we get there, it *is* very crowded. The clansmen stay on the station during the day, and then separate between the three stations at night. They do that in order to keep the families together. The blokes didn't like sleeping separate from their women and children."

"Wise," Rachel commented.

"While they appreciated the idea of everyone on one station, they didn't like the idea of separating family members."

"When does Charlie get in?" Delaney asked. "I'll bet the villagers are anxious for him to get back."

"Jiemba is waiting for him, Val, an' Angel," Adoni explained. "They should be coming in a few hours."

"Good."

"Your people are good," Adoni said to Rachel. "I can't believe you almost got everyone on the same flight, or at least coming in around the same time."

"Part of that was weather, plane transfers, and I'm sure all of it was a God thing," Rachel said. "We left within an hour or so of each other. I'm kind of surprised Charlie, Angel, and Val's flight didn't come in at the same time."

"That's not a flight I would want to be on." Adoni shook his head. "Charlie's not too happy with Angel. And with his pop being murdered, I'm sure he's *real good* company right now."

"Yeah, not so much." Rachel shook her head. "Pretty sure Val's just trying to get through the flight. He wasn't happy with Angel either."

*   *   *

"Okay, seriously, we *have* to talk. I don't know when we'll get the chance to do it again…uninterrupted," Angel said to Val.

Charlie had long-since put on a headset to tune Angel out, and went to sleep…or at least pretended to until he fell asleep. Val tried, but Angel was in the middle seat, and kept bugging him. He envied Charlie, who had the window seat. With his leg in a cast, though, Val wanted the aisle seat so he could rest it in the aisle.

"I really don't want to talk to you," Val finally said, after she continuously bugged him for most of the flight.

"You need to talk to me. Josh and Jon said you might change teams. I wanted to talk to you to find out why?"

"Are you kidding me?" Val asked, jaw dropped. "With everything that happened, is that a serious question?"

"Talk to me," Angel pleaded.

Crossing his arms, Val snapped, "I'm not really sure you want me to."

"I do. I'm a big girl. I can take it."

"You certainly don't act like it!"

"Seriously. Please talk to me? Tell me what's going through your mind."

Val raised an eyebrow. "You *really* want to know?"

"Yes," she insisted.

Turning toward her, he said, "You betrayed everything that our team stands for when you took matters into your own hands. It was a selfish and prideful move. In doing so, you are responsible for the loss of Danny; for Derek being paralyzed; and for the myriad of other injuries that occurred in order to rescue your self-centered behind!"

Stunned, she gulped, but didn't say a word.

"You acted like a spoiled brat in Russia. You decided to put your own wants before the team. That is *not* what a leader does. Jon and Josh work together, making decisions for what is best for the team as a whole. And when we worked with Mark, Derek, and Nico, they always asked our opinions. We pray before every mission. We put the needs of the team ahead of any personal benefit. *That* is how a team of A.N.G.E.L.s are supposed to operate."

"I understand."

"No. I don't think you do. What you did hurt each one of us in ohhhhh so many ways!"

"I know. I also know we're heading into something that could go really bad, and I don't want any bad feelings still between us."

"I don't know that you can fix this that fast."

"Val, I'm really sorry for pulling such a stupid stunt. Trust me when I say that I paid for it dearly, and have learned from all of this. While I know there is nothing I can say or do to fix it, I want to let you know that I will do my best to put the team first in everything we do from now on. I don't want a rift between any of us. I know there are a lot of people angry with me, but I really don't want you to be among them. You have a tender heart, and I'm sorry I hurt you so deeply. If I can be so bold as to ask your forgiveness…" Val went to object, but Angel put her hand up to stop him before she continued, "If I can be so bold as to ask your forgiveness, *with* the understanding that while you may forgive me I know I will be on serious probation, I would appreciate it. I know I have a lot to prove, and I intend to do so."

Val studied her for a moment, while he rubbed his chin in thought. "Let me pray about it, and I'll let you know."

"I'll take it!" Angel said, pleased.

"In the meantime, we'll be landing in a few hours. I'm going to get some rest while I still can."

"Good idea," she said, putting her head back as well. While she was relieved to have the conversation, she knew it would be a long journey to earning the trust back of the entire team. She would have to take it one person, and one day, at a time.

*   *   *

When Charlie, Val, and Angel arrived at the station, they were greeted by a mob of people, especially those anxious to see Charlie. With his hands in the air to settle everyone, Charlie yelled, "Please, everyone calm down. We will meet…*after* I talk with the others. Let me breathe and get caught up, and then we *will* sit down."

Objections were heard from the group, but Charlie pushed through into the main house. "Good grief!" he said, as he stumbled into the house after tripping over someone's foot. "Seriously! I feel bombarded and overwhelmed."

"I'm sure." Nico stood, from where he was sitting on the couch and gave his friend a hug. "Really sorry about your pop, mate."

"Thank you. At this point, stress is at an all-time high," he said, sitting down on the chair, dropping his head in his hands. "Please fill me in on what you know."

"Why don't you eat something first?" Kit offered. "Willow, please get him his plate from dinner?"

"Yes, ma'am. Want me to get Val and Angel's as well? They're making their way up the walk," Willow pointed out. The rest of the A.N.G.E.L.s were already scattered about the living room.

"Please?"

"Done," she said, and left for the kitchen.

She brought Charlie his plate a few moments later, before running back into the kitchen for Angel's and Val's. She returned just as they made their way into the house. Sitting on the stairs, since it was the only space left, the pair quietly ate their dinner while they listened.

"Okay, mate, here's what all we can piece together," Nico started. "About four days ago, Daku was out collecting herbs when he saw Allen. Not sure what was going on, he took him to the elders. They said while Allen spoke, his eyes shifted, and he became a different person."

"He's not a person at all!" Charlie snapped. "What were they thinking?"

"They figured that out a little too late. When they asked him to leave, Allen cut your father's throat. Then, Allen took off before they could catch him."

"Bloody hell!" Charlie said, looking toward the ceiling to stop the tears.

Nico shook his head at Charlie's outburst. "Charlie."

"I'm sorry. I know you don't like that, but…seriously! He didn't deserve to die like that."

"I agree, but you can't talk like that here," Nico pointed out. "You shouldn't talk like that at all."

Charlie took a deep breath, and slowly let it out before he said, "Okay, give me the rest."

"After your father passed, the clan buried him, and then packed up and high-tailed it out of there. They didn't want any more surprises."

"I understand."

"Then, once they got to Alice Springs, they called here. Me, Pete, and a few others went and got them."

"What shape are they in?"

"Terrified." Nico said, as he sat back in his seat next to Kit, resting his arm over her shoulder. "And rightly so. Serenity Wells, along with the Australian A.N.G.E.L.s, have been able to shield them and the other clans, for a long time."

"Unfortunately, we can't shield them anymore," Charlie pointed out. "I hope they don't go after any more clans."

"I don't envy you, friend," Nico said, "but you have some people to calm."

"I don't know if I can protect them."

"You can't, and you don't have to."

"What do you mean?" Charlie asked.

"God will protect them," Rachel said in understanding. "You are one of His. Those people out there are yours. You're also an A.N.G.E.L., and since you are, they are also under the protection of the A.N.G.E.L.s."

"How am I supposed to work as an A.N.G.E.L. and protect my clan at the same time?" Charlie asked, distraught.

"Charlie, while you will always be an A.N.G.E.L., your time as an A.N.G.E.L. in the field is now complete," Rachel said firmly.

Stunned, he looked up at her with tears in his eyes. "That's my calling."

"Your calling has shifted, and you know it," Rachel challenged. "Your new calling is to lead your clan with everything you have learned. Usher them into a new season of change. *That* is your new calling."

"But, I don't want to abandon the A.N.G.E.L.s."

"You're not abandoning us. That's not who you are. You are moving on. Just like Mark, Derek, and the rest of *your* A.N.G.E.L. team, you are all moving forward. You have all survived and thrived, saving and being a blessing to those who are His over the years. You have all earned a blessed retirement. That includes Ethan and Kat, too."

Charlie took a deep breath of air. After he slowly let it out, he said, "You have your mother's wisdom."

"Thank you. I'll take it as a compliment," Rachel said, smiling at her mom. Kit smiled back, weakly. Frowning, Rachel asked, "Are you feeling okay, Mum?"

"Not really," Kit admitted.

"Go take a kip, love," Nico encouraged. "We have a few busy days ahead of us. We head into town tomorrow for your treatment the next day, and then the wedding the day after that, with Christmas two days later. Better get your rest now," he said, resting his hand on her leg, rubbing it as she lay on the couch.

"I guess," she said, and then slowly headed upstairs.

"Let me help you," Nico said, and ushered her up the staircase.

When they were out of earshot, Josh turned to Pete, and demanded, "You've played coy long enough over the phone. Spill it! How is she *really*?"

"She would kill me if I said anything," Pete said, shaking his head as he shoved his hands in his pockets. Leaning on the wall, he explained, "She *really* wouldn't like the report to go out to everyone here."

"We're family," Josh insisted. "Everyone in here is considered family."

"Fine," Pete relented. "She's not doing well."

"Elaborate, please?" Rachel pressed, upset.

Pete sighed, as the demeanor of the room shifted. "I know she had a fluffy robe on, but when you see her tomorrow, you'll notice she's lost *a lot* of weight."

"Like, *how much* weight?" Josh asked.

"Like, at least thirty pounds of weight, which she didn't have to lose in the first place," Pete elaborated.

"Wow." Rachel shook her head. Jesse reached over, grasped her hand, and gave it a gentle squeeze. She squeezed back in appreciation.

"She can't keep anything down, outside of the occasional cracker. There isn't even a recipe of herbs I can put together to help her either. That's not to mention the major damage the treatments are doing to her body. She's losing her hair, and her nails aren't looking healthy…well, whatever nails she has left, anyway."

"She's not going to be happy with you that you told," Nico said, coming down the stairs. Sliding between Angel, Val, and Katia, seated on the lower staircase, he retook his seat on the couch.

"You try telling Josh and Rachel no," Pete said, sorrowful. All of the emotions he tried stuffing over the last two days finally catching up with him, Pete snapped, "We've lied to them for weeks! They're here now, Nico. They're going to see it for themselves."

"Do Caleb and Leah know the true extent?" Rachel asked. Letting Jesse's hand go, she grabbed her arms in a self-hug, as tears slowly flowed down her cheeks.

"Rachel," Nico's heart broke for his daughter. "Rach, please don't cry."

"You lied to us!" Rachel yelled. Standing, her body shaking, Rachel balled her fists to her sides, and demanded, "How could you do this to us?"

When he took a step toward her, Rachel bolted out the front door.

"I'll…" Jesse pointed toward her as he made his way out the door.

Dropping to the couch, Nico hung his head, clasping his hands together behind his neck. "I don't know what to do anymore. I feel like everything is collapsing around us. Charlie's clan is in distress, Kit's health is failing, and we're supposed to have a wedding here in the next few days. Then two days after the wedding is Christmas. With all of this going on, we're supposed to still keep an eye out for the other side?" Looking up at everyone, he asked, "How are we going to do this? When will we catch a break?"

Charlie knelt in front of Nico and took his hand. "You are my brother. What you go through, I go through. What I go through, you go through. We are in this together. That is how we are going to do this."

"That goes for us too," Jon pointed out. "As A.N.G.E.L.s, and the extended family of the A.N.G.E.L.s, we're all in *all* of this together. Divide and conquer. You let *us* handle the other side. Charlie, you focus on your clan. And, Nico, you look after your family."

"I'm watching my love slowly die right in front of me," Nico confessed, pained, as tears slowly crawled down his cheeks. "It's the worst thing I've ever been through in my entire life."

"Nico, we are all bound together spiritually and emotionally. We're all hurting, but in a few days, we will celebrate," Angel encouraged, moving over, and kneeling in front of Nico.

"How can we celebrate when everyone is hurting so badly?" He asked Angel.

"You can do this. Celebrate the love between your daughter and her love. They will be starting their lives together. If there can be a bright spot amongst this darkness, we all need to embrace it," Angel explained.

"Kit will barely recover from her treatment, but she *will* be there for Leah's wedding," Charlie continued. "She will also be there for Christmas. Enjoy the time we have with her."

"What are you saying?" Josh asked, surprised by the last statement. "We're not going to lose her! She'll have *plenty* more Christmases with us!"

"Josh, you need to talk with your brother," Pete said. "Caleb's out in the barn."

Narrowing his eyes at Charlie, Josh challenged, "Why?"

"Just tell him I said to tell you. You won't like what you'll hear, but you *will* hear the truth."

Taken aback for a moment, Josh looked around the room before he left for the barn.

"He won't like what he's gonna hear," Pete warned.

"None of us have liked what we've heard lately," Nico pointed out. "And, I have a feeling it won't get too much better anytime soon."

*   *   *

"Rachel!" Jesse said when he finally caught up to her.

"He *lied* to us!" she shouted through her tears. "When we talked on the phone, he flat-out *lied* to us! How could he do that to us…to *me*?"

Jesse didn't say anything. He just grabbed her to hug her. She fought him for a few moments, hitting his arms, but he held onto her, not letting her go. After a few more moments, she dropped her head on his shoulder, and sunk into him, sobbing. "He loves you," Jesse comforted her. "He doesn't want to hurt any of you. He's trying to figure out how to keep you focused on your job, while trying to hold it together himself."

"She's going to die!" Rachel choked out. "She's going to die, and where will I be?"

"Doing what you're supposed to be doing."

"This isn't fair! This isn't right!"

"I know."

"I don't know what I'm going to do," she said, wrapping her arms around him, holding him as much as he was holding her.

"You're going to go in and give your dad a hug. He needs it as much as you do," he said, brushing her hair out of her face when she looked up at him. Gently wiping the tears off her cheeks, he continued, "Then, you're going to support your sister when she marries the man of her dreams. Afterward, we're going to celebrate Christmas, and then we'll help Charlie with his clan. Hopefully, we can complete all of this before New Year's hits."

"I don't know if I can do all of that."

"You can, and you will. Do you know why?"

She sniffed. "Why?"

"Because one of the many reasons I love you, is that you always do the right thing, and this is the right thing to do…for everyone." When Rachel shook her head, Jesse explained, "You are a strong woman, who I am proud to call mine. I know you can do this."

Bottom lip trembling, Rachel asked, "What if she doesn't make it?"

"Then, you will see her when you reunite with her in heaven. Until that day, you will stay focused on what God needs you to do. He placed you in this position because he knew you were strong enough to do it. While a lot of this is a surprise and a shock to us, it's not a surprise *or* a shock to the Lord. He already knew it would happen. He already has a plan in place for *all* of this. Think about it. Scott has the station across from your family's station, and they are Christian. Koala Pass is a Christian station as well. He knew Allen would go off the rails, and take out Charlie's dad. He knew all of this would happen, so He made sure Seth and Claire bought Akoonah station, and that their son, Scott, would take it over. He made sure there was already a bond with Koala Pass with the marriage of Caleb and Willow. That way when Charlie's clan came, they could be spread throughout the three stations, and Serenity Wells isn't overwhelmed or overrun. He made sure there was not only a family and best friend bond between the stations, but also that strong Christians run all three stations. He knew Allen would take out Charlie's dad. He knew what the other side's plan was before they even conceived it. He knew what all the players were going to do. God *also* knew all of this would happen right in the middle of Kit's medical issues *and* Leah getting married."

"When did you get so smart?"

"Well, ya see, there's this girl whom I adore, who also happens to be very wise. So, you could say that I've learned from the best."

Rachel chuckled, before she started crying again.

"Aww, sweetheart." Jesse wrapped his arms tighter around her and kissed her head, as she sunk into him again, quietly sobbing. "God's got you covered."

"How can I do this?"

"With God on your side, you can be scared and brave at the same time, knowing He's got this. You can take things one at a time, letting Him lead your steps. You soak in the time you have with each person while we're here, creating memories to last you through until the next time…especially with your mom."

"I love you."

"And, I love you. You have a beautiful heart and soul. Let God take those qualities, along with all the gifts we have, and create a perfect match against the other side. When this is all over, we'll need a vacation," he joked.

"I don't know about that. Mum's issues will be going on for a while."

"Here's hoping. With each passing day, she will be suffering, but the longer she holds on, the better chance she has of beating this. It will get worse before it gets better."

Rachel didn't respond. She couldn't. The more she thought about her mom, the more she cried. While she cried, she prayed for mercy for her mom. She actually prayed if God was going to take her, that He would do it quickly, so she *wouldn't* suffer. She wanted her mother released from the chains that bound her of this vicious disease.

Chapter 3
Price of Chains

The next morning, Rachel gave her mother a hug before Kit and Nico took off for the hotel. The treatment would be the next morning. They hoped to be back by the following morning, or at least in time for the wedding that afternoon. Taking into consideration Kit's treatment schedule, Finn and Leah scheduled an afternoon wedding.

"She doesn't look good at all," Rachel commented, as the family stood on the porch, waving at them as they pulled away.

"No, she doesn't," Josh agreed. "We need to bathe her in prayer until she beats this thing."

"*If* she beats this thing," Caleb pointed out.

"She will," Josh said confidently.

"I pray you're right." Leah frowned. "I have a bad feeling, though, that she may not."

"Let's pray you're wrong." Rachel glanced sideways at her, before looking back at the truck driving off the station. "I don't know what I'll do if she doesn't make it through this."

"You'll do what God needs you to do," Leah insisted, sitting on the rail of the front porch, while the other three each took a seat on one of the three rocking chairs on the porch.

"God not only made you one of His A.N.G.E.L.s, but you're also leading a team. He has confidence in you and your abilities, or He wouldn't have placed you where He placed you."

"But, how can I keep my mind on what I'm supposed to focus on, knowing Mum's throwing up her innards an' basically getting nuked every week? You all made it sound like she had doctor's appointments each week. She looks rough! I can't imagine it's going to get any better," Rachel said, hoping they would understand her concerns. "I mean, honestly! How am I supposed to be on this team, lead, *and* have a relationship at the same time?"

"Let's take these one at a time," Josh started. "You'll keep your relationship, because you two are magnets. You are stronger together than when you're apart. You were made for each other. You will help each other through a myriad of issues…including this. Trust me, I wish I had someone t' lean on through this. I wish I had someone t' hug an' hold me when I needed it."

"I see your point, but that is on you," Rachel pointed out. "You could very easily ask one of those beautiful ladies of the A.N.G.E.L.s out."

"Actually…" Josh's voice faded, as his face flushed in embarrassment.

"Really?" Rachel smiled. "Who?"

"I kind of like Zahra. She's spunky, feisty, beautiful, brilliant, and is intuitive. We've had multiple conversations over the time I was grounded, so to speak, at the Haven. I also love her gorgeous brown eyes."

"The one from Egypt?" Rachel asked.

"That's the one."

"She's pretty! Isn't she IT, though?"

"Yep."

"Smart *and* pretty," Caleb said, resting his hand on his chin. "And, *why* haven't you asked her out yet?"

"Well, *that* would require us to slow down enough to do so, *and* be in the same country."

"Good point," Rachel agreed. "Maybe when we get back."

"What's that going to do to Angel?" Leah asked. "Isn't she hooked on you?"

"Just because she's hooked on me, doesn't mean I'm hooked on her," Josh pointed out, slight irritation in his voice. "Just because *she* decided that she likes me, doesn't mean *I* have to like her and do what she wants. I'm not someone's toy that they can pick up and play with whenever they want. I'm my own person."

"This is true. Good point."

"I also made that perfectly clear to her back in Russia. Nothing has changed since then. Well, that's not true, it's actually worse." Josh rolled his eyes. "She *really* needs to clean up her act."

"Talking about me?" Angel sheepishly asked, coming around the side of the house.

"This is a private conversation," Josh snapped.

"I was taking a walk, and just thought I heard my name," Angel said innocently.

"We'll talk later. Please let us talk as a family for now," Josh asked. "There are still some things we need to clear up *as a family.*"

"No need to be rude about it," Angel huffed.

When she didn't move, Josh grumbled, "Obviously I do, because you're still standing there."

"Hey, Angel!" Sasha called from the stables with a grin, as he came out.

"There's your friend. You may want to talk to him. Since your friends are in short supply at the moment, you may want to be nice to him," Josh pointed out.

Leah looked at him, surprised. "That was mean!"

"She needs to clean up her act, and spying on others won't help," Josh said, sitting back in his chair, crossing his arms.

"Okay, okay." Angel put her hands up in surrender. "I'm going," she said, and ran over to Sasha. Together, they headed out to the fields.

"Seriously, that was downright mean!" Leah accused him when Angel was out of earshot.

"She and I need to have a conversation, but not until Rachel's issues are worked out," Josh said, turning back to Rachel.

"Me?" She gaped. "What did *I* do?"

Caleb raised an eyebrow. "Have a meltdown, perhaps?"

Rachel rolled her eyes, while Josh refocused the siblings, "Right, so we've talked about the relationship portion of the statement, now for the rest. You are team lead, because God has confidence in you, and so does your team."

"As far as you being an A.N.G.E.L.," Leah added, "*you* got the call, and *you* said yes. If you don't want to, that's a conversation you have to have with God and the archangel."

"As far as you staying focused on your job while things here seem to be spiraling, we've got it covered," Caleb explained. "You do what you do. If things head south, we'll let you know and deal with it together."

"Oh, like you've been honest *so* far," Rachel accused.

"We were on orders from Mum and Dad!" Leah defended herself.

"What if we promise to never lie or even stretch the truth again?" Caleb asked. "Would that help you?"

"Immensely!" Rachel agreed.

"Good. Now that we've got that settled," Josh stood, "I have another issue to tackle."

"Ha! Good luck with that one, brother," Caleb got up and headed into the house to help Willow, while Josh headed off the porch to go find Angel.

Nibbling on her nails, Rachel watched her brother walk off toward where Angel and Sasha were watching the horses in the paddock. "Some chains will cost more than others to break," she said aloud to herself, before deciding to look for Jesse.

*   *   *

When Josh walked up to the pair next to the paddock, he asked, "Sasha, would you mind if Angel and I talked for a bit?"

"That would be up to Angel," Sasha shrugged. Turning to her, with his Russian accent still laced within his English, he asked, "Angel?"

"Please? Josh and I need to talk some things out."

"I will be in the barn with Pete when you are finished," Sasha said, before heading off toward the barn.

Leaning on the fence, Josh said, "I know I've been cruel lately, and I need to apologize to you for that."

"Thank you," Angel said. "And, I need to apologize to you for a lot of things."

"Please, let me finish first? Then you can have the time to say whatever you need to. Agreed?"

Angel just made a gesture for him to go on, as she hopped onto the fence for a more comfortable position. It allowed her to look at Josh when she needed to, but also out toward the station if she needed to refocus. She figured this would be a heavy conversation that would probably need a lot of refocusing.

"When you first drove up to the station on that day so long ago, I admit, I was initially attracted to you."

Angel grinned. "I knew it!"

"Please?" Josh asked, starting to feel his blood pressure rise already.

Angel covered her mouth. "Sorry," she said through her fingers.

"Thank you. Anyway, the more I got to know you, I started to see things I didn't like. While I *do* appreciate your looks, it's more the heart and soul I focus on. You know you've struggled with this." Angel just nodded, so Josh went on, "Then, you wrestled with the archangel over these same issues for literally hours. I thought *sure* you had dealt with them. So, as a team, we headed to England. When we lost Aden Knight in England, I think that threw you for more than you were ready to admit."

"It did. I agree."

"Having said that, you are not a normal team member. You were *team lead*. As team lead, it was your job to focus us, *not* pitch a fit and desert us, creating an even bigger mess than we were already dealing with in Russia."

"Again, I'll own that. I agree."

"I'm obviously not telling you anything you don't already know here, or have not already been told. Here's where it gets personal."

Angel winced.

Josh took a deep breath, before he said, "I'm my own person. I know who I like, and do not like being pushed into anything…especially a relationship. Rachel told me what you said to her when we were in Dallas, about throwing the mission we went on in her face. That was not cool. From that point forward, I kept a closer eye on your actions *and* your motives. Now, don't blame her. Blame yourself. Had you cleaned up your attitude and actions, this would be a very different scenario right now. When you're on, you're on point. When you're off, you're off base so far, it's not even funny."

"I know," Angel admitted. "Unfortunately, it's an all or nothing with me."

"Exactly! You need to find balance. Look, Angel, I *tried* to talk to you about your issues, and tell you after a while I just wasn't interested. I'm sorry, but your attitude is not what I'm looking for."

"What *are* you looking for?"

"Honestly?"

"I thought we *were* being honest."

"Okay. I'm looking for a strong Christian woman, who has the brains and intelligence to match anyone out in the field. If she's cute, that's a bonus. But, here's the thing, I've known women who, at first glance, are a little on the homely side, who turn out to be some of the hottest women I know due to their personality. And, I've known some drop-dead-gorgeous women, whose personality disgusted me, making them downright hideous. To me, it's not the outside, but the inside that counts."

"Well, you have both."

"Thank you. I appreciate that. You, unfortunately, need to work on your inside."

"And, my outside isn't all that attractive anymore either. It's all scarred up."

"Angel, if you and God clean up what's on the inside, it won't matter what the outside looks like to the right guy. I promise! Besides, those scars prove that you were stronger than whatever tried to take you out. Own that!"

Smiling, she nodded. "Thank you."

"Now, having said all of that, I need you to know that I *will* be talking to some other women on the teams. I do have one in mind, but I don't want to say anything without talking to her first."

Looking down, Angel responded, "I see."

"You have a great guy who's been looking at you, and is completely enamored with you, but you've been too busy looking at me to see him."

"Sasha?"

"Yes. Angel. He's completely infatuated with you. He's defended you on so many levels, that you have no idea! He's strong. He's a Christian. He's got the heart of a lion, and will look after his lioness with a ferociousness not to be equaled. What do *you* think of Sasha?"

"To be honest –"

Josh raised an eyebrow. "Thought you said that's what we were doing?"

"I did, and I am." Angel nodded. Then she admitted, "I actually like him too."

"Geez, girl! Then go get him!"

"I want to make sure we're okay first."

"Angel, that's going to take a while." When she cocked her head to the side, Josh explained, "As far as us personally, we're fine. As far as us as a team, that's going to take some time to repair. Even then, it won't *ever* be the same. What you did was inexcusable."

"I understand."

"You've got your work cut out for you, but you're up for the challenge. I have faith in you. You can do this. And, when you're back to full strength, mentally and spiritually, we'll all have a chat with Michael, the archangel, and see what we can come up with. In the meantime, you need to mend fences with Val. He's not happy."

"I'm aware. We had a rather strong conversation on the plane."

"You need to take the hints, without us getting rude with you. If you don't, we're going to get rude with you again, and it will tear apart this team."

"I don't want that."

"Neither do we. We're bound together by spiritual chains. The spiritual chains are a good thing. It forces us all to work together. That's the price we pay for the chains we forged together. You are bound even tighter with your personal chains though, some of which are not good. If it helps you to get a mental picture, where one goes, the whole team goes."

"That *does* help."

"And, in keeping with the picture, because you are so tightly bound with those personal chains, we have to carry you until they are broken. We are only as strong and as fast as our weakest member."

"Which makes us all pretty slow and weak at the moment," Angel admitted.

"Work *with* us and not *against* us...*please.*"

"I will. Oh! Speaking of work, I have an idea."

Josh apprehensively crossed his arms. "Uh-oh."

"No, this is a good thing. You know how both sides have a box?"

"Yes."

"What if I were to locate the other side's box?"

"That would be *extremely* helpful!" Josh's face brightened at the thought. "But, how do you plan on doing that? It's been lost for decades."

"I have a friend who may be able to help. Would it be okay if I contacted him, and we worked to find the other box? Using my archeology skills, along with his lab and research skills, we actually have a shot of finding it."

"I think that's a great idea! I'll talk to Jon about it and let him know what you're doing."

"So, it's okay if I go on my own for a bit?"

"Yeah. Just keep me posted. At least a text or two per day once you leave."

"Done!" Angel said, excited. "Can I take Sasha with me?"

"Umm, let me talk to Jon on that one. Sasha's strong, and can sense the other side. Both of those may be good to use on your quest, but I want to make sure we, as a team, are on the same page. Let me call a meeting of our team tonight. Then I'll let Rachel know what's going on."

"Great!" Angel's face lit up. "Thank you for trusting me! You won't regret it!" When she jumped off the fence, she gave him a quick hug before running for the barn.

"Oh, I hope this is the right thing, Lord," Josh prayed, looking toward Heaven. "I don't want to send her on a fool's errand. Nor do I want to send her to her death. I know she feels she needs to prove herself, but I don't want to feed into separating the team."

"You are not separating the team. You are merely sending them on a separate mission," the archangel said, suddenly appearing next to Josh.

Not fazed by an archangel of the Lord suddenly appearing next to him anymore, Josh asked, "So, this is a good thing?"

"Let her use her talents. The young man she wants to bring in will be a valuable asset to both teams."

"Who is it?"

"His name is Spencer Schmidt. He is the son of Scott and Stacey Schmidt from Pine Crest, Ohio. They have an amazing story of their own, but Spencer needs to find his own way. Kit actually knows Stacey and Scott. She was in their wedding."

"Really? Does Angel know that?"

"No. Kit is also not aware of him, so caution is to be utilized. Spencer's contact with Kit is to be limited. He may recognize her from wedding photos of his parents."

"Otherwise, this is okay?"

"Yes. Once Angel, Sasha, and those with them locate and retrieve the other box, the balance of power will shift toward us. If the A.N.G.E.L.s have possession of both boxes, then that puts the other side at a disadvantage. The box gives them a false sense of confidence. Take caution, if they lose that, they will become more agitated and desperate. I will do my best to protect and guide you, but you all need to be on high alert."

"Can we trust everyone here? We're kind of on shaky ground as it is, spread between three stations."

"The only one you can truly trust is the Lord. You focus on doing what He wants you to do, and let Him sort the rest out."

"Yes, sir," Josh said. "Thank you."

"Angel has her own chains to loosen. Once they break, she will be freer to be herself."

"You mentioned her and Sasha. Who else is to go on Angel's mission?"

"Val is to stay here. He is not ready to go out yet. He also has much to learn from Pete."

"Agreed. What about the rest of us?"

"I feel you may want to let her do this with only Sasha and Spencer. The rest will be needed here."

"I understand."

"With fewer on the mission, there is less danger of getting caught. Remember this. It will serve you well."

"What do we have to do to take care of the situation in the Outback?" Josh asked.

"Your counterparts will know what to do. Go speak with Jon, and then with your team. Angel and Sasha must begin their journey in a few days."

"Yes, sir. Thank you."

"Know that you go with the Lord's blessing."

"Thank you," Josh said, and then watched as Michael streaked back into the sky. Shaking his head, he sighed. "I'll never get tired of that."

*   *   *

"You want *what*?" Jon asked, stunned, as he and Josh were talking, sitting on the front porch of the main house.

Josh defended himself. "The archangel said it was a good thing."

"Can we trust her? We're *supposed* to be teaching her to work *within* the team."

"We're sending her with a partner in Sasha."

"We're giving up Sasha too?" Jon's jaw dropped. "Why not just send half the team with her?" He threw his hands in the air. "How is this being productive as a group?"

"Calm down and think about this," Josh said. "While we're focusing on the other side in the Outback, they're focusing on us. Angel and Sasha can sneak in the back door, so to speak, and grab the other box. With the other box in our possession, the NOC list is together. That means we won't have to keep looking over our shoulder, wondering if the other side is a half-step in front of us."

"How?"

"Before, we knew the city and the last names, but had to guess the country. The other side knew the country and the first names, so they would just have to sit and wait for us to lead them to the A.N.G.E.L., like in the case with Aden Knight."

Sitting back in his seat, Jon ran his fingers through his hair in thought, before resting his chin in hand. "I guess you're right. If we let her do this, how are we going to bring her back into the team when it's over? The whole point of the discussions we've had with her lately have centered on how she abandoned the team in order to prove herself. In doing this, isn't she doing the exact same thing?"

"Yes...and no. She's doing this with our blessing, and she's going to stay in constant communication with us throughout the assignment. She's also not alone. Sasha and Spencer will be with her."

"That's the other thing. Who is this Spencer? Can we trust him?"

"The archangel said we're supposed to let her do it. He also said Spencer will be a valuable asset to both teams. We need to meet as a group to make sure everyone is on the same page.

Should I tell her and Sasha it's okay, and have her contact Spencer?"

Dropping his head in his hands for a moment to think, Jon finally nodded in agreement. "We need to let her prove herself. She's cleaning up her own mess if she creates one, though. We can't stop what we're doing to go rescue her."

"Agreed. She, Spencer, and Sasha are on their own. We can't help them. Our hands are full enough on this end."

Taking a deep breath, Jon slowly let it out before he nodded in agreement. "Go ahead."

"Okay, let Katia, Isaac, and Val, as well as Rachel know about the meeting tonight. Rachel can tell her team later," Josh said, walking off the front porch. "Angel's got this."

"I hope so." Jon called after him. "If something happens to them, we're going to have some explaining to do to my parents." When Josh was out of earshot, Jon added, "And, *that's* a conversation I do *not* want to have!"

Chapter 4
Rattling of Chains

"You're really going to let me?" Angel squealed, as she clapped her hands in excitement. "You trust me to do this?"

"Angel," Josh said, resting his hands on her shoulders to calm her, "there is a lot of pressure being put on you to do this. We can*not* help you if you guys get in trouble out there. You are on your own. Now, while we have them occupied, you three need to slip in under their noses to locate and retrieve the other box. You'll need to research, and track it all the way back from World War Two, to where it is now. You, along with Sasha, and if Spencer's willing –"

Dumbfounded, she looked at Josh, "How do you know his name?"

"The archangel."

"Oh."

"Look, if the three of you can do this successfully, while we take care of everything else, we may actually have a shot at pulling this off with limited damage. If that happens, we may finally come out ahead for once."

"I am willing," Sasha said, face brightened with excitement. "Then I will not have to worry about her getting hurt."

Angel blushed in response.

"Look, I get that you two are considering starting something, but keep the mission in mind. Delaney and Joe, Jacob and Cori, and Rachel and Jesse are really good examples of how to do this successfully," Josh advised. "They look after each other, but put the team first in how they operate."

"This is true. We must stay focused on the mission," Angel said.

"Remember," Josh cautioned, "we are trusting you with a very important mission. You are to keep in constant contact with us. Do you understand?"

"Yes, sir!" Angel agreed, with a grin. "We can do this!"

"Starting with the statement of 'we' over 'I,' is a great way to start." Josh smiled, with a nod of approval. "I have a good feeling about this plan. The archangel said God blessed this mission as well."

"Great!" Angel grinned even bigger. "I'll get in touch with Spencer."

"Who is this Spencer?" Sasha asked.

Grabbing his hand, Angel said, "No one for you to worry about. He's a friend from college. Good guy, but not my type."

"What *is* your type?"

"You," she said with a wink, before they walked off to go contact Spencer.

"Lord help him," Josh chuckled, shaking his head, as he headed back to the house.

*   *   *

"Thank you for coming tonight. I know Charlie's in a meeting, and there are multiple other things going on within the stations tonight as well," Jon said to those in attendance. As he spoke, Jesse, Jacob, Joe, and Delaney walked in. "Hi, guys."

"Having a meeting without us? Not very team-oriented of you," Jacob pointed out, as he took a seat on the steps. The others were seated throughout the living room of the main house.

"Who told you about the meeting?" Josh asked.

"I did," Rachel said, matter-of-factly. "What goes on here affects them as well. I thought it was only fair to let them in on it too."

"Okay. Sorry for not alerting you," Josh apologized. "We wanted to explain it to our team first, but if your lead says to have you here, you're welcome to come. We want to be united, not divided."

"Thank you," Jacob said, satisfied. "Carry on."

Chuckling, Jon told them the situation, explaining who would be separating from the group.

"Are you sure this is a good idea?" Val asked when Josh finished. "United we stand, divided we fall."

"If they are separated from us, what will happen if something happens to one, both, or all three of them?" Joe asked. "We can't help them."

"I agree," Katia said. "This worries me."

"The archangel said they were to do this," Josh explained. "Besides, we've been doing things as a team since we got together. If we are to pull this off successfully, we need to do something different than we've done previously. Angel, have you gotten ahold of Spencer?"

"Can we trust Spencer?" Delaney asked before Angel could answer. "We don't know him."

"I do," Angel said. "And, yes, he said he'd be on his way here in the morning. He said he would do some research tonight. He's excited. He's kind of like a treasure hunter, with lab-geek background."

"That's kind of cool," Isaac said.

"He's really nice, and he's a Christian too."

"When do we need to pick him up?" Jon asked.

"Not tomorrow, but the day after, around eleven in the morning."

"Good. That's the morning of the wedding," Josh said. "Everyone will be here in one place."

"That's going to be a tight schedule," Rachel commented. "Hope he knows he's coming in for a wedding first."

"He does," Angel said. "Sasha, Spencer, and I will get together the day after the wedding to see what he's found out, and then we'll make a plan from there."

"That'll be a few days before Christmas," Jacob pointed out. "Are you going to be here for Christmas?"

"I would think so. We have a lot of research to do. We may be going back and forth to town during that time."

"That's not a bad idea. The more you can track here, as opposed to being in the field, the less likely you will be to get caught," Jesse said.

"True," Sasha agreed. "This will make me feel more comfortable."

"Keep in mind, Angel, that you don't fully know Sasha's skill set yet," Rachel warned. "And, Sasha, keep in mind that her skill set is strong. She may not need as much protection as you think."

"Yes, ma'am," Sasha agreed.

"I agree," Angel said. "That's the other thing I want to find out before we go. We're going to have to do some testing, so I know what you can handle."

"Test away!" Sasha said with a smile.

"That makes me a little more comfortable," Rachel said, nervously nibbling her nails. "This whole thing feels like it's coming to a head, though. I feel like something dark is coming our way, and we don't know when it will hit."

"I agree," Val spoke up. "There is something dark building on the horizon. When it will break, is not known. It's coming from the Outback, though."

"Duly noted. Angel, Sasha, you both will be responsible for bringing Spencer back in one piece," Josh warned.

Angel and Sasha nodded in agreement.

"Good. Now that we're all on the same page," Josh said, pleasantly surprised that Angel didn't get upset once, "we need to figure out what we're going to do about the issue with wedding security, station security, and the situation in the Outback. Nothing personal, but I want to be proactive, as opposed to reactive."

"I agree," Jon concurred. "I don't like waiting to see what they will do. I like to be on the offense, not the defense."

"Yes. This is not my preferred way to operate either," Katia agreed. "What is the plan?"

Just then several guys, along with Charlie, walked up onto the porch and into the living room. "Hey, Charlie!" Josh said with a smile. "We were just having a meeting."

"I am aware," Charlie said, stepping into the middle of the group with the twelve men in tow. "We are here to volunteer."

Jon furrowed his brow. "Volunteer for what?"

"May I?" Daku asked Charlie. Charlie motioned for him to go ahead, so Daku stood before Rachel, Jon, and Josh, and said, "We are only but a small piece of the Kingdom of God, but He has seen fit to put us under your protection. While we appreciate that, we are strong men who want to protect our clan. We are few, but we are strong. We have many useful skills that will help in taking out the evil in the Outback."

"Take them out?" Rachel asked, wide-eyed. "Are you aware of what you're asking to do? There are a lot of them out there!"

"They are many, and we are a small band here in this room, but Gideon and his army were also a small band as they fought the Midianites…and won. David was tiny in his battle against Goliath. God has a way of making the less than superior, stronger than even they thought possible. We are here to fight for not only our village and clan, but for the other clans as well. Use us," Daku pleaded.

"We can't ask that of you." Josh shook his head. "You all have families to protect."

"Actually," Joe said, as a vision finished playing out in his mind, "they are *exactly* what we need."

"What are you saying?" Rachel asked, horrified. "You can't be serious! We volunteered for this. We don't have children or spouses. These innocents have families to take care of. Our job is to protect the innocent, not send them into the fire. Have you lost your mind?"

"Bear with me here." Joe stood. He squeezed Delaney's hand, before he walked over to the group in the middle of the room. Looking to Jesse, he asked, "If we get too close to the other side, what will happen?"

Jesse shrugged. "They'll sense us."

"Exactly! And, what will happen if any of these villagers, minus Charlie, goes near them?"

Jesse narrowed his eyes as he tried to follow Joe's train of thought. Shaking his head, he said, "Nothing." Then, a picture started to form in his mind, and he completely understood. Grin on his face, Jesse exclaimed, "Oh! That's an excellent idea!"

"I do not understand," Daku said, confused.

"Brilliant!" Charlie grinned, following Joe's train of thought.

"Please explain?" one of the villagers asked.

"As an A.N.G.E.L., when the other side gets close, Jesse and Sasha can sense them. This goes for the other side in sensing us as well," Charlie told the clansmen. "When a normal human goes near, neither side senses them."

"Okay," another villager said, still not following. "I do not understand how this will benefit us."

"That's a great idea!" Delaney said with a smile. "You, my man, are brilliant!"

"Someone, please explain?" Daku asked, agitated.

"If we're going to have a remote chance of planning a sneak attack of any kind, we need someone who the other side will not sense," Rachel explained. "So, for example, if you guys plant explosives in or around their base, and when you are all clear, we blow it, they'll never see or *sense* it coming."

"Oh! I see!" Daku grinned. "Will we be able to take out those who killed our chief that way?"

"Very much so," Charlie said. Then he furrowed his brow. "In order to do this, you will all be put in grave danger. I do not know if I am comfortable with this anymore."

"I believe this is our choice," Daku said. "As Chief, it is well within your right to stop us, but it will not bode well for clan relations. We must avenge Chief's death, as you must as his son."

"I agree."

"Then, you will train us and allow us to do this?"

"Technically, Jacob needs to train part of you, while the others are trained by us to protect those who are setting the explosives," Rachel pointed out. "Jacob, is there something you can come up with that will take an entire mountain down, yet give them enough time to get away?"

Jacob laughed. Then he looked at them, stunned when he figured they were asking him in earnest, and said, "Oh, you're serious?"

"Yes. You have to train them to execute the explosives, yet give them enough time to get in and out safely. Can you do that?" Rachel asked, again.

Jacob sat for a moment, rubbing his chin, deep in thought. "How many people will I have?"

All twelve men raised their hands.

When the clansmen looked at Charlie, he shook his head, as he explained, "I cannot be a part of that portion of the mission. I must stay back with the A.N.G.E.L.s. They will sense me coming. I can come with the team to help protect, but from a distance."

"All right." Jacob finally agreed. "I can work with them. The timing will have to be precise. Once we take out the center of gravity, or hub, the rest should fall…or at least run around lost for a while before the power vacuum sucks up the stragglers."

"We can do it," Daku said confidently. The others nodded in agreement.

"Do we know what the mountain looks like?" Jacob asked.

"We know about where it is," one of the village men offered.

"We can take a trip for recon after the wedding," Josh suggested. "That won't be a problem."

"It'll take a few days out, and a few days back," Rachel said. "Those who go will miss Christmas."

"This is more important," Jon insisted. "Josh, you and Rachel stay here to celebrate Christmas with your family. I'll take the guys."

"I will go too," Charlie volunteered.

"No, you are staying here with your people," Rachel asserted. "They *need* you."

Jacob raised his hand. "I'm going."

"Me too," Jesse said. "You'll need me to sense if the other side is close. I'm more honed in on this skill than Sasha.

Besides, Sasha will be with Angel and Spencer here on the station."

"I will go," Katia volunteered.

"I would prefer you stay with the women," Rachel said. "You, Delaney, and I can stay with the women and children. The men staying can help protect, but with their culture, women look after women."

Delaney nodded. "Agreed."

"I will stay," Katia reluctantly agreed.

"I'll go," Joe volunteered.

Delaney squeaked in objection, but didn't say anything else.

Joe turned and knelt in front of Delaney. Taking both her hands into his, looking deep into her eyes, he said, "I realize this is our first Christmas. We can celebrate it on our own before we go. Trust that God has us all in His hands, and will bring us all back safely. We *need* to do this. My gift of visions will be extremely helpful in the field. We don't have Val's Spiritual sight, so we'll need my gift out there. Y'all will have Val here with his Spiritual sight to keep you safe here on the station. We need to strategically split the group."

Feeling a pit in her stomach, Delaney reluctantly nodded. "I understand. Just know something doesn't feel right. Is there any way you all can do the recon from here? I don't like being separated from you."

"You need to look after those here. Angel and Sasha will be here, but they have a mission of their own. With those going out with us, I need to know that you're here looking after everyone else. Use your gift to put the pieces together. You can do this, Delaney. And, hopefully, we can catch a break after this is over."

Delaney finally nodded.

"Good. Now that's settled. Daku and Charlie, will you guys come into the dining room with us, and bring a map please?" Rachel asked. "The Outback is a big place. We need to narrow down where you're looking."

Most of the group split off, while Rachel, Jon, Josh, Charlie, and Daku went into the dining room. Spreading a map out onto the table, Rachel asked, "Okay, can anyone show me the actual location of the village?"

"Right here," Charlie pointed on the map.

"And, where did we find Angel?"

"Around here," Charlie said. "And when we drove to the village, we drove this way. Angel came into camp this way," he said, narrowing down the area. "In the shape she was in, I cannot imagine she walked all that far."

"Where's Joe?" Josh asked, looking around.

"He's with Delaney. Let them be." Rachel waved him off. Then she went to the door, and called Katia, Isaac, and Jacob inside. They followed her back into the dining room.

"Can either of you help with a possible location?" Charlie asked. "This is where the village is," he said, pointing out each place on the map. "This is where we found Angel. And, this is the direction she came from."

"Do we have a topographical map of this area? About ten miles around the area from where Angel was found?" Jacob asked.

"Give me a minute," Rachel said, and ran upstairs. She came back down in a matter of minutes with an iPad. She used the search engine to find a topographical map of the area. Then she lowered the area to a fifteen-mile area.

"There," Jacob said. "This is where it has to be located."

"How can you tell?" Katia cocked her head to the side. "This map is confusing."

"Check the elevation. This is the only portion of the area big enough, and high enough, to have what Angel described walking out of. Plus, it's in line, albeit a crooked line, to where our campsite was right here."

"Okay, this is our target. We need Jesse so we don't get too close and set off alarms by them sensing us," Jon said. "As *soon* as he even remotely feels the other side, we're going to have to pull out. Jacob, take binoculars with you. We'll let you and Jesse go out a little ahead, so you can look at it as much as you can."

"I have an idea. Let me get ahold of Cori and Kai, and see if they can send us some satellite pics of the area," Jacob suggested. "If their crew can get it detailed enough, we will only need to go out there for the deed. That way the other side won't get suspicious."

"That would be great!" Josh grinned. "Call Cori."

While the others continued to talk, Jacob went to the kitchen to call Cori.

"Haven," Cori answered on her computer.

"Hey, Cori," Jacob said with a smile, as he thought about her.

"Hey, love!" Cori's grin equaled Jacob's smile. "Miss you!"

"Miss you too. We're planning some things here, and wanted to know if you could get some information."

"Give me a minute to secure the line," she said, and immediately went to work to scramble the line in case someone was listening. "Okay, we've got five minutes. What do ya need?"

"If I send you an area on a map, would you be able to get me as detailed a satellite photo as possible for that area?"

"We can get you a picture detailed enough to distinguish the different men, women, and children on the ground if you want it," Kai said from across the room. "Just don't ask us *where* we got it."

Cori laughed. "Yes, we can get you a detailed map. Rachel has her computer, yeah?"

"Yes. Well, her iPad anyway."

"That'll work. Send the coordinates to the email, and I'll send you back the maps."

"Thank you. Hey, Cori?"

"Yeah?"

"Can we talk alone for a minute?"

"Clear the room," Cori said loudly.

The IT people headed upstairs, with Kai as the last. He made sure to say, "I'm it," before he went out the door, closing it behind him.

"Okay. We're alone," Cori said, scratching the top of Charm's head.

"I'm really sorry we can't spend Christmas together."

"I know. There's always next year."

"Well…" Jacob said slyly.

With a knowing smile, Cori asked, "What did you do?"

"Reach under your desk."

Cori reached under her desk. Feeling around for a few moments, she finally found the tiny box duct-taped to the bottom of the desk. "When did you…?"

"Before I left," he said, finishing her thought. "I snuck down and did it when everyone was asleep," Jacob admitted. "Now, since I won't be around a phone on Christmas, go ahead and open it."

Cori pulled the tape off the box. Unwrapping it, she felt a velvet box. "What *is* this?"

"Open it," Jacob encouraged.

Opening the box, Cori felt the bracelet. She giggled when she realized it was in braille. "Seriously? You are awesome!" Cori gushed.

"What does it say?"

"It says, '*If God is for us, who can be against us. Romans 8:31.*' My favorite verse! Thank you!"

"Now, just because I can't be there, know God is with both of us. He's bigger than any of this."

"Thank you, Jacob," Cori smiled, as she wiped her tears. "I've never known someone as sweet as you! You'll have to wait until you get here to get yours. Seems I'm not as sneaky as you," she said, with a smile.

"Always a pleasure to be yours, my lady!" Jacob said with a grin. "So glad it worked."

"Me too! Okay, our time is limited. Send me the coordinates, and we'll see what we can do."

"Great. Thank you! Hope to see you soon!"

"Maybe for New Year's?"

"Here's praying!"

"Hey, Jacob?" Cori asked.

"Yes?"

"I hope you know I'm infatuated with you."

"Yep! As I am with you!"

"Be safe!"

"Always. I'm in His hands," Jacob said, and then hung up the phone.

"Well?" Josh asked when Jacob walked in with a smile. "Did it work?"

"Did what work?" Rachel asked.

"He left something for her." Josh winked at Jacob. They were roommates, so he knew.

"Yes." Jacob grinned like a little kid at Christmas. "She loved it too!"

Josh gave him a high-five. "Well done, mate!"

"Thanks!" Jacob's smile looked like it would never go away. "Oh! I need to send the coordinates to Cori via the email."

"Here ya go," Rachel said, handing him the tablet.

While Jacob worked on that, the others made a plan for security through the wedding and Christmas. If they could hold off the other side until then, they were confident they would be able to get the jump on them.

*   *   *

"They are all in place," one of Cassius's minions said, walking up to Cassius, Calliope, and Korax.

"Wonderful!" Cassius said, clapping his hands together in excitement. Turning to Calliope, he instructed, "You need to take care of your portion of the plan. Right now, she is vulnerable. She is also unprotected."

"Who is?" Korax asked.

"She is our secret weapon," Calliope smiled, as she rubbed her hands together, "and the best part is that she does not even know it!"

Korax raised an eyebrow. "How could she not know?"

"It was one of our experiments when she was here under our control," Cassius explained. "You must understand there is more than one plan in place at all times."

"Oh, I do. So, who is it?" Korax asked.

"That is for *me* to know, and for *you* to find out. Want to take a trip with me?" Calliope nudged Korax. "I could use some back-up."

"I do not think you need back-up, but he *is* a good cover," Cassius agreed. "You leave in the morning. I will get Gamigin to assist in taking down the stations. Once everyone is together for the wedding, my ingenious plan will be in place. I will take out those A.N.G.E.L.s, as well as three stations that are His at the same time. The fact that the clansmen are there as well is a bonus! It will strike fear in the remaining clans, and will force them to follow and worship me. Oh! This could not have worked out more perfectly!"

Half bowing, Calliope praised Cassius, "As usual, you are the master."

"Go execute the plan," Cassius waved her and Korax off.

When they were out of earshot of Cassius, Korax asked, "Where are we going?"

"Where we can wreak havoc," Calliope replied with a smile.

"Oh! I love it when you get that look on your face!" Korax smiled. "You have a devious mind that comes up with brilliant ideas!"

With a wink, she reminded him, "I am a muse. That's part of my job description."

Chapter 5
Shake the Chains

"I'm so nervous!" Leah confessed. "I know Dad and Mum are supposed to be here before the wedding, but the fact that they're not here yet scares me."

"She had a rough treatment," Rachel said, as she fixed Leah's hair. They were upstairs in the room.

The wedding was to take place within an hour. The arch was decorated with greenery, poinsettias, pinecones, holly berries, and white lights in front of the main house. There was also white tulle loosely wrapped around the arch. The chairs were set out in several rows, divided by an aisle for the wedding party to walk down. "Dad took her to a salon so she wouldn't have to do anything but show up. You're just going to have to trust that his tux fits."

"I don't like the unknown," Leah admitted.

"No kidding," Rachel said with a smirk. "There. Done!"

"Thank you! It looks amazing! That dress looks great on you as well!"

"Red *is* a good color. Where are the other bridesmaids?"

"Hi guys," Delaney said, as she and Katia walked into the room. "Everyone is just about ready."

Looking around the room, Katia asked, "Is there not supposed to be more in here? Who are the bridesmaids?"

"They should be here any minute," Leah said. "Anna, Willow's older sister, is one. She'll be bringing her daughter, Taylor, to be a flower girl. Meanwhile, Willow is another. She and Lily are getting ready in the next room. Lily will walk down with Taylor. Then the third is Skye, a girl from school."

"You two still talk?" Rachel asked, surprised, as she finished her own makeup. "I knew she was one, but I didn't think you two were that close."

"Yes. It seems that she and Finn were friends in college. Small world."

"What's she been up to?"

"She got married last year. She's about eight weeks pregnant."

"Really?" Rachel looked at her, astonished. "That was quick."

"We're planning to start as soon as possible," Leah said, and looked to Rachel for her reaction.

"Great! Mum & Dad will look forward to a new little one in the family. I'm glad you guys waited. I don't think they could have handled any controversy at the moment."

"I know. Trust me. It *wasn't* easy! We finally reached a point where we refused to be alone, because we knew it wouldn't end how we wanted. I wanted to wait until we were married. I will admit that he hasn't waited. It was when he was in high school, before he met God."

"I see. So, you guys talked it out, right."

"Yes."

"Then, that's what's important. As long as you two are fine, then what anyone else has to say doesn't matter."

Smiling in relief, Leah admitted, "I was afraid you would be judgmental."

"Judgmental?" Delaney raised an eyebrow. "Rachel isn't judgmental at all."

Rachel smiled. "Thank you!"

"It is true," Katia said. "There are few people I can say that about, but you are one of them."

"I appreciate that," Rachel said, sitting on the bed next to Delaney.

"You both look amazing," Katia mentioned.

"As do the two of you," Rachel commented. Then, looking back at Leah, she continued, "Leah, it's not my place to judge. God's the ultimate Judge. You've waited, and *very patiently*, I might add. I'm proud of you!"

"Proud of you too! Some of the girls in high school gave me grief, saying that we would both be pregnant before getting our diplomas."

"Really?" Rachel crossed her arms. "Can I guess who it was?"

"Why would they say that?" Delaney asked.

"Yes, that does not seem nice," Katia added.

"People can be cruel as teenagers," Leah said. "In any culture."

"This is true," Katia agreed.

"Pretty sure you can guess who it was, though, Rach," Leah hinted.

"Would it happen to be Erin, Sally, and Margo?" Rachel asked.

"Yes, it would."

"And, if memory serves me right, didn't *they* get pregnant in high school, or shortly thereafter?"

"Yes, ma'am!"

"I'm glad we're doing it right," Rachel said, turning back to the mirror. "I think it creates a better bond within the couple."

"I agree," Leah said with a smile, as the door opened.

"Okay, go gently give Aunt Leah a hug," Willow said, walking into the room with seven-year-old, Lily. "Be careful not to mess up her dress or makeup."

"Yes, ma'am!" Lily said, and then ran over to Leah and gave her a hug.

"Lily! You look so beautiful!" Leah exclaimed when Lily ran into her arms.

"You look like a princess!" Lily grinned, lightly playing with Leah's veil.

"Are you ready to do your job with Taylor?"

Lily put the veil down. "Yes! Where is she?"

"She's on her way," Willow said. "She called from Koala Pass about five minutes ago. As a matter of fact, I'm surprised —"

Willow was cut off when eight-year-old Taylor burst into the room, and ran over to Lily. The two hugged, before they gushed over how both looked like princesses as well.

"Okay, then, I reckon your mum's behind you?" Willow asked, glancing into the hall. "G'day, Anna! How ya goin'?"

"Been a rough day, but we're here. Is Skye here yet?" Anna asked, walking into the room.

"Not yet. Mum's not either."

"Actually, she is," Anna said. "She's downstairs in the living room until it's ready to start. She's lookin' *extremely* pale and frail."

"She just had a treatment yesterday. This was pushing it, but she said it would be fine. I *knew* it was too close," Leah said, beside herself.

Rachel leaned down, and whispered in Lily's ear, "Go get Pop. Tell him that Aunt Leah's upset about Nana."

Lily just nodded before she bolted from the room for the stairs.

Willow cocked her head to the side, and asked, "What was that?"

"Back-up," Rachel said with a wink.

Delaney stood, pulling Katia up with her, and said, "We'll head back down now, since it's getting a bit crowded up here."

"You all look amazing!" Katia added. Right before she closed the door, she added, "See you down there."

It didn't take but a moment later to hear Lily bounding back up the stairs, with Nico in tow. "G'day, all…*you beauties!*" Nico said with a grin, as he was caught in the middle of his sentence. "You all look great!" Then he got a good look at Leah, "Except you. Aren't you supposed to be the best-looking one here?"

"Thanks, Dad," Leah said, tongue-in-cheek. "You're such a comfort."

"Skye just got here. Why don't you all go to the room next door to finish getting ready, so I can talk to the bride?" Nico asked.

Once the room was cleared, Nico pulled a chair up next to Leah and took her hands into his. "Tell me what's got you frownin' on what's supposed to be the happiest day of your life?"

"Anna said that Mum doesn't look good. I knew it would be too close to her treatment for this, but her treatments are on Fridays, and Chrissie is on Monday. We had to schedule it so everyone could make it. There was no other way around it."

"Leah, this is the way you had to schedule it. Your Mum wanted you two to have at least a day to yourselves before you came back for Chrissie," Nico explained. "Don't ruin it for the both of you by being upset. Yes, she had a rough treatment, but she wants you to enjoy this day for the both of you. This is your day. Don't let her condition spoil it."

"Dad, is she – is she going to make it?"

"Lord willing. If not, we'll see her when we join her in Heaven later."

Tears welling in her eyes, she explained, "A world without her, though? I can't imagine it!"

"Oh, don't do that! Rachel won't be happy if you ruin your make-up," he said, passing the tissue box to her. "She'll have to start all over again. Look, Possum," Nico said, referring to Leah's nickname, "you have always worried about everyone else but yourself. As a matter of fact, your Mum and I couldn't ask for more caring, strong, and considerate children. I thank the good Lord every day for each of you."

"You used to call me that when I was little, but we're not so little anymore," Leah reminded him as she smiled and blushed. "Haven't heard that nickname in a while."

"Regardless of your age, you will *always* be my little Possum. Rachel will *always* be my little Pumpkin. Josh will *always* be Squiddley, while Caleb will *always* be Diddley – and he has four little knee knockers of his own! Point is, no matter how old you are, you will always be our little ones. As our little ones, we want you to be happy. We know this world can be difficult at times. So, whenever possible, we will do our best to make whatever makes you happy happen. You will too, when you get some of those little squirts of your own."

"I know. Thank you."

"Having said that, yes, your mum isn't in the best of shape, but come hell or high water, she was *not* going to miss this!"

"Will she make it through the whole day?"

"I can't answer that. What I *can* say with certainty, is that she will do her best, and *will* be there for the actual wedding portion."

"Thank you, Dad," she said, giving him a hug.

"You're welcome, Possum. Just know that you've only got a few minutes before I have to give you away. And, by *no* stretch of the imagination is that an easy thing," he said sternly. "We are allowing him to take you as his wife. He will be responsible for you and any little ones you may have. He has to answer to me, along with the Almighty Lord for you all as well. I have the utmost confidence that he is up to the task, though. I know you guys have plans to move to the city after Christmas, but know our doors are always open to you and yours."

"I know."

"And, I *do* believe it is written somewhere in the Bible that you *must* spend at least one week a year at the station."

"Really?" Leah giggled. "And, what's that reference?"

"Somewhere in the book of Nicolas," he said with a wink.

*   *   *

There were some threatening clouds in the sky above, but the air was still, and hanging around at a decent temperature. With the music playing from the speaker, the bridesmaids walked out of the house first. The groom and groomsmen waited patiently at the arch for their counterparts to join them.

Once the bridesmaids reached the arch, Rachel stepped out, with the flower girls following close behind, dropping red rose petals as they walked down the aisle. In a red fitted dress that went to the ground, Rachel looked stunning!

As soon as Jesse saw her, he wanted to stand and wait for her, but he wasn't among the bridal party. She was to be paired up with Finn's brother, Owen. He was glad they were as strong a couple as they were, because from what he knew, and when he spoke with Owen, Owen seemed to be a bit a player, and he was sure Owen would hit on Rachel.

When Rachel was to the front, the music shifted, and everyone stood. The groom wasn't the only one beaming when Leah stepped out. Rachel was proud of her sister. Leah looked stunning! This was her day, and Rachel would do everything in her power to make it a great one for her. They waited over four years to get to this point, and she wouldn't let anything mess it up.

Nico proudly walked down the aisle with his daughter on his arm. He knew he was blessed to have such a wonderful family!

Kit couldn't help the smile that filled her to her soul, as she watched her loving husband walk her daughter down the aisle to get married from her seat. While she didn't have the strength to stand, she had a front-row aisle seat in order to see everything. With all Kit and Nico had been through in their lives, they had many good points as well, and this was one of them. Despite how she felt, she was happy to be there on that day for Leah. She prayed to make it for whenever Josh or Rachel got married…*if* they got married.

To Leah, this felt like a dream, from which she never wanted to wake. The fitted sweetheart neckline bodice that hung just off her shoulders and flowing tulle skirt accentuated her figure. The bodice of her dress was covered in sequins, and the dress was all white, with the exception of the hand-sewn designs along the bottom in red. The designs were done by Charlie's clan. It was tradition in their clan to sew scenes to remind the bride of the advice given to them the night prior. The clan women got ahold of the dress a few days before, and the night before the wedding, they explained each design to the bride-to-be. It was a tradition they held dear, and Leah would never forget what each design meant.

Once Nico and Leah reached the front, Charlie asked Nico, "Who gives this bride away?"

To which Nico responded, "Her mother and I do." Once he said that, he lifted the veil and gave Leah a kiss on the cheek before replacing the veil. Then he took a seat beside Kit.

Rachel suddenly got a good look at Kit, and furrowed her brow in concern, but quickly smiled at Leah, as she took her bouquet from her. Leah and Finn joined hands, while Charlie commenced the ceremony.

There was the greeting, followed by a song sung by Anna. Then, about halfway through, Charlie explained, "It's my understanding that Finn and Leah have written their own vows. Finn, you may go first."

Taking both Leah's hands into his, facing her, Finn explained, "Way back when, in college, when you first walked into one of my classes, you caught my eye. Your smile lit the room. Your eyes danced with excitement of a new journey. It was then that I knew I wanted to get to know you. Then, the more I got to know you, the more I wanted to know. You have a caring heart for those close to you, and often look out for those who you don't even know. You are a fantastic veterinarian, a great worker at the soup kitchen and homeless shelter in Queensland each week, a wonderful sister and daughter, and an even better girlfriend, fiancé, and I have no doubt you will be an amazing wife. I look forward to growing older with you, experiencing everything through your eyes. Every promise I make today to you, and before all of these witnesses, I do so willingly, and wholeheartedly. You are my joy. It will be my honor to have and to hold you from this day forward, and to enjoy the everlasting with the Lord and with you after our time here is finished. You are my other half, created by God, just for me."

Leah smiled and blushed at his kind words. Once Charlie nodded toward her, she said, "I remember that first day as well. It was the start of our forever after. It has been an incredible journey with you to this point, and yet, it has only just begun. Your strength of character is only matched by your strength in God. I am amazed each and every day for the gift God gave me in you. You are everything I ever wanted in my other half, including things I never even thought possible. I'm grateful God brought us together. He has a plan for us, and I cannot wait to see what it is! I look forward to exploring this life with you. Every promise I make today, I make willingly and wholeheartedly. You are *my* joy. And, it will be *my* honor to have and to hold you from this day forward, and to enjoy the everlasting with you after our time here on earth is finished. You are my other half, created by God, just for me," she finished, and then looked toward Charlie to continue.

As she spoke, Jesse started shifting in his seat, extremely uncomfortable. Turning to Sasha, who was sitting next to him, he whispered, "Are you feeling okay?"

Furrowing his brow, Sasha asked, "Yes. Why?" Then, he felt it. It felt like tiny bugs crawling all over him. As it quickly escalated, he said, "Maybe not."

"If there is anyone here who objects to this marriage, speak now or forever hold your peace," Charlie announced.

Jesse and Sasha both stood, on high alert, looking around to see where the feelings were coming from.

"Jesse? Sasha?" Rachel asked, looking at Jesse. Seeing the alarm written on both of their faces. Instinct took over. "A.N.G.E.L.s on your feet!" She shouted, as she dropped the bouquets onto the ground. Pulling the knives from their sheaths under her skirt, Rachel searched the tree line around them. At Rachel's reactions, the other A.N.G.E.L.s stood, pulling their weapons from their hiding spots on their bodies.

It didn't take Nico but a split second to figure out what was happening. "Everyone take cover!" he shouted. "Women and children to the main houses!" He scooped Kit up in his arms, and ran inside the house, with Pete on his heels to help guard the main house.

As everyone scattered between the three stations, the A.N.G.E.L.s took positions to defend all three stations. Within a couple of minutes, the A.N.G.E.L.s were joined by the male station hands at each station as well as the younger and older men from the clan.

Rachel, Jon, Josh, Nico, Jesse, Charlie, and Caleb all had radios, as they spread between the three stations. "In position on Serenity near the main house," Rachel confirmed into her radio, as she took her shoes off, deciding fighting barefoot may give her more of an advantage than fighting in heels.

"We're safe," Nico acknowledged. He was holed-up with the women and children in the main house watching the front door, while keeping an eye on Kit who was on the couch. Pete and Val had the back door.

"Koala Pass is in position," Josh said over his radio.

"As is Akoonah," Caleb confirmed.

"Head's up. They are very close, and there are a *lot* of them," Jesse warned, as he was on the other side of the station from Rachel.

Within moments, they heard what sounded like a bee swarm. The trees around the stations were instantly alive with creatures from the other side, rushing the stations. There were flying and crawling creatures of nightmares, mixed with demons, and Unnaturals.

Sudden streaks of light burst from the clouds. Heavenly angels, along with a couple archangels, appeared in front of the rushing horde of the other side. The heavenly angels were quickly joined by the station hands and A.N.G.E.L.s to hold the line, away from the main houses on the stations.

The fighting was intense. Rachel got cut multiple times, but stood her ground. She was relieved to know that the other side didn't bring guns. They fought with knives, swords, bow and arrows, and their hands…or anything else they could get their hands on. The A.N.G.E.L.s and those on their side did the same.

Talons swiped; knives plunged, sliced, or scraped; rocks were thrown; and arrows flew, but each side was equally matched…until those with Nico in the main house, and those in the other main houses, were joined in prayer by those around the world who were compelled to pray.

*   *   *

Woke from a startled sleep, Casey jostled Mark. "Mark! Wake up!"

"What? What's wrong?" he asked, groggy. Looking at the clock, he groaned. "It's midnight. What's wrong?"

"The team needs prayer," she insisted.

Suddenly, there was a knock on the door.

"Come in!" Mark called out, as he sat up in bed.

Cori poked her head in, and explained, "We were all just woken up. The team needs prayer."

"Got the message. Assemble everyone downstairs. We'll be down there in a second."

"You got it!" Cori said, and closed the door behind her.

When she was gone, Mark and Casey got out of bed. Sliding his slippers on, he mentioned, "Looks like we've got a long night ahead of us. If it's big enough to wake the house, then the team is in serious trouble."

"I agree," Casey said, standing. Giving Mark a hug when they both got to the door, Casey said, "We have to trust them to the Lord."

"He's got this," Mark said, and then they went downstairs to join the others in prayer.

* * *

A young teacher in Queensland was working on her lesson plans, when she felt an overwhelming urge to pray. Setting aside her lesson plans, she went into her bedroom and found her Bible. Lying prostrate on the floor, with her hands and head resting on the Bible, she prayed for those in the world who needed the Lord. Not knowing exactly who it was that needed prayer, she prayed for the safety of the Lord's saints, and for protection by the Lord's angels for those who needed it.

* * *

Woken from a deep sleep as well, Juan, who was one of the OG Mexican A.N.G.E.L.s, woke his wife Claudia. "Sorry, love. I know it's two in the morning, but a team out there needs help. We need to pray."

Rolling out of bed, knowing the protocol, Claudia phoned all of the other Mexican A.N.G.E.L.s, before joining her husband in prayer.

*   *   *

In Pine Crest, Ohio, Stacey Schmidt shuffled to the bathroom, bleary-eyed. Focusing on the clock, she saw that it was three in the morning.

"Stace!" Scott called out in alarm.

Not even going to the bathroom first, Stacey ran back into the bedroom.

Both looked at each other, and at the same time, they said, "Spencer's friends are in trouble!"

"We need to pray," Scott said.

"Agreed."

Kneeling next to the bed, the pair joined hands as they prayed for safe travels for Spencer, and safety for his friends.

*   *   *

A young boy was out sitting on the beach, watching the waves from the backyard of his Hawaiian home around nine, when he felt it. Adjusting his position, he got on his knees, resting his folded hands on lap. Not sure who to pray for, he simply soaked in the Lord's presence, allowing Him to guide his thoughts.

*   *   *

On a mission trip for her youth group to Belize City, Belize, a young, teenage girl was woken from a deep sleep around one. Unsure as to whom to pray for, but compelled to wake the others to pray as well, she knew her mission and woke them.

The youth leader didn't take but a moment to get everyone together before they joined hands in prayer.

*   *   *

A young family was on safari at Kruger Park in South Africa. Driving around, they enjoyed looking at all the wildlife already spotted. It was nine in the morning, but the mother didn't care. She had her husband pull over, and, with the windows closed, the young family of five joined hands in prayer.

*   *   *

It was ten in the morning in Jerusalem. A teenage boy was on the way to the store to pick up breakfast items for his family, when a wave so overpowering hit him, and he dropped to his knees right there in the street in prayer.

*   *   *

As each person in the world felt compelled to pray, joining those already in prayer, the Heavenly angels glowed brighter. The strength the prayers of the saints gave them, allowed them to push the line back toward the trees.

The other side realized what was going on, and pushed forward even harder. As the battle grew even more intense than it was, Rachel blew a piece of her hair that fell into her face out of the way, looked toward Heaven, and called for help, "Lord, help us!" Then, she jumped on the back of one of the demons and slashed its throat.

As the demon fell to the ground, two others grabbed Rachel, each one holding one of her arms, on either side of her. Within a split second, Rachel heard the high-pitched scream of an arrow as it whizzed by her head, hitting one of the demons right between the eyes. At the same time, another arrow pierced its heart. Stunned for a split second, both Rachel and the other demon looked up to see Jarrah and Barwon, both ranch hands from Serenity, each fire-off two more arrows. The arrows pierced areas that were mortal wounds on the other demon. It stumbled back for a moment, before it went to lunge at Rachel. By that point, both ranch hands were beside Rachel, and Barwon finished it off, while Jarrah grabbed Rachel's arm, pulling her out of reach.

Slightly shaking her, Jarrah yelled, "Rachel! Focus!"

"I…" She shook her head as she watched the two demons burst into flames before disintegrating into ash. "Thank you, but…" she said, and instinct took over. Shaking free, she ran for another demon, face transfixed on taking out the creatures from the other side to protect the station.

Before she got too far, Jarrah pulled her back. "Are you focused?"

"Yes. They caught me by surprise. Won't happen again. I want to get back in there. Let me go!" she ordered. It was at that moment that the clouds burst open with rain. "Seriously?" she said, looking toward the sky. It was then that she noticed the angels with swords surrounding the main house, and knew those in the main houses were safe, no matter what happened out there that day.

"They came down when the others came. They are around all the main houses, since they contain the women and children," Barwon explained.

"Good."

"*You* should be with them," he pointed out, raising an eyebrow at her.

"No," she insisted. "My job is out here."

"Your dress is already destroyed," he commented. "I do not want to be the one to tell Nico that you are gone with it."

Looking at the shreds that were left of her beautiful dress, Rachel got another burst of determination. *They messed with her sister's wedding!* "My job is to defend the innocent. And, while my dress may be a disaster, I'm alive!" Rachel said with a smile and a twinkle in her eyes. Before they could say another word, she ran toward an Unnatural, who was fighting with one of the clan members.

This went on for hours. Rachel didn't think it was ever going to end! Her arms and legs felt like rubber. She pushed beyond what she thought she could, while fighting earnestly.

Just when she was about to drop, there was a loud clap of thunder. While some from the other side retreated for the tree line, others still stood their ground. Those who didn't run were struck down where they stood, when lightning from the heavens struck in multiple areas, blinding everyone, creating a wave of death for the creatures of the other side as it went out from the lightning bolt.

Then, an even louder clap of thunder instantaneously went off, quaking and shaking the ground all around them. Rachel covered her eyes as she dropped to her knees, unable to stand any longer. When she finally looked up, her body was shaking uncontrollably. Looking around them, she saw it was still pouring rain, but there was not one from the other side alive in the fields around them. As a matter of fact, they all looked as if they were struck by lightning. Their bodies were charred and smoldering for only a moment before they burst into flames, and then dissipated into piles of ash.

Amazed, she looked around to see everyone as stunned as she was. There were murmurings from people trying to figure out what had happened, and others were making sure people were okay.

"Rachel?" Jesse's voice came over the radio.

"I'm fine. You?" she asked, still sitting on the ground, head in her hand.

"I'm a little beat up, but no worse for the wear."

"What about everyone else?" Rachel asked. "All stations, please check in."

"The main house is fine. We were protected," Nico said.

"Akoonah is stable. We had quite a few losses," Caleb explained, "but we're still standing. The main house is unharmed."

"Koala Pass is in the same position as Akoonah," Josh said. "Give it a few moments before we abandon the stations for Serenity. I don't know if I trust there won't be a second wave."

"Same here," Rachel said. "And," she looked around to see a few bodies here and there of station hands or clansmen, "looks like we're in the same position as Akoonah and Koala Pass. Dad, have Pete and Val get the medical bags ready. I'll be in to help in a bit."

"Copy," Nico said into his radio. He turned to see Pete standing in the doorway of the living room. The women and children were sent upstairs into the rooms to pray when the battle started. "Did ya hear?"

"Yes. I've already got two bags in the barn. I was worried after the whole clan coming here, that something big may happen. I have been preparing for two days."

"Good man."

"Do you...do you know if my boys are okay?" Pete asked, rubbing the back of his neck as he paced. "Don't tell Victoria. Tell me first. If anything happened to any of them, I need to be the one to tell her."

"Understood." Glancing at the radio, afraid to find out whom they'd lost, Nico finally said into the radio, "Request from Pete for the status of his boys."

"Stand by," Rachel said. Looking around, she called to Barwon.

When he got over to her, he helped her stand, and stabilized her when she went to tumble. "Whoa! You need to get to the main house. I know you just healed from broken ribs. I don't know that you were fully up for this."

"I am. God gave me the strength I needed. He always will. Do you know where P.J., Nicky, David, and Joey fought?"

"Two were near Jesse's end of the station, one was here, and the other ran to Akoonah."

"Jesse, there are supposed to be two near you. Caleb, one is at your station. I'll look around for the one here," Rachel said.

"Copy," both Caleb and Jesse responded.

What felt like forever, while Barwon walked with Rachel through what remained of the battlefield, they found multiple people who needed medical attention, and calculated five dead. They finally located Joey up in the north field.

"Joey?" Rachel asked, when she saw him standing alone.

He turned toward them, almost in a daze.

"Joey, are you okay?" Barwon asked, running over to him. Looking him over, he asked, "What's wrong, boy? You don't look too worse for the wear."

Joey just turned, facing Akoonah station, as a tear crawled down his cheek. Rachel saw what he was looking at, and quickly scrambling over the fence. Once over, she ran over to where Joey's brother, David, lay motionless on the ground. "What happened?" Rachel shouted, as Joey and Barwon moved closer to her. Her heart raced while she reached down for a pulse on the motionless seventeen-year-old. Sighing, she then asked, "Why weren't you two in the main house?"

"He-he said it was our duty as the Chief's nephews to fight," Joey explained, bottom lip trembling. "I never saw anything like it before! The creature was black, with scales and wings, and..." his voice faded as he shuddered.

When Rachel turned David's body over, she saw the unmistakable markings of talons from a demon. The slash marks were across the young man's throat and chest. With the emotional toll of the day finally boiling over, Rachel's shoulders dropped, and she burst into tears.

Pete and Victoria's children were born and raised on the station. She knew them since their births. Remembering the loss they'd already experienced in losing a couple children when they were younger, along with the Chief less than a week ago, she didn't want to have to be the one to tell them of this as well.

Grabbing the radio off her side, hands shaking, she pressed the talk button, "T-this is Rachel. Um, Joey is fine. Shaken, but fine. Caleb, I found the one who was on your station. Has anyone located P.J. or Nicky?"

Hearing what Rachel didn't say over the radio, tears immediately ran down Nico's cheeks. He understood, from Rachel's statement, that David was no longer with them. "What's your location, Rachel?" Nico asked, beside himself, as he saw Pete drop to his knees, before dropping his head into his hands, rocking on the floor.

"North field with Barwon."

"Nicky's fine," Jesse finally came over the radio, just as Nico ran out of the house for the north field.

"P.J.'s actually here at Koala Pass. He's shaken, but okay," Josh said over the radio.

Nico didn't respond. He just sprinted toward the north field, focusing on the three figures he saw near the fence on their knees, between Akoonah and Serenity. As he scrambled over the fence, he slowed down when Joey turned toward him.

The tears streaking the young boy's face instantly broke his heart. Nico just grabbed Joey and held him while he sobbed.

"We need to get him back to the main house," Rachel said between tears, "to Victoria and Pete."

Nico shook his head. "Just a minute." Still holding Joey, Nico felt the fifteen-year-old's body shaking as he cried uncontrollably. He knew Joey didn't want his father to see him like that, so he just held him, and would let Joey cry it out.

"Want me to take him back, boss?" Barwon asked. "You three can stay until you are ready. I feel I need to take the boy home to his parents."

Nico nodded, so Barwon went over and scooped the young man's body from the ground. The gentle giant cradled the boy, as he carefully scaled two fences before heading toward the main house.

"I'm sorry, Dad," Rachel said, distraught. "If we weren't here –"

"Things would have been worse," Nico cut her off. "We have been a target for a long time. You, along with the heavenly angels and the clansmen, fought them off, protecting the women and children. You are *not* responsible for this."

"Leah's wedding." Rachel shook her head. Then a thought struck her. "Are Leah and Finn okay?"

"Don't know about Finn, but Leah's a mess. Your Mum's not doing well either. This has taken quite a toll on them."

"Charlie?" Rachel said into the radio.

"Go ahead," Charlie answered, much to Rachel's relief.

"You were the only one with a radio I hadn't heard from. Making sure you were okay," she explained, as she wiped the tears off her face. She knew she needed to regroup, and help clean everything up from the disaster created by the other side. Working her way out of the field, toward the main house, she knew Pete and Val would need her nursing experience to help.

"I'm physically okay, but furious, as are the other clansmen. This plan had better come to fruition sooner than later. They crossed another major line today," Charlie warned, anger evident in his tone, as the sound of wailing slowly grew from around the stations. "We've had enough!"

The men watching the houses finally released the women from the houses, unable to hold them back any longer. The children were still held in the homes until the adults could get everything cleaned up.

Rachel left her dad and Joey still crying in the field. She knew she needed to get back to help with the clean-up, and that they would need her to bandage people. As she neared the main house, she saw the arch coated in blood, with the bouquets trampled at its base.

Kneeling, she gently picked up what was left of Leah's bouquet, and pulled out any flowers that looked decent. Using her knife, she cut off part of the tulle from the bottom of the arch. Looking around the arch, she pulled off some greenery, along with holly branches, and put them together with the flowers she salvaged. Using the tulle she cut off, she wrapped the stems of the tiny bouquet and tied the ends in a bow.

As she was fluffing the bow, she heard someone call her name. She looked up to see Jesse running across the field toward her. As tired as she was, to see him lifted her spirits. "Jesse," she breathed out.

When he got to her, he put his hands on the sides of her face, and looked her over. Her hair was a disaster, and had multiple twigs sticking out of it. She had dirt in her hair, and on her face, along with dried blood. Her dress was torn, and in some places either shredded or missing. "Are you hurt?" he asked, continuing to look her over.

"Just in the heart," she said, shaking her head. She glanced at the flowers in her hand. "Poor Leah and Finn. This was supposed to be a day of celebration for them. That's not to mention those lost." Looking back up at Jesse, as tears poured down her cheeks once again, she said, "David's dead. He was only seventeen."

"I figured by what you said," he said, and gently kissed her forehead. Then, looking around, he added, "People are going to need help."

While he wrapped his arms around her, Rachel mumbled through her tears, "This day is…I have no words." She shook her head. "The loss."

"Why don't we go help?"

Looking up at Jesse, she explained, "I need to see Leah first. I can't do anything for Pete or Victoria, but I can for Leah."

He nodded, as he brushed off the tears from her face. "I understand. I just needed to see you were okay. There are a lot of people who were shaken to their core today. I think I need to help."

"I'm going to talk to Leah first, and then I'll head on over to help Val and Pete."

"Good idea. And, Rachel?" he asked, lifting her chin.

"Yeah?"

"I love you."

"I love you too," she said, and kissed his lips before he ran off.

Fixing the flowers as much as she dared, she made her way into the main house. When she stepped in, she found the children huddled in the living room, whispering amongst themselves in three different groups. She glanced into the kitchen, to find it empty, before heading up the stairs. "Leah? Are you here?"

"In here," Leah called from their parents' room.

When she walked in, she found Leah and Kit on the bed. Kit looked like she could barely keep her eyes open. Her skin was pale, and she looked even more frail than normal. Leah's eyes were red from crying, as she lay on Kit's shoulder, with Kit's arm around her.

"Hi," Rachel said quietly.

Leah rolled over to see what she had in her hands. "What's that?"

"It's what I could salvage. I know it's not much, but –"

Leah burst into tears when she realized what Rachel did. "That's so sweet!" Shaking her head, she added, "This day is not at all what I imagined. Not even close."

Going over to the bed, Rachel handed the bouquet to Leah, and said, "Maybe Charlie can finish the ceremony later? That way you guys can try to piece together what is left of this day."

"No. The stations are a disaster. People need help. Besides, I just wanted to be with Mum for a bit. I need to change before I head outside."

Just then, Rachel realized there was blood all over Leah's dress. "What is…" her voice faded. "Is Finn okay?"

"He got hurt, but he'll recover."

"Is it your blood?" Rachel asked, horrified by the thought as she looked over her sister.

"No." Leah pushed her hands away. "It was an Unnatural. I was angry that they stormed my wedding, and killed five of them on my own."

Rachel couldn't help the laugh that escaped her mouth, and quickly covered her mouth with her hand. "I'm sorry."

"No." Leah finally smiled. "It *is* kind of funny when you picture it. Gives new meaning to Bridezilla," she said in a chuckle. She sighed, and then mentioned, "I don't want *this* day to be remembered as the day we started our forever after together. I want *that* day to be happy."

Taking Leah's hand into hers, Rachel suggested, "What if we do it on Christmas? That can be a day of double celebration.

Besides, if Finn forgets your anniversary, he's got a present for you regardless, so he won't get in trouble."

Leah giggled. "This is true."

"What if I talk to Charlie about it later, and you talk to Finn?"

"Okay," Leah agreed.

"Good," Kit said, grabbing Leah's other hand. She gave it a gentle squeeze as she said, "I need to get some rest. Please go help the others?"

Both girls leaned down and gave their mom a kiss on either cheek before they headed to change and then out to help.

Chapter 6
Chain Reaction

After the three stations met on Serenity Wells Station, Pete, Rachel, and Val set off to bandage those who needed it, aided by some of the clanswomen, while the rest of the women got food and watched the children. The men were spread through the three stations on different duties. Some collected those who passed in battle, and took them to the front of Serenity's main house to be mourned; while others dug graves at the burial ground on the station, or helped with general cleaning of the stations from battle.

"Are you okay to join the others?" Nico asked after he let go of Joey. "Your Mum will need a hug from you. While you are the youngest male, and have a few sisters sprinkled in there as well, I happen to know you're her favorite."

"Thanks," Joey mumbled, wiping his face from his tears.

"You are a brave young man. I don't know if I would have faced what you did today when I was fifteen."

"Yes, you would have," Joey said, as they ventured toward the main house. "You are one of the bravest men I know. The stories Dad tells of you in The States with the FBI are exciting!"

"I still think you're mighty brave," Nico said, draping his arm over Joey's shoulder as they walked.

"Thanks, Uncle Nico. That means a lot coming from you."

"I need to ask you a favor."

"What's that?"

"There will be a mission in a few days that some of the clansmen are going on." Stopping in front of him, Nico put his hands on Joey's shoulders and bent down to look him in the eyes. "Now, I *know* you want revenge for what they did to David, but I want you to promise me that you will hang back and protect the women and children here on the station."

"But –"

When Joey went to object, Nico cut him off, "With the loss of your grandfather, and now your brother, among the others lost today, I don't think your family can handle anymore. I am going to ask the same from P.J. and Nicky as well, so don't think I'm doing it just because you aren't eighteen yet. I think you are a fine, brave, and strong young man. I just saw your dad's reaction to the loss of your grandfather and your brother less than a week apart…so close to Chrissie no less. Please don't make them mourn another?"

Joey thought for a moment. Looking around the battle-torn stations from the top of the hill where they stood, they could see it all. The reactions of those who lost loved ones, along with seeing those injured, and remembering what he felt at hearing about his grandfather, broke his heart. Joey finally relented, nodding in response.

"Good. Thanks, mate," Nico said, and they resumed their walk back to the main house. The silence between them had an understanding of the agreement between the two, as well as the bond that was between the pair. Nico was not looking forward to the conversation between he, P.J., and Nicky, but he was not about to let Pete or Victoria experience what they did today, any time soon, if he could prevent it.

* * *

The priority for the rest of the day was caring for the wounded and burying the lost. That night, while Rachel, Val, and Pete still tended to the wounded, the clansmen not hurt cornered Charlie in the barn.

"We need to do something *now*!" one man shouted.

"We cannot wait for them to attack again!" another shouted.

"After the loss of the Chief, and now this, it cannot be put off any longer!" another man yelled.

"We cannot just sit here and do nothing! This was a deliberate attack that *must* be answered!" came from another man, as the roar from the others shouting various things all at the same time, grew in intensity.

More of this type of shouting went on for over five minutes before Charlie got the crowd of men under control. "MEN!" Charlie roared when he had enough. "Sit down and let us talk *to* each other, not *at* each other!"

When the men calmed down, they were too anxious to sit, so Charlie climbed onto a wooden box so he could see everyone. He saw Jesse, Jon, and Josh slip in the back just in

117

case Charlie needed back up. Nodding in appreciation toward them, he then turned to the clansmen, and said, "Please, let us speak about this like gentlemen." When they calmed once again, he explained, "I am just as angry as you. I have lost not only my father, but my nephew, and multiple other men that I am responsible for this week. It has been difficult for *all* of us. The A.N.G.E.L.s are working on a plan, but we need to use patience –"

The noise level erupted above what Charlie could control, so Josh let out a high, shrill-pitched whistle that got everyone's attention and irritated the horses. When everyone turned around, Josh took a step forward and explained, "Gentlemen, this is a chess match. They have made some serious moves, but we will be the ones to win the match. We need to be strategic in our countermoves to achieve this. All of our lives, and the lives of everyone we care about, depend on it. We were shaken, but not broken. The Haven is currently working on getting us the information we need to execute a plan. We only need to exercise some understanding that while a strike will not happen tomorrow, a strike *will* happen in the next several days that will be precise, surgical, calculated…and will cause immense damage and devastation to the other side. Can we count on you to watch our backs while we make the plan?"

Some of the men nodded, but others shook their heads, while others threw their hands up in frustration.

Putting his hands in front of him, in a manner of showing trust and surrender, Josh took a few more steps toward the group until he was right in front of them. "We need your help in this plan to make it successful. If you leave on your own, the plan we discussed as a group in the main house will not come to fruition. Jon needs to work with some of you on training, while Jacob works with others on how to execute his portion of the plan. If we work together, instead of tearing each other up or going off on our own, we *can* win this. Will you join us?"

After a few tense moments of debate among the clansmen, the original twelve from the meeting in the main house stepped out of the crowd. Daku said, "We will join you. We will work with you to take them down." Then he looked at the remaining fifteen, and asked, "What say you?"

In what seemed like several more tense minutes, finally, one after the other moved over to the group with Daku. The last remaining man looked at Daku, then Charlie, and then looked at Josh, and asked, "We *will* take them out, right? My son was killed today as well. I will *not* let his blood go unanswered!"

"Yes. We need your help, though," Josh explained. "Just like Sasha and Jesse knew when they were coming before we saw them today, giving us a few precious moments to get some to safety, and others into position, the other side can do the same in regards to us. You see, Sasha and Jesse can feel when the other side is near. They have people on their side who can do the same thing. Because of this, we need you men to do for us what we cannot. We'll be detected if we try it on our own. We will be there for when your portion of the mission is complete, or if something should go wrong. While I have no doubt regarding the ability of everyone here, we don't leave things to chance…we leave them to God."

"What if I don't believe in God?" the man challenged.

"Jarli," Charlie said, coming down from the box he was on, "just because you do not believe in God, does not mean He does not believe in you. Let us talk, while these men continue without us. Josh, do you have this?" When Josh nodded, Charlie offered to Jarli, "Perhaps I can set your mind to ease if you give me just a little of your time?"

Jarli only nodded in response, so he and Charlie went off to speak privately. When they were away from the others, Jarli said, "Your father spoke to me multiple times, but I have a difficult time accepting what he said as truth. Especially with what all we have seen lately."

"Actually, I would counter that *with* all you have seen, you, of all people, *should* believe. You have seen Michael, the archangel. You have seen demons. You have seen people possessed by the dark side of this. You saw creatures of the night that plague people's night terrors in real life, and physically fought them. Why is it you resist?"

"Because I do not want anything to do with *any* of this!"

Leaning on the fence of the horse paddock just outside the barn, both men looked out over the vast acreage of Serenity Wells Station, deep in thought. Charlie prayed and meditated on the scenery before him for a few minutes, before a moment of clarity by the Spirit came to him. When it did, he stated, "I'm afraid you may have a misconception I need to clear up for you."

"Oh, really?" Jarli asked. "What's that?"

"While you think you have a choice of joining the fight or not, I present you with the truth that you are already *in* the fight. You are *already* on a side. You have to choose to leave that side to come to the light, or stay where you are…on their side."

"What are you saying?" Jarli asked, wide-eyed. "Are you trying to tell me that I am on the side with those creatures from today? No way! I would never choose to fight *with* them!"

"Yes. I am speaking the truth," Charlie's answer hung for a heavy minute before he explained, "You see, back in the beginning, when Adam and Eve committed the first sin, communication between God and man was broken. After that, it took a blood sacrifice from a perfect animal to atone for sin. Then, Jesus got together with God, and they figured out a way to repair the communication between God and man, as well as make a way for humans and God to spend eternity together. There had to be an ultimate blood sacrifice, though, from One who was perfect. The only One who fit that, was Jesus. You know the story of when Jesus was born of the Virgin Mary, right?"

"Yes."

"Well, have you heard the story of Jesus Himself?"

"A little, I am afraid I am not very well educated in this area," Jarli admitted. "I know He was born, and that the king at the time tried to kill Him. The King had all the babies less than two years old killed in order to try to kill Jesus as well. Jesus and IIis family went to Egypt for a bit, before returning once it was safe. Then I heard stories from Chief about the miracles that Jesus supposedly did. Did He really do all those things?"

"All those things and more!" Charlie smiled. "Jesus was amazing! The most amazing thing He did, though, was when He gave His life for His people...past, present, *and* future."

"What does that mean?"

"That sacrifice I mentioned earlier?"

"Yeah."

"When Jesus came, He *knew* what His ultimate job would be…and that was to give His life for mankind."

"So, you are saying that the blood sacrifice they had to give to atone for sin, was Jesus?"

"Yes."

"But, why?"

"Let me back this up a bit," Charlie said, thinking through how to explain it all. "In the Bible, in Romans 6:23, it says, *'For the wages of sin is death; but the gift of God is eternal life through Jesus Christ our Lord.'* When Adam and Eve sinned, that created the break between God and Man. You see, Satan used the vulnerability of Eve, and the weakness of Adam, to bring sin into the world. This broke God's heart, but the break had to happen. John 3:16 and 17 explains it pretty well. It says, *'For God so loved the world, that He gave His only begotten Son, that whosoever believeth in Him should not perish, but have everlasting life. For God sent not His Son into the world to condemn the world; but that the world through Him might be saved.'* Jesus fixed the communication between God and man by His sacrifice. He did not come here to judge us, but to save us. Remember when I said you were already on a side?"

"Yeah."

"Because of sin, we are born on the side of Satan, along with those creatures you saw today. That's your team, so to speak. Satan wants us to stay on his side, so he does his best to keep it a secret that if you do not choose Jesus and God, you are automatically on Satan's side."

"But, how is that fair?" Jarli asked, stunned. "I did not pick that side. How can you say that God loved the world if we are stuck on Satan's team?"

"You are *not* stuck on Satan's team. Through Jesus' sacrifice, we are given an option. Because Jesus gave His life, we now have an option of leaving that team. But, if we do not choose to do this before we pass, we will forever be in hell with Satan and his followers. When we choose to follow Jesus and God, we have the promise of eternal life with Them."

"Interesting," Jarli said, leaning against the fence. "So, what do we have to do to switch sides?"

"That's easy…well, sort of."

"Do not confuse me, please?"

"Okay, well, here is the thing. You see, yes, Jesus did die. Yes, He did pay the penalty for our sin on the cross. That was a sacrifice He knew was coming, and He did it willingly."

"Did He have a choice?"

"Actually, He did. He is the Son of God. If He did not want to, He did not have to. He *chose* to go through with it, even though He knew *exactly* what was coming. He was tortured, beaten to the edge of death, and then hung on a cross to die. Having said that, there's another portion of this reality. He died, but rose from the grave three days later, and is still alive today."

"Bullocks!"

"Jarli! Do not let anyone else hear you say that!" Charlie chastised him. "That language is not allowed on this station."

"My apologies. But, seriously, mate. You expect me to believe that?"

"Would you believe it if I told you that over five hundred people saw Him walking around *after* He died on the cross?"

"Give me the straight truth."

"I am! I can show you in the Bible where it says it!"

"All right. Show me later. Go on," Jarli said, crossing his arms, still doubtful.

"Jarli, He is God, the Son. God is omniscient, omnipotent, and omnipresent. He is, was, and forever will be. He is here for us at all times, everywhere."

"If He's so all-powerful, why does He care about me? Why would He?"

"Because He loves you."

"How am I supposed to believe that? I don't see Him here."

"Let me think on how to explain this," Charlie said, letting the Spirit guide his thoughts. "Before He left, Jesus wanted to give His twelve apostles, who He had been teaching during His time on earth, a gift. He gave them the Holy Spirit."

"Oh! I heard of that one!"

"Right. The Spirit is the part of the Trinity, Who helps guide our steps."

"Doing that Christian talking I tease you about again. What does that mean?"

"What?"

"Trinity?"

"God is three persons in One. He is the Father, The Son, and The Holy Spirit."

"I'm confused."

"The easiest way I can describe it is like an egg. There is the eggshell, the egg white, and the egg yolk. All three make an egg, but they can be separated, and be useful by themselves."

"Oh! That's interesting. Okay, so to make sure I'm following you, you are saying that Jesus is the Son of God?"

"Yes."

"And, He came to earth to be a sacrifice, so we do not have to do the blood sacrifices anymore to pay for our sin?"

"Yes."

"And, He died on the cross for that sacrifice, but –" He put his hand up to stop Charlie from interrupting. "…but He rose from the grave, so He's alive?"

"Yes."

"Here on earth?"

"No."

Throwing his hands in the air, Jarli snapped, "Well, where is He then?"

"He is in Heaven with God, waiting for us. In John 14:3, He says, *'And if I go to prepare a place for you, I will come again, and receive you unto Myself; that where I am, there ye may be also.'* In other words, He's making a place for us in Heaven. He's getting ready. And, He'll come back one day. When He does, He'll take all of us, who are His, back to Heaven with Him, so we can enjoy eternal life, glorifying God together."

"And, the other option? What does that look like?"

"Well, Matthew 13:50 describes it by saying, *'and throw them into the blazing furnace, where there will be weeping and gnashing of teeth.'* Revelation 20:13 and 14 says, *'The sea gave up the dead that were in it, and death and Hades gave up the dead that were in them, and each person was judged according to what they had done. Then death and Hades were thrown into the lake of fire. The lake of fire is the second death.'* Jarli, it is not a pleasant place."

"How long will they have to be in a lake of fire?"

"Forever."

"Serious?"

"Yes. In fact, in Matthew 10:28, it tells us, *'Do not fear those who kill the body but cannot kill the soul, but rather fear him who is able to destroy both soul and body in hell.'* In Revelation 14:11, it describes it in saying, *'And the smoke of their torment rises forever. There is no rest day or night for those who worship the beast and his image, or for anyone who receives the mark of his name.'* As a matter of fact, Thessalonians 1:8 and 9 puts it as, *'in flaming fire, inflicting vengeance on those who do not know God and on those who do not obey the gospel of our Lord Jesus. These will suffer the punishment of eternal destruction, separated from the presence of the Lord and from the glory of His might.'* You see, just like there is a chain reaction of everyone wanting vengeance for what happened to Chief, and what happened today, there was a chain reaction to the sin that was done by Adam and Eve. That chain reaction caused everyone to be born onto the other side's team. Jesus came and fixed part of it, but we are not puppets. He wants us to choose willingly to follow Him. And, if we do, we are to be loyal to Him, and have a relationship with Him for the rest of our lives. He craves that kind of relationship with us. Just like you want to have a relationship with your children, God wants to have a relationship with us. The only way to do that is through Jesus. He's the go-between."

"I think I have it…with one exception. How do I change sides?"

"All you need to do is ask. Matthew 7:7 says, *'Ask, and it shall be given you; seek, and ye shall find; knock, and it shall be opened unto you.'* In other words, you only need to pray and ask for Jesus to come into your life."

"That's it?"

"Yep. Romans 10:9 says, *'If you declare with your mouth, "Jesus is Lord," and believe in your heart that God raised Him from the dead, you will be saved.'* So, once you believe, your name is written on a list in Heaven, and you have effectively changed teams."

"I see," Jarli said, leaning down, snapping a piece of wheat. Chewing on it in thought, he continued, "So, if we do what Josh wants us to, and something happens while we are out there, when we die, if our name is on that list, then we will go to Heaven?"

"Yes, but this is more than a one-and-done."

Looking at Charlie, Jarli raised an eyebrow. "What do you mean?"

"This is for life. If nothing happens to you, and you come back, and your name is on that list, you have a responsibility."

"What responsibility?"

"We are to tell others, just like I am telling you right now. We are also to listen for the Spirit to guide us, and show us the plan God has for us. We *also* have a responsibility to keep up our relationship with Him daily."

"So, it's not just what He can do for me, but what I can do for Him?"

"Exactly. Just like every relationship here on earth. He wants to have a relationship, not a 'what's in it for me' moment. He wants you heart and soul. He also wants you to want Him heart and soul."

"Well then, I think I have some thinking to do."

"Just know that your time is limited, as some may have sadly learned today."

"I understand. Tell the others I will join you on this mission. I have some thinking to do on my own."

"Just please do me a favor and let me know your decision before we go? Whether you choose to pray and believe on Jesus or not, is up to you. I would like to know what your choice is."

"Why?"

"If something is going to happen, I want to know whether I will see you again or not."

"I see," Jarli said, shoving his hands in his pockets. "All right. I will let you know."

"Thank you," Charlie said, standing up. "I love you as my brother, but I need to get back with the others. Who knows what they are doing to Josh."

Jarli chuckled as Charlie took off for the barn. With a lot on his mind, he stood, shoved his hands in his pockets, and headed out onto the station to do some deep thinking.

Chapter 7
We Forge the Chains We Wear in Life

"Mom, Dad, we wanted to know if you had a few minutes to talk?" Leah asked, as she and Finn walked up to where Kit and Nico were resting on the porch rocking chairs early the next morning after breakfast.

"Of course. Even with everything going on, you are our daughter, and a priority," Kit said. She looked worse today, than she did the day before. All of this was taking a lot out of her.

"We've talked, and while we know generally speaking, Christmas time is for family," Finn started. "However, with what happened yesterday, we were wondering if it would be okay to get married tonight…on Christmas Eve." Seeing the stunned look on their faces, Finn quickly explained, "I know we were supposed to be married yesterday, then in Cairns today, to be back for Christmas on Monday, but everything is pretty much already here. And while we didn't want yesterday's events to mar our wedding day, we *do* want to reserve Christmas Day for family. We also want to do it when we're *sure* everyone can be here. With Josh and Rachel's schedules, that's a toss-up if they can even get back here for a set date."

"Exactly," Leah jumped in after seeing the look on her parents' faces. "Rachel talked to me about the possibility of

Christmas Day, but we want a day that is just for us. It still gives us a reason to celebrate without stepping completely on Christmas. We also know the teams are going to be taking off the day after Christmas, and we wanted to get married while friends and family are still here."

Taking a moment of thoughtful prayer before he replied, Nico glanced at Kit, who nodded, before he stood and walked over to the couple sitting on the railing. Wrapping his arms around Leah, before extending his arm out to Finn, who happily hugged him as well, Nico said, "We would be *happy* to have your wedding here tonight." Looking at both of them, he asked, "Are you *sure* you want to do it tonight, though, with all of the events from yesterday? I need to caution you that many are in mourning."

"Then we need a reason to celebrate," Leah said with a smile.

"What are you going to do about dresses?" Kit asked. "Rachel's is ruined, and your dress, along with the other girl's dresses are disasters. We don't have time to get them cleaned and fixed."

"While yesterday looked like a horror show, I'll admit, it doesn't change our resolve to be wed," Leah explained. "I don't care if we get married in jeans and T-shirts, as long as we get married. Life is too short to be stuck in formality." Taking Finn's hand into hers, Leah declared, "I love this man, and only want to be his wife. We both want our lives started together."

"Can you do all the arrangements?" Kit asked. "I need to take a nap if we're about to be up late."

"I'll get Rachel and the clanswomen to help me. Pretty sure my other bridesmaids, along with the women of the other two stations can help throw it together as well," Leah said, her countenance brightening.

"Well, it'll look like a zombie apocalypse with all the walking wounded, but the day is yours," Nico said. "I gotta help Caleb with the station. Kit, go grab a kip. Take as long as you need, love," he said, and then kissed her on the head before he ran off onto the station.

"I need to tend to some of the injured animals from yesterday," Finn explained. "You take the day to get everything ready. All I ask is that you tell me where, when, and what to wear, *with* some notice."

"You got it!" Leah said, and then gave him a kiss before he took off for the barn.

"You got a good one," Kit commented, as she slowly stood, bracing herself with the chair arms.

"Thank you, Mum," she said, looping her arm through Kit's to assist her into the house once she got up. She also helped her mom up the stairs to her room.

"I appreciate your help," Kit thanked her.

As they took one step at a time, Leah confessed, "I feel the need to tell you that we are also getting married before anything happens to you."

Kit stopped on the stair she was on, and looked at her daughter. "What do you mean?"

"Mum, let's be honest. You aren't lookin' so good."

"I don't feel so good," Kit admitted.

"Let's get you upstairs to bed, and then we can keep talking."

"Okay," Kit relented.

As Leah helped her mom up the stairs, her heart broke. By the time they made it up the stairs, and down the hall to Kit's room, Kit looked beyond exhausted.

Sighing, Kit said, "I don't think I should be this tired, and was hoping to not be in this much pain. I feel like my body's on fire most of the time."

Taking her hand, Leah sat on the bed beside her. "I'm sorry you're in so much pain and agony. If I could take it from you, I would."

"I know you would, but I wouldn't let you," Kit said with a wink. "It's the parent's job to take the pain from the child, not the other way around."

"I still feel horrible. It breaks my heart to see you like this. You were so strong only a few months ago. Was your…was your mum like this too?"

"Worse," Kit said. "I was only seven, but I remember it well."

Leah wrapped her arms around her mother. "I'm so sorry."

"It's okay, honey. I'll either pull through, or you'll see me when you join me in Heaven. If I don't make it, I'll be with my mum until y'all can join us later. I'll be getting things ready for you. You see, I'm okay either way."

"I'm not," Leah said, as a tear slowly crawled down her cheek. "I want to see you with my kids, like you've been with Caleb's. I want them to know you. I know it's selfish, but I want you here."

"That's not up to me, Possum," Kit said, gently. "That'll be up to God."

"Then it's my prayer that you stay."

"As long as it's by His will, and not ours."

*　　*　　*

The day flew by with a flurry of activity. While Leah and the women of the clan, as well as the stations, kept everyone fed and focused, they also got the wedding arrangements completed. A few had to make a run to town to finish or buy something that got ruined. Even though it was Christmas Eve, they did their best to make the day special for Finn and Leah.

While everyone else got ready for the wedding, Angel and Sasha, driven by Pete, went to get Spencer. His plane was delayed, much to Angel's relief. She didn't want him walking into the disaster that happened the day before, or its aftermath. He may have just turned around, and got back on a plane for the United States!

"There he is!" Angel said, visibly excited to see him.

Sasha's stomach lurched at her excitement. He hoped she felt the same for him, as he did for her, but time would tell. Seeing a handsome, blonde-haired, green-eyed young man coming down the terminal did not help his anxiety. While Sasha was relieved Spencer appeared strong, due to their mission, he wasn't happy at Angel's visible thrill at seeing him.

Spencer looked to be around six foot, and carried himself like he could handle himself in a fight. Sasha half-wished he was the geeky, scrawny lab guy he imagined. When Angel wrapped her arms around Spencer in a hug, Sasha cringed.

"It'll be okay, mate," Pete said, noticing Sasha's countenance. Resting his hand on Sasha's shoulder, he assured him, "She likes you. I can tell."

"Did you see the smile on her face when she saw him?"

"Yes. I saw her face when she saw *you* when you all got here together too. She likes ya, mate. Trust me."

Folding his arms in front of him, Sasha said, "Time and God will decide that."

"Keep that thought in mind. Here they come," Pete mentioned. Sticking his hand out to shake Spencer's, Pete said, "G'day! I'm Pete. How ya goin'? I trust you had a good flight?"

"A little rough," Spencer admitted, shaking Pete's hand. "The plane had issues in LAX that cost me an extra day. Thankfully, they gave me flight credit for the return flight."

"I am Sasha," Sasha said, shaking Spencer's hand. "Thank you for coming to help."

"Well, with what Angel explained to me, how could I not?" Spencer beamed, fascination evident, as they headed to baggage claim. "Is there really a box from around the time of Christ out there for us to find?"

"Sort of. It's more from His apostles," Angel clarified.

"Do you really have one of them?"

Eyes wide in shock, Sasha asked, "Angel! You did not really tell him that, did you?"

"I had to in order to explain what was in the other one," she said in her defense.

Shaking his head, Sasha crossed his arms. "That was not good. The team will not be happy with you."

"Look, Angel and I were close in college. We didn't have any secrets," Spencer explained. "While I know your group has many secrets, I also needed some information prior to coming out. I may be lab tech, but the archeological perspective of this is insane."

"If we find it, you cannot tell a soul," Sasha warned.

"Just being able to touch it will be more than enough for me," Spencer assured him. "You have to understand the thrill it will be to see what's in it! When she told me, it blew my mind!"

"How do *you* know what *exactly* is in it?" Sasha asked Angel.

"The Colonel told us," Angel said matter-of-factly.

"I see."

"Do *you* know what's in the boxes?" Angel asked.

"I do. When I told my godmother what we were doing, she told me what was in them."

"What do you mean you told her?" Angel asked, shocked. "How could you?"

"Seriously?" Sasha challenged, taking a step toward Angel, as they stopped in the middle of the walkway. "You are *seriously* going to say that to me? My godmother is an A.N.G.E.L., same as us. Spencer is not. Which one of us may have overstepped in this situation?"

Angel took a deep breath. This was not how she wanted this conversation to go. Obviously, they would need to work on communication. "I'm sorry. You're right."

Pete's jaw dropped. The fact that she did not fight him, stunned him.

"Thank you. Now, where is your luggage?" Sasha asked Spencer.

"Over there in that one." Spencer pointed out the carousel. "The luggage hasn't started yet," he said, as they headed toward where the luggage would come out. "Look, I didn't mean to start anything. I'm excited. It's not every day, or even in the average dig, that you come across the items Angel mentioned. I don't plan on telling anyone. I'm just thrilled to be a part of this."

"What did you find out?" Angel asked, as she reached for Sasha's hand, relieved when he accepted hers into his.

Quietly, Spencer explained, "From what Angel told me, John and Peter had the box that you guys are in possession of, while Paul and Timothy took the other one. I tracked it from the beginning. I'm sure that's how the other side, as you call them, found it in the first place. I tracked their missionary journey, and went on from there."

"I know you did a lot of work, but what if we take it from another angle? What if we look where we think it was last?" Angel asked.

"You know?" Sasha asked, surprised.

"I'm betting, if they're like us at all, they kept it close. I have a feeling they may have had it in Black Rock."

"You seriously going back there?" Pete asked, dumbfounded.

"Possibly. If you recall, regarding my parents' past, there was also another place here where there was a cluster of them in Queensland. They may have hidden it there as well."

"How do we know they didn't do what we did?" Sasha asked.

"What did you do?" Spencer asked, pulling both of his bags off the baggage carousel.

"We buried it," Angel explained. "A small handful know exactly where, but we all know it's buried somewhere, and is still in our possession."

"You buried it?" Spencer asked. "Are you serious?"

"You wouldn't be able to see it even if we had it," Angel explained. "I'm afraid that's only for the inner circle."

"No problem," he said, as Pete took one of his bags, and Spencer carried the other. "I'll do what I can to help."

"Did you find anything else?" Angel asked.

"I found Paul and Timothy's potential resting place, but that's not pertinent to finding the box. Did you guys find anything out?"

"We've kind of had our hands full," Angel explained. "Rachel's sister is getting married today."

"Oh! So, we're going to a wedding?" Spencer asked, pleasantly surprised. "I love weddings!"

"You would," Sasha said under his breath. When he did, Angel squeezed his hand hard, so Sasha let it go, and shoved his hands in his pockets. When Angel shot him a look, he narrowed his eyes back at her, daring her to challenge him again.

Looking back at Spencer, she said, "So, needless to say, we've been a bit busy since we got here."

"You did not tell him what happened yesterday?" Sasha questioned.

Angel narrowed her eyes at Sasha, before turning back to see Spencer raise an eyebrow at her. As they put Spencer's luggage in the back of the truck, Angel said, "There was an incident."

"An *incident*?" Pete said, blown away, unable to keep quiet anymore. While they got in the truck, he said, "That was more than just an incident!"

"I'm trying not to scare him here," Angel said on a sigh as Pete headed toward the station.

"You need to be honest with him," Pete scolded her.

"What happened?" Spencer asked.

"There was an attack on the three stations," Angel explained. "People were lost in the attack."

"What *kind* of attack?"

"An attack from the other side."

"Meaning?"

"Demons, Unnaturals, and creatures of the night."

In wide-eyed horror, Spencer's jaw dropped as his heart raced. "You're serious?"

"It was bad," Sasha admitted. "It was originally in the middle of Rachel's sister's wedding, which is the reason it is postponed until today."

"I see," Spencer said, processing this new piece of information. "You said it would be dangerous. I was thinking human danger, though."

"Still interested?" Sasha asked. "It's not too late to take you back to the airport."

After a moment of long, heavy silence, and everyone else holding their breath, Spencer finally said, "Yeah. I'll do it."

Sasha and Angel let out a sigh of relief, while Pete just shook his head. "Are you sure you know what you're walkin' into, mate?" Pete asked. "This stuff is the stuff nightmares are made of, only *you're* dealing with it face to face. There is no turning back once you come toe to toe with one."

"No, I'm not sure, but I'll find out what I'm made of if we run into them. It beats doing standard tests, though. The idea of figuring out the puzzle is what propelled me to be a lab tech in the first place. This is a bigger puzzle than normal." Chuckling, he added, "Not sure if I'll be able to go back to normal lab work after this, but we'll see."

Angel giggled. "It'll change your perspective of the world. That's for sure."

*   *   *

"You look great!" Rachel said when she walked into her sister's room. "I know it's not what you wanted, but you at least look comfortable in this dress."

Smiling, Leah looked beautiful in her white textured cami maxi dress. It was a layered drape design with a scoop neck, and the dress rested at ankle length. She wore the sides of her hair up with a handmade headband, made of natural flowers from around the station.

"What's Finn wearing?" Rachel asked, dressed in a khaki version of Rachel's dress.

"He's wearing a white shirt, similar in texture, with tan pants. It's a lot more casual than I wanted, but I feel it'll be a lot more relaxed as well," Leah explained.

"Here's praying it doesn't get interrupted again either."

"We're hoping and praying God will protect us through tonight *and* Christmas."

"When are you two taking off for your honeymoon?"

"We're not exactly sure. Yesterday kind of messed up the plans. Dad really needs Finn and me here for the animals. Once we're comfortable with their status, we'll probably go."

Resting her hands on Leah's shoulders, Rachel explained, "This is your time. Some station will always need you two somewhere in Queensland. Take the time for you two now."

"I want to, but Finn's not comfortable. We're one of the only two Vets in the area. We actually made the stations nervous when they found out we were getting married," Leah smiled. "They're afraid we'll move to the city and make too much money to care about the stations."

"Pretty sure, knowing you, you set their mind at ease."

"Oh yeah. They're still waiting for us to say something, though."

Anna knocked on the door and walked in, wearing a tan dress, similar to Rachel's. The three of them, along with Willow, went to town that morning to get the dresses. "Hey. How are you doing?" Anna asked. "I know with your other friend bailing, that you've had a rough morning."

With the events from the day before, Skye chose not to come to the wedding. She left town, pretty shaken up.

"I don't blame her. I'm actually surprised *you* decided to come back after yesterday," Leah said, grateful.

"Oh, you are not getting rid of me that easily." Anna smiled. "This is too important."

Willow snuck in behind Anna, along with Lily and Taylor.

Leah smiled. "Well, at least *most* of my bridal party is here."

"We only lost one." Rachel shrugged. "Have to admit, that's not too bad. The odds were not in our favor, but God saw differently. Today is your day. Besides, how romantic is it to have your wedding anniversary on Christmas Eve?" Rachel sighed. "So sweet!"

"I think so too. He's the best present God ever gave me," Leah said. "I'm almost hoping Charlie decides to skip the formalities, and just asks us to do the vows and be done."

"Awww." Willow looked up from straightening Lily's dress. "Don't be like that, Leah. This is a day for you guys to remember with joy, not in trepidation."

"After yesterday, wouldn't you be scared?" Leah asked, rubbing her arms.

Willow stood. "Let's pray right now for the Lord's protection? Will that put your mind at ease?"

Leah nodded.

The four women, and two girls joined hands in prayer for the night's events. They prayed for protection for all in attendance, as well as for the stations. Then they took a few minutes to pray specifically for Finn and Leah, and the life God had planned for them.

"Feel better, Auntie Leah?" Lily asked, giving Leah a hug.

"Yes, little one. Thank you," Leah said, kneeling down, giving her a hug back. "You have a precious heart. Don't ever lose that."

Lily grinned. "I won't."

"The others just pulled in from the airport. Are you ready?" Nico asked, poking his head in the door.

"Yes. I was ready yesterday. I'm *more* than ready today," Leah pointed out.

"Fair enough," Nico said. "I'll be back up to get you all in a tic," he said, and disappeared.

"I'm glad you are all here. Thank you," Leah said to Willow, Rachel, and Anna.

"Wouldn't miss it," Rachel said.

"You know I'm always here," Willow agreed.

"And, we wouldn't miss it either," Anna said, resting her hand on her daughter, Taylor's shoulders.

"You know me, Auntie," Lily piped up. "I'm always up for dressing pretty!"

"Yes, I do," Leah said, gently touching Lily's face. She looked from Taylor to Lily, as she said, "Now, we don't have rose petals today. The women gathered flowers from around the station for you to drop. Please do your best to get them to the side of the aisles, that way I'm not stepping on full flowers?"

"Sure!" Lily agreed.

"No worries!" Taylor agreed as well.

Hearing a knock on the door, Leah stood. "Come in."

"It's time, ladies," Nico said with a smile. "You all look great!"

"Thank you!" The ladies all said in unison.

As they headed downstairs, Leah had her arm looped through Nico's. "You look nervous, but no worries. The Lord's angels showed up and surrounded all three stations a few minutes ago," Nico assured her.

"Good. That's what we prayed for," Leah said, relieved.

"The archangel said they would be here through the morning after Christmas to protect us, and give us rest, and time to plan the attack."

"So, we finally get a break?" Rachel said over her shoulder.

"Much deserved," Nico pointed out.

"Too true!"

"Oh! Since Skye's not here, Finn's groomsman, Adam decided to sit in the audience. Anna's husband, Caleb, and Owen are still upfront."

"Is he okay with that?" Leah asked.

"Yeah. He didn't want to look awkward up there by himself, so he said he'd be fine sitting with the others. Finn said he could still sit with everyone at the head table, though, so he was happy."

"Good."

"He just wants you both to be happy…as do all of us."

Hearing the violin being played by one of the station hands, Leah said, "It's time."

Anna and Willow went down first. Then, Lily and Taylor went down behind Rachel. Once Rachel and the girls were at the front, the station hand changed the tune for Leah and Nico to walk down.

As soon as Finn saw Leah, his heart leaped! Yesterday she was beautiful, but today, she looked more like herself. He appreciated her natural beauty.

Once to the front, Charlie started the ceremony. To Rachel, Finn and Leah looked to be in absolute bliss as they said their vows, prayed over each other, and lit their unity candles. Then the moment finally came for Charlie to pronounce them husband and wife.

"I now pronounce you husband and wife, you may now kiss the bride," Charlie said to them. After they kissed, Charlie turned them to the three stations and clansman, and said, "Ladies and gentleman, it is with the utmost pride, that I present to you Mr. and Mrs. Finn Walker."

Cheers were instantly heard, that echoed through the stations. The animals even reacted to the noise. It went on for a few moments, until Finn walked back down the aisle with Leah, and they headed toward the barn, which was cleaned out and set for the reception. They were followed by Owen and Rachel, Caleb and Willow, and finally Anna and Josh.

Once everyone moved to the barn, the women set out the meal, and a fun time was had by all!

*   *   *

Around ten that night, Jesse finally got Rachel away from the head table, and they went outside. "Whew!" Rachel said, with the permanent grin she had on her face from the point that he saw her walk down the aisle. "Great, but tiring!"

Taking her hand, he mentioned, "They look so happy."

"After yesterday, pretty sure all three stations needed this. It was a brilliant idea!"

"I'm just glad you and Josh were able to be here for it. With the way our life is, I wasn't sure that would be a possibility."

"I had faith that God would let us be here."

"You look amazing, by the way."

"Thank you!"

Letting go of her hand, he moved behind her and wrapped his arms around her waist. Looking down to the barn from the top of the hill, Jesse sighed, and then said, "Someday, I would love for that to be us."

"Lord willing."

"How long do you want to wait? While I'm not in a rush, I don't want to miss out either."

"I understand. How about if I let you know. I know we just officially started, but –"

"But we've been inseparable since the first day I saw you," Jesse finished her sentence.

"Right."

"I remember that day."

"Me too."

"Not the way I do. As soon as I stepped out of the Jeep, and saw your golden hair blowing in the wind, with those amazing blue eyes, I hoped and prayed you were the one joining us." He sighed. "You are beautiful not just on the outside, but absolutely stunning on the inside as well. Your strength of character is matched only by your faith in God."

"That's honestly the sweetest thing anyone has ever said to me," she said, turning around in his arms to face him. When she did, she draped her arms around his neck, and looked into his eyes for only a moment before she kissed him. While it started as a peck, Jesse moved his hands to her waist, and leaned in for a deeper kiss.

Rachel's mind went blank, as they took a few precious moments for themselves. Lost in the kiss, they didn't even hear when Leah and Finn walked up.

"Can't leave you two alone for a minute," Leah finally said with a smirk.

Rachel jumped, and then quickly turned around, still in Jesse's arms. They waited all night to spend some time together, and neither wanted to let go.

"You scared me," Rachel commented.

"Not much scares you. You're usually on alert," Leah observed.

"With the Heavenly angels here, I'm relaxed for once."

"Well, we were coming to tell you that we're going to take off. Dad and Mum rented us a room in town. And, unbeknownst to us, they booked us a trip for our honeymoon."

"Probably because they knew we wouldn't do it on our own," Finn pointed out.

"He knows you're responsible, and would stay where needed," Rachel explained. "That attests to both of your hearts."

"That was sweet! Thank you!" Leah smiled. Giving Rachel a hug, she said, "We've already said good-bye to everyone else. Thank you so much for being here."

"I'll be here whenever you need me…if the Lord wills it," Rachel clarified, "I work for Him."

"I know. I'm grateful for the protection as well."

Hugs were given, and then Leah and Finn headed back to the barn to be sent off on their honeymoon.

"I'm so happy for them," Rachel said, watching the celebration as they pulled away.

"Me too. I'm also glad for our one-on-one time, though. With the way our life is, time like this is precious."

"We're still heading into a storm," Rachel warned. "Yesterday was bad, but Joe told me earlier today that there is more ahead."

Jesse sighed. "It is a heavy burden we bear."

"We forge the chains we wear in life. In this case, I am happily chained to the Lord…no matter where that leads us."

"And, today, we witnessed another pairing, as Leah and Finn were chained…in a good way," Jesse pointed out.

"Some chains are good, some are not so much," Rachel commented.

Jesse kissed her cheek from behind. "Well, I'm happily chained to you."

"And, I am happily chained to you as well."

"Good. Remember this good feeling. Tomorrow may be Christmas," Jesse said, "but tomorrow night we'll be planning an attack for the next day. More lives may be lost before this over."

"Angel, Sasha, and Spencer will be taking off that next morning as well. The Lord only knows how that venture will resolve."

"Do you think everyone's ready?" Jesse asked.

"I hope so," Rachel said. Then, with confidence, she added, "Regardless if they are or not, God's got this. He's stronger than any of this."

"And for that, I am grateful."

Chapter 8
Untangle the Chains

"Auntie Rachel!" Lily ran into Rachel's room, which also had Katia and Delaney in the room. Rachel was in a double bed, and Katia and Delaney were in a set of bunk beds. Bounding through the air onto Rachel's bed, Lily landed, and then planted a kiss on her aunt's cheek. "My brothers will be fixin' t' follow if you don't come down now. Pop-pop said to bring Delaney and Katia too."

Laughing, Rachel tickled Lily for a moment before she asked, "Is that the mission you were sent on?"

"Yep!"

"Okay, okay," Rachel said, sitting up in her bed. "Let me wake the other two up."

"We're up, love," Delaney said, rolling toward Rachel. "Young ones are always so full of energy, yeah? Care to share some of that?"

Giggling, Lily shook her head, and said, "Noooo."

Delaney sighed. "Can't blame a girl for trying."

As Rachel flipped on the lamp, Katia's head peeked over the top bunk, and she let out a groan. "I remember this feeling from the orphanage. The little ones loved Christmas...*and* waking us up," she said, as she covered her head with the pillow.

"Well," Rachel slid on her slippers, "you'd better take the warning. Jasper, Ben, an' Zach are not nearly as quiet as Lily. We got a warning before the second wave was sent. We'd better act on it."

"Those blokes are full a' energy." Lily agreed. Rolling her eyes, she added, "Sometimes too much energy!"

"This is the first Christmas I am away from sestra," Katia mentioned, climbing out of the top bunk. Once on the ground, she slid her feet into her slippers while she donned her robe.

Delaney was a little slower. She sat up for a few moments to get her bearings first. "Well your sister's going to have her hands full with the wonder twins over there."

"You can call her later," Rachel promised, as she headed out the door, holding Lily's hand. "Until then, you'd better hurry. Dad's patience wears thin before sending in the second wave."

"Go ahead. I'll be there in a minute," Delaney said to Katia.

"Better hurry. Rachel's warning does not seem encouraging," Katia cautioned.

"I'll be there in a minute," Delaney said again, and Katia left her, closing the door behind her. Delaney pulled out her Bible from her suitcase. She flipped to her life verse, Isaiah 41:10, *'So do not fear, for I am with you; do not be dismayed, for I am your God. I will strengthen you and help you; I will uphold you with My righteous right hand.'*

When she finished reading her verse, she turned the photo over that was marking its place. It was of Delaney on her graduation from college with her friends. She sighed. Her family abandoned her so long ago, she forgot what it was like to have one. Once she turned eighteen, she finally confessed to her family, which was of a different religion, that she was a Christian. When she refused to renounce her Christianity, she was excommunicated from the family. She rarely saw them in town, and if she did, they turned and walked the other way. Her friends *were* her family, and this new family God gave her in the A.N.G.E.L.s, she would protect with her life.

Shoving the photo back into the Bible, she rested it on her pillow before heading downstairs. What she walked into, she would never forget. It was like something from a greeting card. Something that only happened in her dreams!

At some point during the night, the presents seemed to have doubled. There was a stocking for each one of them (that wasn't there the night before either), actually filled. There was even a breakfast feast already on the table kept warm by small burners.

"What is all this?" Delaney grinned, pleasantly surprised. "I *know* what this place looked like last night, and this isn't it!"

"Welcome to a Sullivan Family Chrissie!" Nico said, gesturing to a spot left for her next to Joe on the stairs. "We've been waiting for you!"

Delaney blushed as she sat down. "Thank you!"

Taking Delaney's hand into his, Joe quietly admitted, "We're all stunned. Seems they've been planning this since they found out we were coming."

"I've never had this before! Nothing like this, anyway."

"I have not since my parents passed," Katia said, from the other side of Joe. "Our Christmas was always small before they passed, though. I have never seen anything this big except on television."

"I promise you that your sister is experiencing the same size Christmas," Angel said from the other side of the room. "Our parents make Christmas big!"

"Good!" Katia smiled. "I want her to have a good one too."

"Let's start with the stockings," Kit said to Nico.

"Jasper, would you like to pass them out?" Nico asked his grandson.

"Would I!" Jasper's face lit up. Running over, he quickly got all of the stockings passed out before taking his seat on the floor with the other kids.

"Go ahead," Nico said, and everyone dug into their stockings.

Each person got several candies, snacks, and small trinkets. Delaney didn't care what was in it. She was grateful to have received anything at all. It was a few years since she properly celebrated Christmas.

Once they finished, the special treat for the group was when the kids passed out a cupcake, with three candles in each one. Nico, Josh, and Rachel helped light all the candles, so the wax wouldn't melt too much before they could eat them, and then everyone sung "Happy Birthday" to Jesus.

When they finished singing, everyone blew their candles out. Once they were all out, and the candles were being collected, Nico explained, "The three candles represent Jesus. Since He always was, always is, and always will be, the candles represent His past, present, and future. While you eat your cupcake in celebration of our Savior's birth, I'll read Luke 2," he said, opening his Bible. After he finished reading Luke 2:1-21, he said, "There are three very important things we celebrate each year as Christians. It's the beginning, being Christmas; the end, being Good Friday; and the forever after, being Resurrection Sunday. All three are crucial. As we head into the upcoming year, keep in mind all of the things God shows you. Remember everywhere Jesus walks with you. And, don't forget all that the Spirit guides you to…and through. Life isn't easy, no matter what path you walk. Jesus walked it, so He understands. He made sure you were never alone. You not only have Him, but the family in Christ. Blood makes you a relative…loyalty makes you family. Thank you for enjoying our family celebration with us this year," he concluded, and nodded toward Lily, who got up and passed out all the presents.

Each A.N.G.E.L. received a present, and of course, the children each got multiple. Inside the boxes for each of the A.N.G.E.L.s, they received a leather-bound journal, a packet of nice pens, and a thin pocket Bible, which easily fit in their back pocket.

Kit cleared her throat before she explained, "In life, there are many stories not told – mainly because they are forgotten. With your adventures, we didn't want you to forget anything…or any*one*. Keeping a journal also reminds you how far you've come, especially on those days of discouragement. You all have a higher calling than most. He has already shown that to you multiple times. Before you go on your mission tomorrow, please take some time today to write down what you have already experienced in your life up to now. If you need another journal, please do not hesitate to ask for one. We have many in reserve. The reason we ask you to do this, is so when you head out in the morning, it is fresh in your minds as to Whom you serve. He has already won the battle. You are just following through what He has planned so long ago."

Words of appreciation were expressed from each member of the A.N.G.E.L.s.

"Know that you are always bathed in prayer each day as well," Nico added. "There is a little note from Kit and me in each of your journals. In the meantime, Josh would you mind praying over breakfast?"

"Sure," Josh agreed.

Once finished, they enjoyed a wonderful breakfast. Afterward, the children played with their toys and games they got for Christmas, Willow cleaned up, Kit went and took a nap, and the A.N.G.E.L.s met together, with Nico, Charlie, and Pete. The group met at Pete's house for privacy.

"What's the status?" Nico asked the group, as they sat down.

"Cori, Kai, and company were able to get what we needed for satellite photos, and I have a plan in place," Jacob explained. "Some of the explosives are currently doing their thing to be ready in the morning. A couple nights ago, after the meeting in the barn, I met with what will be my team. I explained in detail what they will need to do."

"Are you confident they are ready?" Charlie asked.

"Actually, yes." Jacob nodded. "They are fired-up, but know what's at stake."

"Next?" Josh asked the group.

"After the same meeting, we met with the remaining men, and explained what their part would be in covering for those carrying out Jacob's plan," Jon explained. "I have a few concerns regarding a couple of them, but for the most part, they seem ready. After a couple days ago, I am confident they can handle themselves."

"What are your concerns?" Charlie asked.

"There are a few who are *too* fired-up, if you catch my drift. I'm afraid they're not only going to be out there to execute the plan, but also are potentially out there for a death wish. The losses sustained a couple days ago hit many of your people harder than you realize."

Charlie furrowed his brow. "Meaning?"

"Meaning my gift is knowing what people are feeling," Jon reminded him. "I can tell you that all of your people have had their world turned upside down, only to have to battle their worst nightmares the other day, and suffer even more loss. They have lost family and friends…not to mention their Chief, and their home, in a matter of a few weeks. We're used to being uprooted and thinking on the fly. We're also used to what is truly out there. They are not. Plain and simple – they are country folk, thrown into a battle they did not even know existed."

"What is their emotional status?" Charlie pressed.

"Terrified, horrified, yet full of resolve…with exception of the few I mentioned, who have a death wish."

"Which are those?"

"I'll tell you after the meeting. That may be more of a Chief thing to deal with than an A.N.G.E.L. thing. If they still have that tomorrow morning, though?" Jon shook his head. "They need to stay on the station to guard it with the others. We can't have anyone going in with their own agenda. They all need to stick to the plan in place."

Charlie nodded. "I agree."

"So, what *exactly is* the plan?" Rachel asked. "I know we came up with a tentative, but I have yet to hear the final."

Spreading the maps out onto the floor, the group surrounded the maps so everyone could see. Jesse started, "We drive to this point, and leave the vehicles, along with five people to guard them."

"Which five?" Delaney asked.

"You," Jesse said to her, "along with Joe, and three of Charlie's guys. Angel, Sasha, and Spencer leave in the morning for their own mission. That will leave me, Jon, Josh, Charlie, Rachel, Jacob, and Isaac to go with the rest of Charlie's group."

"What about me? Where am I to be in this list?" Katia asked.

"We really need you to stay and guard the station with Val," Jon said. Seeing her disappointment, Jon explained, "Look, we know just how strong you really are, Katia. We need you to keep things safe here while we're gone. Please don't be upset or offended."

"No fair." Katia crossed her arms. "You *know* what I feel. I do not know how you feel."

"Am I *that* bad to hang out with?" Val asked, jokingly.

"No," Katia said, looking down, shoulders dropped. "I just do not like to be left behind."

"Don't look at it as that," Jesse said. "You're going to be in charge of the safety of three stations. We already know they have a target on them. That's why someone has to stay back. Val will be here, but he's still compromised."

"*Really* don't like that term," Val snapped. "Makes me feel like an invalid."

"Could you have done battle the other day?" Jesse challenged.

"No."

"Then you certainly cannot do battle in the field if need be. I need Katia here to not only keep an eye on the station, but to protect you," Jesse explained. "Imagine this. You're the only A.N.G.E.L. on the station, and some members of the other side attack the stations. Could you honestly do anything other than what you did the other day?" Jesse asked.

"No."

"Katia, what would happen to the stations if it were just Val left here?"

"It would not be good," Katia admitted.

"Then, *you* need to come up with a security plan, that will be in place until we return," Jesse said.

"So, you are leaving me in charge of the men and women here on these stations?"

"Yes," Nico jumped into the conversation. "Pick the men you want on security from the station hands of all three stations. Meet with them today. Get a schedule set to cover all three stations for a few days…longer if we need it."

"I can do that," Katia said, her countenance brightened.

"Thank you," Nico said appreciatively. "That takes a lot off of me."

"Now, what about Angel, Sasha, and Spencer?" Charlie looked at Angel for her update.

"We've actually done quite a bit already. Well," Angel blushed, "actually *Spencer's* done quite a bit. He did some research before he came."

When Angel nodded toward Spencer, he explained, "The scrolls that Paul and Timothy originally had were in clay pots. Those pots were then placed in a wooden box, with whatever was with them, for transport purposes. They remained in the box from around 1000AD-1500AD. From there, the knights in charge of the box transferred it to a chest for better protection. From what I could tell, they remained in that chest until 1700AD, before being shifted to a trunk, and shipped with their protectors to separate locations. That's where the boxes were first separated."

"You were able to track them from that long ago?" Joe asked, stunned.

"Yep. Then in the mid-1900's, when your Colonel and Hawk got ahold of their box, the second box's location was a mystery…and still is today."

"How did you track it?" Delaney asked, fascinated.

"I followed the history from the Paul's and Timothy's missionary journeys, and went from there," Spencer explained. "Now, I lost them both somewhere in the World Wars."

"Which is where ours was lost until the archangel got it to the Colonel and Danny," Josh added.

"Right. My question is, where is the other one? Most of the time, it was in some sort of stronghold. Your 'other side,' as you call it, seem to keep it close. You guys, I understand, store it in a safe place, which is wise. From what I gather, the more you move it, the easier it is to detect."

"That's our theory as well," Josh agreed. "As for the other side, there have been a few main strongholds in Australia, or at least they have been in the past, along with the one we are going after tomorrow."

"May we have a list of those?" Sasha asked.

"Sure," Josh said.

"Does anyone know what some of the other strongholds are around the world?" Angel asked.

"Pretty sure your dad would be the one to ask regarding that," Nico suggested. "He and Derek are among the old guard A.N.G.E.L.s who have been all over, right?"

"Yep," Angel said. "I'll call him when we're done here."

"Sounds good. Now, Jacob, where are your guys planting the explosives?" Nico asked.

After Jacob pointed out the positions, and Josh showed where the crew would stop and wait until Jacob's crew was ready, they took over three hours to bathe the missions in prayer.

Both missions were crucial to helping the A.N.G.E.L.s, and they knew if they could execute both of them, it would benefit A.N.G.E.L.s all over the world. They knew they had the prayers of the other A.N.G.E.L.s, along with the saints going with them as well.

*   *   *

"Haven," Cori answered the phone with the computer.

"Cori, this is Angel."

"Stand by," Cori said, smacking Kai on the arm, who scrambled the communication in case anyone was listening.

"You're clear," Kai said after he was finished.

Cori turned back to the computer. "Go ahead, Angel."

"Is my dad around?"

"Yes. Stand by," Cori said. "Hey, Hanif, can you go get Mark and Jerrod?" Cori called to one of the other computer people.

"Yep," he said, and disappeared up the stairs into the Haven, only to return with both guys moments later.

"How much time do we have?" Mark asked Cori, as he and Jerrod came down the stairs, with Chief on Jerrod's heels.

"Five minutes. Then she'll have to call back. I want to keep it under that for safety purposes," Cori explained.

"Got it," Mark agreed. Taking the call off hold, he said into the microphone, "Hey, Angel! What's going on over there? How are things after the fall-out?"

"Christmas morning was a celebration, and this afternoon was planning. Tonight, will be mourning until everyone leaves in the morning for Alice Springs. Meanwhile, my group heads toward Cairns in the morning."

"Got it. Well, Merry Christmas!"

"Thank you! While I love you, I actually called for a reason."

"Better make sure to talk to your mom before we get off," Mark warned. "I don't want to be in the doghouse because I got to talk to you on Christmas, and she didn't."

"I understand," Angel said with a chuckle. Then she quickly cleared her throat before she asked, "I was wondering if you knew other locations of strongholds of the other side from around the world."

"Yeah."

"Is there a way you can give them to me?"

"Ummm…" Mark thought for a moment. "Stand by," he said, putting her on hold. Turning to the others on the team, he asked, "Would it be better for me to just say them over this, or send it in an email?"

"Email can be intercepted a lot easier than just saying it," Kai pointed out.

"Yes. Cori has it scrambled right now. Tell her now," Hiro added.

"How much time do we have?" Mark asked Cori.

"Call her back," Cori said, as she began typing on her computer. "That will give me a chance to bounce the signal all over."

Getting back on with Angel, Mark instructed her to get a pen and paper and sit by the phone. Calling her back about ten minutes later, he said, "Hey, Angel."

"Okay, got a pen and paper. How long do we have?" she asked.

"Ten minutes at the longest. I will let you know if you need to cut it sooner," Cori said, resting her hand on the braille keyboard, while listening to a separate system on her computer. She hoped to stay ahead of anyone trying to listen in on their communications.

"Fair enough. You ready, Angel?" Mark asked.

"Go ahead."

"I don't know if they're still there, but one of them is near Inamura Rock, near Okutama, Japan. There was also one in the old electric plant near Niagara Falls in New York state. The next one I can remember is near Chernobyl in Russia. Please be extremely careful in that area."

"I will. Anymore?"

"Yes. Behind the Iguazu Falls in Argentina."

"Which one?"

"That's your department…if they're still there."

"Great," Angel groaned. "Any more?"

"The trace has started," Cori announced, keeping her fingers on her keyboard.

"Got it," Mark acknowledged before turning back to Angel. "Angel, there's one in the Kruger National Park in South Africa. These are very dangerous places. They're dangerous without the added danger of the reason why you're going there."

"I understand."

"Black Rock was one, and there was another one in Cairns as well."

"Got it. Mom told us where the one in Cairns was," Angel confirmed. "Thank you!"

"Three minutes," Cori announced.

Jerrod watched the lines connect on Cori's computer screen. "They're tracing quickly."

"Yeah," Cori said, keeping her fingers on her keyboard, "They're a little too good. Mark, get off with her, and I can set up a better web for them to untangle."

"We have to hurry, Angel. Listen, you are all in our prayers until we hear from you again. Please make it sooner than later. Your mom is worried, but trusts God. She said she was okay with not talking to you today. She doesn't want you to hear the concern in her voice," Mark confessed. "Know we're all praying for you, and are waiting to hear how it all plays out. We trust Him to care for all of you, and to carry all of you through this."

"Then keep trusting Him. Love to all. Please pass love to Mom and the twins. I have to go."

"I understand. We love you all."

"Bye," Angel said, and hung up.

"Good job," Cori said. "They only had a few more until they found us. You got off quick enough."

"They'll be okay, Mark. God is bigger than any of this, yeah?" Kai encouraged.

"I know. It just concerns me."

"You cannot be in more than one place at a time, but God can…and is," Hiro pointed out. "And, if I remember, Rachel said you were retired, so that means your place is here."

"Your English has improved…almost a little too much," Mark said, shaking his head. "All right. I have to fill in Casey on what they're doing. While she said she understands not being able to talk to her, I know it kills her."

"She will understand," Hiro said. "She is an understanding woman."

"I hope so," Mark said, and headed upstairs.

After he closed the door behind him, Hiro crossed her arms, and warned, "Discernment is one of my gifts. We need to pray. There are many reasons to be of concern."

Jerrod looked at the young A.N.G.E.L.s in the cyber cave, and reminded them, "We *always* need to be in prayer. Until the Lord returns, concern is the call of the day. The enemy never sleeps."

*   *   *

Everyone was up early the day after Christmas. After breakfast, most of the clansmen and women went to the graveyard to mourn their lost, prior to the clansmen leaving for the mission with the A.N.G.E.L.s.

While they did that, the A.N.G.E.L.s worked together to pack for the trip. It would take them a few days to get out to the location. The first target was a hotel in Alice Springs that night. Meanwhile, Angel, Sasha, and Spencer were to head into Cairns to start their search.

"So, I'm thinking we should work backward," Spencer suggested.

"What do you mean?" Angel asked.

"Well, you said your mom was taken captive in Cairns, right?"

"Right."

"Let's check there. There's no sense in starting from the beginning. In the past, they moved it with them. If we check in Cairns, then Black Rock, and then where the others are heading, we can avoid potentially unnecessary travel."

"Good point," Sasha said. "I agree with this plan."

"Okay," Angel said, processing the idea. "The one question I have is, how to check these places? Do we just waltz on into them?"

"We have to think like them," Sasha said. "Where would they hide it in these places?"

"Well, I know Black Rock is a disaster area, so that will be a challenge to search."

"We will do our best," Sasha encouraged. "God will lead us."

"Okay. When we get to the hotel, I'll call my mom and dad and get a more exact location for Cairns."

*   *   *

Travel for both teams was long and arduous. While Sasha, Angel, and Spencer's team talked most of the way, catching Spencer up on the history of the A.N.G.E.L.s, the other portion of the teams, spread between five trucks, was less talkative and more pensive. They were going to where they *knew* the other side resided. They *knew* what they were walking into, and prayed they would all make it out alive. Landing in Alice Springs for the night, they ate and went straight to bed, knowing they would have to get up bright and early the next morning.

*　　*　　*

Victoria Stanton and her partner, Shawn O'Brien, hid behind a boulder that lazily rested on the sandy beach with their hearts pounding out of control. Under normal circumstances, the serene scene of the moonlight dancing off the waves of the Waterfront in Cairns would serenade them in a romantic moment that love stories were made of. The breeze coming off the saltwater would add to the surroundings, creating an ambiance that ignited many a passionate moment between lovers. However, this moment was something of nightmares.

Over the years as an A.N.G.E.L., God had graced them with numerous glimpses of His boundless love and mercy, but what they saw was something beyond unnatural. She looked to be that of a woman in her late fifties, and under normal circumstances they wouldn't have thought twice about her – but the form inside her sent chills down their spine. The tall, thin frame of this beautiful woman would normally send out the comfort of a woman who had lived her life and would guide other women through the trials life threw at them, but the form inside the woman marred and mangled anything that got in its way, creating an enigma of unmistakable significance. She was the queen bee of a swarm of evil that had only one thing in mind – to annihilate the A.N.G.E.L.s. If they succeeded, it would create a void in the world that would allow evil to have a stronghold on the inhabitants of the planet it would never release. It was up to the A.N.G.E.L.s to keep the balance of power in check.

The pair were the lookout for the American A.N.G.E.L.s while they went in to rescue two of their crewmembers. This situation was not abnormal since A.N.G.E.L.s from the various units had crossed paths over the years in regards to missions, but this one was different. This one made the hair on the back of their necks stand on end, as a paralyzing terror surged through their bodies. They had never seen or felt anything of this magnitude before, and to know it was in their backyard horrified them beyond words. *How could something have formed and functioned of this immense size and they not know?*

"We need t' get to Hawk and warn him," Victoria whispered in the dim moonlight.

Shawn nodded in response. He wanted to stay as silent as possible. He adored his partner, Victoria, and admired her skill over the years. She could take a man even of Mark English's size down in a matter of seconds, and it brought a sense of pride to know she was his love.

Victoria gulped and her heart skipped a beat when she heard a stick crack about fifty feet away. She didn't want to die. She and Shawn had formally begun a relationship only a couple of months ago and the last thing she wanted to do was lose him...or worse yet, the thought of him having to watch her die broke her heart. She didn't want to imagine the pain either scenario would cause them.

Shawn rested his hands on her shoulders and whispered, "I love you with all my heart. You are a source of strength for me." Her body shook under his hands. He knew it would take a miracle of God to pull them from the impending doom that surrounded them.

They would use themselves as a distraction so the other four A.N.G.E.L.s could get away. Hearing the alarm in the voices of those within the warehouse, the pair instantly knew those inside realized their prisoners had escaped. Shawn sent in a couple rounds through the front window to pull the attention away from the back of the warehouse where he knew the others were making their escape.

Several large men ran out of the concrete hive and made a beeline in their direction. Even though the floodlights were a good hundred yards away, they watched in alarm as a tall fair-haired woman's eyes shifted to pure black. Their hearts skipped a beat. At that moment, they knew. Time momentarily stopped for the two A.N.G.E.L.s, as their eyes were opened to what was around them. They saw the true form of not only the demon, but also of the legion that possessed her followers.

They bolted for the boat they stashed as a get-away vehicle. It was nestled in the Cairns Wharf, tucked away from any prying eyes. They made it to the waterfront before they heard them closing in on them. While the distance to their escape was not far, it felt like a thousand miles.

"We need to run," Victoria whispered, grabbing his hand, though he stopped for a moment.

Looking at the blond-haired beauty before him, he was in awe. Her expressions did not give away a hint of how lethal she could be. She was a walking weapon. Deadly, and a steel core that could freeze even the hottest area in The Outback if she put her mind to it, but now she looked like a scared child. "You have to be strong. We will make it."

"I love you," she whispered, resting her hand on his strong jawline. His reddish-blond hair complemented the freckles that danced across his nose. Only the A.N.G.E.L.s and those he worked with in the military knew the man before her had killed many men during his lifetime, even though he did it from one to two hundred yards away in order to help others escape. He was the best marksman of the Australian A.N.G.E.L.s, yet he had a heart of gold. He would do anything for anyone who needed him – that included giving his life.

"You go. Get the boat ready."

She shook her head in alarm. "I can't leave you."

"You have to. I'll distract them while you run. I want you to run as fast as those gorgeous legs of yours will carry you. Don't look back. Get to Hawk and tell him. He has to know."

"What will happen to you?"

"Don't worry about me. I will either meet you in Heaven or in the Outback."

She looked at him blankly for a moment as their reality sunk in. He was going to sacrifice his life to get her to safety. "I can't let you do it."

He grabbed her face as he held it close to his. "You have to. Only one of us will have a chance. We won't be able to make it out together. They will get us if we try. Go down Wharf Street until it crosses Spence Street. Turn right. Spence Street dead-ends into the wharf. Get out of there as fast as you can and don't look back. Do you hear me? Don't look back."

She heard him, but she shook her head as she felt the color drain from her face. What was he saying? If she did that, then she knew she would never see him on this planet alive again. "You're not fighting flesh and blood."

"I know what they are."

"You won't survive."

"But you will. Don't argue with me about this," he insisted.

Victoria leaned forward and kissed him with every ounce of love she had for him. She knew the kiss would have to last them a lifetime. She prayed she would be wrong and that God would protect them as He often did in the past, but there was a feeling of foreboding that churned deep inside her.

He returned the kiss with the love he had for her. He knew what he was doing. He would protect Victoria with everything in his power. He would start as soon as he saw the first one in his site until that was no longer an option. Then he would step into the line of fire. He had to give her enough time to get to the wharf and get away.

"I love you. Now go," he said, feeling the pit in his stomach wanting to take over his emotions, but he forced it back down.

"I love you too...with all of my heart. May God have mercy on you, my love."

"God will have mercy one way or another. I am one of His. He will cither call me home or allow me to see those beautiful blue eyes of yours once again here on Earth. May He keep you safe."

"A prayer from both of our lips to God's ears," Victoria whispered.

They held each other one last time, before Victoria looked around the rock to make sure her way was clear. Not seeing any movement, she bolted toward the road, knowing Spence

Street was but a few precious blocks away. If she had to, she would cut through Marlin Parade to get to the dock.

As she ran, she heard the distinct pop of Shawn's rifle, and knew the firefight had begun behind her. The stride of her long legs covered the ground before her as she felt she might have made a mistake leaving Shawn. She remembered his words, "Get out of there as fast as you can and don't look back. Do you hear me? Don't look back."

Massive rounds of gunfire erupted from where she left Shawn. Her stomach lurched when the barrage of gunfire came to an abrupt halt. Tears stung her eyes and her heart skipped a beat. She turned down Spence Street. She knew her lover was sitting in the peace and comfort of The Lord, but how could he leave her there by herself to continue the fight without him?

The wharf. It was in her sights when a horrific sting pierced the back of her right thigh then another bit into her left shoulder. She fell to the ground and skid about five feet, with sand splattering into her face. She spit it out and wiped off her face as she pushed up and ran, creating a cloud of dust around her. The wharf was less than five feet away. She didn't look back. She didn't want to know how close they were to her.

Her feet thumped across the wood of the wharf as adrenaline surged through her body, carrying her further than she would be able to go on her own. With each step, visions of her life flashed before her eyes. God had protected her and granted her many exciting adventures that allowed her to save numerous lives in His name throughout the years. He allowed her to be a part of plans that helped His children out of situations they would not otherwise escape. She was part of an elite force for not only her government, but more importantly, for The King of Kings and Lord of Lords. She took pride in the work He granted her over the years.

Another capsule of searing heat grazed her head. She dropped off the wharf into the water. A peace enveloped her at hearing God's words clear in her mind, "Before I formed you in the womb I knew you, before you were born I set you apart. You have done well My good and faithful servant. Come home."

…Angel sat upright in her bed, breathing heavily, as a mixture of sweat and tears poured down her face. *Was that real? Could that have been what really happened the day her parents were rescued?*

The names were right, she was sure of that. *Was it real, or a dream from the story her mom told her before they went to bed that night when she and her mom spoke?*

Remembering the feeling Victoria felt, she shook her head. *It had to have been real. It was a dream, given to her by God. It would lead them in their journey the next morning.*

Sliding out of bed, she quietly went to the bathroom and closed the door. She didn't want to wake the guys in the bed next to hers, but she couldn't sit there with all the feelings swirling inside of her. The love Victoria and Shawn felt for each other was unmistakable. *Jesse and Rachel have that love. So do Delaney and Joe. Cori and Jacob weren't there yet, but they were on the way. Would she ever find that love?*

Washing her face, she then dried it with a towel and looked in the mirror. *Life, as far as they knew, for an A.N.G.E.L. wasn't always a long one. Would God bless her with that feeling for another before she was called home?*

Shaking her head, she looked back at the mirror. The scars coating her arms and legs reminded her of her time in the caves. A shudder went down her spine as her own screams echoed in her ears.

Covering her ears, she shook her head. "No," she whispered aloud. "No, they're not real! I'm free! God will keep me close to Him." Looking in the mirror, she glared, and said a little louder, "Get thee behind me, Satan! You have no power over me! I am one of God's children! I am covered by the blood of Jesus!"

As the overwhelming feelings slowly faded, she took deep, cleansing breaths. When she put her hand on the door to go back to bed, there was a light knock on the door, and she jumped.

Heart still racing, she slowly opened the bathroom door to find Sasha standing there. "Are you okay?" he whispered. Then he got a good look at her, and stepped into the bathroom, shutting them both inside. Resting his hands on her shoulders, he said, "I know you are not okay. What happened?"

"I-I had a dream. That's my gift...or curse...depend-depending on how you look at it," she stammered. "You see, God gives me dreams for when I need them."

"What is this dream that has you scared and shaking? You have no color in your face."

Resting her hands on his wrists, she confessed, "Will I live long enough to find true love?"

"What?" Sasha asked, confused.

"This dream. It showed me the love between two people. It's a love I have never felt before. I have seen it in my parents, and in some of the other A.N.G.E.L.s, but I have never felt it myself. I know I am going to die earlier than most people. I just want to feel that love first."

"Why do you think you will die earlier than most people? Where did that come from?"

"You know as well as I do, that as an A.N.G.E.L. our life spans are short here on earth. I knew this when I stepped into it. It doesn't mean I don't still have those natural desires."

"Of course you do. You are human," Sasha said, not completely following her train of thought. "What does this have to do with a dream God gave you? Was there information in this dream?"

"Yes, but the feelings were intense!"

"I am sorry you had to experience this dream," he said, wrapping his arms around her, hugging her.

As she cried, she tried to explain, but there were no words. She could barely form a thought, except to remember Victoria's feelings. Understanding that was not the intention of the dream, she stood. Sasha draped his arms around her waist, as she admitted, "There's a lot going on in my head."

Chuckling, Sasha agreed, "Now *this* I understand. Want to clear some of it?"

"I don't want to wake Spencer. He's had a long couple of days."

"We could go out to the balcony?" Sasha offered. "We can talk quietly, so as not to wake him. It is only three in the morning. It would not be fair to wake him this early."

Angel nodded, so they went through the room to the patio, grabbing a couple blankets from Angel's bed to wrap in on the way through. Once settled, Angel looked out at the ocean from their fifth-floor hotel room patio.

"It helps to actually talk," Sasha said after ten minutes of silence.

"I guess I'm wondering what God has for me."

Chuckling again, Sasha explained, "None of us know that answer. Only God."

"I know. Sometimes I just wish He would share part of it with me."

"That is something you know He cannot do. Well, it is not that He cannot do it, it is that He chooses not to do it. He calls us to live by faith, not by sight."

"I know," Angel agreed. Then she looked over at him and added, "That doesn't mean I have to like it."

"You *are* a stubborn one," Sasha teased, with a smile. "It is that stubbornness that I enjoy about you."

"It *is* my best and worst quality," Angel admitted. "And, it often gets me into trouble."

"Yes. I can see this."

Stunned, Angel pointed out, "You don't have to agree with me!"

Laughing, Sasha nodded. "Yes, I do. I tell the truth. Whether you like it or not. I would rather hurt you with the truth, than comfort you with a lie. My godmother taught me that at an early age. It is my motto."

"I guess I need that."

"You are strong, and will need a strong man as well," Sasha explained. "Not to control you, but one who can handle your...oh, what is the word?" he asked, struggling to remember. "Oh, yeah! Spunkiness. Yes, that is what Joe called it."

"Joe said I was spunky?"

"At the very least. Feisty, stubborn, strong-willed, and obstinate were some of the other words I have heard in reference to you." As Angel's eyes grew wide and her face got red, Sasha explained, "This is not a bad thing. Please do not take it like that."

"How can I not?" she demanded.

"Because, those are the qualities I love about you."

"W-what?" Angel asked, confused. "Those are not normally good things."

"In my case they are. You see, I am strong as well. I do not want a weak woman. I want a woman who I *know* can handle herself, so I can take care of business. I admire the strength within you. You have been through much already. That stubbornness saved your life...as well as your soul. That obstinate, strong-willed, feisty personality allowed you to stay strong when the other side tried to brainwash you. Without those qualities, you would have folded, and could have faced the same fate that befell Allen."

Thinking through his words for a moment, Angel took in the view before them. The clear night sky held tons of stars, along with a harvest moon, which reflected off the ocean before them. The dull roar of the continuous ebb and flow of the ocean, as it came onshore and then receded, took over her thoughts for a few moments. "Does God ever put two strong people together? If so, what does that look like?"

Furrowing his brow, Sasha did his best to explain his train of thought, and hoped it coincided with hers, "The chain of command, so to speak, in the household, is God as the head, the husband as the second, then the wife, followed by the children. If you end up with someone less strong than you, it will put your household out of balance. You will overtake them in the chain of command…and they will let you. You need someone who will embrace those strong qualities, and work *with* you, instead of trying to control you. You still need boundaries, because your husband will need to answer to God for your actions, so keep that in mind. If you land with the correct man, you can be strong…*together*. You can bring out the good qualities in each other, instead of battling for power. Once you embrace each other, your strengths, and the chain of command, all will come into balance." Taking her hand into his, he continued, "Use the force of nature you are for good, and not for a power struggle. You *are* a leader, or God would have never put you in that position in the first place. You need to get your mind in the right place to assume that role once again."

"You think I can?"

"I *know* you can. I think this will be a good test. It will show not only the A.N.G.E.L.s, but also *yourself*, that you can work *with* a team, and not *against* it. The more you untangle those chains you carry, and loosen them, the freer you will be, to become the leader God intended you to be. It is up to you as to when you will be that leader. In order to accomplish this, you need to listen to God, and not yourself."

"Don't I need to trust my instincts?"

"*Within* the team, yes. Do not fight with them. Take a lesson from Rachel in learning the strengths each team member has, and delegating each to that strength. Also, Rachel takes the opinion of others in the team as well when making decisions. When a team feels that they have a voice, they stand behind that person more because they know they care."

"I can see that."

"Where is your hope?"

"My hope is in God."

"Are you aware of the acrostic H.O.P.E., and what it stands for?"

"Actually, haven't heard that one yet," Angel said, curious.

"The *H* is for 'higher power.' The *O* is for 'you have to be open to change.' The *P* is that you 'have the power to change.' And the *E* is to 'expect the change.' You see, the higher power is God. You have to be open to God to change your heart. You have to know that the power is within you to change – the Holy Spirit. And, the hope of all hope is that you have to expect that change to happen. *That* is your hope. When you rely on Him for everything, instead of yourself, things *will* change…and for the better, I might add."

"I'm sure. I'm just so used to doing it myself. I always imagine the worst possible outcome, and try to compensate for it."

"While that is not a bad thing, try relying on God for things. When you make different decisions, different opportunities will open up. When you make a plan, knowing already what His plan is, things will work out. For example, the dream you had tonight?"

"Yes?"

"Well, God showed it to you for a reason. You have a glimpse of His plan. What was the dream? Was it about love?"

"Not totally. It was when my parents were rescued. He showed me where the building is, and what the area looks like around the building."

"Then, he obviously wants us to go there, right?"

"Right."

"So, what do you know from this?"

"I know where it is, and what exactly happened that day."

"So, you also know possible dangers as well, yes?"

"Yes," Angel agreed.

"But, you *also* know God showed it to you, so you know what we are walking into, yes?"

"Yes."

"Then, God is with us in this plan," Sasha concluded. "We stay on guard, but allow Him to guide us on this mission. He is trying to show you, I think, that He approves."

"Good line of thinking."

"Now you must hope that God will show you the rest, and have faith that He is behind us."

"I do."

"More so now that you have had this dream, right?"

"Right."

"Good. Now, how do you feel?"

"Like I wish it wasn't only three-thirty in the morning," Angel said, rolling her eyes. "I don't want to wait until Spencer wakes at six."

"What if we just rest here on the patio meditating in prayer?" Sasha suggested. "We can listen to the glory God created in the sea, and watch in the morning how He cares for even those creatures around us. If He cares for them, how much more will He care for us?"

"Tons!"

"Then you will have even more hope, yes?"

"Yes," Angel said, feeling as if a weight was lifted off her soul. She felt a couple chains she had been carrying around, drop, as she looked from the ocean, to Sasha, and back again.

Seeing the smile on her face, Sasha put his hand out for her to take, which she gladly did. Giving it a squeeze, they both sat in silence, as they prayed to the Lord, thanking Him and praising Him until the sun rose that morning. The stunning colors of pink and blue were quickly replaced by bright peach, yellow, and gold until Spencer woke at six that morning. Angel headed into the day with a renewed hope!

*   *   *

"Glad you guys could finally join us," Isaac said with a smirk when Rachel and Delaney, finally came down for breakfast that next morning in the hotel.

"We had to pack," Rachel said, going to get her breakfast from the breakfast bar. "We also took long showers, knowing it could be a while until our next one."

"Good idea," Charlie said, finishing the bite of scrambled eggs in his mouth. "It could be a while until we get a decent meal, too."

"Good point," Delaney said, scooping an extra spoonful of scrambled eggs onto her plate. Then she got a piece of toast, along with a couple sausages.

Sitting down, the girls joined hands in prayer before diving into their breakfasts.

"Where are your bags?" Joe asked, standing up a few minutes later, after finishing his meal.

"In our room," Delaney said, pulling the key card out of her pocket, handing it to him.

"Is everything ready to be loaded?"

"Yep."

Giving her a kiss on the head, he then grabbed a couple guys to load the vehicles, while the others finished eating their breakfast. Once finished, they checked out, and loaded into the vehicles for the second leg of the trip.

This portion would take them deep into the Outback, and that much closer to their goal. They would camp out that night, and then, early in the morning, make their move on the stronghold of the other side. They were nervous, anxious, but trusting in the Lord to complete this mission. Knowing the archangel said this mission was blessed, gave them some comfort. If He didn't bless it, they wouldn't be doing it!

Chapter 9
Cast Off One's Chains

"Mom said it was near here," Angel said, looking at the map.

"There." Spencer pointed toward the docks. "She said your friend Danny lost his two people over there near the docks."

"Shawn and Victoria," Angel said somberly. Her heart racing, she looked toward the end of the street to a large vacated building, as portions of the dream flashed through her mind. "It's there."

"How can you be sure?" Spencer asked.

"Because I had a nightmare about it last night," Angel explained. Squinting to see better from the distance they were, she said, "It *looks* vacated. Do we dare go in?"

"I do not think God brought us this far to run. Do you?" Sasha asked.

"No. But, I *do* think we need to be on our guard. We need to go in cautiously. Man, I wish we had Val with us. With his gift is spiritual sight, he could tell us if it were empty or not."

"You've mentioned before that your spiritual gift is dreams," Spencer said to Angel. Then he turned to Sasha and asked, "What's yours?"

"I have visions, and I sense when the other side is near," Sasha explained. "When they are near, my skin crawls as if there are bugs scurrying all over it, and it gets more intense the closer they are to us, as if they are biting."

"Can you feel anything now?" Angel asked.

"Not at the moment."

"Let us know if you sense *anything at all*," she said. Then, taking a deep breath, she added, "Okay. It's now or never."

Sasha grabbed Angel's hand, and courageously said, "Then let's go."

As the trio approached the warehouse, Spencer kept a close eye on any movement around them. The brick was covered in ivy. Multiple windows were cracked or shattered, where the locals had thrown rocks at them. When they neared the warehouse, Spencer noticed even the door looked cracked and broken in places. It was only being held onto the frame by one of the three hinges. What was worse than the condition was the smell. It smelled of more than just mold and mildew. It smelled of death. The stench was so strong it offended his senses. "Shew!" he said, covering his nose, as they walked up the stairs to the door.

"It does not smell pleasant," Sasha said, using his inner arm to cover his nose and mouth, while still holding Angel's hand.

"You know, maybe we need to rethink this," Spencer suggested, going to turn back around.

Angel let go of Sasha's hand and grabbed Spencer's arm. "Where's that adventurous spirit I'm so used to seeing?"

Glancing up at the size of the building, he admitted, "After hearing the stories around the station, I have to admit that I'm actually scared."

Resting her hands on his shoulders, Angel reminded him, "The archangel said God has blessed this mission. He wouldn't have told us that if he was sending us to our death."

"What about the other team? They're blessed as well, but they don't know if they'll all make it out. Just because it's blessed, doesn't mean we'll all make it out alive. It just means that it'll be successful."

"While this is true, please understand that I wouldn't have called you if you weren't mission-critical. We don't bring people into the fold just for kicks. We don't share our secrets just to take them on a mission to die. This *is not* a suicide mission. This is a mission for the Lord God Almighty. He is the One we all serve. Trust Him, Spencer."

Sighing, Spencer debated in his head for a long moment. Rubbing his forehead, the stress was evident.

"Spencer, you are here with pure intentions," Sasha said, stepping between Angel and Spencer. Angel stepped to the side to let him speak. Resting his hand on Spencer's shoulder, he explained, "We are all offered a choice. No one is forcing you to come with us. I *did* see the excitement in your eyes when you spoke of this mission. Can you honestly tell me you do not want to do this?"

"No. I do, but..." his voice faded, as he looked at the massive building before him.

"You do not think we are afraid as well?" Sasha asked.

"You?" He asked, surprised. "*You* are afraid? You don't look like you're afraid of anything!"

"Oh," Sasha chuckled, "there is much I am afraid of in this life." Crossing his arms, he explained, "I am afraid something will happen to Angel." When he said that, Angel blushed. "I am afraid something will happen to my teammates. I am afraid something will happen to my godmother. To let you in on a secret, I am even afraid of scorpions! Those little things are tiny, silent, and have a rude sting." When he said that, Spencer chuckled. "Seriously! Have you ever thought about them? Prior to coming here, the worst thing I was afraid of in the creature world was the wolverine or the Karakurt spider! Now that I have become an A.N.G.E.L., the only things that scares me are scorpions…and that spider. You see, once you've faced the other side on a regular basis, facing the worst of what the other side can throw at you, the rest is minuscule."

Shoving his hands in his pockets, Spencer said, "Yeah. I can see that."

Leaning against the front of the building with one of his feet braced on the wall, Sasha said, "There is a lot we will face. There is a lot that will scare you. You have the comfort of knowing that whatever is thrown at you, even if it ends in your death, that you will be with Jesus once it is over and done."

"So, you're saying that up to and including death is just a transition?"

"Yes. Albeit a sometimes painful one. Yes, it is a transition. That is how you need to look at it. You need to be bold for the Lord. Jesus was bold for you, up to and including His death. It is the least we can do for Him."

Taking a deep breath, Spencer slowly let it out as he took another good look at the building. Finally, much to Sasha and Angel's relief, he said, "Okay. He called me, and I answered 'send me.' I need to follow through with it, despite my fear."

"Delaney once explained to me that there are a couple meanings to fear. One of them is 'Forget Everything And Run,' and the other is, 'Face Everything And Rise.' Which one do you want to do?" Angel asked.

"I want to face everything and rise, with Christ beside me," Spencer said. "Okay. Let's do this!"

Turning back toward the dilapidated door, Angel rested her hand on the handle. With a barely audible voice, Angel whispered, "Lord, please be with us."

The door creaked when she pushed it open, almost falling off the remaining hinge. The breeze from the ocean kicked up the dust inside, and shifted multiple spiders from their secure homes about the warehouse. The sunlight pierced through the thick air, showing the dilapidated innards, along with a multitude of rats that ran for darkness when the light invaded their solitude.

"Homey," Angel said as she flipped on her flashlight.

"I, uh, think we should stay together," Spencer stammered. "It-it's a bit creepy. I wouldn't want you to become afraid."

"Oh, I'll be fine," Angel said with a smirk.

"Okay, fine. *I'm* afraid," Spencer admitted.

"I agree that we should stay together. We are stronger together," Sasha concurred.

Turning his flashlight on, Spencer reminded himself, as well as the other two, "Together we stand, divided we fall."

"True that, brother," Sasha said, turning on his flashlight as well.

Each step they took caused trepidation. The floorboards creaked under their feet, threatening to give-way at any second. As they entered each room, they searched in hopes of finding some sense of direction as to where the box was located, if it was held in the warehouse at all.

Among the debris were piles of ash throughout the building, which Angel instantly recognized as the leftovers of demons. Angel just about jumped out of her skin when she stumbled across a severed hand on the floor. She wasn't sure how much more her heart could take. The walls, tables, and chairs were coated in suffocating amounts of dust, and cobwebs were strewn about entire doorways at some points.

Angel screamed when a spider, about four inches in diameter dropped in front of her from the ceiling. She tried to move, but her feet were frozen to the floor. As the color drained from her face, Sasha swooped in, broke the spider's stream, and dropped it onto the floor. When he stepped on it, it crackled under his foot, and Angel shuddered.

"What was that?" Spencer asked, stunned by the noise.

"Spider," Sasha explained.

"What kind of place has spiders that crunch underfoot?"

Sasha shrugged. "I have seen bigger on the station."

"That-that was….umm…oh my word!" Angel said, pale, heart racing out of control.

"It is dead, Angel," Sasha explained. "I killed it. See?" he said, shining the light on the dead carcass.

"Th-that one is, but when you s-see one, there's a myriad you c-can't see," she stammered, as she looked around for more. "Maybe Spencer had the right idea."

"I understand you are scared," Sasha tried to calm her down, "but we have a lot of work to do, and it starts with us clearing this building."

"Angel, you told me we are to trust God in this," Spencer reminded her. "Are you going to face everything and rise?"

"Rachel told me of yet another definition for fear," Sasha said. "This one may help you both. It is 'False Evidence Appearing Real.' You see, there is nothing of which to be afraid. This building was abandoned long ago. The only thing to fear are those creatures that call it home. The other side is not in here, or my skin would be crawling."

"Right." Angel nodded. Motivating herself, she continued, "False evidence appearing real. There is nothing to fear here. God's got this!" Looking toward the Heavens, Angel reminded the Lord, "While I trust you, I am, and probably always will be terrified of spiders!" Taking a deep breath in order to get her emotions under control, she slowly let it out, as she rested her hands on her hips. Shaking her head, she said, "I don't understand how they always find me. Why do the creepy things always seem to find me?"

Noting that Angel got herself under control, Spencer continued his search of the room. "I guess they're just attracted to you," he mentioned, opening a cupboard. When he did, he gasped, as a skeleton fell forward shattering on the ground at his feet. "Um, okay. Well, *that's* disturbing."

"Especially since it is not a pile of ash," Sasha commented, as he went over to some shelves to dig through.

Raising an eyebrow, Spencer asked, "Meaning?"

"The pile of ash means it is from the other side. That is what those ash piles are all over the floor. The demons usually burst into flames, before dissolving into a pile of ash when you kill them," he explained. "They usually look something like those," he said, pointing to several piles around the room.

"Interesting. And the fact that it's a skeleton means…?" Spencer pressed.

"It means it was a human," Angel said, crouching in front of an old, dusty chest. Blowing on it to clear some of the dirt from the latch, Angel covered her mouth and coughed at all the dust that instantly invaded the air and her lungs. She took a moment before looking in to find rolled pieces of parchment paper. "What are these?"

Spencer and Sasha leaned over her shoulder to see several large rolls. As Angel picked one up, another spider dropped from it. She screamed and jumped back. "Seriously!" she exclaimed, her chest rising and falling in rapid breaths.

Spencer crunched it beneath his foot. "Got it."

Picking up the scroll, Sasha said, "It should be fine, but just in case…" Unrolling it on the ground, they found a map with the different Australian territories.

"Merciful Mother of our blessed Lord!" Angel said, getting a good look at it, color slowly draining from her face.

"What?" Sasha raised an eyebrow at her.

"Unroll another one," she ordered, studying the one already rolled out.

He unfurled the next one, to find the North American continent.

"Sweet fancy Moses!" she said, heart skipping a beat when she saw the one Sasha unrolled.

"What?" Sasha asked, getting impatient. "What do you see?"

Angel gulped. "One more to be sure."

Spencer grabbed two just to make sure she wouldn't wait again before explaining. He unrolled the Europe and Asian continent maps next to the one's Sasha already unrolled. Angel's eyes widened even more, so Sasha grabbed the last one, which had the South American continent on it, and unrolled it as well.

Angel gasped. "Sweet Jesus! I'm going to have heart failure before this is over!" she said, shaking her head.

"Seriously, Angel!" Spencer snapped. "Spill it!"

"Look at all the marked areas on the continents," Angel said, pointing them out. When she got to the North American one, she pointed directly to an area marked just outside of Reno, Nevada.

"Oh no," Sasha groaned, finally figuring out why Angel was in such a panic. Snatching the Europe and Asia one from Spencer, he groaned again. "Godmother," he whispered, pained.

"What is it?" Spencer demanded, getting frustrated. "Care to share…*anyone*?"

"These are marked where the A.N.G.E.L.s live…past *and* current," Angel explained.

"How can they know the current if…?" Spencer's voice trailed mid-sentence as a thought hit him. He grabbed the North American map from Sasha and searched his home near Cleveland, Ohio. "Why is *mine* marked? How did they know I would work with you?"

"The scrolls," Angel said, looking down at the maps. Glancing up at Spencer, she said, "And, it's not that you are just working with us. This means you are now one *of* us. *You are an A.N.G.E.L.* according to this map."

"What does *that* mean? Don't I get a choice? And, are you saying the scrolls have my name on them too?"

"There was a Schmidt listed on the American one, but I never connected that it was *you* who would be the Schmidt," Angel explained. "I thought it may be further down the timeline, because it wasn't in the immediate list. I guess I was wrong."

"The Lord is the *Only One* Who knows it all. You can be wrong, Angel. My bigger concern is not if you are right or wrong. My bigger concern is that *all* of the A.N.G.E.L.s have a literal target on them," Sasha said, worry evident in his tone. "And, if the scrolls are here, that means they will come back to this place to get them."

"So, are these the scrolls we're looking for?" Spencer asked, looking in the chest. "I don't see the other items you mentioned."

"These *are* scrolls, but not the ones we're looking for," Angel clarified. "We'll take these with us, but the scrolls we're looking for hold *much* more value to the other side than these. They are half a N.O.C. list that goes on for centuries."

"So, if I'm following you correctly, and from what you've told me, *their* list, for example, would have Pine Crest and Spencer on it?" Spencer asked.

"No. It would have America and Spencer on it," Angel corrected. "Ours had Cleveland and Schmidt on it."

"So, because Pine Crest is a suburb of Cleveland, that's how it was listed?"

"Yes. Our list gives us the main city, or if it's not near a big city, it gives us the actual town, along with the last name. Theirs has the country and the first name."

"Then, how do they know *exactly where* in Russia my godmother is?" Sasha demanded. "They either have a spy amongst us, or they know something we do not."

"This would actually explain…" Angel's voice trailed as she grabbed the Europe and Asia one from Sasha, and looked at England. There was a mark on London, with a red mark over it. Grunting in frustration, she stood. "They only had to follow us to find the exact person. They know the city too. I don't know how, but they do!"

"We have to find their scrolls to balance the knowledge," Sasha insisted. Grabbing the backpack off his back, he rolled and stuffed the scrolls into it. They were too big to be tucked all the way in, so they stuck out of the top. When no one else moved, Sasha insisted, "Sooner than later."

They gathered their bags, and their wits, and continued to search the building, room by room. When they walked into the fourth room, Angel had a vision hit her mind so hard, it threw her. She gasped as she braced herself on the wall, wide-eyed, while the vision played out right in front of her like a violent movie…

A woman walked in who looked to be about fifty or fifty-five years old, but very fit – she was the one from Angel's dream the previous night. The woman was thin, around six feet tall, had light brown, almost blonde hair, and bluish-gray eyes. She pulled up a chair next to a young version of Angel's mother, Casey, who was securely tied to a chair in the middle of the room. The woman sat on her chair backward, resting her chin on her crossed arms on the back of the chair.

"Hello, sweetie," she said to her with a thick Australian accent. Casey barely got her eyes open – her head was still swirling out of control from the sedation she experienced when they were kidnapped. "My name's Jacki. Are ya comfy?"

"Not really," Casey mumbled.

"How about ya wake up a bit more, love? We need t' talk."

Casey struggled for a couple more minutes to fight off the drug they gave her hours before, until she was able to pick her head up to look at her.

"There, that's better, don't ya think? Now, how about you tell me a story?"

"About what?"

Jacki got off the chair and leaned down so she was less than three inches from Casey's face. She jerked Casey's head back by her hair, and said, "Yer brother took a box of mine, and I want it back. Where is it?"

"I don't know." What she said was true. At one point, Casey knew where it was located, but at that moment, she had no idea if the Colonel had moved it or not.

Jacki took Casey's head and slammed it into the headrest, making her nose bleed, before pulling Casey's head back to look up at her. "How about you cooperate with me? Your friend didn't and he's not looking too good right now," Jacki said, referring to Mark, who looked horrible when Casey saw him only minutes before, when he was dragged into the room where she was originally held.

When Casey didn't say anything, Jacki picked up a syringe from the table that already had a liquid in it. She pulled up Casey's shirtsleeve and jammed the needle into her arm, emptying the stinging solution into Casey.

Casey gasped and gritted her teeth, but didn't yell, as much as she wanted to. She didn't want to give Jacki the satisfaction of knowing how much it hurt her.

"We'll just let that soak in a bit before we try again," Jacki said, tossing the syringe onto the table behind her. She then sat backward in her chair again and rested her folded arms on the back of it. She watched Casey, as she impatiently drummed her long nails on the back of the chair.

Within seconds, Casey's head started spinning. "Whoa!" She shook her head, fighting to clear it. Objects were blurring and melting together, and she saw flashes of light around the room, while she struggled to form a complete thought.

Jacki reached up and tucked a piece of Casey's hair behind her ear. "You're a pretty one. No wonder my son liked ya."

Casey looked at her in confusion. "Your son?"

"You would know him as Hunter Morgan."

Casey looked up toward Heaven and screamed in her head, *"Oh, God please help me! If she knows he is dead, I will be in more trouble than I already am."*

"Tsk, tsk, tsk, it would be a shame t' mess up that pretty face for him. He thinks the world of ya."

Casey struggled to get her brain back under control. "What did you do to me?"

"Just gave ya a lil' something to make ya tell me the truth. Sodium Pentothal is a handy little thing that helps in situations like this," Jacki said, and got up and walked behind Casey again. She grabbed Casey's hair and jerked her head back so hard that Casey thought she was going to break her neck. "Where is your brother's strongbox?" she demanded.

"I don't...." Casey closed her eyes, feeling her stomach lurch. Swallowing the vomit that wanted to come up, Casey moaned, "I don't know."

"Well, maybe you need a lil' persuading," Jacki said, and slammed Casey's head back down on the headrest again, before walking back over to the table. Deliberating for a moment, Jacki then went back over to Casey and untied her hands. She flipped Casey backward on the bench, and retied her hands above her head. Jacki then went over to the sink and filled a bucket of water. As she walked back, she nonchalantly flipped a towel over her shoulder. "Let's see how resistant you really are. I don't wanna mess up that pretty face. Hunter will get upset." She winked. "He wants you when I'm through with you."

Casey's heart raced in fear, pumping the drug through her system faster. She tugged and squirmed to get free of the ropes with everything she had, feeling them cut into her wrists. Unfortunately, there was no escape.

Jacki took the towel and placed it over Casey's face, before she slowly poured water over the towel. Casey knew what was coming and held her breath as long as she could.

After a couple of minutes, Casey shook her head but the soaked towel clung to her nose and mouth. Casey gasped for air. When she did, Jacki continued to pour the water until Casey inhaled it and started choking on it. She kept this up until a black cloud overtook Casey, rendering her unconscious.

When Casey woke, Jacki was leaning over her with the towel over her shoulder and a fresh bucket of water. "Wanna tell me where the strongbox is now?"

The tears stung Casey's eyes, as she looked from the bucket to Jacki and back again. "I don't know. I really don't know!"

"It was in *your* possession. Either you tell me, or we are going to go a couple more rounds."

Casey vigorously shook her head, unable to come up with an answer that would remotely satisfy her. Jacki put the soaked towel back on her face and she poured the water once again. "No-no-no-no-no-no-no-no-no-no," Casey begged. Struggling to get air, Casey once again inhaled the water that flooded her nose and mouth. She prayed for some type of intervention to stop this, but the answer was drowned out by the sound of water cascading onto the ground, and the gurgle of Casey's objections while Jacki continued to pour.

"Tell me where the strongbox is," Jacki demanded.

"Don't....know," Casey whimpered. She barely got the words out before the water invaded her body beyond her control and she passed out.

When Casey woke up once again, the towel was still on her face.

"Ya got another shot at this. Bet your head hurts, huh?" Jacki asked.

Casey only nodded in response.

"Tell me where the strongbox is, and I'll stop."

Casey moaned. "I don't know."

"Sure ya do. You're a resistant lil' thing. Let's try this again," she said, before she proceeded to pour the water again. This time, though, the water was hot.

Casey screamed. She jerked her head side-to-side in an attempt to get away, as the hot water coated her face, suffocating and burning her.

"The strongbox, love," Jacki pushed. "Where is it?"

Casey shook her head, so Jacki continued to pour. Casey tried to spit out the water only to inhale more as Jacki continuously poured. Casey could only hold on for so long before she passed out once again.

Jacki did this over and over, several more times. Casey's hands had lost feeling in them quite some time ago, and her head spun, yet throbbed in pain. She wasn't sure how much more she could take, and worse yet, there was no end in sight.

As her mind spiraled out of control, Jacki drowned and revived her over and over again. If Casey knew where the box was, at that point she would have told her. It seemed almost never-ending. She thought about making something up just to appease Jacki, but her mind wasn't even working well enough to come up with anything believable.

After drowning her, and bringing her back to life over a dozen times, Jacki decided something a little more drastic and permanent might be needed. She took a few moments to look at the tools and weapons that were on the table, as Casey once again lay unconscious, water dripping on the floor around her.

Jacki went back to Casey and positioned her unconscious body in the original position she found her in when Jacki arrived. Once Casey was secured, Jacki picked up both Casey's tank top and outer shirt, rolling them up to expose her back. Then she sat on the chair in front of her, waiting for her to wake again.

After several minutes, Casey woke, spitting up water. Her hair and clothing were soaked. A chill ran down Casey's back, as Jacki had the air conditioning turned down to about sixty-five degrees.

"Did ya enjoy your nap?" Jacki sneered.

Casey shook her head.

"Then, are ya ready t' tell me *who* has the strongbox, since ya don't seem to know *where* it is? After all, it *is* mine, and I want it back."

Casey shook her head again. She shuddered, as water ran in streams down her bare back.

"Hmm, then maybe ya need a lil' reminding." Jacki got off her chair. She went back over to the table and picked up a whip. Drawing it back, she flicked her wrist, landing the whip directly in the middle of Casey's back.

Casey couldn't help it. She let out a horrid scream as Jacki dragged the whip across her back, slicing into her cold, wet skin.

"Now," she asked again up by Casey's ear, "are ya gonna tell me where your brother's strongbox is since it's not in your storage shed?"

"I don't...." Casey took a deep breath as she gritted her teeth. "I don't know where it is!"

Jacki didn't say anything. Brewing, she lashed at Casey's back again with her whip three more times. With each point of contact, the whip sliced into Casey's skin, ripping it to shreds. When she was finished, Jacki went back in front of Casey. Resting her hand on the side of Casey's face, she jerked Casey's chin toward her. With tears pouring down Casey's face, Jacki demanded, "Does that feel good?"

"Nooo," Casey moaned.

"Do you want me to stop?"

"Yesss."

"Then tell me what you did with your brother's strongbox?"

"I didn't."

"Who did then?"

"I don't know what he did with it."

"Who?" she yelled.

"He took it."

"WHO?" she roared.

"I don't know where."

"My patience is running thin with you. I'm trying t' take it easy on ya since you're an innocent in this," Jacki said, as she paced in front of Casey. "All ya have t' do is tell me where it is, or who has it, an' I'll stop."

"I don't know!" Casey yelled, struggling to think clearly through the pain and agony.

Jacki stood in front of her for a moment. "I don't believe you!" she said, before slapping Casey hard across her face, dragging her fingernails across Casey's cheek. Casey immediately felt the blood drip down her cheek. Jacki knelt in front of her and tightly held her chin so Casey faced her. "Now, I don't want t' do any more damage to your beautiful face, so why don't ya help me by telling me where the box is."

"I don't know!" Casey screamed. The salt from her tears stung the scrapes on her face, and she could feel the cuts on her back from where the whip landed, drizzling the blood into small streams, cascading over the pieces of torn flesh.

Jacki got up and went behind Casey. Drawing her whip back again, she beat her with it. The lashes landed across the other slashes, slicing deeper into Casey's skin as she whipped her six more times.

Casey's horrific screams echoed through the building. Between the ten lashes, the poundings to her head, the water torture, and the drugs...Casey couldn't think straight. She went in and out of consciousness like some horror movie she couldn't escape. She prayed that God would either make Jacki stop, or God would take her home. She wanted it to end either way.

Jacki leaned down and whispered in Casey's ear, "How about now? Do ya remember where the box is now?"

Casey slowly shook her head with a moan.

"Ya know, your back looks pretty bad. Maybe I should wash it," Jacki said, and walked over to the table. Picking up a bowl, she took it to the sink. Running the hot water until it was steaming, Jacki then filled the bowl before adding salt. Looking at Casey, she added more for effect.

Casey stared at her in wide-eyed horror. Jacki was going to put *saltwater* on the open wounds. "No, please!" Casey begged as her body trembled in fear. "Please don't!"

Jacki slowly walked over, stirring the salt into the hot water to dissolve it. "I won't…if ya tell me where to find my box."

Casey anxiously looked from the bowl, to Jacki's face, in terror. "I don't know," Casey said, heart pounding in desperation. "I'm sorry! I don't know! *I don't know*!"

"Tsk! Tsk! Tsk!" Jacki shook her head. Pouring the contents of the bowl down Casey's back, Jacki let out this hideous cackle.

The howling scream Casey let out was a high-pitched, shrill scream of pure pain and agony.

"Angel! ANGEL!" Sasha shouted at Angel. He and Spencer unsuccessfully tried for several minutes to bring her back from wherever it was she had gone. Placing his hands on the sides of her face, he got within inches, and shouted again, "ANGEL!"

"I-I don't…" Angel shook her head, unable to get the horrific scream out of her mind. Tears streaked her face, as she remembered what her mother went through on that day. She heard the stories, and saw the scars, but to see it play out right in front of her was a whole other experience!

"Angel!" Spencer shouted. Standing to the side, he put his hand on her arm, and loudly said, "Angel, come back to us!"

"Angel, please!" Sasha pleaded with her. "Please come back from wherever it was you went."

Angel gulped, wide-eyed. "Wow. That was…I-I don't know."

"What *was* that?" Sasha asked, his hands on Angel's shoulders, relieved to have her back.

"I think that was a vision. If this is even remotely close to what Joe experiences, I don't know how he does it!"

"What was it?" Sasha asked again.

"It was of my mother, *here* in *this* room. This is where Jacki tortured her."

"Whoa," Spencer let out in a whisper, as he took a step back to give her air. "Intense."

Shaking her head, Angel wiped the tears off her cheeks. "What that woman did to her was inhumane! Mom told us the stories, but to see it right before me was a whole other level!"

"I need you to focus on me for a minute," Sasha said, placing his hands back on the sides of her face, making sure she looked at him, and him only. "We are in the middle of Cairns. We need to search this place in order to move forward. I know what you saw was traumatic, but we need to keep moving."

Angel nodded. "I understand." Taking deep, cleansing, breaths, she forced herself to focus. Continuing the search, she periodically looked over her shoulder, feeling as if she were being watched. She finally shook it off as ghosts of the past.

Moving dust covered shelves, knocking on walls coated in web and debris, and looking under every table and bed, the trio scoured the entire warehouse…unsuccessfully.

"Great!" Spencer said, when they finally exited the building. Brushing the dirt and spider webs off his arms, he declared, "I'll need about three showers to get rid of all of this grime."

"At least," Sasha agreed.

Since the vision, Angel was unusually quiet. She only nodded in response.

"Back to the hotel?" Sasha suggested. "What if we spend the night before heading to Black Rock tomorrow?"

"Good idea," Spencer agreed. "It's a good thirty-some hour drive to Black Rock. If we take off early, and drive through the night, we can get there the day after tomorrow."

Sasha nodded in response, before he rested his hand on the small of Angel's back. "Need to talk?" he asked her.

Angel shuddered. "That scream was…" Her voice faded. "That was my mom. That woman could have killed her."

"I am sure the Spirit let the A.N.G.E.L.s who were there on that day know just how important your mother was to the Kingdom."

Angel furrowed her brow. "What do you mean?"

"She was mother to three future A.N.G.E.L.s," Sasha simply said. "One of them is still destined to lead one of the teams. The other two are leaders in their own right. The same thing applies to Rachel and Josh's mother. It is my understanding that she had multiple horrific incidents that almost killed her as well. God knew both women would be crucial to the future of the A.N.G.E.L. teams."

"Good thing God already knows the plan," Spencer added. "That helps in keeping us focused on Him when we can't see the next step."

"Good point," Sasha said, as they got into the car.

With Spencer driving, they headed back to the hotel. "We didn't find any evidence of a box in the warehouse. Where do you think it was when that woman and her followers were there?"

"Maybe there was another location in use at the time?" Angel offered.

Spencer nodded, deep in thought, "Possibly. Or maybe it was in one of the other locations your dad mentioned."

"That's possible too," Angel agreed.

"Regardless, we need to find out where it is now," Sasha said.

"Agreed," Angel said, with a sense of determination in her voice. "Our teams are counting on us. Future A.N.G.E.L.s are counting on us...now more than ever!"

Chapter 10
A Link in the Chain

"You start school next week," Casey said to Liliya, Katia's sister, as they were eating dinner a few days after Christmas in Nevada. "Are you ready?"

"I think I am as ready as I can be," Liliya said with a shrug. "Katia is doing her own thing. I need to do the same."

"I agree. Speaking of doing your own thing," Derek said, cutting his steak, "what is your outlet?"

"What do you mean?" Liliya asked, confused.

"Well, for example, Jesse is an artist. That is how he deals with things. Jon's outlet is usually physical exercise. Angel's is running. What do you do to alleviate stress?"

"I do not know. I have not had freedom to choose this."

"We could explore different outlets to find it," Derek suggested. "You have been through a lot, and I know you and Casey have worked through quite a bit of it, but you need something for the daily stresses."

Casey nodded. "I agree. You are about to dive into a new environment. While we are putting you into a private school for now, you have many cultural things to work through. The stress will seem overwhelming at times."

"This I know. I also know you have all worked with me in many areas over these last few months in order to…how did you say it?" she asked, snapping her fingers. "Oh yes! To catch up. Thank you."

"We'll go shopping for your school supplies tomorrow, and we'll pick up your uniform when we visit the school," Casey explained. "I got the school supply list, and paid for your uniforms when I registered you a few weeks ago. While school actually starts on the fifth, we'll be going in on the fourth for you to meet your teachers. That's when we'll get your uniforms as well."

"This is wonderful news!" Liliya grinned. "New school. New name. New country. New me!"

"Yes. This is why you need to find your outlet," Derek pressed. "Too many changes."

"When will *we* get to go to school?" Allie asked.

"Yes. I want to meet other kids our age," Callie agreed.

"While you two are doing well, we'd like to keep you out of the school system for another year. Let us get Liliya going first. It will be easier for her to get into a college with an actual high school diploma and testing. Besides, I'm not ready for you little ones to go to school yet," Casey said to them with a wink and a smile.

They grinned, before continuing to eat.

"While this is all well and good, have the ground rules about talking about home life been laid out yet?" Mark asked Casey.

Casey shook her head. "Not yet."

"That needs to be a priority. We need to protect the home life if we're going to be sending kids into the school system. The A.N.G.E.L.s need to be protected."

"I will protect the A.N.G.E.L.s," Liliya insisted. "You are my family. My sestra is an A.N.G.E.L. as well. I will never do anything to harm any of you!"

"Not intentionally," Mark said. As soon as he did, Liliya's jaw dropped, and her face flushed red in anger. "While the intention may not be there, we need to set boundaries. We are all linked together. What one does affects us all."

"I *will never* do anything to harm *any* A.N.G.E.L.!" Liliya raised her voice. "To say otherwise is an affront to me! I do not like that!"

"I'm sure. You have to understand," Mark calmly explained, "that the other side has ways of putting things in your mind. Also, as a teen, you may want others to accept you. You may say something just to get attention."

"That's enough," Casey said before taking a bite of her potatoes. When she did, both Mark and Liliya looked over at her, stunned. "We can talk more about that tomorrow. For tonight, let's just relax and enjoy our time," Casey said, hoping to tone down the anger and anxiety she felt from both Mark and Liliya. "We don't have many more family nights before school starts. We need to enjoy them. We have also agreed to never go to bed angry. In order to do that, for tonight, we need to table this conversation until tomorrow."

"Agreed," Mark said, "but, tomorrow we need to talk."

*   *   *

Deep in the heart of the Outback, the group heading toward the other side, finally reached their destination around two in the morning. As they disembarked their vehicles and stretched, Rachel looked out at the vast countryside in awe. "God's work is amazing," she said on a sigh.

"I know. The limitless creatures, among the various plants and scenery He created amazes me every day," Jesse agreed. "We've been all over the world, and each place is unique in its beauty and creativity. I don't know how the Lord does it!"

Taking a moment to look around and make sure they weren't overheard, in a low voice only heard by Jesse, she said, "We have to blow it."

"What? The mountain?"

"Yes. That's the only way to contain them and take out a massive chunk of their kind. I only pray Cassius, Korax, and Calliope are in there when it's blown."

"While I don't like it any more than you do, I agree. We have to get the scales balanced again."

"Without balance, our world will tumble into the darkness."

"Agreed."

"Okay, let's join hands in prayer before we depart," Rachel said louder, in order for all to hear. "We need to make sure our Lord and Savior walks with us this early morning into this mission, and that He blesses our steps."

"The battle is His!" Charlie declared.

"Not ours, but for *His* glory!" Daku shouted.

"For the blood of our fallen!" another clansman yelled.

Joining hands, the nine A.N.G.E.L.s, along with the fifteen clansmen, made a giant circle around the vehicles. "Father, we come before You as Your soldiers. It is only by Your guidance and strength that we take on this mission today," Rachel started. "We ask You to go before us, and make a way. We ask that You go before us, where angels fear to tread. We ask for Your hands of protection for all of us here, as well as those A.N.G.E.L.s, and Your saints spread throughout this vast world You created. We are in awe of Your strength and abilities, and know that You are bigger than any of this. We know that we only go forward with Your blessing…"

As she continued to pray, and each person after her, saints around the world were led to stop what they were doing, and to start praying.

*   *   *

Anastasia, up in St. Petersburg, Russia, was getting ready for bed when she felt the call. Getting down on her aged knees, she rested her clasped hands on the bed, and bowed her head in prayer. Knowing her godson, Sasha, was out there with the A.N.G.E.L.s, she prayed every day for them. However, this was something stronger. This was something deep within her that she hadn't felt for a long time. This was something world-changing.

*   *   *

Being that it was eleven in the morning in Reno, Nevada, the A.N.G.E.L.s, along with the English family members were just sitting down to an early lunch, when they all felt it.

"It's time," Jerrod said knowingly.

"I think we all feel it," Kai said, looking around the table.

"We need to fast and pray until the battle is finished," Akio announced, setting his silverware down.

"Yes. While this food looks good," Hiro said, "we need to save it for later and pray now."

"Agreed," Casey said, getting up to put it away. "You all go pray, while I clean up, and I'll join you when I'm finished."

"I'll help," Jerrod jumped up.

"No. You go with them," Mark said, as the rest of the group broke up into smaller groups. Derek and Mark took Liliya, Allie, and Callie, and headed upstairs. Meanwhile, Jerrod (with Chief) took Hiro, Kai, Hanif, Akio, Cori (with Charm), Raphe, Zara, and Toby, and headed out to the back deck.

Getting down on their knees in prayer, with their hands lifted toward the Heavens, each prayed in their own language to the Lord, but spoke in one voice of agreement as to the safety of the team, and the outcome of victory.

* * *

Meanwhile, down in Mexico, the Mexican team felt the same pull. It was around one o'clock in the afternoon, so they stopped what they were doing and either went to their vehicles, or if they were home, to their living rooms, and prayed for the safety of the A.N.G.E.L.s. While they were not one hundred percent sure what was going on, they knew by the burden that it was big, and prayed accordingly. Even though it meant possibly being late back to work from lunch, they would remain in prayer until the Spirit lifted the burden. While they may not know the ending result, they prayed for the Lord's will and direction, and the faith to accept the results.

* * *

Little, eleven-year-old, Lauren Knight in London, England had finished her dinner, and was working on her homework around seven at night when she felt it. It felt like a pit in her stomach. Her heart raced as she looked around the room. After the loss of her brother, Aden, several months ago, creatures plagued her nightmares. The slightest sound out of the ordinary sent her back to that day with fear and trembling.

Suddenly, before her, stood an angel. "Hello, Lauren. My name is Michael. Do not be afraid."

Speechless, she stared at him, as the color drained from her face.

"Lauren," he said, kneeling in front of her, resting his arm on his knee, "I am an archangel of the Lord God Almighty. I am aware of what you faced on that fateful day, and am here to tell you that you have angels watching over you, sent by the Lord. Do not worry. There are angels fighting daily on your behalf."

"W-what happens if they lose?" Lauren's voice quivered.

"You are blessed, young one. The Lord has amazing and wonderful plans for you. Hold onto that promise."

"I will."

"Now, some of those you met on that day are in trouble. That feeling you have inside you is not a bad feeling. You will need to learn the difference between the bad and good feelings. The Spirit, at this moment, is asking you to pray for the Lord's A.N.G.E.L.s. They need your prayers."

"Why me?"

"Every prayer of the Lord's children comes with power and strength as they rely on the Lord. They give the heavenly angels the strength they need to continue to battle. The Lord God relishes in the prayers of His children. You must learn to listen for the Spirit's voice to tell you when to pray, and for what to pray. You will be an incredible prayer warrior. This is, unfortunately, a gift that is being neglected the more the instant gratification generations grow. The more people are distracted by the world, television, and social media, the less they listen for the Spirit's voice. Every child of the Lord needs to know what His voice sounds like in order to follow Him."

"I know. I am afraid of what else is out there, though," Lauren admitted.

Resting his hand on her knee, Michael explained, "You, Lauren Knight, will be an A.N.G.E.L. one day, if you choose to answer the call when it is put on your heart. If you so choose to answer the call in the positive, the Lord will need His children to pray for you one day. You are more aware than most that we do not fight against flesh and blood, but against the powers of darkness. Do not let Aden's death mar your soul beyond help. Use it to fuel your passion to spread the Word of Lord with strength and fortitude. Do not cower. You are a child of The King. You are a princess among men. You are a link in a chain that binds us all together as one."

"Thank you," Lauren said through her tears of joy. "I will listen."

"Then start right now. The A.N.G.E.L.s need you."

* * *

As the sun rose, Alani rested on the beach in Honolulu. Doing her devotions on the beach in the morning had become a habit she cherished each day. Seeing the muted tones of blue and pink slowly shift into brilliant hues of gold and peach was the joy of her day.

The sun had been up for a few hours, and her devotions were finished, but she felt led to stay on the beach for a bit longer that morning. Around eight o'clock, she felt the heavy presence of the Lord like she had never felt before in her thirty-five years of life. It overpowered every sense. As the world blurred around her, she had visions of a mountain blowing up deep in the heart of the Outback, and instantly bowed her head in prayer.

Even though she didn't know those in trouble, she knew one of her brothers or sisters in Christ needed her.

*   *   *

Deep in the jungles of Africa, a young native boy was out with his friends exploring. Stopping short, one of his friends ran into him. "Whatcha doing?" the young boy's friend demanded. "I almost tripped over you!"

"We need to pray."

"You're serious? The others are leaving us," he said, gesturing toward the group of young boys walking out ahead.

"We *need* to pray," the young boy said again.

"Pasi," the young boy said, shaking his head in frustration, "if we stop, then we will lose the others."

"It is not the others I am concerned with losing, Tanner. Someone is in trouble, and they need us to pray. Are you telling me that you do not feel it? The others are not Christian, but you are. I know it is our secret. I am not trying to let the secret out. I am trying to help those in trouble. You can either stay and pray with me, or you can go with them. I am choosing to stay and stand with others in prayer."

Looking from Pasi, to their group of friends in the distance, Tanner debated in his head. He felt the pull, but he didn't want to lose his friends.

"You two coming?" one of the boys from the group called back when they realized the two lagged behind.

A verse popped into Pasi's mind, and as Tanner debated, he quoted Matthew 16:24, *"Then Jesus said to His disciples, "Whoever wants to be My disciple must deny themselves and take up their cross and follow Me."* This is your chance to make the choice for Him. What do you choose?"

Tanner looked from Pasi to the group of boys, and back again. Looking back to the boys, he called, "We are staying. You guys go ahead. We have something we need to do."

A grin crossed Pasi's face as his friends took off without him and Tanner. "Want to pray now?"

"We need to," Tanner said, as they ran off on their own.

*   *   *

A young girl around college-age was resting in her bed around midnight, when she felt it. Not bothering to flip on the light because she was blind, she rolled out of bed. To her, it felt like a stomachache, but she knew exactly what it was she was feeling. It was the Lord telling her to pray.

She grabbed her blonde hair, shoving it into a ponytail holder before she braced her hands on the dresser. Hearing her mother watching television in the other room, she knew she would have time by herself, so she felt around for her headset and iPod. She would often listen to praise and worship music in order to concentrate on her prayers. The music shut out the rest of the world and allowed her to concentrate only on Him.

Making her way back to the bed, she sat on it. Tucking the headphones in her ears, she turned the music on and sat for a moment. That's when she saw it. In her mind, she saw the men heading toward the mountain, and then…she saw what happened next.

Alarmed, she bowed her head and prayed in earnest for those in the vision. Knowing she would not know the end of the story, she focused on the characters, and prayed for them. She would pray for them until she felt the Lord tell her it was enough.

Knowing it would be a long night, she lay down in her bed, with one hand resting on the iPod on her chest, and the other tucked behind her head. When she ran out of words, she would just hum or sing the worship music. Either way, she knew the power the prayers and praise held in the eyes of God. She understood that being with Him in that moment is what was needed.

*   *   *

"Amen," Jesse said, as the prayer circle ended with him. Looking to Rachel for direction, he asked, "Next?"

"Next we begin the hike. Those coming with us, pack up and let's head out. The Lord goes with us this morning," she announced.

Delaney, Joe, and three of Charlie's clan were left at the trucks, while Jesse, Rachel, Jon, Josh, Charlie, Jacob, Isaac, and the remaining clansmen with them, took off into the Australian Outback.

"I wonder how Angel and the guys are doing?" Joe said after several minutes of pensive silence, as he and Delaney leaned against the jeep. Charlie's guys were clustered together, talking amongst themselves, but kept a continuous eye for movement around them.

"Well, we haven't heard anything yet, so hopefully that means they're staying out of trouble, yeah?"

"Let's pray!" Joe rolled his eyes. "That girl can find trouble in a convent!"

Delaney giggled.

"Seriously! I've never known someone so trouble-prone!"

"She brings a lot of it on herself," Delaney pointed out. "Here's praying she got that sorted, more for Spencer and Sasha's sake."

"From your lips to God's ears." Joe sighed. "Honestly, we don't need any more trouble. This is going to be bad enough."

"We can't let the attack on the stations go unanswered," Delany said, taken aback by Joe's statement.

"I agree. I am just not one that goes looking to blow up God's handiwork."

"Meaning?"

"Meaning it's not the Outback's fault the other side chose to have another hideout out here. If we could somehow surgically remove them from the mountain, instead of blowing another mountain, I would rather do that. God created that mountain. The other side has tainted the beauty of it. We already blew one up on the other side of Alice Springs. I don't want to blow another one up. It will forever change the countryside when it's blown."

"While I agree, we *need* to do something!" Delaney insisted.

"I agree. I only wish it could be less dramatic. I'll be glad when things slow down a bit," Joe admitted. Taking her hand, he explained, "I'd like to enjoy some time with you, without having to worry that we'll be attacked. It would be nice to just relax."

"It's been a while," Delaney agreed, giving his hand a squeeze. Looking out toward the direction the rest of the group had departed, she observed, "We can't see them anymore. Time to stop talking, and pray again, yeah?"

"Yeah. Go get Charlie's guys so we can start. The sooner the better. I know the stations have had people in prayer since we left. We need to join them again."

*   *   *

At Serenity Wells Station, there was a group of ten to fifteen people praying at any given moment, and had been since the groups departed. Katia was working on a security schedule at the dining room table when she felt it. Hearing Val hobble in on his crutches, Katia didn't look up. She just asked, "You felt it too?"

"Yep. Time for the stations to pray."

"I am boosting security. The stations are on a tiny staff doing the bare minimum until this is over. It is time to ramp up the prayer from all three places."

"I'll tell Willow to alert the stations. When I get back, do you want to pray together?"

"Actually, I would like that," Katia said with a smile.

Val's heart leaped at her smile. He couldn't help the grin that spread across his face. Leaning against the doorway, he said, "While I know you didn't want to stay here, I'm glad you're here with me."

"Me too," Katia said, as her face flushed. "You are nice."

"Thank you."

"You are also not as rough as the others," Katia observed.

"And, *you* are tough as nails," Val said, "but have a soft side as well."

"Thank you for noticing."

"I noticed it the first time I met you, when you burst through the restaurant. You were a firecracker then, but I saw your passion for your sister."

"Really? I would have thought I was a…what's the word?" Katia asked, struggling to remember the phrase. "Not a tight gun?"

"Loose cannon?" Val offered.

"Yes! That's it! I would have thought that you would have called me a loose cannon."

Val hobbled back over to the table. Sitting on the bench beside her, he confessed, "Katia, I've liked you from that first moment I saw you. At this point, as your friend, I respect the force of nature that you are. I am pleasantly surprised that, with everything you've gone through in your life, that you're honestly still sane."

"There are times I wonder if I am sane," she said in a chuckle.

Val grinned as he shook his head. "That smile."

"You have a nice smile too," she confessed. "You have a peace about you. When you smile, your dimples stand out, and you look cute."

"Thank you!" Val said appreciatively, before feeling the tug again. "Look, I want to talk more, but right now we need to get the stations in prayer. Can we talk more at a later time?"

"Of course. Where am I going to go?" She gestured with her hands in the air. "I am in charge of the security for three stations."

Val smiled. "This is true. And, right now, Pete and I are in charge of the medical portion for the three stations."

"And, we are *all* in charge of prayer!"

"Yep!" Getting up, he headed toward the kitchen. Stopping in the doorway, he paused and looked at Katia…only to see her watching him.

*   *   *

After their adventure in the warehouse, the trio in Queensland took multiple showers, ordered room service, and then retired to sleep for the night. The next morning around five, a nightmare invaded Angel's sleep once again…

"You are now a part of *our* group!" a demon hissed at the twins, while they cowered in a cage in the cavern at Black Rock.

"We want Mommy!" Allie shouted through her tears, as Callie just trembled where she sat.

What they witnessed since they were taken were things of night terrors! The mafia boss had his man take them, and then he turned and sold them to Calliope and Korax. Korax was in his human form at the time.

Once taken, they were whisked away to Australia, only to be dumped into a cage when they arrived at Black Rock. They hadn't eaten the entire trip and had only received water. Once they arrived, a loaf of bread was thrown into the cage with them, along with a bucket of water and a ladle.

Dirty, hungry, confused, upset, and just plain terrified, the twins watched in horror as Korax turned into a bat-like creature, with blackish-red scales, talons for nails, and yellow-green eyes that seemed to bore a hole into their very soul. Young and innocent, the two did not know what to do…except cry.

Calliope sung to them, in hopes of calming them. Finally able to get them to sleep, she then set to begin their brainwashing. Day and night, the creatures taunted the twins. In the middle of it all, Calliope would then swoop in and shew the demons away, giving them a break. She would then sing the twins to sleep over and over again. Her goal was to get them to rely on her. Once that was achieved, the rest would be easy.

About three days into it, Allie woke one morning, gently jostling Callie. "Wake up, but be quiet," she whispered.

"What?" Callie asked, as she struggled to focus in her sleep state.

"I want Mommy."

"Me too. How do we get out of here, though?"

"Mommy taught us to pray. She said God is with us wherever we are, right?"

Wide-eyed, Callie asked, "You think He's here? Even in this is a scary place?"

"I think we need to pray and see if He is here."

"Okay."

Allie grabbed Callie's hands, and she prayed in the voice of a whisper, "Dear Jesus, we need help. It is scary here. Mommy said you would be here if we asked. Please help us?"

"SILENCE!!" a demon hissed, when the hair stood on the back of its neck. "We do not do that here! If you pray, Calliope will not like you anymore, and you will be completely alone. Is that what you want?" it asked, coming right up to the cage. When the twins scurried to the back of the cage to get away, the demon smiled an evil smile. When it did, saliva dripped from its fangs. "I could eat you for a snack!" it hissed. Reaching in, it swiped at them, barely missing them. It snagged its talon on Callie's skirt, tearing a piece of it off. Taking a deep inhale of the cloth, the demon sneered as saliva dripped from its mouth once again. "Delicioussssss!"

"Go away!" Allie yelled, while Callie just sat there in shock.

"If Calliope was not here, you would be mine!"

"But, I am," Calliope said, walking into the cavern with a loaf of bread under her arm. "Back it off, and leave them alone."

Scurrying to a corner of the cavern, the demon kept an eye on the little girls. Allie could see that it was serious about eating them!

After sliding the bread through the bars of the cage, Calliope sat on the ground while they hungrily ate the bread. The twins were coated in dirt, their hair was a rat's nest mess, and they ate as if they had not eaten in days. It was the gratefulness in their eyes where Calliope centered. They were starting to bend. A sinister smile formed on Calliope's face while she watched them eat. She had plans for them. Big plans! The sirens she created so long ago could be resurrected in these two if given enough time. She only needed a few more days before she could start. She needed the twin's spirit more susceptible to her will. She needed them pliable and relying fully on her.

Angel sat upright in bed and looked around. Glancing at the clock, she saw it was only five-thirty. *"Why am I suddenly flooded with these dreams? What is God trying to tell me in this one?"* she thought to herself. She was relieved that while it was scary, and she could feel what the twins felt, it wasn't anywhere near as bad as the other nightmares she experienced lately.

Pulling her legs up, she glanced over at the sleeping Spencer and Sasha. Both were resting peacefully, and for that, she was grateful. This lack of sleep was not helping her at all, but she would press on for the team. Knowing she needed to clean up her reputation, she reminded herself that this wasn't about her, it was about the team.

"Why are you awake?" Sasha whispered.

"Oh!" she said, resting her hand on her chest, as her heart raced. "You scared me. You were asleep a second ago."

"As were you when I went to the bathroom about an hour ago," he countered.

"Had a nightmare about when the twins were held in Black Rock."

"Do you remember much about the layout?"

Angel shook her head. "No. And, even if I did, Jacob blew it up. It would be completely different now. We're going to be relying on your sensing ability again."

"Pretty sure that's a constant. I'm more concerned with getting lost."

"We can take chalk in. One color going in…different color coming out."

"Good idea. Why don't you get some rest? We're not getting up for a few hours."

"Might as well get up now," Spencer said, rolling over, facing them. "We're all up. If we get started now, we can there faster. It's going to be a long drive."

"Good thinking. Besides, the longer we wait, the hotter it gets," Angel pointed out. "This isn't some cooled warehouse. This is Black Rock."

"True," Sasha said, getting up. Grabbing his clothes, he then went into the bathroom.

When the door closed, Spencer moved to Sasha's side of the bed to talk to Angel. "Okay, what's going on with you two?"

"What do you mean?"

"I mean you two are considerably closer. Is there something going on?"

"Maybe," Angel said with a shy smile.

"Nice!" Spencer grinned. "He seems like a nice guy. He also seems strong. You need both. The guys you went for in college were horrible choices!" he chuckled, while rolling his eyes. "Seriously! You could have done *so* much better than Jaime Renfield!"

"Well," she shrugged, as her face flushed, "he *seemed* nice."

"You should have asked me. I would have told you he was a cretin."

"I know." She sighed. Then she smiled as she added, "Sasha seems like a good guy."

"Yes. He does." Hearing the bathroom door open, Spencer got out of bed to grab his clothes. As he walked by Angel, he leaned down and said, "Just don't screw it up!"

Angel stuck her tongue out at him, and he laughed as he went into the bathroom, and Sasha took his place back on the bed.

"What was that about?" Sasha asked.

"Just Spencer being Spencer."

"Was there anything ever between you two?"

"No. He really liked Dina Evans. She had her eyes on someone else, though. He's a good guy. Maybe he will hook up with another one of the A.N.G.E.L.s?"

"Possibly. Why do you two not hook up, as you call it, now?"

Looking over at him, confused by that question from him, she answered, "Because I'm interested in someone else."

Lying down on the bed, facing her, he smiled and blushed, before asking, "Oh really? And, who would that be?"

She shrugged, playing coy. "Another one of the A.N.G.E.L.s."

"Who?" Sasha pressed.

"Your turn," Spencer said, coming out of the bathroom.

"Have to wait and see," Angel said, getting off the bed. Grabbing her clothes, she headed into the bathroom.

"Wait and see about what?" Spencer asked, flopping on the bed next to Sasha.

Lying back, Sasha interlaced his finger behind his head, as he looked toward the ceiling, with thoughts of Angel. "She is trying to hide that she likes me."

"How do you feel about her?"

He sighed. "Love at first sight."

"Really? How do you know?"

"Cannot get her out of my mind. God had this spunky young lady cross my path, and I was history! If she chooses me, I will do my best to make a good partner for her. She is a rare gem…only she does not fully understand that, I do not think. She thinks she needs to impress people, but she is impressive as she stands. God is not finished with her yet." He glanced over at Sasha, and added, "He is not finished with any of us, or we would not be here."

"This is true."

Looking back up at the ceiling, Sasha continued, "Where she sees scars, I see strength. Where she sees the need to impress, I already see an impressive young lady. Now," he glanced back over to Spencer, "I am not blind to the mistakes she has made in trying to impress. I only wish her to see herself as God and I see her."

"Well said," Spencer agreed. "She *is* quite impressive."

"How come you two did not get together?"

"I think of her more like a sister. She's not really my type, but we get along great."

"Is your type among the women of the A.N.G.E.L.s?"

"I haven't seen too many of them." Spencer shrugged. "If God allows me the honor of having a wife, I'll be thrilled. If he doesn't, I'm content with just Him and me."

"That is a great way to think. I was the same, until Angel crossed my path."

"God works in mysterious ways, my man," Spencer said, patting Sasha on the arm.

"This is true."

"Ready?" Angel asked, coming out of the bathroom. "We have like a thirty-three or thirty-four-hour drive ahead of us."

"Let's pack up and go," Spencer said, heading over to his suitcase. "We have a lot of road to cover, and time is ticking."

*   *   *

"Time keeps passing, but I feel like we haven't gone anywhere," Rachel said, and then drained a bottle of water, as they continued to walk deep into the Outback. They were making the journey in the dim light of the early morning. The sun was nowhere in sight as of yet, and wouldn't be for several more hours.

"We didn't want the jeeps close, so it's going to be a bit," Jacob reminded her. Turning back toward where they'd walked from, he shook his head. "Can't even see them anymore."

"Whose idea was this?" Rachel asked.

"Yours. You said you didn't want them to hear the Jeeps," Josh said, as he shifted the weight of his backpack.

"Okay, then are we almost there? This looked a *lot* shorter on paper!"

"Don't whinge," Josh said, as he wiped the sweat off his forehead. "We'll get there when we get there."

"Fine," Rachel huffed. Stopping, she cocked her head to the side. "Wasn't that mountain over that way earlier?"

Everyone stopped and studied it for a moment.

"I think you're right," Jacob said, and then began looking around. "Did we shift direction at some point?"

Jesse pulled out his compass. Lining it up with the mountain, he shook his head. "When did we shift? We're off. Look."

"Just redirect us to where we need to be," Jacob grumbled. "This is a long enough hike without redirection."

Pointing toward the left, Jesse said, "That way. I'll keep it open so we don't shift again."

"We're going to have to either find our initial trail again, or I will have to revamp the initial plan a bit," Jacob mentioned. "This direction may be only a little bit off, but it's off enough to make a difference."

"We weren't *that* far off." Jesse rolled his eyes. "It was just that we've been a bit off for a long time. A bit off for a long time, makes a lot of difference in the long-run."

Walking for what seemed like hours, but was only around forty-five minutes, they finally neared an area with several trees. Crouching behind them, Rachel asked, "Anything yet, Jesse?"

"No."

"Good. Then we're far enough out. Jacob? Are they ready?"

Jacob gathered his men, and they made a circle. He went over the plan once more, and then sent them on their way. "Why do I feel like a father sending his children to their doom?"

"They are all scared, but in a healthy way, even the ones you were worried about. They feel courageous, yet resolved. They'll do their job. God's with them," Jon said confidently, as he sat down next to a tree and pulled his breakfast out. When everyone looked at him, he said, "What? It's going to be a bit until we know anything. Would it be better to stand around stressed, or fuel up with food, while sitting down to rest in case we need to run later?"

"Good point," Jesse said, and sat down next to him. The others followed suit, not taking their eyes off the small band of men heading toward the mountain carrying explosives. As they each prayed, they nibbled on their food.

Rachel kept an eye on the group through binoculars while she ate her sandwich and prayed in her mind, hoping *she* wasn't sending the men to their doom.

Chapter 11
Tightening the Chains

The long drive through the Australian roads down toward Black Rock were gorgeous, but Angel knew what was going on in the Outback, as did Sasha and Spencer. They were aware of the timeline, and that it was going on at that moment.

While Spencer drove, Angel and Sasha took turns praying aloud for over three hours, before they finally turned on Spencer's iPod, containing worship music. They figured worshipping and praising the Lord would take their minds off what was going on in the Outback, yet keep them in the forefront of their minds at the same time.

*　*　*

The teams were divided in two groups of six. Each man of Jacob's team had one man beside him, keeping guard over him until the explosives were planted. After that, they would make their way back to the A.N.G.E.L.s...hopefully before they went off!

Silence was key, and as Aboriginals, they had this skill almost engrained in them. Learning techniques to accomplish this as young children, they could be stealthier than most. This enabled them to be good hunters as well.

As they neared the mountain, Daku noticed figures on the top of the mountain. It was then that music began to reach their ears. Daku grabbed his earplugs that Jacob gave each man in order to protect their hearing in case the explosives went off early. They were instructed to put them in as they neared the mountain. What Jacob didn't know, was that he would also be saving them from another fate.

Most of the men got their earplugs in quickly enough, except Parri. His soul was immediately engrossed in the music he heard. His partner and cousin, Woorin, tried to put them in for him, but he punched him, and ran toward the music.

The songs of the Sirens on top of the mountain pulled him toward it with such force, he didn't hear or see anything else. The song seemed to overtake every sense. All he could focus on was that music…that beautiful music.

Without warning, he was surrounded by three demons, hissing and clawing at him. They ripped him limb from limb, until the only thing left of him was shredded clothing and body parts…while his friends and family looked on in horror!

More resolved than ever, the teams and Woorin, made their way to their destinations in stealthy silence. Their feelings of resolve were mixed with mourning and anger, but they pressed forward.

Woorin, the member of the pair from Jacob's team, knew what he had to do, even without the backup of protection from his cousin, Parri. Jacob was clear in their mission. He was a strong leader, who instructed them well.

Keeping an eye in every direction for more traps, they made their way to their assigned placements. In and placed without any further incident, those on Jacob's team lit the fuses of their homemade explosives before running for their lives.

It was when they ran that the demons around the mountainside noticed them, and ran for them as well.

"Crickey! They're in trouble!" Rachel scrambled from her spot on the ground.

The others followed suit, and ran toward the remaining eleven. Knowing it didn't matter anymore that the other side knew they were there, the A.N.G.E.L.s ran as fast as they could to help the clansmen, and to keep the remaining creatures of evil in the mountain until the explosives went off.

Reaching them at the mid-point, wide-eyed, Daku exclaimed, "They are here!"

"Run! We've got this!" Josh shouted in the chaos.

"No!" Daku stopped in his tracks, resolve taking over once again. "We will stay and fight."

"You have done your part, now let us do ours," Jon insisted.

As soon as he said that, the explosives began to go off in succession around the mountain, just as Jacob planned. "Brilliant!" Jacob smiled. Then his eyes went wide, as he saw the incoming twenty or so demons headed their way.

"Go!" Josh said again to the clansmen.

"No!" Daku shouted.

"Go!" Charlie ordered.

Reluctantly, Daku, and the remaining clansmen ran toward the tree clearing to wait for the A.N.G.E.L.s. Daku stopped mid-way to watch, as the demons neared the seven A.N.G.E.L.s. Several stopped with him, while the remaining finished the run.

"I knew you would be near!" a demon hissed at Rachel, as it clawed at her. "This is *your* doing!"

Rachel jumped back just in time, before she ran at it, knife in hand. Without another word, she slashed its throat. Then she continued on behind it, and plunged the knife into its side. As it dropped to the ground in flames, she turned to the next one.

Jesse lunged through the air, feet in front, landing his feet on the chest of the demon racing toward him. As it dropped to the ground, Jesse flipped it over, lifted its head, and jammed the knife into its neck. When he pulled the knife back out, the black blood instantly coated the ground around them. With his knee in its back, Jesse held him there until the demon began to flame up. Jumping off, he turned toward the one going after Jon, while the one he just killed turned to ash. Meanwhile Jon was in a wrestling match with the one he was fighting, until Jesse pulled the gun from the holster in his jeans and shot it in the head.

When the gun went off, there was suddenly a burst of explosions in the distance. Everyone stopped, stunned at the amount of the debris that shot up into the air. Jacob's explosives obviously set off something within the heart of the mountain, sending ash and debris in every direction.

A rock hit Rachel, sending her back several feet to the ground, knocking the wind out of her. Curling up in a ball, she hoped to protect her body from any more harm.

As the rocks and debris rained down, it knocked out some of the demons, killed others, and injured the rest. The A.N.G.E.L.s did their best not to get killed from the debris, and prayed for God's protection from anymore injury.

*   *   *

When it began to settle, Daku, and those with him ran up to the group. They killed the remaining demons before going to the A.N.G.E.L.s to check for injuries.

While Daku and his clansmen killed the demons, Isaac crawled over to Rachel, and asked, "Rach? Are you okay?"

With blood coming down from the side of her head, she slowly sat up and nodded. Looking shell-shocked, she looked at the bodies, debris, and ash for her team members. "Jesse?" she asked weakly.

"Not sure. I kind of have my own issue," Isaac said, nodding toward the broken bone in his lower leg. The blood soaked his jeans from where several rocks landed. He also had scrapes and bruises already forming all over him.

Rachel slowly got up in a daze, searching for Jesse. She walked by Charlie and Josh, who were being taken care of by a couple clansmen for cuts and scrapes. Turning back to Isaac, she saw a couple more run to his side to set his leg, and then braced it. Looking around, she felt her world swirl around her. "Jesse?" she asked again to no one in particular. Her voice sounded hollow, even to herself.

Jon grabbed Rachel's ankle. She jumped as she looked down at him. "Help me!" he gasped. There was a boulder on his mid-section.

Rachel knelt down to push the rock off, when Jacob suddenly appeared next to her. With cuts on his arms, Jacob helped her push the boulder off Jon, but with a bit of a struggle.

"Ribs," Jon groaned in pain once they finally got it off him. "Do not move me."

Rachel's nurse training kicked-in. "Punctured lungs?" she asked, almost on automation.

Jon nodded, as he struggled to get air.

Noticing the blood coming from his mouth when he coughed, Rachel turned to Jacob, and asked, "Do you have a lighter?"

"Always," Jacob said, handing it to her.

"Don't suppose you have a straw or pen?"

He pulled the pen from the ground where it fell from its normal place behind his ear, and handed it to her.

She handed him her knife. "Sterilize that with your lighter," she instructed, as she stripped the pen. While he ran the flame up and down the blade, she felt around Jon's ribs. Once she found what she was looking for, she grabbed the sterilized knife from Jacob.

"Wait! What are you doing?" Jacob asked, in horror.

"Saving his life. Now shut up!" she snapped, as she felt around again. Finding the exact location, she took a deep breath, said a prayer, and cut into Jon's side. As blood poured out of the cut, she quickly inserted the pen casing, and was relieved when Jon starting breathing a little easier. Taking off her overshirt, leaving her in a tank top, she wrapped the over shirt around the pen casing, and turned to Jacob. "Hold this in place," she instructed. "Do *not* let go until a paramedic of some kind comes and takes him to the hospital."

Jacob nodded. "Yes, ma'am."

Rachel took a moment to turn Jon onto his injured side, despite his objections.

"What are you doing?" Jacob asked. "Isn't that going to make it worse?"

"No. It'll help the blood drain out, and keep it away from his good lung." Turning to Jon, she instructed, "Just don't move anymore. With your broken ribs, I don't want any more damage. This will help you, though."

Jon just nodded in response, as he groaned in pain.

Rachel stood and looked around at the devastation that surrounded them, beside herself. Relieved that the remaining demons who escaped the explosion were now piles of ash, her concern was for those on the teams. The fact that no one from the other side was left alive was one of the few things going for them.

Grabbing the satellite phone out of her backpack, she dialed Delaney.

"Looks like it went pretty high," Delaney said, answering the phone.

"It did. We need to be airlifted out of here, though. Jon needs immediate help."

"What shape is everyone in?" Delaney asked, grabbing a pen and notebook from the jeep.

Delaney wrote down exactly what Rachel said to her, "At the very least, Jon has a punctured lung. I have a pen case inserted into his lungs, enabling him to breathe. He has multiple broken ribs, and I'm pretty sure there is some internal bleeding. He needs help as soon as possible."

"Right," Delaney said, nodding to Joe, who got on his phone, calling Alice Springs. "Go on," she said, while Joe called for help.

"Isaac has a broken leg. It's currently set. There are others with multiple cuts, scrapes, bruising, and…" Rachel stopped and gasped. "Jesse," she breathed out.

Delaney gulped at Rachel's reaction. "What, um, what's Jesse's status?"

When she asked that, and the way she asked, Joe looked over, heart skipping a beat. He told the hospital to hold on, while he listened to the phone Delaney had in her hand.

"He's-he's unconscious and not moving," Rachel squeaked out. "I need to get to him, but…" her voice faded, as her feet froze in place and she wobbled. Pushing back the black cloud that wanted to overtake her, she simply said, "We need help."

"Done," Joe said, and took his phone to the side to continue talking to Alice Springs.

"Rachel," Delaney said, as calmly as she could muster, hoping and praying to cover her own worries, "you are a trained registered nurse. You are made for this. You need to go to Jesse and tell me his injuries."

"So much blood," Rachel said, tears pouring down her cheeks, as she wavered in place. Shaking her head in despair, she admitted, "I can't."

"You can. You have to. You may be the only one out there who can. Rach, Jesse needs you."

"I need *him*," she admitted. "I don't know if I can do this without him."

"You can, and you will. Your strength is in God, not in Jesse. He may be your love, but God is your strength. C'mon, one foot in front of the other, yeah?" Delaney encouraged.

"There are four guys around him right now. He-he's not moving."

"Rachel!" Delaney snapped. Everyone with them turned to Delaney, stunned. "Rachel Sullivan, pull up your big girl pants, and go help your man!"

"I…yes," Rachel said, weakly. "I…I need…" Rachel dropped the phone, as she collapsed on the ground, surrendering to the black cloud.

Jacob grabbed the phone with his free hand, while still holding onto the shirt on Jon's chest, grateful to feel Jon's chest rising and falling…even if it was staggering. "Delaney, this is Jacob. Rachel just passed out."

*　　*　　*

"Rachel!" Kit sat upright in bed from her deep sleep. Struggling to see the room around her from her nap, Kit felt her way to the door, heart racing, and mind spinning. "Nico!" she called from the top of the stairs.

When there was no answer, she grasped the stair railing, slowly making her way down the stairs as her world spun around her. "Nico!" she called again. When he didn't answer, she called out, "Willow!"

Willow came out from the kitchen where she was doing food prep. "Mum?" Willow asked. Rushing to Kit's side, helping her down the steps to the couch, she asked, "What's wrong? You look shaken."

"Where's Nico?"

Willow took her radio off her belt, and called, "Caleb? Is your dad around you?"

"Yes. What's going on?" Caleb's voice came back over the radio. "Have you heard from the teams?"

"No. Your mum is down here, shaken. She keeps asking for Nico."

"He's on his way," he said. Letting out a whistle, every ranch hand in the area looked up. "Pop! Mum needs you at the house!" he shouted to his dad across the field.

While Nico ran for his horse, Caleb took off for the main house on his. They arrived only seconds apart. "What's going on?" Nico asked, as he dismounted.

"Dunno. Willow said Mum needs you," he said, as they headed into the house.

When they walked into the house, Kit looked up at Nico, and he saw that she had absolutely no color to her skin. It was almost gray, and she was literally shaking. Kneeling in front of her, Nico said, "Talk t' me, love."

"Rachel's in trouble," Kit's voice quivered, as she trembled in her seat.

"She's on a mission," Nico encouraged. "She's in God's hands."

"She needs help!" Kit insisted. "God woke me. They need help. We have to get to Alice."

"You are *not* going to Alice Springs!" Nico snapped. "You'll be lucky to get back upstairs."

"Nico," Kit pleaded. "I need…" Kit wavered in her seat, but Nico grabbed her shoulders, steadying her. Turning to Willow, he ordered, "Call an ambulance. Get her to a hospital! Caleb, we have to get to Alice Springs."

"You go. Take Pete with you. I'll go with Mum to the hospital and keep you updated," Caleb said, as Willow ran into the kitchen to call for an ambulance.

"They'll be here in fifteen minutes. They're on their way back from another call," Willow explained, coming back into the living room a minute later.

"Suffocating," Kit said, gasping for air, as the world continued to spin around her. "Feels like chains are weighing my chest down, tightening around me. The chains are tightening." Kit cried. "The teams are in trouble, Nico!"

Nico wrapped his arms around Kit. "I can't go to Alice. Caleb, you grab Pete and go to Alice. I'm going to the hospital with Kit."

"Yes, sir," Caleb said, and ran out of the house. It wasn't until the door closed behind him, that he let a few tears escape out of his eyes. As he raced to the west field on his horse for Pete, the tears streamed down his cheeks. He felt as if the world around him was collapsing. "Pete!" he shouted, as his horse jumped the fence, heading straight for Pete, who was on his horse.

"What's going on?" Pete asked, furrowing his brow. "I heard the call. Do I need to go to the house?"

"No. We need to go to Alice."

"Springs? Why? Are the teams out there in trouble? Do we need more people?"

"Mum said the teams need us," Caleb explained, as the sirens from the ambulance could barely be heard in the distance.

"Caleb?" Pete asked, not moving a muscle. "Is your mum okay? Is that ambulance for Kit?"

"Yes, it's for her. She's in bad –" was all Caleb got out, before Pete took off for the main house on his horse at a full sprint.

Pete's horse was moving so fast, that his horse sailed through the air, scaling the fence without missing a beat. All anyone saw from a distance was a streak of dirt getting kicked up from Pete's horse, closely followed by Caleb on his horse.

As they made it to the house, a cloudburst cut loose, dropping one, then two, then moved to sheets of rain within seconds. "Seriously?" Caleb yelled, looking at the sky.

Getting down from their horses, now soaked, Caleb and Pete ran into the house. They found Kit laying down on the couch, unconscious, gray, and looking more frail than normal.

"She's in a bad way," Nico said, tears slowly going down his cheeks. Shaking his head, he admitted, "I don't know how much more she can take."

Pete didn't care that they were men, he knelt down and hugged his friend. "We'll get through this, mate…all of this. We've been through worse."

"I don't think so," Nico said, hugging his friend tighter. He didn't want to let go. That was what he wanted to do to Kit, but he was afraid he would break her.

"They're comin'," Caleb said, hearing the sirens getting closer.

Just then, the kitchen phone rang. Everyone looked at each other, scared of what the call would bring. Willow shook her head before she darted from the living room to answer it. When she returned after only a moment, both men stood, moved next to Caleb, and braced for impact.

"That was the Haven. Delaney called them. Joe's been on the phone with Alice Springs. They were too close to the mountain when it blew. From what Delaney said, that Jacob said, his explosives set off a chain reaction deep within the mountain that no one could predict. When it did, most of the mountain blew, sending debris for miles."

"The team?" Nico asked, rubbing the back of his neck. He wasn't sure how much more he could take. "Rachel? Josh?"

"Well, from what Jacob could tell her –"

"Jacob? Why not Rachel?" Nico asked, sensing there was something she wasn't telling him.

"She passed out."

"Um, okay," Caleb said, going over to Willow. Resting his hands on her arms, he bent down so she was looking at him. "Tell me *exactly* what she said."

Her eyes were brimming with tears as she explained, "Rachel's unconscious. Josh, Charlie, and Jacob have cuts and scrapes. Jon has a punctured lung, and broken ribs…at the least. Rachel got him stable before she passed out. Isaac has at least a broken leg." She stopped, and looked up at Caleb, tears slowly crawling down her cheeks.

"What about Jesse?" Nico asked, understanding what she was trying not to say.

"They lost Parri before the mountain blew. The demons got him," she quickly said.

"What about Jesse?" Nico pressed.

"He won't wake up," she admitted. "They can't get him to wake up. They can't get Rachel to wake up now either. They're going to life-flight the injured to Alice."

"Willow?" Caleb said slowly. When she shifted her eyes back to him, he asked, "Is there anything you want to tell me?"

She nodded before she shook her head. Bottom lip trembling, she confessed, "They don't know when or *if* they can get Jesse *or* Rachel to wake up. Jesse has been unconscious since the explosion. Once Rachel passed out, they couldn't get her to wake up. Delaney said that Jacob said there was blood coming from her head."

*   *   *

"Do not fear," the archangel, Raphael, said suddenly appearing in the backseat beside Angel.

Angel screamed, while Spencer struggled to keep the car under control enough to get it to the side of the road, jerking his iPod out of the radio system as the vehicle came to a screeching halt. Meanwhile, Sasha just about jumped out of his seat.

"Holy Christmas!" Angel shouted, as she grabbed her chest. "Who are you?"

"I am Raphael, your brother's guardian angel," he simply responded. "I am also one of the Lord God Almighty's archangels."

"And *what* are you doing here?" Sasha asked, recovering from the shock, while Spencer still tried to get a grip on what he was seeing in the backseat.

"Michael sent me."

"Why?" Sasha asked. "Are we in trouble?"

"The other team needed him, and he sent me to keep you all safe," he explained, as Angel realized he was sitting there in jeans and a tan T-shirt shirt, holding a long jacket on his lap.

"Where are your wings?" Angel asked, recovering from the shock as she tried to look behind him.

Raphael fanned them out behind him, covering the back window. When he did, Spencer's eyes widened so big, Angel was surprised they didn't pop out! "Ummm…" was all Spencer could get out, heart racing.

"Okay, so you are coming with us?" Angel asked, confused.

"Yes."

"You stated that the other team needed Michael?" Sasha asked.

"Yes."

"Um, why?" Spencer asked, and then gulped when the archangel looked at him.

"They are in need of him and the other angels to protect them until help arrives."

Narrowing her eyes, Angel challenged, "If you are who you say you are, then who is Jesus?"

Raphael smiled, "He is the Lord and Savior Jesus Christ, Son of the Living God."

Nodding in approval, Angel then asked, "What happened to the other team?"

"You are to concentrate on the mission before you," Raphael explained. "Michael will attend to the rest of the team."

Angel narrowed her eyes at him again, and demanded, "What happened to the other team?"

Raphael smiled again, amused. "He said you would be a challenge."

"Who?" Angel asked.

"Michael." Turning back to Spencer, he instructed, "Please continue our drive."

"No," Angel asserted. When Spencer looked from her, to the archangel, and back again, Angel asked once more, a lot sterner in her tone, "*What happened to the other team?* They are part of us. We are *all* a unit. What happens to one, happens to all. Tell us, or we are going nowhere."

"You will go where the Lord tells you to go," the archangel said, matching her tone. "Do *not* forget Whom you serve."

"I know Whom I serve," Angel said. "I also know that two of my brothers were on that mission."

"They are in the Lord's hands," Raphael responded.

"Tell me!" Angel insisted.

"I am afraid I will have to agree with Angel on this. We do not move unless we get information on the status of our teammates," Sasha said. "That is a must. They are our family. Yes, we know they are in the Lord's hands, but if there is something we should know, I do believe you should tell us."

Sighing, Raphael glanced at each one in the car before he looked toward Heaven, and listened for a moment. Closing his eyes, his face glowed for a few minutes, before going back to the regular color. Nodding, he opened his eyes. "The Lord instructed me give you this message. He stated that there were injuries sustained during their mission. While their overall mission was a success, multiple team members are being taken to the hospital."

"Who?" Angel demanded.

Raphael shrugged. "Well, all of them."

"What shape are they in?"

"That is all the Lord has instructed me to reveal. He stated that yours is to trust in Him, and Him only, and to follow through with *your* mission. Both missions are to be carried out and completed. They are both critical. The other team completed theirs. It is up to you three to complete yours as well. You must do this to restore the balance of power."

"He doesn't *need* us to do anything," Spencer challenged. "He is God. He *wants* us to do this."

"You are correct. Very good, Spencer," Raphael nodded in approval, as he tucked his wings against his back, and slipped his jacket on to cover them.

Spencer slowly pulled back onto the road, while Sasha looked on the map to find out where they were located, and what direction they needed to head. Angel, still in the backseat, was burrowing a hole in the archangel with her eyes.

Turning toward her, Raphael said, "I thought your brother was a challenge." Then he chuckled, as he added, "I do not envy *your* guardian angel. Ariel has an immense amount of patience and endurance, but even with her helpers, she has her work cut out for her with you."

Sasha and Spencer couldn't stifle their laughter on that one, but did their best for Angel's benefit.

"You come in here and tell us our team is in trouble, but to keep driving as if nothing is wrong. Michael, the one we're used to taking orders from, is so busy that he couldn't come himself, but we're just supposed to move on," she said sarcastically. "*Why* would we do this?"

"Because the Lord commands it. You follow the Lord, not Michael."

"Can we at least call the Haven to find out the status of the others?"

"No."

Angel grabbed the satellite phone from her backpack. When she tried to dial it, the phone remained silent. Wide-eyed, she picked up her cell phone, and noticed that there was no service. "Sasha? Spencer? Do either of your phones have cell service?" she asked them, angry and desperate at the same time. If the angel was blocking them from contacting anyone, it had to be bad.

"Nope," Sasha said, looking at his phone. Then he picked up Spencer's, and said, "His does not either. I am using the paper map to navigate us. We lost GPS several cities back."

"Are *you* responsible for this?" she accused Raphael.

"You are not in control," Raphael said with a peaceful smile.

"Is someone dead?" Angel demanded, heart rate racing.

"You will find out the status of your teammates once you complete your mission…not before."

"Oooooo! You are more infuriating than Michael!" she growled, balling her fists.

"And *you* are not in control," Raphael said again.

"I'm enjoying this." Spencer grinned, periodically looking at them in the rearview mirror.

"Keep your eyes on the road," Angel snapped.

"Reverting back already?" Raphael challenged.

"How do you know about my past?" Angel asked, as her face flushed in embarrassment.

Laughing, Raphael took a moment to respond. With a grin, he reminded her, "There are two things you need to recall. Number one, may I remind you that I am your brother's guardian angel? I have been with Jonathon since the time of his birth. Your past is intertwined in his. I have watched you grow up as well. Number two, may I *also* remind you that I am an archangel of the Lord God Almighty? Michael is an archangel with me. While we do not know everything, there is much we *do* know and are aware of over time. I have seen much since my creation."

"Now, that last statement is a bit mind-blowing," Spencer admitted. "I get the rest, but I can't imagine all you have seen since your creation." He sighed, shaking his head. "That's a *lot*!"

"Yes, it is." Raphael smiled. He leaned forward in his seat, and asked, "Would you like to know how *you* are connected to the A.N.G.E.L.s, Spencer?"

Spencer offered. "I would think it's through Angel."

"While that is true, there is an earlier connection you may not be aware of," Raphael explained. "You see, when Kit was younger, she went by another name...Katie. Katie went to college in Cleveland, Ohio with your mother, Stacey. At the time, Stacey was known by Stacey Spencer, hence your first name."

"Really?" Spencer asked, stunned. "Kit knew my mother?"

"Stacey counseled her after the loss of young Katie's roommate. She was also at your mother and father's wedding. She was in the bridal party," Raphael pointed out. "Now, having told you this, it is not information you can share with your mother. It may put Kit's life in danger. The reason I shared this with you, is to point out that you may not always know the connections, but the Lord does know them. There are plans in place that have been in place for centuries. They have been around long before you were even a thought in your mother's mind. Nothing takes the Lord by surprise."

"Are my brothers alive?" Angel asked, crossing her arms. "Can you at least tell me that?"

"Yours is to find out once your mission is complete. Until then, you are to trust the Lord with them," Raphael stated.

"Seriously?" Angel asked, stunned.

"This is a lesson in control...and *Who* is in control." Raphael said. Then he added, "Just a hint, it is not you."

Rolling her eyes, Angel sighed as she said, "My brother must love you."

Raphael grinned. "He does. He says he is glad I have a sense of humor. Your human sayings amuse me."

"Well, I am not amused at the moment," Angel said, rolling her eyes again.

"Angelina, have you not learned by now just Who is in control?"

"Yes."

"Then, why do you continue to challenge Him? Trust the Lord with the lives of your teammates. More hangs in the balance of this world than the lives of the A.N.G.E.L.s."

"Meaning?"

"Meaning that you *need* to find those scrolls."

"Can you give us a hint?" Angel asked. "Will we find them in Black Rock?"

"You may," Raphael said, and then shrugged. "Then again, you may not."

"How long do you want to continue to be with us? Help us find the scrolls quicker, so you can move on," Angel said. "If they're not there, then where are they?"

"We are to follow the path before us. We will find them in the time the Lord deems appropriate."

"Oh my word!" Angel threw her hands up in exasperation. "Sasha, can we switch seats?"

"Nope," Sasha said with a smile. "There are some lessons that only the Lord, it seems, can get through to you."

"What?" Angel narrowed her eyes at him. "You're supposed to be on my side!"

"You are still challenging the Lord. Spencer and I are fine with continuing on with the mission without knowledge of the status of the team. You are the one pushing. Knowing an archangel is in the vehicle with us, actually brings me comfort. I do not understand why you are fighting with him."

"I'm not!"

"Yes. You are," Raphael agreed with Sasha. Then he added with a smile, "And, I can do this for weeks, months…even years if you wish. I promise you that *you* will give out before I do."

Spencer and Sasha burst out in laughter. They couldn't help it with that statement.

Angel crossed her arms in a huff, and sat back in her seat.

"Continuing to stew is still fighting. I do not bend to this behavior any more than Michael," Raphael pointed out.

Glaring at him, Angel snapped, "Fine. I trust you."

"I do not believe that any longer than it took for you to say it," Raphael shot back.

"Ooo! I *really* like him!" Spencer snickered from the driver's seat.

"That was *so* very not helpful!" Angel snapped at Spencer.

"Angel," Spencer said, matter-of-factly, "There is no version of this where you come out on top. Just accept that he's with us, and that the Lord is with us in this. You are *not* in control. Let the Lord take care of the other team."

"Again, *so* not helpful," Angel grumbled.

"Actually, *very* helpful," Sasha countered. "Philippians 2:14 reminds us to *'Do all things without grumbling or complaining.'* It sounds like *you* are not listening."

"Actually, wanting to be in control is more of a fear thing," Spencer explained.

Angel sighed, rolling her eyes, "You're a lab tech, not a psych major."

"Can I give you a little unsolicited advice?" Spencer asked.

"You give another kind?"

"I'm here voluntarily. Don't take your anger out on me. Listen," Spencer said, "if you remember, my mother *is* a psych major, and actually has her Doctorate in Psychology. When I was younger, and some things started happening, I kept trying to take control of anything I could. You see, when one is afraid, they have a tendency to grab control of everything. They feel if they can control something, it will be easier to face everything. Having said that, you're supposed to face everything with the Lord *by your side*, and *then* rise. The verse she pounded into my head to combat the control thing was Revelation 1:17, which says, *'Then He placed His right hand on me, and said: Do not be afraid. I am the First and the Last.'*

In other words, He started it and He *will* finish it. *He* is the One in control."

"Well said, young Spencer," Raphael said proudly. "Your mother has taught you well."

Spencer grinned. "My father has too."

"Okay. Just give me some time to cool down," Angel mumbled, as she sunk into the seat.

After a few moments of silence, Spencer asked Sasha, "How long do we have?"

"Twenty more hours."

"Great!" Angel clicked her tongue. "So, over twenty hours of silence."

"Not silence," Spencer reached down and reconnected his iPod, and turned it back on. "Twenty hours of praise and worship."

Raphael grinned. "*Now* you are speaking my language."

Chapter 12
Heavy Chains

"What's her status?" Anna, Willow's birth mom, asked, sitting down next to Nico in the waiting room of the hospital.

With his head dropped into his hands, he just shook it. "Don't know. No one will tell me anything. They just keep telling me that a doctor will be with me as soon as he knows anything."

"Was she awake when you got here?"

"No. She went unconscious at the house. No matter what they tried, she wouldn't wake the entire ambulance ride."

Anna let out a frustrated sigh. "Okay. What about Rachel and the rest of the crew? Have you heard anything from them?"

"No. Caleb and Pete are on their way to Alice. It'll take a good day to get there. Until then, if they call Willow, she's supposed to call me."

"What about the Haven? Have they gotten ahold of the other team yet?"

"No. The other team seems to be on radio silence. Not sure why they suddenly went silent either. That makes me nervous, especially knowing Angel's in charge of that group. Honestly, this whole thing has turned into a complete disaster." Looking over at her without lifting his head, he admitted, "While I know the Lord is the One in control, I feel like I'm carrying around heavy chains that I can't get rid of." Sitting up, he further explained, "It's like with each scenario, someone handed me a big, hundred-pound chain to carry, and I can't put it down anywhere. I just have to sit here with them on my lap, unable to do anything about them."

"Pastor will be here as soon as he can. He will help you with some of that. He's at the station, calming Willow down. He said he would come as soon as he got her under control. She's a bigger mess than you."

"I know. She and Kit are close."

"Look, I know she thinks of Kit as a mum. I also know, being her birth mum, that she felt abandoned for a while, until my parents explained the entire situation to her. There is nothing I can do to thank you for saving her all those years ago, except to sit with you today until we know Kit will be okay," Anna said, resting her hand on Nico's shoulder. "You both are close to my heart. You are like family. Technically, you *are* family through marriage."

"Agreed," Nico said, before he dropped his head back in his hands, shaking it again. After a few minutes of silence, he turned to Anna, and admitted, "I don't know what I will do with myself if something happens to her."

"You're going to continue living, knowing she is with the Lord, waiting for you to join her. And, until you do, you have your children, along with your grandchildren, to look after and guide."

"Rachel." He shook his head at the reminder. "They said there was a lot of blood pouring from her head wound."

"That's actually a good thing. It's my understanding that it is better out, than forming a blood clot in her head."

"I know."

"Nico, do you believe or depend on God? There *is* a difference."

"I know. And, both. My heart is God's, but it's Kit's as well. She was the gift given to me by God Himself."

"And, He has given you many wonderful and happy years together."

"Doesn't mean I'm done yet."

"What if she is?"

The question heavily hung in the air for several moments before Nico responded, "What do you mean?"

"She's told me that her body continuously feels like it's on fire. She battles throwing up more than she's taking in every day. She's lost an immense amount of weight that she didn't have to lose. You could probably snap her bones like a twig with the lack of nutrients in her system."

"Are you telling me that I can't be selfish in this?"

"I'm trying."

"I-I can't," Nico admitted, shaking his head again, as the tears finally released, crawling down his cheeks. "I'm sorry. I can't. I need her to fight."

"She *has* been fighting. Have you not seen that?"

"I have! I also know she has more fight in her."

"She's fighting for *you*. She's fighting for *all* of you. You guys are always telling her to fight. She doesn't want to disappoint you. Maybe once, just once, one of you can tell her it's okay if she wants to move on," Anna said, tears pouring down her cheeks. "I love her with all my heart, but if I experienced even a remote amount of the pain she does on a daily basis, with no end in sight, I don't know that I could do it!"

Nico dropped his head on his folded arms, as he slid off the chair, sobbing. "I can't." He shook his head, as his heart shattered into pieces. "I just can't. I love her too much."

"Then, love her enough to let her go be with the Lord if she chooses to. Give her the choice."

"I can't do it."

"You have to at least consider it…for her sake. She's fighting with everything in her."

"What if she doesn't have enough in her?"

"Then she will be watching from Heaven as she prepares a place for you with Jesus."

Nico just shook his head, dropping it back onto his knees. Silently sobbing for several minutes, he was lost in thoughts of Kit until he was interrupted.

"Mr. Sullivan?" a doctor said, standing in the doorway.

Nico sniffed and wiped his nose as he stood. Wiping his hands on his jeans, he then went over and shook the doctor's hand with his other hand. "I'm Nico Sullivan."

"I'm Dr. McDougal. Your wife is in the critical care unit. There are limited visiting hours in that ward. I'm sorry." As soon as he said that, Nico's stomach lurched. "I can't promise that she will pull through. I wish I could, but she's in really rough condition. I've spoken with your doctor, and he agrees that before she can have any more treatment, she needs to get stronger."

"But, won't she get weaker before she gets stronger? How is she supposed to beat this if you discontinue the treatment?" Nico asked, heart racing to the point that his heartbeat was almost overpowering his ability to hear anything else around him.

"Mr. Sullivan, while I understand your concern, she needs to get stronger before she can have any more treatments. It may only take a few days to get her strong enough. Your doctor will phone you later, but he is confident with some time here in the hospital, that we can get her to finishing her treatment program. She may only need to take a week or so off."

Rubbing the back of his neck, Nico's world started to blur around him. As he paced in front of Dr. McDougal, he heard Deuteronomy 31:8 go through his mind, *"The Lord Himself goes before you; He will never leave you nor forsake you. Do not be afraid; do not be discouraged."*

Nodding in understanding of what the Spirit was trying to tell him, Nico asked the doctor, "So, you're saying it's up to her?"

"It's ultimately *been* up to her. According to the doc on your case, he said that she's a fighter. Give her a few days of rest, so she can fight once again."

Nico anxiously crossed his arms, and then rubbed his chin. "You think she'll make it?"

"I *think* I've already answered that."

"I see. I see." Nico nodded. Stopping his pace, he looked up and asked, "When can I see her?"

Glancing at his watch, Dr. McDougal explained, "Visiting time is in a few hours, and you can only see her for about a half-hour. In that ward, we try to keep the visiting down to a minimum."

"Can we get her out of that ward?"

The doctor shook his head, confused. "Why would I do that?"

"What your file on her doesn't say, is that we've been inseparable since we got married almost thirty years ago. Because of that, when we *are* separated, it doesn't end well for either of us."

Crossing his arms, Dr. McDougal asked, "What are you telling me?"

"That if I am not in the room with her, she won't get any better." Anxiety ramped back up, Nico prayed in his head for strength. When he did, the Spirit whispered John 14:27 to him, *"Peace I leave with you; my peace I give you. I do not give to you as the world gives. Do not let your hearts be troubled, and do not be afraid."* Nodding again, a thought struck Nico. "I'll tell ya what…what if I make you a deal?"

"I'm listening."

"If, when she wakes, she asks to have me in the room with her, you will either make that happen, or transfer her to make it happen. If she doesn't, then we'll follow your plan of action, and I'll abide by hospital policies…no fighting."

Rubbing his chin in thought, Dr. McDougal mulled over the deal in his head.

With the doctor taking too long to answer, Nico explained, "We're inseparable, because we're soul mates. If she doesn't ask for it, I'll abide by your rules. If, when she wakes, you explain the visiting hour schedule, and she objects, then you will either get her transferred or figure out a way to make it so I can be in there for her. Deal?" Nico asked, sticking his hand out for the doctor to shake.

After hesitating a few more moments, Dr. McDougal finally shook his hand. "While I'm not totally comfortable with this, I understand that the will and the heart are stronger than any medicine I could give her. If you are as close as you claim, it would not be in her best interest to keep you separated. Now," the doctor said, not letting Nico's hand go, "if I *do* arrange to have you in the room with her, you must promise me that she will get rest."

"Done!" Nico grinned, as they shook on the second part of the deal.

Crossing his arms over the file, Dr. McDougal said, "You have me intrigued. While I have not seen it often in my years of practice, I *have* seen it. I'm curious if this is another one of those cases."

"Trust me. It is. Thank you, sir," Nico said, shaking his hand once more before going back over to Anna.

"That was brilliant!" Anna encouraged. "Well done! Kit would be proud! I thought you were done for when he said you could only see her a half-hour every few hours."

"My only prayer is that she wakes soon."

"I have a feeling it'll be a while. Until then, we'll pray," she said, putting her hand out.

They joined hands in prayer for the A.N.G.E.L.s on their way to the hospital, those still on their mission, and for Kit to pull through…all per the Lord's will.

*   *   *

"What do you mean you can't get ahold of your team?" Mark demanded of Akio, Raphe, Toby, and Zahra. "Your job is to stay in contact with them."

"Sir," Toby started, taking a brave step forward, "what you don't understand is that it isn't on our end. We can't even track their cell phones. It's like they've been suddenly wiped off the grid."

"We cannot even highjack their car," Zahra explained.

"I think that's *lo*jack," Jerrod corrected her, as he stood beside Mark.

"Right!" Zahra agreed. "That's it. We cannot find it anywhere."

"We have even attempted to track their route using satellites, to see if there are any accidents along the way," Akio pointed out. "There is not one."

"To be honest, we have even had Cori and Kai try to find them," Raphe mentioned. "They're nowhere."

"Really?" Mark asked, stunned. Turning toward Cori and Kai, who were on the other side of the cyber cave, he asked, "The wonder twins can't find them either?"

"No, sir," Kai said, shaking his head, not taking his eyes off his computer. "Their vehicle is nowhere on the road at all. We were able to track it up until about an hour ago, and then *poof*...it's gone!"

"Has anyone attempted to call out for help from our friend?" Mark asked, crossing his arms.

"Yeah," Cori said. "He's not answering either. Pretty sure his hands are full with our team."

Stroking his chin, Mark nodded. "That's a strong possibility."

"Sirs, if we hear *anything,* we will alert you immediately," Zahra assured them. "In the meantime, please go back upstairs and rejoin the others in prayer. It is of the utmost importance that prayer continues."

"I agree. Thank you, Zahra," Mark said.

"I'm staying down here with this crew," Jerrod said, taking a seat. "I'll still be in prayer, but I'm going to hang out down here."

"Sounds good," Mark said, and disappeared up the staircase, closing the door behind him.

As soon as the door closed, the team let out the breath of air they were all holding. With having to explain to Mark that there was no way to find Angel, after last time, they were honestly terrified. They were relieved when he didn't fight them on leaving the cyber cave.

"For everyone's sake, we need to find Angel, Sasha, and Spencer," Toby mentioned, as he headed back to his computer.

"More for theirs, than for ours," Akio commented. "We do not know their condition."

"After the other team almost got blown up, it makes me nervous that we cannot contact them," Zahra said. "What makes me even *more* nervous, is for the other team, with Rachel and Jesse not waking up. Hey, Cori or Kai, would one of you mind getting ahold of Delaney or Joe to check on the status?"

"No." Hanif shook his head. "We are under strict instructions by Joe to not call them. They will call us."

"Well, that stinks!" Raphe said, shaking his head.

"They do not want us...what is the word?" Hiro asked Hanif.

"Nagging," Hanif said. "They don't want us nagging them for information.

"Right! That is the word. We are to wait and pray."

"Doesn't mean we won't stop looking for the others, though," Cori said over her shoulder.

"That goes without saying," Toby agreed. "I just pray we get some sort of an answer soon. While we're not super close yet, they are still our team. We are to watch over them as the Safe Haven. Not hearing from either of them makes me nervous."

"Just focus on what you are good at," Jerrod said. "As the Haven, we are only support. As support, there are many facets to your position. It isn't just computers. It's prayer. It's keeping an eye out, so when they call, we have answers. As support, your jobs are to anticipate what they will need. You can't do that if you're stressed."

While they sat there processing what Jerrod said, each one heard Matthew 6:34 in their minds being whispered by the Spirit. As they did, Jerrod quoted it aloud, *"Therefore do not worry about tomorrow, for tomorrow will worry about itself. Each day has enough trouble of its own."*

"There is a game Cori and Kai taught us about verses," Akio said. "What was it?"

"Are you talking about the Challenger/Aggressor game?" Jerrod asked.

"Sort of…well, a portion of it anyway," Cori said. "Down here, we do verses on certain subjects, and see how many we can think of that we have memorized regarding that subject. Let's do verses on peace. I think we need to calm our anxiety with peace."

"Agreed," Zahra said. "I will start. John 16:33 says, *'I have told you these things, so that in Me you may have peace. In this world you will have trouble. But take heart! I have overcome the world.'"*

"Ooo! Good one!" Akio said with a smile. "I am going to keep going with John. John 14:27 says, *'Peace I leave with you; my peace I give you. I do not give to you as the world gives. Do not let your hearts be troubled, and do not be afraid.'"*

"First Corinthians 14:33 says, *"God is not a God of confusion but of peace,'"* Hiro said, and then grinned that she got it correct when the group gave her thumbs up.

"What about Second Thessalonians 3:16?" Cori offered. "It says, *'Now may the Lord of peace Himself give you peace always in every way.'"*

"Don't forget Numbers 6:24 through 26," Kai said, "It says, *'The Lord bless thee, and keep thee: The Lord make His face shine upon thee, and be gracious unto thee: The Lord lift up His countenance upon thee, and give thee peace.'"*

"I got one for ya," Jerrod said, sitting back in his seat. "On deployment, when there were downtimes, I would memorize scripture. Ephesians 2:14 through 18 brought me comfort many times. It reads, *'For He Himself is our peace, who has made both one, and hath broken down the middle wall of partition between us. Having abolished in His flesh the enmity, even the law of commandments contained in ordinances; for to make in Himself of twain one new man, so making peace; and that He might reconcile both unto God in one body by the cross, having slain the enmity thereby; And came and preached peace to you which were afar off, and to them that were nigh. For through Him we both have access by one Spirit to the Father.'"*

"Okay, I'm impressed!" Kai said, and half-bowed.

"That was brilliant…and comforting," Cori applauded.

"*That* is the Word of God," Jerrod said. "It can be comforting when you are in fear. Whatever you need, you've found out through the game, it is in the Bible."

"I have another one," Hanif said, still searching on his computer for the team. "There's also Philippians 4:6 and 7. It says, *'Be careful for nothing; but in everything by prayer and supplication with thanksgiving let your requests be made known unto God. And the peace of God, which passeth all understanding, shall keep your hearts and your minds through Christ Jesus.'* He is everywhere…even everywhere we cannot be or see. He is the true Overwatch. He is the One in control."

"Amen!" Raphe agreed. "One more I would add to the list is Colossians 3:15, which says, *'Let the peace of Christ rule in your hearts, since as members of one body you were called to peace. And be thankful.'* I, for one, am thankful for not only the family of Christ, but the family we have found in the A.N.G.E.L.s. Yes, we are still getting to know each other, but our bond is in the Lord. He will solidify us together in Him with time."

"Double Amen!" Kai cheered. "Okay, last one, and then the praise and worship music comes back on. Agreed?"

"Agreed," they all said in unison.

With his hand on the button to start the music, Kai quoted, "Proverbs 16:7, which says, *'When a man's ways please the Lord, He makes even his enemies to be at peace with him.'* Guys, God's got this. We only need to trust Him, yeah?"

"Yes. Take it to Him, and leave it there," Akio said, excited. "He will guide our thoughts, feelings, and fingers. He is stronger than any of this."

"Amen!" Cori agreed. Just then, her computer beeped. "Hiro, go grab Mark. Delaney's calling."

*　　*　　*

"I wish I could tell ya more," Delaney said over the satellite phone on speaker, as she Joe, Josh, Charlie, and Jacob surrounded her in the waiting room, so everyone could hear.

"Well, that the status hasn't changed is at least *something*," Mark said. "I wish it was more, but any news is information at this point. Um, we *do* need to let you guys know something," Mark said, and then took a deep breath, knowing the conversation would not be an easy one.

"What's going on, Mark?" Josh asked.

"We haven't been able to find Angel, Sasha, or Spencer."

Josh furrowed his brow. "What do ya mean you can't find them?"

"We lost them," Jerrod stepped in. "They disappeared about an hour or so ago. No one can find them at all. Not even Cori or Kai."

"Neither Cori, nor Kai can find them?" Jacob asked, astonished. "How can *they* not find someone, unless…" Jacob's voice faded, as his face went pale.

"Don't go there, mate," Josh said, resting his hand on Jacob's shoulder. "We don't know what's going on."

"One does not need to know what is going on to know that the Lord God Almighty is in control," said Michael, the archangel, as he walked into the waiting room in tan pants and a white T-shirt, with a long jacket on.

"Do *you* know what is going on?" Charlie asked him.

"Who is that?" Mark asked.

"Michael, the archangel," Cori said. "I recognize his voice."

"Very good, young Cori," Michael said, pleased.

Cori beamed. "Thank you, sir."

"Back to my question. Do you know what is going on?" Charlie asked, again.

"Do not be afraid for Angel, Sasha, or Spencer. The archangel, Raphael, is with them," Michael explained. "He will keep them protected."

"Is that why we can't even find their vehicle?" Kai asked.

"Yes. You will be able to locate them once they complete their mission. Until then, no one on this planet will be able to find them."

"I see," Mark said, mulling over the archangel's words. "So, they're safe?"

"Yes."

"Thank you. Now what about Jon, Jesse, Isaac, and Rachel?" Mark asked.

"Isaac only sustained a broken leg," Michael explained. "Jon will have a bit tougher road ahead of him. He, in time, will recover."

"Jesse?" Mark pressed. "Rachel?"

"That has yet to be determined."

"What?" Mark's face flushed red, he sat back in a chair, stunned. "What does *that* mean?"

"That means I do not know the outcome of their situations as of yet. Mark, you must continue to trust as you have done faithfully through the years."

"Yes, sir," Mark said, and then dropped his head in his hands. Then he asked, "Can I at least come out there?"

"No. You must continue to trust from where you are. Your fellow A.N.G.E.L.s around you will continue to encourage and lift each other up. Prayer is key. The control is not yours. This, you *must* learn."

"The control has never *been* mine," Mark said, running his hands through his hair. Standing, he started pacing. "Thank you for calling. Please keep us posted."

"There is another situation, of which you are not aware," Michael said.

Mark threw his hands in the air. "What now?"

"Kit is in the hospital. She is unconscious."

Cori gasped, while Mark sat down in his chair again.

Jerrod groaned, but his medical training kicked in, and he asked, "What's her status?"

"She is in the critical care unit right now."

"What's her prognosis?" Jerrod pressed.

"That has yet to be determined."

Mark took in a deep breath of air. Dropping his head on his hands, he slowly let the air out.

When he didn't say anything, Kai got on the microphone, "Thank you. Please keep us posted on that situation as well. We won't bug you, but please don't leave us in the dark either."

"Agreed," Michael conceded. Then he said, "Mark, Jerrod, trust them to His hands."

"Always have," Mark mumbled. Then, as an added thought, he mentioned, "Please take care of everyone, and let Nico know we are thinking and praying for him as well."

"Will do," Joe said.

"Do you guys need me to come out there?" Jerrod asked.

"No," Michael said. "You are needed to keep everyone focused at the Haven. We have things, as you say, under control here."

"Fair enough," Jerrod said. "Know you are all in our thoughts and prayers."

"Thank you," Jacob said, grateful.

Just then, Jon's doctor came into the waiting room.

"Gotta go," Joe said. "We'll keep you updated."

"Thank you," Mark said, and Cori cut the line.

"Are you all here for Jonathon English?" the doctor asked, surprised. Not only were the A.N.G.E.L.s in the waiting room, but so were the clansmen. They were not leaving until they knew everyone was okay.

"Yes, sir," Charlie stepped forward. "What news have you?"

Crossing his arms over the file, he explained, "Mr. English is heavily sedated, but resting comfortably. What that young lady did out there saved his life. Her quick thinking gave us the time we needed to get in there and repair the damage as much as possible. He will need to remain here for several days. With his cracked ribs, and the sensitivity of his lungs, I don't want to risk him puncturing the lung again."

"I understand. And, Isaac Braham?" Charlie asked.

"He has a broken leg. They are casting it right now. He should be released within a few hours."

"And, Rachel Sullivan?" Joe pressed.

"She is currently down in surgery. A CAT scan revealed that she has a subdural hematoma."

"What *exactly* does that mean?" Delaney asked, not sure if she wanted to know the answer.

"Basically, her surgeon is going in and drill a small hole in her skull." When he said that, Delaney gasped. The doctor continued, "This burr hole, as we call it, will then have tubes placed in it to drain the hematoma."

"I'm not a doctor, but that doesn't sound good," Jacob said, slowly rubbing his forearms.

"Please know that eighty to ninety percent of patients who have this surgery maintain significant brain function. Having said that, we will need to keep her in here for a while to watch out for any seizures, permanent muscle weakness or numbness, or brain herniation."

"English, please?" Joe asked, getting frustrated.

"We need to look out for the side effects listed, as well as a potential for inflammation on her brain."

"Won't that potentially cause a coma?" Charlie asked.

"Potentially. That is why we are keeping her in here."

"What are the *potential* long-term effects?" Delaney asked, getting frustrated at having to pull the information.

"There are multiple possible long-term effects. We will have to wait until she wakes to discuss this, *and* any long-term plan of action."

"What about Jesse English?" Jacob asked, *really* not wanting to know the answer. If Rachel was this bad, and she was awake at one point, knowing Jesse never woke, terrified him.

"I'm sorry, but he is in the critical care unit. He is currently in a coma. The injuries he sustained were extensive. We have yet to fully ascertain all of his injuries at this time, and do not wish to hazard a guess."

"Is this, like, one of those medically induced comas?" Delaney asked.

"No, ma'am. We're hoping he wakes soon on his own."

"Oh," Delaney said, beside herself.

"Does Jon know about his brother?" Charlie asked.

"Not yet. We thought he should recover a bit before we talk to him about his brother. He has asked multiple times, but we sedated him so he won't know until he wakes, *and* we're confident he can handle the news."

"We'll contact the family," Joe said. "That's actually who we were just talking to when you walked up."

Reaching in his pocket, the doctor pulled out his card and handed it to Joe. "I have already been in contact with them multiple times. However, if you have any questions, please do not to hesitate to contact me."

"Will do. Thank you, sir."

"Um, when can we see everyone?" Jacob asked, arms crossed, tears brimming his eyes. He kept looking up at the ceiling, refusing to let them fall.

"You can go see Isaac now. Wait. Let me correct myself. Only two at a time can go see Isaac right now. The rest will have to wait out here. We cannot have this many people traipsing through the emergency room."

"You guys go. I'm going to call Mark," Joe said, waving the phone.

"I'm staying with Joe," Delaney said.

"I'm going," Jacob insisted.

"Me too," Charlie said.

"Why don't the two of you go? Delaney and I can call the Haven, Nico, and keep an eye on the crew over there," Joe said, nodding toward the clansmen, who were sitting around the waiting room. Only Woorin was quiet, as he sat in the corner, tears slowly crawling down his cheeks. Everyone else was talking amongst themselves but clearly looked in mourning. "I think someone may need to talk."

"I agree." Charlie nodded. "If you need me. Call."

"Yes, sir," Joe said, and watched as Jacob and Charlie went through the doors with the doctor toward Isaac's room. Turning back to the clansmen, Joe said, "We need to contact a few people. Please stay right here. We'll be right back."

When they just nodded, Delaney tugged on Joe's arm to leave. Once outside, Delaney explained, "They're a bigger mess than I thought they would be."

"They lost *another* member. Up until two and a half, three weeks ago, they were tucked safely in the Outback. The worse they had to worry about was the flora and fauna. They're now painfully aware of just what is out there, and what the other side actually looks like. It doesn't surprise me that they are thrown for a loop. I'm more concerned with the reactions I'm going to get on the other end of these calls."

"It's not going to be pretty."

"You are not alone," Michael said, suddenly appearing next to them in the same outfit from earlier.

"Nice digs," Joe commented.

"It helps to not stand out in the middle of town."

"You are about seven feet tall. Pretty sure you stand out anywhere you go," Joe pointed out.

"This is true," Michael said, sitting on a bench to help disguise his height. "I will be with you when you make the calls. Then I must return. I have angels with Rachel and Jesse, but I feel the need to be directly with them."

"Do you know if they'll make it?" Delaney asked, nervous about even asking the question. "The doctor didn't seem too optimistic."

"That has yet to be determined."

Delaney sighed, rolling her eyes. "You're as comforting as he was, yeah?"

"I am sorry I cannot answer your question. I am, as you say, in the same boat as you. Only the Lord knows the answer to this one."

"Really?" Joe said, surprised. "You usually know *everything* when it comes to the A.N.G.E.L.s."

"I am afraid, in this case, I am at the Lord's mercy as well."

"Interesting. That's a new one."

"We are not omniscient."

"No. But, you *do* know a lot."

"We do. However, we only know what is revealed by the Lord. We are His messengers. We are not superhuman."

"Let's be realistic," Joe said, "You're a bit more than *just* a messenger. You are an archangel. You are the warrior of archangels at that. We know who you are."

"While this is true, I am still at the mercy, and under the Lord God Almighty. I am at His bidding."

"Agreed. As are we. Well," Joe said, dialing the Haven, "Let's get this over with."

294

Chapter 13
Weak Link

After multiple brutal conversations with the Haven and the station, Joe, Delaney, and Michael went back into the hospital to wait with the others. Once settled, Michael pulled Woorin aside, and spoke with him while they waited, in order to ease his mind from the heaviness of losing his cousin on top of everything else.

Once Isaac was released, the group went to a hotel for the night, mainly to wait for Caleb and Pete to come get the clansmen. They would take everyone, along with Charlie and Isaac, back to the station. Katia and Val would mainly take care of Isaac. They would also help Charlie care for his people, and watch the stations until the others returned.

In the meantime, Josh, Jacob, Delaney, Joe, and Michael would stay in a hotel near the hospital to keep tabs on the remaining three. It was up to Rachel, Jesse, and Jon as to the timeline. They would stand in prayer until they woke.

*   *   *

"Mrs. Sullivan, my name is Dr. McDougal," the doctor from the emergency room said to Kit, as she finally woke in the critical care unit. "Your doctor, Dr. Foster, is having me give him updates. He was here earlier, but you were still unconscious."

"Please call me Kit. Where's Nico?" Kit asked, even sounding weak to herself.

"He'll be in soon. I wanted to have a chance to explain to you what was going on before he came in."

"What happened?"

"It seems your body got overwhelmed, and decided you needed a break. You are currently in the critical care unit."

Kit cleared her throat as she looked around. "I see."

"Now, down here, visiting hours are limited to a half-hour every few hours. They don't want visitors tiring out the patients."

Kit shook her head. "No."

Dr. McDougal shook his head, confused. "What do you mean 'no'?"

"Need..." she shifted to a more comfortable position, which was difficult with all the monitoring equipment and IV, "...Nico. Need to have him with me."

With a smirk, Dr. McDougal said, "He said you may say something like that. Now we have a deal I will need to fulfill."

Kit raised an eyebrow.

Chuckling, Dr. McDougal explained, "Well, it seems that you two are connected. He said you would go downhill if you couldn't have him in the room. We made a deal that if you objected to the hours down here, that I would figure out a way to move you. Having said that, I already had my suspicions, due to the way I initially found him in the waiting room." When she cocked her head to the side in question, the doctor waved her off, and continued, "He was very distraught. Anyway, I made arrangements to have you moved to ICU. Up there, you will have a nurse for your room, and only one other. That way you can get the attention and care you need. You can have your husband in there as often as you want. As for other visitors, we need to keep them to a minimum. No more than two people in there at a time…meaning your husband and one other."

Kit nodded in understanding.

"Is that an agreement?"

"Yes, sir."

"Good." The doctor smiled. "I like it when patients are cooperative. Now, your prescription is rest. We're going to keep you in here for a few days, monitoring you until we're comfortable enough to give you another treatment. And, then we'll keep you for a few more days to see how you handle it. In other words, make yourself comfortable. You'll be in here for a while. It seems you weren't getting the necessary rest at home, so you now have a forced vacation."

"I see," Kit said, taking in the information. "And the feeling of being a marionette?" she asked, holding up the monitoring leads.

"Those have to stay. They help to keep tabs on you. Sorry. You'll have to feel like a marionette for a while. Consider them extensions of yourself for a bit."

"Great." Kit rolled her eyes. "Um, when can I see Nico? I need to talk to him."

"I'll go get him. You are quite the insistent one about him."

"We're connected."

"I understand. I'll go get him."

While he was gone, Kit soaked in her new reality. She went from bad to worse in a matter of a few days. She wasn't sure how much more could have gone wrong, but she would fight until the Lord took her home.

"Rachel?" Kit asked, as soon as she saw Nico.

Nico walked up to her, rested his hands on the sides of her face, leaned down, and kissed her lips. "I missed you."

"I missed you too. Rachel?" she asked again. Her heart monitor picking up speed.

"Kit, if you don't calm down, I'm going to have to ask him to go," the doctor warned, watching the monitor. "You don't want that, do you?"

"No," Kit said, tears forming in her eyes. "I just need to know about our daughter."

"She's in surgery," Nico explained. "We won't know anything until the surgery is over."

"What happened?" Dr. McDougal asked.

"She was in an accident in Alice Springs. She and another young man, Jesse," Nico said, looking down at Kit, "are currently unconscious. As I said, Rachel's in surgery for a subdermal hematoma, and Jesse is in a coma."

"What's Jesse's last name?" the doctor asked, taking out a pen and paper.

"Jesse English. Rachel's is Rachel Sullivan."

"And they're at Alice?"

"Yes."

"I have a good friend out there. Let me see what I can do to get you information."

"That would be great!" Nico said, relieved.

"I also have some colleagues who may be able to lend assistance. Let me get back to you on this. In the meantime, they are moving you to ICU shortly."

Nico smiled. "Really?"

"Deal's a deal!"

"Brilliant! Finally, something's going right!"

*   *   *

Once Kit was settled, she and Nico knew it would be a long ride until she was in the clear. While they knew it was for the best, it was not an easy task to keep Nico penned up in the hospital room with her, but both knew Kit wouldn't make it without him.

*   *   *

"Okay," Dr. McDougal said, coming into Kit's room a few hours later.

"You have news?" Nico stood. Anxiously shifting from foot to foot, he asked, "Is it good or not so good?"

"Well, I got ahold of a couple colleagues over at Alice. I also spoke with some here regarding their cases." Not waiting for Kit and Nico's reaction, the doctor explained, "A few from here are on their way to Alice Springs right now to take a look at both of them. Once there, they will consult with their doctors and figure out a plan of action. At this point, it's up to them. Depending on how hard they fight, will depend on if they pull through."

As soon as he said that, Kit's heart rate skyrocketed.

"Kit, you need to calm down. I am doing my best to keep you updated, but you can't keep doing this when I give you information."

"But-but, she's our baby!" Kit said, tears flowing down her cheeks. "You're not supposed to outlive your children!"

"Kit, they're in God's hands. They have always been in His hands," Nico said, bending over so he was close to her face, as he rested his hands on her shoulders. "Pray for God's will. Depending on how they wake up, they may wish they were dead. We can't predict the condition they will wake up in. We do know, though, that God and Michael are looking after them."

"Michael?" the doctor asked.

"A very close family friend."

"I see. I don't know the names, but I know there are multiple people who have been there for them since their arrival."

"Yes. He's among them," Nico said confidently. Then turning back to Kit, he reminded her, "They are the Lord's. They have always *been* the Lord's. They answered the call. It's up to Him as to how this plays out."

"I just don't want –"

"I know what you want, but we don't always get what we want," Nico said, cutting Kit off. "I want you out of here, but that's not going to happen anytime soon."

"It's *really* not going to happen anytime soon if you don't calm down," the doctor warned, keeping an eye on her monitor. "You're going to find yourself having heart issues on top of everything else. As it is, you have me concerned."

"I-I'm fine," Kit said, pushing the doctor away. "I'll be fine. I just need to cry."

"You can cry, but calm down. You have one minute, or I'm going to get you something to calm you down," the doctor warned.

Taking a few moments to calm down, Kit got herself under control.

"Good job. Now, if I hear anything else, I will let you know. Until then," he looked at Nico, "Keep her calm."

"Yes, sir," Nico agreed.

"My colleagues, who are going, are at the top of their fields. Those who are currently at Alice are brilliant doctors in their own right. They couldn't be in better hands," the doctor explained.

Nico looked up. "They couldn't be in better hands. They're in God's."

* * *

After several days, they finally released Jon to Michael, Jacob, Delaney, Josh, and Joe. Caleb came to Alice Springs and took him back to the station to recover. He brought Val with him, just in case something happened on the way home.

This left Jesse and Rachel still in the hospital. There were people literally praying all over the world for the pair, especially those at the Haven and the stations. Kit and Nico continued to keep them in prayer from her hospital room as well.

*   *   *

"I am excited to meet my teachers," Liliya said, as she, Mark, and Casey went to the school to finalize all Liliya's paperwork, gather her uniforms, and meet her teachers. Despite what was happening on the other side of the world with Jesse and Rachel, Liliya would still begin school the next day. They left the twins at home with the cyber cave team and Derek and Jerrod, so they could enjoy some time with just Liliya.

"You will have a fresh start here. No one knows you," Casey pointed out.

"Yes. All they know is that we adopted you," Mark continued. "All they *need* to know about your sister, is that she travels for a living. The twins are being homeschooled, because we wanted to give them a jumpstart in school. That is all anyone needs to know regarding our family."

"And, my back story, is that you found me through the adoption agency, and wanted to give me and my sister a better life," Liliya recited. "I got it. I will not mention any of the family's extracurricular activities cither."

"What does your sister do?" Casey asked. "You said she travels for a living. What does she do?"

"She is in the Army," Liliya explained. "This means she will be gone for long periods of time. I just will not mention *which* Army," she said with a sly smile.

303

Resting his arm over her shoulder, Mark gave her a gentle squeeze, as he said, "Very good, Lily."

"I think I would like to stick with Liliya. That is what I am used to," Liliya explained. "Katia and I talked, and we want to keep some of our past. Our first names hold our heritage and were given to us by our biological parents. You guys, as our heart parents, will be taking care of us for the rest of our lives, therefore we will keep our last name of English."

"We can totally respect that," Mark agreed.

"And, I think it's wise to hold onto your heritage," Casey said. "It makes you unique. You don't want to 'fit in' anywhere. Be an original."

"I agree," Mark said. "That means that you are a limited edition. I can promise you that there is no one else like you in this school. I can also promise that you will find the friends God wants you to have if you just listen to His voice."

"I know from personal experience that starting a new school can be tough. My brother was in the Air Force, and we moved every few years. And, try explaining the situation of no parents?" Casey smiled, shaking her head. "Jack did his best, though, and I always appreciated that."

"He was one of the good ones," Mark acknowledged. Then shaking his head, he added, "Man, I miss that guy! Keith and the Colonel, too!"

"You still have Uncle Derek," Liliya pointed out.

"This is true. And, I have my love," Mark said with a twinkle in his eyes, as he looked at Casey. Grabbing her hand, they walked into the office.

"May I help you?" the secretary asked. Then getting a good look at them, she smiled. "Oh! I remember you! The new student. We don't get many of those for second semester. I'll let the principal know you're here."

As she disappeared into the office, Mark rubbed the back of his neck. The hair on the back of his neck stood on end, and he was instantly on alert. "There's an Unnatural here," he whispered to Casey and Liliya.

"In *here*? In a school?" Casey asked, stunned. "Where?"

"I don't know. I just know they're near. While I'm not as sensitive as Jesse and Sasha, the older A.N.G.E.L.s always knew when there was one around. It's like our skin goes on edge. Being at the Haven, I haven't felt it in a long time, but the feeling is unforgettable."

The secretary walked out of the office, and said, "We got a new principal over break. Unfortunately, Mr. Dickenson passed away with a heart attack. Mr. Fulton is our new principal, and his wife is one of your teachers." The secretary smiled, as she then ushered them into the office.

Sitting across from Principal Fulton, Mark couldn't help feeling on edge. Grateful to know the former principal died of natural causes, he figured he could relax with the new one. "Morning, sir." Mark shook his hand.

"Morning." Korax shook Mark's hand before both men sat down across from each other. Korax felt it when the mountain was taken out. He and Calliope had escaped the explosion by getting set up in Reno. He would have to disguise his disdain for the people in front of him for the sake of the plan, but revenge was first and foremost on his mind. "First off, welcome to our school," Korax smiled. "We are pleased to have you join us."

"Thank you," Liliya mumbled. There was something familiar about him, but she couldn't put her finger on it. Noticing the photo on the desk, she asked, "Is this your wife?"

"Yes. Calli will be one of your teachers," he explained.

"She's stunning!" Casey said, surprised by the beauty in the photo.

"Yep! We joke that I married up. She's my better half," Korax said, pleased that the brainwashing Calliope did while they had Liliya worked. If she didn't recognize Korax or Calliope, he was sure Calliope would be able to execute their plan. His main concern was Mark. He felt Mark as soon as he walked into the school. He was certain Mark felt him as well.

"Well, not to be rude, but we have two more at home we have to get back to. I know we have some things to do here, though," Mark said, squirming in his seat, his skin feeling like bugs were crawling all over it.

"Completely understand. I'll have Sally give you the tour and introduce you to Liliya's teachers. We will also have a little more paperwork to fill out. And then we'll see you tomorrow, young lady," Korax said, standing to shake Liliya's hand.

When she shook his hand, Liliya quickly pulled it away. There was something about him that she didn't like. She felt dirty shaking his hand. "Thank you," she mumbled before they left the office.

"Ready for your tour?" Sally asked, as she saw them come out of the office.

"Yes, please?" Casey asked. Glancing at Mark and Liliya, she had an uneasy feeling. Then she saw the uniforms on the desk. "Are these Liliya's?"

"Yes. There are five uniforms, two sets of gym clothes, a jacket, and a folder with a map of the school, as well as a welcome pack inside," she said, gesturing toward the clear plastic bag on the counter. "She will need a backpack tomorrow, a notebook, and pens. She'll get all of her books tomorrow. Oh! And, here is your locker," she said, handing Liliya a piece of paper. "The combination of the locker is on the paper. Do not worry, it is changed each time a new student is to take possession of it. We don't like it when people steal from others, so we make it difficult to do so. The head janitor is the only one with a master key."

"Good to know," Mark said, pleased. "Is her schedule in the folder as well?"

"Oh, yes! Here. This will allow you to see your day," she said handing Liliya a computer printout of her schedule. Sally had a copy as well, in order to follow the schedule. "Let's start with your homeroom, and homeroom teacher."

They went through the schedule, and on the last class, they walked into Mrs. Fulton's class. "Mrs. Fulton, I'd like to introduce you to your new student. She starts tomorrow," Sally explained. "Liliya English comes to us all the way from Russia."

"Russia? Really?" Calliope said, standing up when they walked in. As she shook their hands, it felt like lightning shooting through her, but she remained composed in order not to mess up months of planning. "Welcome, Liliya," she said, when she got to her. Shaking her hand, she looked right into Liliya's eyes, as she said, "Welcome. Shalom," Calliope said, still holding Liliya's hand. "Are you excited to begin tomorrow?"

Liliya cocked her head to the side before she took her seat. After a moment, she responded, "Yes, I am excited to start tomorrow."

Mark felt extremely uncomfortable in the principal's office, but in this room, it was almost beyond what he could handle. As everyone took their seats, Mark asked, "Um, if I may interrupt, where are you from?"

"My husband and I came in from Kansas," Calliope simply responded, hoping to offset Mark. She knew who he was, and she was pretty sure he felt that she was from the other side. While she planned to see Liliya, she never planned to actually see Mark.

"Really? And before that?" Mark asked, sitting back in his seat, studying her.

Calliope knew she was in trouble, so she followed her instincts, and got up from her seat. Leaning on the front of her desk, she crossed her arms, and explained, "We have traveled extensively in our marriage, due to my husband's job. Maybe we have run into each other somewhere along the way. What do you do for a living?"

"I was Air Force special operations," he explained. "If we ran into each other in my job, it would not be for good reasons." Leaning forward, Mark asked, "This is a private Christian school, correct?"

"Of course."

"Then, who is Jesus Christ to you?"

Calliope gulped. Resting her hands on her desk, she explained, "He is the Son of God."

"And, is He your Savior?"

"Would I be able to work here if that was not the case?" Calliope answered, without really answering the question.

Mark sat back in his seat, narrowing his eyes at Calliope for a moment, before he said, "Our daughter's name is Callie. Not many have that unique name."

"No. They don't."

"Mark," Casey said, resting her hand on Mark's arm, "you are pushing."

"I know," Mark said, not taking his eyes off Calliope's. He knew if he pushed hard enough, and she were an Unnatural, her eyes would shift. When they didn't, he said, "You have to understand that Liliya is our daughter, and we want to make sure she is well taken care of."

"We will take excellent care of her while she is entrusted to us for her education," Calliope said, relieved to not have to answer any more questions from Mark.

"Thank you," Casey said, appreciatively.

After receiving her books, the group went back to the office to fill out a little more paperwork before leaving. Once outside, Mark said, "There are Unnaturals in there. I am *sure* of it. I don't know how I feel about sending you back in there to go to school."

"By your actions, you think it's the principal and Mrs. Fulton?" Casey observed.

"I don't know. While I didn't push the principal, I did push Mrs. Fulton, and she didn't budge," Mark said, confused.

"What do you mean by budge? What is that?" Liliya asked.

"Well, when someone says they didn't budge, that means they didn't move. In this case, when an Unnatural is pushed, their eyes, at the very least, will shift to black before returning to their normal color. If pushed hard enough, they will shift to their true selves. I don't understand why her eyes didn't shift, though. I was sure she was one of them, and a high one at that."

"Maybe because she is not an Unnatural," Liliya said with a shrug, as they got in their truck. "I feel very comfortable with her. It is him I do not like."

"I don't care for either of them," Casey said. "What I *do* care about is Liliya. Are we sure we want to send her to school when we are uncomfortable with who may be teaching her?"

"Oh! Please do not make me stay home. I want to go to this school. I will not be alone. There will be other students there. I do not feel I will be in danger."

"I'll make you a deal," Mark said, thinking, "if you feel the least bit uncomfortable at school, you tell us. If not, and we find out, you will have to be pulled until you go to college. If you do tell us, we may be able to find another school for you to attend. Deal?" he asked, as they were on the way home.

"Deal!" Liliya grinned. "I want to experience American high school before going to college."

"It's more college that I am worried about. At least this way we can help you navigate social skills while you're still at the house," Casey pointed out.

"I will not disappoint you," Liliya promised.

"Honey, we love you as if you were born of us. You are one of ours. We *chose* to have you in our family," Casey explained. "You are one of our daughters. Just be yourself."

"I will!"

"Then they will love you, as we do!"

"Just make sure to keep the A.N.G.E.L.s out of any conversations. This may take some quick thinking on your behalf," Mark said, "but, I know you can do it. You're a smart girl. Use that street smarts you gained in Russia to keep you on your toes, and keep you safe."

"Am I not safe here?" she asked, surprised.

"You are safe at the Haven. Out in the real world, you face the dangers everyone else faces."

Thinking on Mark's words, Liliya said, "I am grateful Katia stayed behind this time to watch over the stations. While I am worried for Rachel and Jesse, if something happens to Katia, I do not know what I would do."

"You would live your life the way it was intended. You *do* have family now," Casey explained. Then she added, "I just wish Rachel and Jesse would wake up."

"We may not want them to wake up," Mark said.

"Why would you say that?" Casey asked, stunned.

"Depending on the amount of brain damage either sustained, they may not want to wake up either," he explained. "Brain damage can be a tricky thing."

"That's our son!" Casey said, wide-eyed.

"I am aware of that. I am also aware of what certain damage can do to the psyche when you're used to functioning at a certain capacity."

"They will adjust if there is damage."

"If they can. Depending on how much, will depend on if they are a vegetable when they wake or not." When he said that, the looks on both Casey and Liliya's faces made him further explain, "Look, I'm just being real with you. Casey, you've been in the medical field. You understand what happens. Liliya, you are almost an adult. You have actually more life experience than some adults I know. You both have to understand how this works."

"I do," Casey said cautiously, "I just don't want to lose hope. Jesse's our son. Rachel is a great Christian influence over many."

"They're also A.N.G.E.L.s, and we're known for having short life spans," Mark reminded them.

"I understand that, but –"

"But, nothing," Mark dismissed Casey, cutting her off. "Their lives are in the Lord's hands. We have no say in the matter. Our job is to pray for them, for those looking over them, and for the doctor's whose care they are under. The rest is up to the Lord."

"I don't want to be reminded of this," Casey said, holding back the tears.

"I do not either," Liliya added. "It is bad enough that I cannot talk to Katia every day. I already know she could be in trouble every time she leaves. I do not want to think about losing anyone else."

"We are *all* potentially in trouble every time we leave the Haven. This world is an evil place. The only reason the Haven is safe is because the Lord put His angels around the property, so we have a safe place on this planet. The world is scary! The sooner you realize this, the better off you will be. The *only* One you can fully trust is the Lord," Mark said. "Now, I'm one-hundred percent positive there is an Unnatural in your school. If we are to trust you to attend, you can*not* be alone there. Have someone near you at all times. Do you understand?"

"I do."

"And, we cannot send someone to guard you either."

"I understand."

"Then, every morning, we will pray for protection before we take you to school. I know God gave us this warning for a reason."

Casey looked from Mark to Liliya, and gulped. "Then, we'd better listen."

*   *   *

The next morning, Liliya got up and ready for school, with a thrill of excitement. Allie and Callie were happy for her, but they would miss their new sister. It seemed just as they gained siblings, they lost them to the A.N.G.E.L.s or to life in general.

Ever since losing their mother, they quickly learned not to take life for granted.

After prayer, Casey and Liliya went to the van, so Casey could take her to school. They were met by an angel. She was around six-foot-five, had long blonde hair, sky-blue eyes, and was wearing a tunic, with a belt around her waist. The belt contained a sheath with a sword in it.

"Do not fear," the angel said.

"Oh, honey, we're used to you guys," Casey said with a smile.

"You may be, but I am not," Liliya said, jaw-dropped.

"Have you any news for us?" Casey asked.

"I was sent by Michael to warn you of danger in Liliya's school," the angel replied.

"We're aware," Casey said appreciatively.

"You are not aware to what extent."

"I'll be fine," Liliya said. "I do not want to stay home. I want to go to school."

"There is danger there," the angel reiterated.

"I know, but I will be fine. There will be others there," Liliya pushed.

The angel stood in front of the driver's door of the van, not moving. "You are in danger, Liliya."

"I have free will, correct?" she challenged.

Casey looked from the angel, to Liliya, and back again, before suggesting, "Maybe we should look into another school."

"No," Liliya insisted. "I want to attend this school. I am comfortable at this school. I am ready. Please do not make me change schools before I even start?" she begged Casey.

"Will she be okay today?" Casey asked the angel.

"That is not known. That is not the message. Michael was warned, and sent me to warn you that she is in danger at that school. Michael would have told you himself, but he is staying with Rachel and Jesse, along with the others at the hospital."

Nibbling on her nails, Casey debated in her head. Finally, she said to Liliya, "I think we need to talk to Mark about this."

"Free will," Liliya challenged.

"Excuse me?"

"Do I not have the free will to go to the school I choose?"

"Not necessarily. That's not how this works. If Mark and I do not feel you are safe, we do not have to take you."

"Then you will have to homeschool another, and I will not be able to take my testing for college. Please, Casey?" Liliya begged. "I really want to go to this school! I feel like I've been trapped here for the last few months. I want to be able to breathe."

Hurt, Casey asked, "We're suffocating you?"

"In a way, yes. I'm never alone here. I can never be just me, without having to make sure I am doing the right thing so I don't get kicked out."

"Who said you had to do the right thing to stay here? We just want you to be you."

"Then, let me go."

"Is she in danger today? Or is this something that can wait a few days until we can enroll her in another school?" Casey asked the angel.

"That is not known to me. I am only a messenger. I do not see the future. The choice is yours, but she *is* in danger at that school," the angel said, and then disappeared.

"See? She is gone. Please just take me today? We can then have the weekend to sort this out. Please do not make me miss the first day of school? It is difficult enough starting over, but having to do it after the semester begins will make it that much more difficult."

"Let me talk to Mark for a moment. When I return, I will let you know what he says. His word stands," Casey warned, and then went back into the house.

Knowing what his answer would be, Liliya took off running down the driveway toward the main road. Once there, she headed in the direction toward town to go to school. She was barely a mile from her home, when a car pulled up beside her. It was Mrs. Fulton.

"Liliya? Why are you running? Did something happen to your family? Are you in danger?" Calliope asked.

"No, Mrs. Fulton. I just want to get to school."

"I'll give you a ride," Calliope offered, with a gentle smile. "Hop in."

Once inside, Calliope grabbed her hands, and immediately began to sing. As soon as she did, Liliya went into a trance. After a moment, Calliope said, "Shalom, young one." This was a trigger phrase. When Calliope said part of the phrase yesterday, she saw the effect on Liliya, and knew finishing the phrase would activate her. "Do you hear me, Liliya?"

"I hear and I obey," Liliya said, in an automated voice response.

Calliope smiled a sinister smile. "This is what I want you to do…"

*   *   *

"Liliya!" Mark shouted out the window of the van, and then sped ahead of Liliya before pulling over. Running up to Liliya, he noticed she was walking in a daze. Resting his hands on the sides of her face, he asked, "What happened? What's wrong?"

"I do not know. I do not want to go to school today," she said, shaking her head. "I do not want to fight with you, or have you upset with me. Please forgive me?"

"We forgive you. Look, if Michael sent an angel to warn us, and knowing there is an Unnatural there, we don't feel it's safe for you to go to that school." Resting his arm over her shoulder to escort her back to the car, Mark asked, "Do you want to be homeschooled, or do you want to go to another school?"

"I do not know. I only know I need to go home."

Stopping, Mark stood in front of her. "Liliya, please look at me. What happened to you?"

Finally looking up at him, she admitted, "I do not know. I just know I would like to go home."

"Okay," he said, walking her over to her side of the car. As he opened his door, and helped her in, he was certain something had happened, he just wasn't sure what. He was grateful however, that she wasn't going to fight them on not going to the school anymore.

Chapter 14
Loosen the Chains

That night, Liliya was especially quiet. After dinner, Cori asked to talk to her. As they sat down on the back deck with Charm, Cori said, "You know, as a blind person, it's all about sound…or lack thereof."

"I cannot imagine."

"And, as a keen observer of sound, tonight you had a lack thereof. In my experience, that calls for sitting down and talking. What's going on?"

"Honestly?"

"You know I'll hear it in your voice if you're not honest."

"I know," Liliya said in understanding. Taking a deep breath, she then explained, "I feel like I have been watched almost continuously since I got here. I feel like I am never alone…and not in a good way. I feel like I need to get out into the real world, instead of living sheltered here in the Haven. You have to understand! Katia and I went into the orphanage at young ages. Because there were two of us, they did not want to separate us. This caused issues in placement for us. However, when Katia was of age, she became my guardian.

From that point forward, we were able to live life with a certain amount of freedom. Yes, this freedom caused issues, but we were free. I do not feel free here. Going to school would have been my chance to breathe. Having said that, I *am* happy here. I just need a little room."

"It's understandable. Have you talked to Mark and Casey about it?"

"After today, I do not think they want me in school."

"I don't think it's that. Kai said he saw you two talking to an angel this morning. That wouldn't have anything to do with Mark and Casey's discussion this morning, would it?"

"You know about that?" Liliya asked, stunned.

"I have super hearing, remember?" Cori said, with a wink. "There's not much in this house I *don't* hear."

"Good to know."

"It's not like I listen on purpose. I just hear it."

"That is okay. It cannot be easy being you. And yes, the angel said I was in danger at the school. I tried to fight it. I was feeling trapped."

"Again, understandable. I feel you may need to have this conversation with Mark and Casey. If you'd like, I'll sit in with you as moral support. That way you don't feel outnumbered," Cori offered. "Technically, it'll be three to two with Charm."

Liliya finally smiled. "That would be great! Thank you!"

"Let's go."

*   *   *

Sitting in the room with Rachel, Josh took her hand into his. He and Jacob were with Rachel today, while Joe and Delaney were with Jesse. "Okay, Rach, this is long enough. Mum and Pop really need some good news. You've been out now for over a week. The doc says that's way too long."

Sitting in the chair on the opposite side of the bed, Jacob asked, "Did the doc give any indication as to when she would wake?"

"That's up to her. *I'm* just letting her know that Mum needs her to wake up. She'll be getting a treatment in a few days, and she needs to know that Rachel's okay. She can't be worrying about her while trying to fight the chemo at the same time. That puts too much stress on her. So, Rach," he said, turning back to Rachel, "It's your turn to do something for Mum. She needs *you* this time!"

*   *   *

As Rachel slept, she had a dream…

Liliya was tucked back behind a boulder just beyond the Haven's property line. Behind the rock was an entrance to a cave. As she ducked in, she flipped the flashlight she had on, and looked around.

Finding the chalk arrow drawn on the bottom of the cave wall, she followed it back to an open area. In the open area was a box...and Calliope!

Rachel's heart rate picked up on her monitor, as she saw Liliya walk up to Calliope, and Calliope said, "Shalom, young one. Do you hear me?"

"I hear, and I obey," Liliya said, suddenly in a daze.

"You are the weak link in the A.N.G.E.L. fortress. You are crucial to exact the revenge of my fallen comrades. This is the box you will use to complete that mission."

"I hear, and I obey," Liliya said again.

Kneeling in front of the box, Liliya took the knife out of her pocket and cut the tape. Opening the box, she almost seemed to be in automatic mode. To Rachel's horror, there was not one, not ten, but about twenty pounds of C4 attached to a device!

Rachel struggled to open her eyes! She had to warn someone! Her body, however, was not cooperating. She was forced to continue the nightmare...

Liliya picked up the heavy box. She navigated her way out of the cave, into the blistering Nevada sun. Carrying the box, after fifteen minutes, she crossed back onto the Haven's property. Keeping an eye in every direction, she slowly made her way to the boulder with the names of the A.N.G.E.L.s painted on it by Jesse. This boulder was out from the house by about twenty-five yards, and she was on the opposite side from the house, so no one could see her.

Remembering Calliope's instructions, Liliya set the explosive, and just walked away like nothing ever happened. Rachel watched as she walked right through the house, merely waving to anyone who acknowledged her presence, and went out the front door. Once Liliya reached the street, which was about three-quarters of a mile from the house, the bomb went off, killing everyone in the Haven, obliterating everything in its path, and even sending Liliya flying into the air.

Rachel fought with everything within her until she finally opened her eyes. The light was the first shock she found. The high-pitch of her heart monitor racing was the second. The third horror she discovered was the tube in her throat.

Josh jumped up from his seat to hold down Rachel's hands as she grabbed for her throat, while Jacob ran for the nurse. They would have to get the tube out before she yanked it out on her own! "Rachel! Calm down!" Josh shouted, struggling to keep ahold of Rachel. "Rach! They need to get the breathing tube out! Calm down!"

The nurse ran in, and within moments, she had the tube out. "If you don't calm down, miss, we'll need to sedate you," the nurse warned, as Rachel still struggled under Josh's grip.

Unable to speak, Rachel knew she had to get the information from the dream to someone! *The Haven was in danger! Was Liliya the weak link they didn't see coming? What had Calliope done to Liliya when she had her? Why didn't*

Angel know about it? Was Angel in the same boat? Would Calliope be able to activate Angel sometime in the future?

Rachel groaned, and shoved her hands down, not moving. When Josh let go, she made a motion for Josh to get her a pen and paper. Her throat hurt too much to speak, but she knew she could write.

While she wrote, the nurse left to get a sedative. While she didn't want to give Rachel one, Rachel's heart monitor was still racing. Rachel needed to calm down, and she wasn't doing it on her own.

Once he handed the pen and paper to her, Rachel wrote, *'Haven in trouble! Bomb!'*

"What do you mean a bomb?" Josh asked in a low voice, so he wouldn't alert anyone else as to what she was writing.

"What kind? How much? And, where?" Jacob asked, looking at the notepad over Josh's shoulder.

'Haven,' Rachel wrote.

"Okay, young lady, if you don't calm down, I will have to give this to you, but I don't want to," the nurse said, picking up the IV line going into Rachel.

To the nurse's horror, Rachel reached over, and yanked the IV out of her arm.

"What are you doing?" the nurse asked, stunned. Grabbing a corner of the sheet from Rachel's bed, the nurse put pressure on the site until it stopped bleeding. "You *do* know I'm going to have to put that back in, right?"

Rachel nodded, and the nurse ran out of the room for what she would need to put it back in. While the nurse was gone, Rachel wrote, *'About 20lbs. of C4! Total loss.'*

"That *would* be!" Jacob said, wide-eyed.

The nurse returned, and using Rachel's writing arm, she quickly inserted the IV needle. As she was taping it into place, the phone on her hip rang. "It's your doctor," the nurse explained, and then stepped out of the room to answer it.

"Okay, you know how this works," Josh said. "Chances are, she's gonna come back in here and knock you out. Who set it off? How do you know this?"

Rachel wrote feverishly, knowing she wouldn't have much time. *'Liliya set it off. Calliope brainwashed her. Angel a sleeper too?'*

"Good question," Josh said. Then he asked, "You said Calliope? Are you sure this is real? Calliope was supposed to be in the mountain."

'Have Casey say to Liliya, 'Shalom, young one.' That should trigger her.'

"Okay, going to have to knock you out for a bit. Doc doesn't like your behavior, nor does he care for how fast your monitor has been going since you woke," the nurse said, picking up Rachel's IV.

"Please?" Jacob begged. "Just give us a few more minutes? We need the information only she seems to know."

"Doctor's orders," the nurse said, and emptied the needle into the IV.

Rachel knew her time was even more limited. Feeling the warmth wash over her, she struggled to stay alert, as she wrote, *'Don't know timeline. Must find out if Calliope was still in the mountain. Think it is real, but not sure. Save them!'*

"We will, Rach," Josh assured her. "We need to go talk to the others."

"She'll be asleep for at least a few hours," the nurse said, watching the monitor, as she kept two fingers on Rachel's pulse. "I will personally keep an eye on her from the nurse's station, and periodically check in until you guys return."

"That would be appreciated," Josh thanked her. Looking back down at Rachel, Josh asked, "Is there anything else you can tell us?"

'Haven totaled,' she wrote. As the medicine took over, she wrote *'Get to Liliya...weak link.'*

*   *   *

"Do you really think it's true?" Jacob asked, as he and Josh headed to Delaney, Michael, and Joe with the notebook Rachel had used.

"I hope not, but it may have been a warning."

"Dreams are not her gift."

"I know. I also know we don't have time to wait for Charlie to get back here. You and I are going to have to go, and leave Delaney and Joe here," Josh said, as they entered the ICU.

"I will be going with you," Michael said, when they walked into the room.

"How do you know?" Jacob asked, surprised.

"I told him," Joe said. "I had a vision that the three of you went back to the mountain. Don't suppose you could tell me why?"

"Is this regarding the danger I sent an angel to warn the Haven about with Liliya?" Michael asked.

"What danger?" Josh asked. "And, why weren't we notified?"

"Liliya was in danger at the school she was set to attend," Michael explained. "You were not notified, because it did not pertain to you."

"Does twenty pounds of C4 blowing up the Haven pertain to us?" Josh asked, angry, as he tossed the notepad to Michael.

Michael scanned the notes, before he disappeared in a streak of light.

"What's going on?" Delaney asked. "Joe just explained the vision when you suddenly appeared at our door."

"It seems we have a weak link in our midst," Josh explained, "and she seems hell-bent on taking out the Haven with about twenty pounds of C4."

"Who?" Delaney asked, stunned.

"Liliya, via Calliope."

"What do you mean? Has anyone called the Haven?" Delaney asked, alarmed.

"We came here first," Jacob said.

"Then go outside and call them!" she ordered. "They need to know!"

Jacob just nodded, and headed downstairs to call the Haven. Hearing Josh get yelled at by Delaney for not calling them as soon as they knew, he barely heard Josh fire back just as he went out of earshot. "So glad I'm not in *that* conversation," he said aloud to himself, as he headed outside.

*　*　*

"Haven," Cori answered through the computer.

"It's Jacob," he responded.

"Just a sec," Cori said, and put him on hold while she scrambled the line. When she came back on, she said, "Great to hear your voice! Actually, it's a relief. You've had all of us worried!"

"I know. I'm fine, though. You guys may be a different story."

"What's going on?" Cori asked, while she smacked Kai on his arm, before smacking Hanif and Hiro as well.

"Does she not know another way to get our attention?" Hanif asked, rubbing his arm. "She seems to enjoy hitting us."

"I don't, but I don't have time either. Someone go get Jerrod. Otherwise, hush!" Cori reprimanded him. "What's going on, love?" she asked Jacob, as Hanif bolted up the stairs for Jerrod.

"According to a dream Rachel had –"

"Rachel is awake?" Hiro asked, excited, cutting Jacob off.

"Yes, now hush!" he said, imitating Cori, who giggled. Getting a serious tone back in his voice, he explained, "We think Calliope is somewhere near you guys."

"She wasn't in the mountain when it blew?" Kai asked, confused, as Jerrod came down the stairs with Hanif.

"Josh, Michael, and I will be going to check that out. Now, please, you guys need to stop interrupting," Jacob said.

"We will. Go on, Jacob," Jerrod said, as Hanif grabbed a pen and paper to take notes.

"Rachel said that Calliope has brainwashed Liliya."

"Liliya?!" Cori asked, stunned. Then, realizing she interrupted him again, she said, "Sorry. Just shocked. Go on."

"Thank you," Jacob said, and then continued. "Calliope has brainwashed Liliya. According to the dream Rachel had, she's going to set off twenty pounds of C4 near the house, blowing it to smithereens…with you all in it."

"What?!" Kai asked, jaw dropped, while Hiro and Cori gasped.

"Jacob," Jerrod said, and then gulped.

"I will alert Mark," Hanif said, running upstairs.

As he did, Jerrod continued, "Jacob, I don't have to tell *you* what twenty pounds of C4 could do to this place."

"No, you don't," Jacob said, just as Mark bolted in from upstairs, with Hanif on his heels.

"What's going on, Jacob?" Mark demanded.

"According to a dream Rachel had…and yes, she was awake, until we had to sedate her again…anyway, she said that Calliope has brainwashed Liliya. I can't remember the phrase she said to say, but she said that Calliope uses Liliya to blow the Haven with around twenty pounds of C4. I know I don't have to tell you either, what kind of damage twenty pounds of C4 will bring."

"Obliteration," Mark said, to the horror of all of those in the cyber cave, as he imagined what that amount of C4 could do to them.

"How do we stop it?" Jerrod asked.

"Well, one is to find Liliya, and sit on her. Hey, Jacob, have you ever seen Calliope?" Mark asked.

"No. Why?"

"I think I have."

* * *

Not finding anything in Black Rock, Angel, Sasha, Spencer, and Raphael were on their way to the location of the mountain. Coming in from the opposite direction from Alice Springs, they parked their car and walked over to what used to be the mountain. They were stunned when, appearing out of nowhere, were Michael, Jacob, and Josh.

"What are you guys doing here?" Angel asked, surprised.

"Where have *you* been? We haven't been able to get ahold of you for over a week!" Josh said, equally shocked.

"Is there something I need to be aware of?" Raphael asked Michael. "I was not expecting to see you here."

"There is much to discuss," Michael said, "starting with searching this pile of rubble for Calliope."

"We'll need to be careful," Jacob warned. "There is no stability in this mess."

"Wait!" Josh said, when everyone turned toward the mountain. "Seriously! Where have you been?"

"I made it so no communication could get through," Raphael explained. "It was part of my mission. Their mission was not to be interrupted."

"So, you have no idea your brother is in a coma, and that Rachel just woke from hers?" Josh asked, crossing his arms.

Spencer, Angel, and Sasha stopped in their tracks. Turning slowly toward Josh, Angel warned, "You had better not be saying that for effect."

"I'm not," Josh said, walking up to her. "Joe is there right now. Delaney's in Rachel's room. Jon is at the station, currently on bed rest for a bit longer. He had a punctured lung. Isaac is at the station with a broken leg. Katia and Val are holding the fort at the station right now, hoping to hear some kind of information. Kit's been in the hospital for days. A lot went on! Seriously, Jacob and I didn't have all these scrapes and bruises last time you saw us, did we? That mountain didn't look like that either."

"Why didn't you tell me?" Angel demanded from Raphael, tears stinging her eyes. With her fists balled at her sides, she stood there shaking in anger.

"The mission had priority," Raphael simply said, and turned back toward the mountain with Michael.

"My brother has been in a coma for almost a week, and I am just *now* hearing about it? This is not right! I *asked* you if there was something I should know!" she shouted at Raphael.

He turned toward her, and said, "Yes. I am aware. I am *also* aware that your lesson in trusting the Lord is still ongoing. Now, we have an assignment we have not completed."

Bottom lip trembling, Angel crossed her arms. A few more tears crawled down her cheeks, as she asked, "Is my brother going to live?"

"That is not yet known," Michael said. "We need to get in here, and see if we can locate Calliope's remains."

"I thought we were looking for the other box?" Spencer shook his head, confused.

"*We* are," Sasha clarified.

"We are also looking to locate Calliope's remains," Michael said. "We need to know if she is in Reno."

"Reno?!" Angel looked at him, stunned. "Are my parents okay? Are the other A.N.G.E.L.s okay?"

"At the moment, yes. We are concerned that she may have brainwashed Liliya. Was Liliya alone with her at any time?" Michael asked.

"Yes. They often separated us."

Michael went up to Angel and set his hands on her shoulders. "Do you remember what she did to you during this time?"

"Some of it," Angel said with a nod. Then she admitted, "Some of it I don't."

"Shalom," Michael said, and then studied her for some sort of reaction. To his surprise, her pupils reacted to the word.

"Does that mean what I think it means?" Josh asked, seeing her pupils react.

"Does *what* mean what you think it means?" Angel asked, dumbfounded.

"We need to know if Calliope is here. If not, she will need to be hunted down," Michael declared. In a split-second, there were streaks of light shooting from the sky, landing all around them. "Search this mountain. If she is here, I want her found! If not, you are to search this globe with extreme prejudice! *I want her found*!"

"What? What's wrong?" Angel asked. When the heavenly angels ignored her, and headed straight for the mountain of rubble, Angel demanded, "*What is going on?*"

"Angel, I am afraid Calliope has done something to you," Michael explained.

"What? What *else* could she have done to me?"

"She brainwashed you," he said. Then, leaning down, he said, "Shalom, young one."

Angel just shook her head.

"That means we do not know the rest of the phrase for you. That was the phrase for Liliya. Josh, Jacob, Sasha, Spencer, keep an eye on her. Sit on her if you have to. I have to get to the Haven. Raphael, you are in charge here," Michael said aloud. As soon as Raphael nodded, Michael disappeared.

"Keep searching!" Raphael shouted. "We have two missions to fulfill!"

*   *   *

"Where is she?" Michael asked, suddenly appearing in the living room of the Haven.

"We don't know," Derek said, wheeling in from the kitchen. "We've searched the entire grounds. They're still not giving up, but we're running out of places to look."

"Where are Jerrod and Mark?"

"They're looking for Liliya. Casey's in the kitchen with the twins, making snacks and coffee. We're not normally up at midnight, so we're pushing our normal times," Derek explained. "Searching for a teenager in the dark is also not an easy task."

"I understand. I will assist," Michael said, and went out to the back deck, with Derek wheeling behind him. Once out there, he closed his eyes, and suddenly, the angels surrounding the Haven began to glow. He glowed as well. The light got brighter, until it almost looked as if it were noon, instead of midnight. "They will find her," Michael declared. "They will contact me when they do."

"Thank you," Derek said, appreciatively.

As soon as he said that, there was activity toward the back of the property. In an instant, Michael was standing beside Mark, Cori, and Jerrod. "What is the commotion?"

"Someone thought they saw her, but we still can't find her," Mark said. "The light is helping immensely, though. Thank you!"

"When you do, you are to say, 'Shalom, young one.' At that point, she will respond that she hears and will obey. Instruct her to abort the previous mission. You are to instruct her to never follow Calliope's instructions again."

"Yes, sir," Mark said.

*   *   *

Finding the cave about fifteen minutes off the property, Liliya ducked in and flipped on her flashlight. Looking toward the ground, it took her a moment to find the chalk arrow directing her down the tunnels to an opening. With each passing minute, her heart rate picked up speed. Knowing she had been discovered at the Haven, she needed her next set of instructions on how to complete her mission now that the circumstances changed.

"Shalom, young one," Calliope said, when Liliya walked into the open area.

As soon as the words exited Calliope's mouth, Liliya went into a trance, "I hear and I obey."

"Why are you here so early, young one? You were not due to arrive for another nine hours."

"It was discovered that you had given me a mission."

"Okay. This is what you are going to do," Calliope started.

Chapter 15
Breaking Free from the Chains

"Are you saying that I'm a sleeper too?" Angel asked.

"I am saying that, if given the correct phrase, Calliope can make you do what she wants," Raphael explained. "It is my understanding that this has happened to Liliya."

"Has anyone told Katia what's going on?"

"I am not aware of who has communicated what information to whom."

"No, she's not," Josh said, as he moved a heavy rock. "We don't want to worry her. She's stressed enough with what all happened here while she was stuck at the station."

"*Someone* should tell her that her sister is being used to blow up the Haven," Angel said. "That's the right thing to do."

"She will be notified when the situation is under control. She needs to learn to let her sister function separately from herself. If she is notified every time Liliya steps out of line, she will not be able to do her job as an A.N.G.E.L.," Raphael explained.

"So, just like you didn't tell me about Jon or Jesse, you're not going to tell Katia about Liliya?"

"Correct."

"You think *I* have a temper?" Angel chuckled, as she crossed her arms. "Have you *met* Katia? She's a spitfire! She also fights extra hard for her sister. She will do just about anything for her. By *not* telling her, you are doing her…and us…a disservice."

"She will be told when it is the appropriate time," Raphael reiterated. "When the Lord deems it, we will tell her. Until then, *you* have a job to focus on."

"Ohhh, I don't think I like you anymore."

"Why change now?" Raphael snapped, as he went to another area to work on getting through the rubble pile.

"That's not a good idea," Josh mentioned when Raphael was out of earshot.

"What?"

"Ticking off an archangel. Ticking off *any* angel for that matter."

"Why?"

Josh cocked his head to the side, and asked, "Are you serious right now?"

"Yes. Why is it not a good idea to make an angel angry?"

"You are *so* much smarter than that question suggests," Josh said, shaking his head.

Angel narrowed her eyes at Josh as she stood her ground.

"Angel," Sasha said, coming up beside her, "I have not dealt directly with them long, but I do not have to in order to understand the power they yield. You are treading in dangerous territory. Do not anger him."

"Think it may be too late for that, mate," Josh said, nodding toward Raphael. "He looks madder than a cut snake!"

"I do not know what a cut snake is, but I can imagine an angry snake of any kind is not good."

"No. It's not," Josh said. Then to Angel, he added, "You may want to be good for a while. I don't think it'll behoove you to upset him anymore."

"Fine!" Angel huffed. "I'll be good."

"I think you may need to go talk to him, too," Sasha pointed out.

Angel rolled her eyes. "I'd rather talk to my laundry."

"I'd settle for you digging in," Jacob said. "All you've done since you got here is complain and be rude."

"Really?"

"Yes. Really," Jacob said, standing up, daring her to challenge that. When she didn't say anything, Jacob continued, "You say you've changed, but all I see is the old Angel."

"Ouch! A little cold out here in the Outback," Angel said, rubbing her arms.

"Cold? More like a polar vortex that *you* created," Jacob pointed out. "Or rather, your *attitude* created. You have an uncanny ability of getting people angry with you. Now, pick up a rock or two and start digging! We don't have all day! The Haven needs to know if Calliope is in here or not."

"Your life depends on it too," Raphael reminded her. "She can activate you at any time."

"Lovely." Angel sighed, before she bent down to move some rocks.

*   *   *

"This is a big campus," Kai said, as they were still searching the Haven grounds for Liliya.

"These awful hours are not helping," Hanif pointed out. "We are sleepwalking. It is two o'clock in the morning.

"Hoping Casey has coffee, yeah?"

"Yes. Or it will be a long night."

"Do you think Liliya would really blow up the Haven?" Akio asked, about twenty feet from Kai and Hanif.

"I don't think she would do it of her own volition," Kai pointed out. "She's too kind-hearted. Having said that, I think Calliope could make her do whatever she wants. She has her brainwashed. All she had to do was say a phrase to activate her. She was a sleeper."

"That's not good."

"No."

"Curious question," Hanif said, as they continued searching the grounds.

"What?" Akio asked.

"Were not Angel and Liliya both held by the same person?" As soon as he asked the question, both Kai and Akio stopped dead in their tracks. When they didn't move, Hanif continued, "It would be prudent to assume, since Liliya is a sleeper that Angel may be as well."

Kai gulped. "I, uh, hadn't thought of that." Taking his phone out of his pocket, he dialed Mark.

"Yeah, Kai, what's up?" Mark asked, answering the phone.

"Hanif just pointed something out that I'm not sure anyone has considered."

"What?"

"Angel and Liliya were both held by Calliope. Angel was actually held *longer*. Wouldn't it be smart to assume Angel is a sleeper as well?"

Mark stopped in his tracks and looked up at Michael. When Michael dropped his head, Mark said into the phone, "I think I need to have a serious conversation with the archangel." When he hung up the phone, Mark accused, "You knew. Didn't you?"

"Yes. We are not aware of the full phrase to activate her, but Angel is, as you say, a sleeper," Michael admitted.

"When were you planning on telling me?"

"We are looking for Calliope's remains in the mountain."

"Calliope's not *in* the mountain!" Mark yelled. When he did, multiple people looked up from where they were searching.

"That doesn't look good," Kai said in a low voice from their position, about fifty yards away.

"I have a feeling the archangel knew Angel was affected," Akio suggested. "And Mark just found out."

"She's right here in Reno!" Mark continued, still shouting.

"You know this for certain?"

"Yes!" Mark said, exasperated. "Why do you think we're searching for Liliya, and not Calliope?"

Clearing her throat, Cori had a hold of Charm's leash, while they searched as well. "May I speak?"

Keeping an eye on the archangel, Mark said, "Anytime you want, Cori."

"Thank you. It is my understanding that Calliope said a phrase and woke Liliya, yeah?"

"Yes," Mark said. "That's how we *know* she is not in the mountain that blew up. She was a teacher at the school. I'm sure of it."

"And, um, it is also my understanding that Angel can be activated as well, yeah?" Cori asked.

"Yes," the archangel said.

"And, Josh, Jacob, Angel, Sasha, Spencer, and other angels are searching the mountain, yeah?"

"Yes. This is correct," Michael said.

"Then, may I make a suggestion that the efforts go toward looking for Liliya, and focusing on Rachel and Jesse, instead of searching a mountain in futility."

"The search on the mountain has two missions. One is to potentially find Calliope, which as you stated, is now a search in futility. The second is to potentially find the box in the other side's possession," Michael explained.

"I see. Now, since you are aware of Angel's potential state, how are you containing said state?" Cori pressed.

"I have Josh, Jacob, Sasha, and Spencer staying with her until I can get back," Michael explained. "It is my hope that they will locate the other box while they are at it."

"That is all well and good, but *what* are you going to do about Angel?" Mark asked.

"Find Calliope."

"Wait. Your solution to Angel being a sleeper is to find Calliope?" Mark asked. "You *do* realize that this could be a disaster in the making! I mean, seriously! We're looking for a teenager, who could potentially be carrying twenty pounds of C4! What damage do you think Angel could do if she is activated without our knowledge?"

"Much."

"Could you be a little more encouraging?" Mark asked, frustrated.

"I am afraid I cannot at this time."

"Ya know, there is another option to looking for her," Cori said.

All three men turned to her, curious. "What are you thinking, Cori?" Jerrod asked.

"Why be on the defense, when we should be on the offense?"

"Clarify," Mark ordered.

"Calliope will want Angel. Angel's her other weapon," Cori pointed out.

"And," Michael started, a plan forming in his mind, "if we can set a trap, we can use Angel as the bait."

"Wait!" Mark objected.

Ignoring Mark, Michael went on, "And, when we find Liliya, we can use them both."

"Stop right there!" Mark snapped. "You are talking about using *two* of *my* children as bait to lure a muse…who isn't even supposed to exist, I might add."

"Legends and myths all have an origination point," Michael explained. "Before you worked on team A.N.G.E.L., did you *really* think angels existed. Or better yet, that you would be working directly with, and talking to, an archangel of the Lord God?"

"Fair enough," Mark agreed. "But, I still don't agree with using Angel and Liliya."

"We have to *find* Liliya first," Jerrod pointed out, as he was near them. "As for Calliope? Keep Angel on a short leash until Calliope comes to us."

"Interesting prospect," Michael said, mulling it over in his mind.

"*Not* an option!" Mark insisted. "Those are my children!"

"It will be up to them," Michael said firmly.

"But –"

"Mark, I hear your objections. First, we need to find Liliya. Angel is currently contained at the mountain, searching for the box. Once we find Liliya, I will speak with her and Angel. It will be their choice."

"Fine," Mark grumbled. Then looking around, he said, "We've searched the entire grounds. What if she isn't on the property?"

"She may not be. We need to keep her and Calliope off the Haven's property at all costs."

"For how long?" Cori asked.

"Until we can search Liliya, and take Calliope into custody," Michael said. "I do not trust Calliope."

"How are we going to kill a muse?" Jerrod asked. "Honestly?"

"I have a myriad of ideas. I have been around for a while," Michael said with a smirk.

"Do you think the other side is building up again?" Cori asked.

"They may be, but those in the Haven will always be protected," Michael stated. "That is the reason for these angels with fiery swords. If you are not an A.N.G.E.L. or a member of the English or Sullivan families, you will more than likely not get on the property."

Kai walked up to the group. "I think we may need to go off the property."

"Why?" Mark asked.

"Because we've searched this place top to bottom. Besides, Calliope can't get on the property, and she knows that. She may be *near*, though."

"With twenty pounds of C4, she only needs to get near," Mark pointed out. "That will make one massive crater, and obliterate anything in its path."

"So, we could literally be standing right here in this spot, and still be killed?" Kai asked.

"Yes," Mark confirmed.

"Michael, with all due respect, can't you just do your thing and locate her?" Kai asked. "It's literally two-thirty in the morning."

Michael disappeared in a streak of light into the sky.

"Was that a yes?" Kai asked.

"Mark?" Cori said, sensing something near. She closed her eyes, and with her Spiritual sight, she saw her.

"What?" Mark asked, still frustrated with the conversation with the archangel.

"She's in a cave. Go that way about fifteen minutes," Cori said, pointing to the east.

"Umm, may I point out that you're blind?" Kai asked. "How do you know you're pointing in the right direction?"

Cori rolled her eyes. "What's my Spiritual gift?"

"You know what? I don't care," Mark said, and ran in the direction Cori pointed. He was closely followed by Kai, Hanif, and Akio, leaving everyone else at the Haven to keep watch along its borders.

"Mark!" Kai yelled, as he stopped, with his hands on his knees. Struggling to take deep breaths, he asked, "What – how do we know how far fifteen minutes…oh goodness!" Kai said, gasping for air. "There's a reason I work behind a computer."

"We don't know," Mark said. "I'm letting the Lord lead."

Leaving Kai and Hanif, while they caught their breath, Akio and Mark continued out into the desert. Akio halted in his steps when he passed a cave. "Mark," he said, "she's in here."

Going to where Akio was, Mark asked, "How do you know?"

"I don't. It's a feeling. Here," he said, resting his hand on his stomach.

"Gut feeling. Okay. I get it. Let's go," Mark agreed.

Pointing the flashlight toward the ground, they headed in. Looking back after a few moments, Mark saw the entrance get considerably smaller from when they first walked into the cave. Turning back toward the tunnel, he took a deep breath and slowly let it out. That's when he saw it. There was a chalk arrow near the floor of the cave. He tapped Akio, and pointed toward the arrow. Then he put his finger to his mouth to tell Akio to stay quiet.

As they moved into the depths of the cave, Mark's heart raced. His years of being in the military let him override his feelings of wanting to panic.

Further in, they finally came to an opening. Lying on the ground near a boulder, was Liliya.

"Liliya!" Mark exclaimed. Keeping an eye in every direction, he cautiously approached her. Reaching down, he put two fingers on her neck...relieved to feel a strong pulse. "She's alive. We need to get her out of here."

"Where is Calliope?" Akio asked, nerves on edge as he continuously scanned the area for surprises.

"Good question. Keep an eye out," Mark said. He then picked Liliya up and flipped her over his shoulder, doing a fireman's carry of her. "In the meantime, let's bail!"

As they went to go back into the tunnel, Mark felt it against his pant leg. *'Click!'* "Oh no," he groaned, not moving.

Akio tried to look around Mark. "What is going on? What happened?"

Mark looked down. When he did, Akio shone the light on his pant leg. Barely visible, was a tripwire. Akio looked back up to Mark, jaw-dropped.

"If I move, this place will blow," Mark said slowly. "I need you to go get the others for help."

"Do you want me to take her with me?" Akio asked, sliding past Mark to get in front of him, being careful to step over the wire.

With sweat beads pouring down his forehead, Mark calmly explained, "Any movement could set this off. Please hurry."

"Yes, sir," Akio said, and quickly disappeared down the tunnel.

As soon as Akio was out of the cave, Calliope appeared from the shadows. "So," she started, and then hummed a bit as she neared Mark. When she got up right next to him, she sweetly said, "I see you're in a bit of a predicament."

Mark fought off the scent that tried to take over every sense, as she continued to hum a tune.

"It won't work," Mark said sharply.

Innocently, Calliope asked, "What won't work?"

"Whatever you are trying to pull. It won't work on me."

"Really?" she asked, running her finger under his chin as she slowly paced in front of him. Stopping, she went to a few inches away from his face, and asked, "Why will it not work on you?"

"Because I am not only in love with my wife, but I am strong in the Lord. Both will keep me focused on whatever you try to pull!"

"Allen said he would be able to resist as well, but we *both* know what happened to him. Hmmm," she said, up near his ear, and then began humming again, running her fingers through his hair.

After a few minutes, Mark rolled his eyes, and said, "You can stop now. You're more like an annoying mosquito, than actually tempting me with anything."

"Aww, you are no fun!" Turning toward the direction of the cave entrance, she heard a noise. "Well, that's my cue to leave. Until we meet again, handsome," she said, and kissed his cheek before she left.

Mark rolled his eyes again as he sighed. Shaking his head, he watched her disappear back into the shadows, just as Akio, Michael, Kai, and Hanif came down the passage toward him.

"She was just here," Mark said. "She went that way." He nodded in the direction she left in.

"Thank you, but we are more concerned with you. She is probably long gone by this point," Hanif said, kneeling on the ground, following the wire to the cave wall to see where it led. "I wish Jacob were here. This is more his line of work."

"What do you see?" Akio asked.

"Probably the same thing I do on this side," Kai said, as he was on the ground, looking on the opposite side from Hanif. "That's a lot of C4."

"Make a crater, huh?" Mark chuckled nervously. "I always hoped to go out with a bang."

"Today is not the day you die," Michael said, assessing the situation.

"Thanks for the head's up. Do you have a way of us getting out of this alive?" Mark asked.

"I do." Turning to the others, he said, "I need you to all run back to the Haven. Get the others, and go into the Haven, down to the basement. This is going to blow, and I do not want anyone near windows in the Haven. They will more than likely blow as well, creating a lot of sharp debris."

Akio, Hanif, and Kai all three stood there, pale.

"That is an order," Michael said, sternly. "Now go!"

"Yes, sir," Kai said, and tugged Akio and Hanif's arms to follow him.

Once they were out of sight, Michael turned back to Mark. "I am going to leave you for a time. I will return with Angel and Raphael."

"Please hurry? She may be light, but with not moving, she's starting to get kind of heavy."

"I will be back as soon as I can. I need the others to be secure in the Haven. I will ensure this is true first. I will also need to assist Derek down to the basement. Will you be okay until I return?"

"I have no choice. If you see a bright light in the distance, you know I couldn't hold her any longer."

"You are an A.N.G.E.L.!" Michael stood and declared. "The saints of the Lord are down on their knees in prayer for you." Suddenly there were two angels, one on each side of Mark. "They will hold you up when you think you cannot stand anymore. Allow them to hold some of the weight."

"Yes, sir."

"I will return," he said, and disappeared.

Mark turned to the angels on either side of him, and said, "Thanks for the help. I don't know how much longer I can hold her."

"You will hold her as long as it takes," one of the angels, Ariel, said confidently.

*   *   *

"How long are we going to keep digging?" Angel asked, and then tossed a large rock to the side. When she did, she looked down and gasped. "Oh my!"

"What is it?" Raphael asked. "Did you find the box?"

"No. I found another actual body," she said, and gulped, as she stared at the dirt-covered hand sticking out of the mound of rocks and rubble.

Josh and Sasha ran over and uncovered the body. To Angel's horror, it was Allen!

"You know him?" Sasha asked, seeing all the color drain from Angel's strained face.

"Th-that's Allen. He's the pastor that…" her voice faded as she looked at his eyes. There was a look of pure terror in them. His body was mangled, cut, and smashed in parts. His face, though cut up from the debris, still showed the horror he knew was about to befall him. "He didn't go to Heaven when he died. He did the unforgivable sin."

"I know. We'll still bury him," Josh said, pulling his body out from the rubble. "It's the right thing to do."

Those around continued to dig, while Josh pulled Allen's body from the rubble, and set it to the side. They found three other bodies through their search, so Josh stacked Allen's with them until they could get them buried.

"How do we know when to stop digging?" Jacob asked.

"When we find the box," Raphael said, determined.

After another twenty minutes of digging, one of the Heavenly angels called out. Everyone ran over, to find a metal box partially buried in the earth, with stones around it as well.

"Is that what I think it is?" Spencer asked, a thrill of excitement ringing through. "That would make all of this worth it if this is *the* box."

"I do believe that is the box," Michael said, suddenly appearing behind them.

Angel jumped, as he appeared directly behind her. "I swear I'm getting a cowbell when we get back to town to put around your neck!"

Chuckling, Michael said, "My apologies." Then he walked up the rubble to the box, and easily released it from its stone tomb. He carried it off the mountain, and set it on solid ground before snapping the lock to open it.

As he lifted the lid, a bright light shone from it.

"That looks familiar," Angel said, remembering when they opened the box in Mexico. They scrambled down the rocks to Michael, circling the box.

"It is the other box," Michael exclaimed. "You have found it."

As Michael went to close it, Spencer objected. "Please? At least let us see what's in it?"

Michael smiled at Spencer's curiosity, and turned it toward them.

Spencer and Angel knelt in front of it, and picked up various items to show the others. Spencer picked up a cloth bag and opened it. Pouring out the contents, there were thirty pieces of silver that slid from their home. "Are these what I think they are?" Spencer asked Michael.

"They are the thirty pieces of silver that Judas was awarded for betraying the Lord Jesus," Michael explained. "Right before Judas hung himself, he threw the money into the temple. Since it was considered blood money, the priests used the money to purchase Aceldama field, also known as the potter's field, or the field of blood. The owner gave the money to Paul afterward. To him, it was cursed, and he wanted nothing to do with it. Paul and Timothy put it in their box."

"Is *this* what I think it is?" Angel asked in awe, as she held up a cup.

"That's supposed to be in Valencia Cathedral in Spain," Spencer said, stunned. With his hand out, he asked, "May I?"

Angel reluctantly handed over the cup.

"Just because they *think* they have the correct one, does not necessarily mean they do," Michael said knowingly, before reaching down to pick up a scroll. Unfurling it, he scanned the list. "This is their half of the list," Michael said. "It has the first name, approximate date on when to find them, and the country."

"We have both lists!" Josh said, ecstatic. "We can find everyone without having to worry about the other side."

"We will deliver this to Katia and Val to place where they deem fit," Michael said.

Before he closed the box, Angel said, "Wait!" Running to Sasha's backpack, she pulled out the scrolls they found in the warehouse. "These need to go in there as well. We need to keep this stuff together."

"Good idea!" Spencer said.

"What are those?" Josh asked.

"Those are maps of where the A.N.G.E.L.s currently are all over the world," Angel explained as she put them into the box. "We found them in the warehouse in Cairns."

Once she put them in, Michael stacked the contents back in the box before sealing it. Standing, he said, "Raphael, Angel, and I need to go. You are free to either return to the hospital to wait with the others, or continue digging this area clear of bodies. The mission, at this point, is complete…and successful. Thank you."

"Where am I going?" Angel asked, while Raphael picked up the box.

"You will need to be secured," Michael said, grabbing her arm before she had a chance to get away.

Angel tried to pull away, but Michael held tightly to her arm, and then grabbed Raphael's before they disappeared.

"Oh, she is *not* going to be happy!" Josh chuckled.

"Talk about being madder than a cut snake!" Jacob laughed.

"Okay, do we stay here, or do we go to the hospital?" Sasha asked.

"Honestly," Josh said, "I say we bury the ones we have, and then go back to the hospital. There really isn't any reason to continue digging."

"Agreed," Sasha said, grabbing a shovel, heading over to start digging.

It took only a moment for the others to join him. Once they finished, they got in Sasha and Spencer's vehicle, and headed for the hospital in Alice Springs.

*　　*　　*

Willow screamed and jumped, heart racing, when Angel, Michael, and Raphael appeared in the kitchen. "Crikey!" She said, and then slammed her hand over her mouth. "Sorry!" She blushed. "You nearly scared me to death!"

"My apologies," Michael said, as Katia and Val suddenly appeared in the doorway. "Hello. I am glad you are here."

"How are Rachel and Jesse?" Val asked.

Before anyone else could say a word, Angel blurted out, "Liliya's been brainwashed as a sleeper in service to Calliope, and so am I." Glaring at Michael, she practically dared Michael to say she was wrong.

Michael gave her a stern look before turning back to a stunned Katia.

Katia gulped, and then asked, "Is she okay? My sestra?"

"She is with Mark right now," Michael assured her, "whom I need to get back to. Before I do, we needed to drop this off with you," he said, gesturing toward the box in Raphael's hands.

"Is that the other box?" Val asked, stunned, as Raphael placed it on the floor. "What's in it?"

"The cup of Jesus from the last supper and the thirty pieces of silver Judas got for betraying Jesus. Can we discuss Liliya and my current condition?" Angel snapped.

"Angelina English!" Michael turned toward her, visibly angry with her. "You will cease speaking immediately!"

Shocked, Angel backed down. "Yes, sir," she said quietly.

Turning back to Katia, he instructed, "You are to continue to look after the station, and you, Val, and Isaac are to find a place to hide the box. Liliya is under my current supervision. You are to continue your mission, knowing she is not in the hands of Calliope." Turning back to Angel, he said, "*You* are to come with Raphael and me back to the Haven. You are not to leave my sight. Do you understand?"

"Y-yes, sir," Angel said, holding her arms.

Michael stood between Raphael and Angel. In a split second, they were gone.

"Hate it when they do that," Willow said, finally breathing normally.

Looking to Katia, Val asked, "Where do you want to put it?"

"I have an idea," Katia said, thinking. Angel told her where the other box was, so her thought was to place it under the casket of Katie MacKenna in the graveyard. She knew the casket was full of bricks, and that there was no body, because Katie MacKenna was also Kit Sullivan.

"Before we do, we need to write down the next hundred years of names, locations, and dates," Val explained. "Every time that box is opened, we are in danger of being found."

"Then, we dig the hiding space first," Katia said. "That way we can write everything down, and get it hidden before we are located."

"Good point. The *last* thing we need is creatures of the night, demons, or Unnaturals crawling all over the grounds again," Val pointed out.

"Yeahhhh, I've had my fill a' them, too," Willow said. Stopping from cooking for a moment, she looked to Katia and Val, and said, "Ya know, it's nothing personal, but I will be glad when you all leave, so we can get back to normal around here."

"No offense taken," Val said. "To us, this *is* normal."

*　　*　　*

Reappearing right beside Mark and the angels, Michael said, "I apologize for the delay. The other team found the box."

"Great news," Mark said. Body shaking, and with sweat pouring down his face, he added, "Can we fix *this* issue now?"

"What's going on?" Angel asked, nervous.

"He has tripped a wire. He cannot move or he will blow up," Michael explained.

"And you were taking time to look through the box?" Angel said, upset.

"Need I remind you to whom you speak?" Michael said sternly. "This is the final time I will remind you to keep your mouth shut. I will no longer tolerate your disrespect."

Angel grabbed her arms, and took a step back in submission.

"Michael, do we release these two?" Raphael asked, referring to the angels on either side of Mark and Liliya.

"They are to remain as a second shield."

"Wait! What?" Angel asked, stunned. "Remain for *what*?"

Michael grabbed Angel's arm, and positioned her right next to her father. The angels on either side of them knelt down on the ground, fanned their wings, and covered Angel, Mark, and Liliya, creating a cocoon of sorts.

Then, Michael and Raphael positioned themselves on either side as well, and covered all in the pack. "Mark, pull your leg back," Michael instructed.

Mark shook his head. "If I do, it will blow."

"We have you protected," Michael assured him, bracing for the explosion they knew would be coming from the rocks on either side of them.

"Please don't let my girls get hurt," Mark begged.

"You are all protected. Trust the Lord," Michael assured him.

As the angels all began to glow, Mark looked down at his leg, and moved it back. *'Click!"* was heard, before a sudden and loud explosion rocked their world! Mark and Angel dropped to the ground, while Mark did his best to keep ahold of the unconscious Liliya.

The explosion was felt in the cyber cave of the Haven. As the ground rattled around them, getting louder by the second, everyone dropped to their knees in prayer. Callie and Allie clutched onto Casey, while she grabbed Cori and Derek's hands. The dogs whimpered, as they cowered next to their handlers.

The explosion shot up into the air. When it did, the blast wave went out devouring everything in its path, turning everything near it to dust and rubble. As it neared the English property, everyone grabbed the hand of the person on either side of them, bracing for impact.

The wave swept across the desert, heading out in a circular motion. Crossing the boundary of the Heavenly angels, the wave decreased immensely. The angels created a wall, taking in most of the force of the wave.

The boulder with the names of the A.N.G.E.L.s cracked in two. The windows of the Haven blew out, as the concussion wave passed through the house. Dishes shattered. Furniture blew. Glass cabinets crackled before the glass blew out, while the wood ones cracked. Down in the basement, computers exploded, as shrill screams and shouts were heard from those in the basement. An immense pressure wave pressed into them and through them on its way through the house.

When it passed out the other side, those in the basement collapsed, unconscious.

By the time it hit the other side of the Haven, near the road, the angels on that side were able to absorb the remaining power the blast held, keeping it contained.

Once the wave cleared, there was a strong absence of sound around the Haven. No one was conscious. Broken glass in the kitchen shifted and fell, shattering on the ground, yet there was no one to pick it up. The grandfather clock in the living room was permanently stopped at three-twenty-two, the time the wave came through. Nothing else moved.

*   *   *

As soon as those who were at the mountain arrived to the hospital, Rachel woke up again.

"Morning," Josh said, walking into the room with Sasha.

"Did you find Calliope?" Delaney asked, as she was the one staying with Rachel.

"No. But, we *did* find the other box," Sasha said, pulling up a chair.

"Good."

Rachel groaned as she struggled to focus. When she went to talk, she grabbed her throat. It felt as if someone put sandpaper down her throat. Making a motion with her hand, her hand then dropped to the bed.

"I'll tell you what," Delaney said, "what if I try to ask the questions that I think you will want to know? If I don't get them, then I'll give you the pencil. Deal?"

Rachel just nodded, as she laid her head back, closing her eyes.

"What did you do with the box?" Delaney asked.

"Michael took it to Serenity Wells," Josh said. "Then he, Raphael, and Angel disappeared."

Rachel furrowed her brow.

"Raphael is another archangel," Josh explained, with a smile. His sister didn't have to ask most of the questions. She was animated enough that he could figure them out. "It seems that Angel and Liliya were *both* turned into sleepers."

Rachel's eyes widened, as her heart rate sped up.

"Careful, or the nurse will come knock you out again," Delaney warned.

Rachel looked at Josh for answers.

"Mark had Liliya, and Michael said he wasn't going to let Angel out of his sight until Calliope was found," Josh explained.

Just then, Delaney's phone rang. Looking at the number, she handed it to Josh. "It's Serenity."

Josh answered the phone, "G'day. It's Josh."

"Hi, Josh. This is Katia," she said.

"How ya goin', Katia?" Josh said, happy to hear her voice.

"We have taken care of the box. Have you heard anything from the Haven? We tried calling, but we cannot get through."

"You can't get through to the Haven?" Josh said, as his mind started racing. "Have you called the other numbers? Like Mark's or Derek's numbers?"

"I have tried them all. I was beginning to wonder if our phone was broken. That is why I called Delaney."

With a sick feeling in his stomach, Josh groaned. "We need to pray. I have a feeling something bad happened."

Delaney looked up at Josh. "Do you want me to see if Joe knows anything?"

"Yes," Josh said, "I have a feeling things didn't go so well at the Haven."

Chapter 16
Chains Broken

"Well, looks like you'll be heading to chemo tomorrow morning," Kit's doctor said, as he walked into the room. "How you handle that, will determine when you go home."

"I understand," Kit said, appreciatively.

"You're here awful late for a doctor," Nico said, looking at his watch. "Don't you have something better to do than to be in a hospital at eight-thirty at night?"

"Yes, but I have some news for you," Dr. McDougal explained.

"That she's heading to chemo in the morning?" Nico asked.

"I didn't say it was excellent news," he said with a shrug.

"Are you sure I'm ready?" Kit asked.

"You've done amazingly well!"

"Well, I thank my nurse," she said, giving Nico's hand a squeeze, as he was sitting in a chair next to the bed.

Grabbing the other chair, the doctor sat down, next to the bed. Chart in hand, he explained, "I gotta be honest with you. I wasn't sure you would do as well as you're doing. I was extremely concerned."

"So were we," Nico admitted, "but God pulled her through."

"Kit, you're a strong lady," the doctor said in admiration. Then, turning back to Nico, he said, "I also just heard from a doctor friend over in Alice. Your daughter has woken up again."

"How is she?" Kit asked.

"He did a physical on her. She has a long road ahead of her. Some of the things she is battling is weakness in her limbs, and some of her memory is scattered. She hasn't been awake long enough to determine if there are more side effects."

"Thank you for your honesty," Nico said. "We really appreciate it."

"Some people don't appreciate my honesty. They call it rude."

"Remember where ya are, mate," Nico said with a wink. "This is 'Stralia. We don't beat around the bush."

"This is true," the doctor said with a smile. Then he nervously shifted in his seat. "Now for the not so good or even okay news."

"Jesse?" Kit asked, feeling like she was on the verge of tears.

"Jesse," the doctor said with a nod. "He has yet to wake. The longer he takes to wake up, the worse his prognosis will be. He has to either wake very soon, or he may not wake at all."

*   *   *

Deep in the cave, Mark moaned as he struggled to gain consciousness. He knew his girls would need him...if they were still alive.

"Mark, open your eyes," Michael said, as he, Raphael, and the other two angels strained to keep the debris from crushing the trio.

"What happened?" Mark asked. The ringing in his ears was only overpowered by the intense pressure on his chest. "Did we die?"

"No. I told you that you would not die today," Michael said, and then groaned. "We need you all three to wake, so we can get out of here. If any of us move, the debris will crush you."

"What if Ariel takes them out one at a time?" Raphael suggested, referring to the angel just under Michael.

"Ariel?" Michael asked.

"Consider it done," Ariel said, and disappeared. When she returned, she grabbed Angel, and then Mark, followed by Liliya. Once she disappeared with Liliya, the other three disappeared as well, and the debris cascaded into the opening, immediately filling it with rock and dirt. The amount of dust and dirt alone kicked up would have suffocated a human. The rock and stone would certainly have crushed them if the explosion didn't vaporize them, but the angels saved the trio.

Appearing right next to the three, Michael knelt down next to Mark, and asked, "What is injured?"

"I don't know," Mark moaned. Then, almost at a yell, he said, "I can barely hear you. My chest hurts, and it's hard to concentrate. I know this feeling. I experienced it in Iraq. Didn't like it then…certainly don't like it now!"

"Raphael, go to the Haven and see how the others are," Michael ordered. Then, as Raphael disappeared, Michael began ordering the other two angels in caring for Liliya and Angel.

*   *   *

Appearing on the deck of the Haven, Raphael was surprised to find the home still standing. Stepping through the sliding glass door, since none of the windows or glass remained after the blast, he stepped over the threshold crushing a pile of glass.

Inside the house, the furniture was tossed about, along with any other belongings. It looked as if the house was ransacked, but Raphael knew it was worse. It sustained major damage from the blast.

Heart racing, Raphael asked the Lord. "Please let me find them alive?"

Stepping over chair and table pieces, books, food, broken dishes, etcetera, in the kitchen, Raphael made his way through the disaster zone that had become the Haven. Finally arriving at the door of the basement…well, the threshold of the door anyway, Raphael took a deep breath. The door to the basement was splintered into pieces under Raphael's feet as he stepped onto the stairs.

There were no lights, and it was around three-thirty in the morning, so it was dark outside. Raphael could hear the sirens in the distance as he took each step, otherwise it was eerily quiet. Not knowing how much time they had until the emergency services arrived, he quickly maneuvered down the stairs. Some were missing, but there were enough stairs for him to get to those in the basement.

Once down there, he pulled out his sword from its sheath, and closed his eyes. It began to glow, getting stronger by the minute. Using it as light, he looked around. They were all unconscious, not moving at all.

Raphael knelt next to Raphe and touched his neck. It was a good strong pulse, much to his relief. He moved from person to person, checking for a pulse. Grateful to find one in everyone to that point, he reached for Allie's neck.

His heart skipped a beat. "No. Please, no, Lord!" Raphael's heart broke. Leaning down he listened to her chest. Feeling Casey stir next to him, he said, "Casey, if you're awake, your little girl needs you."

Casey shook her head to clear it. She could barely hear what Raphael said. "What's-what's wrong?" Casey asked.

Then groaned, as pain shot through her body. Lying back on the ground, she only moved her head toward Raphael. "What is it?"

Raphael pointed to Allie's lifeless body, with tears on his cheeks.

Casey's paramedic training kicked back into gear, and she rolled over and got off the ground, immediately starting CPR. As she did, Raphael laid his hands on Allie's head. Closing his eyes, he spoke to the Lord with his heart, pleading for the life of the young one.

"Please, God! Please help her!" Casey said, doing compressions, before breathing into Allie's mouth. "Come on, Allie! You can't leave us!"

Casey continued the CPR, while Raphael soaked in the peace of the Lord. As he did, he, himself, glowed. Resting his head on Allie's forehead, he continued to pray. Suddenly, he let out a yell and looked toward the Heavens. "Save her!" he shouted.

Hands shaking, Casey continued the compressions on Allie's little body. "Please, God! Please!"

Allie suddenly gasped. As she took a deep breath of air in, Casey let out a sigh of relief.

"Thank you, Lord!" she said, and picked up Allie, cradling her in her arms. Kissing the top of Allie's head, she kept saying, "Thank you, Lord! Thank you! Thank you, Lord! Thank you!"

Raphael, weak from everything he experienced, moved to Callie. He was relieved to feel a pulse in her. Looking to Casey, he said, "Everyone is alive. Help is coming."

"What's wrong?" Casey asked, cocking her head to the side. "You don't look so good."

"It has been a long, hard day. I need to return to the Lord's presence. I will send others here to help," he said, and immediately shot up like a streak of light into the darkness.

Within minutes, several streaks of light shot into the basement. Various angels positioned themselves near those in the basement. Chief licked Jerrod's arm, before dropping his head on Jerrod's shoulder. Charm licked Cori's face. She was delighted when Cori actually opened her eyes. Tail wagging, Charm licked Cori's face and neck.

As each one woke, they experienced the same vicious ringing in their ears. To hear each other, they had to yell. With only some concussion wounds, they otherwise fared well. They did much better than any of the equipment in the cyber cave, or belongings in the house itself.

As the firemen ran into the house, the angels disappeared. Casey and Jerrod called for help for all in the basement.

Once the firemen made their way downstairs, they knew they would be okay.

*   *   *

"We need to get you near the house, so the firemen can find you," Michael told Mark.

"Are the girls okay?" Mark yelled over the ringing in his ears.

"They will be," Michael assured him. "I will have two angels on Liliya until Calliope is found."

"Thank you," Mark said, appreciatively.

"I will take Angel with me. She is in the most danger at this point. You stay on top of Liliya until Calliope is found."

"Understood," Mark said, holding Liliya in his arms.

Resting one hand on Mark, who held Liliya, and his other hand on Angel, the tiny group disappeared from their position in the middle of the high desert. When they reappeared, they were near the boulder.

"Care for her. I will watch over Angel," Michael promised.

Mark only nodded in response.

Without warning, Angel and Michael disappeared. That's when Mark saw in the distance, running from the front of the house, were several firemen. He called out for help. As soon as the firemen reached Mark and Liliya, he knew they would be okay. His only prayer was that Calliope would be found quickly, or he feared he would never see Angel again.

*   *   *

"Your turn, friend," Joe said to Jesse. "Rachel's not doing too well. She could really use the encouragement."

"You should see her," Delaney said, shaking her head. "I had to step out. She was struggling to remember the simplest thing, yet could recall a lot about each of us. She can barely keep her hands and arms up. She's so weak. She really has no idea what happened after the mountain blew. She doesn't even know Jesse's still in this state."

"Ya hear that, bud?" Joe said to Jesse. "Your lady needs you."

"What did the doctors say?" Sasha asked, as he, Jacob, and Spencer walked in, leaving only Josh with Rachel.

"That it's up to him," Joe explained. "Has anyone been able to get ahold of the Haven yet?"

"No," Jacob said. "That scares me...especially after Rachel's dream."

"Where's a blasted angel when you need him?" Joe asked. As soon as he said that, Ariel, one of the angels from the explosion with Mark, appeared. "Well, *that* was convenient. Should have asked for that sooner."

"I have been sent with a message," Ariel explained.

"Well, you may want to say it fast, before you're caught," Delaney said, glancing out at the nurse's station through the window. "People have been in and out of here all day."

"Fear not," Ariel said. "Your friends and family at the Haven are a little bruised and battered, but are okay. There was an explosion, but the angels around the Haven took most of the concussion wave. The Haven still stands. The people are being taken to the hospital to be checked out, but will be fine with time."

"And, Kit?" Delaney asked. When everyone looked at her, she defended herself, "We're getting answers, yeah?"

"Agreed," Joe said. Then he turned to Ariel, and asked, "What's Kit's status?"

"She will be fine, in time. She is getting stronger each day."

"So, she'll beat this?" Jacob asked.

"Yes. She will be fine in time."

"Rachel?" Joe asked.

Ariel's shoulders dropped. "She has sustained permanent damage."

Delaney gulped before she squeaked out, "An-and Jesse?"

Ariel looked down at Jesse. Touching his ankle, she began to glow. "Wake now," Ariel said, as she glowed brighter. "It is time to wake, young one."

Jesse moved his head side-to-side, as he let out a moan. Delaney jumped up in excitement. Grabbing his hand, she said, "Jesse! Are you in there?"

Jesse's eyes fluttered open. Taking in the environment around him, his mind was suddenly overflowing with memories of the trek out to the mountain. Seeing Parri get torn apart by the demons after being lured in by the Sirens, his memories then moved to the battle, right before visions of the explosions happening all over the mountain collided at the same time in his mind! Grabbing his head, he shut his eyes.

Seeing his heart monitor take off, Jacob got up near Jesse's head, and said near his ear, "Don't freak out. Rachel needs you, brother. You need to get control of yourself, so you can help her. Focus on one memory at a time until you get control of them. You can do this. Rachel needs her man."

Jesse took a few deep breaths, as the world swirled around him. *Rachel needed his help. Jacob said that she needed him. What happened to Rachel? What about everyone else who wasn't in the room?* Jesse took a few more moments before he opened his eyes again, and looked at those in the room with him.

Delaney turned to Ariel…to find that she disappeared. "Where'd she go?"

"She must have left during the commotion," Sasha said. "I was looking at Jesse."

"Jesse, man," Joe said, "Rachel's in rough shape. It will brighten her day if you could at least write her a note?" He held up a pen and small tablet. This would also help them determine what shape Jesse was in as well.

Jesse grabbed the pen. At first, he had a little trouble negotiating the pen. Then he grunted in frustration. Taking a calm breath of air, he focused on the piece of paper. He used the pen, and wrote, *'Tell her that I love her. Tell her that we need to take our turn. She should know what that means.'*

"Done," Joe said, standing and leaving the room.

As he headed to Rachel's room, he knew he would be bringing good news. His worry was if he could hide his concern for Rachel when he saw her. Resting his hand on the door, he said a small prayer before he walked into the room.

Rachel was sitting up in bed. When he walked in, she smiled, and tapped the side of her bed.

"I have some news for y'all," Joe said, holding up the paper.

"Have a seat and spill it," Josh said. "We could use some good news."

"Well, some is good. Some is questionable," Joe admitted.

"Spill it," Josh said again.

Sitting on the chair to the side of Rachel's bed, he first read the note from Jesse. When he finished, he said, "He's very concerned for you, but at least has his eyes open."

"P-praise God!" Rachel said, relieved, her arms still resting on her lap.

"So, would you care t' tell me what taking your turn is referring to?" Josh asked.

"Marriage."

Taken aback, Josh asked, "Is he asking to marry you?"

"No. He is s-saying we n-need t' get better, so we can t-take our turn."

"As long as he knows he needs t' ask Dad before he asks you, I'm good," Josh said. Rachel reached over and tapped Josh's hand, letting him know that she understood.

"So, more news?" Joe asked. When Rachel nodded, Joe explained, "Seems we had a visit from an angel. She said that in time, your mom will be fine. She said she will get stronger day by day."

"Bonzer!" Josh exclaimed with a grin. "Anymore?"

"Yes. We know the reason why we can't get ahold of the Haven."

"Which is?" Josh asked, impatiently.

"Well, it seems the bomb went off." As soon as Joe said that, Rachel gasped. "I know, but the angel said that the Haven still stands. She said the heavenly angels took the brunt of the explosion. She also said everyone will be okay. They're a little bruised and battered, but okay."

"Crikey! Any more news?" Josh asked, leaning back in his chair, not sure if he wanted to hear anymore after that one.

"Well, have you told her about the other box yet?"

Rachel snapped her head in Josh's direction and crossed her arms.

"All right. All right. I surrender," Josh said with a chuckle, as he put his hands in the air. "When we were at the mountain looking for Calliope, we found the other side's box. Val and Katia were in charge of hiding it."

Rachel looked back to Joe for more information.

"That's all I got," Joe said, hands in the air. "I'm out of news."

Rachel pointed to the note, and then moved her fingers, asking for more information.

"I don't have any. He wrote this, and I brought it right over."

Rachel leaned over to grab the pen and paper. When she did, she froze and dropped the pen. Suddenly, she gasped, her body dropped to the bed and began to jolt.

"Get the nurse!" Josh yelled, as her eyes rolled to the back of her head and her body convulsed.

Joe ran out and got the nurse. He didn't want to go back in, so he hung out in the hall to make sure she was okay. Shaken by what he saw, he slid down the wall to the ground and prayed for Rachel once again.

It took a few moments, but Josh finally came out. Leaning against the wall, Josh shoved his hands in his pockets. Looking toward the Heavens, he struggled to control his tears.

Joe stood, bracing for impact.

Taking a deep breath, Josh explained, "She had a seizure. It seems they are also a side effect of a brain hemorrhage."

"Josh, I don't mean to be cruel here, but can she go out in the field like this?" Joe asked.

Josh didn't hesitate. He simply said, "No."

"I need to tell Jesse."

"You will do no such thing!" Josh snapped. When Joe looked at him, he said, "You will stay here and watch my sister. I need to find the archangel...or any angel...and get some answers!"

"You got it," Joe said, as he watched Josh storm out of the hospital.

*   *   *

Ramming the door with his hands, the door instantly gaveway for Josh. Inhaling the fresh air, he closed his eyes to get control over the anger within him.

Looking back to the sky, he lifted a fist and shouted, "Enough! We need to talk!"

Not hearing a response, Josh went over and slumped on a bench. That's when he heard in his mind a still small voice say, *'Why are you downcast, O my soul? Why so disturbed within me? Put your hope in God, for I will yet praise Him, my Savior and my God,'*

Josh looked toward the sky. "I know Your voice," he whispered to the Lord. "I know Your words. What I *don't* know is what the plan is here? Rachel is head of her team. She cannot do that in her current shape. This will affect her for the rest of her life."

'Do not be anxious about anything, but in everything, by prayer and petition, with thanksgiving, present our requests to God. And the peace of God, which transcends all understanding, will guard your hearts and your minds in Christ Jesus.'

"I know Philippians 4:6 and 7. That verse was taught to me as a child. I *also* know the first verse, Psalm 43:5. Look, I know you are trying to comfort me, but I'm really confused, frustrated, and even a bit angry. Every one of the A.N.G.E.L.s made it through alive this time, but we may have still lost a critical one in Rachel. Can she still lead if she cannot be in the field? Have we lost her? And if we did, we could also potentially lose Jesse."

Psalm 91:1-2 crept through his mind, *'He who dwells in the shelter of the Most High will abide in the shadow of the Almighty. I will say to the Lord, "My refuge and my fortress, my God, in whom I trust."'*

"So, this is a lesson in trust?" Josh asked, already knowing the answer.

First Peter 5:6-7 was whispered to his heart, *'Humble yourselves, therefore, under the Mighty Hand of God so that at the proper time, He may exalt you, casting all your anxieties on Him, because He cares for you.'*

Standing, Josh said, "Fine. I trust You. I have *no idea* what You're doing, but I know you have a plan. A verse my Mum drilled into my head was Jeremiah 29:11, which, as you know, says, *'For I know the plans I have for you," declares the Lord, "plans to prosper you and not to harm you, plans to give you a hope and a future.'* I know You got this. I know You have a plan, a hope, and future for Rachel. I also know that, *'An anxious heart weighs a man down, but a kind word cheers him up,'"* he said, quoting Proverbs 12:25. "With Your words, you have eased my soul. I will trust You."

*   *   *

Michael slowly crept into the chemical plant with Angel right behind him. He hadn't let Angel out of his sight, and wouldn't until Calliope was dead. He and Angel followed Calliope and Korax into the plant, hoping to finally end this. He knew that it was two against two, but Angel was at a disadvantage. He also knew the Lord had his back. As an archangel of the Lord God Almighty, he knew his strength was solely in God.

Looking through the metal maze of ladders and catwalks, Michael and Angel maneuvered their way around the massive vats of chemicals toward the direction Calliope and Korax headed. The coolness of the metal and the overpowering chemical smells only added to the tense situation. His concern was also for Angel. *While she was trained, could she handle Korax or Calliope without flashbacks, if needed? Would Calliope trigger her? Was she already programmed to do a task and only needed the execute code? This would be a test for Angel as well.*

As they neared the area where Michael last saw the pair, streaks of light suddenly burst on scene, up on a catwalk. Michael grabbed Angel's hand and disappeared momentarily, reappearing next to Calliope. Michael shoved Angel behind him, as he drew his sword. "Surrender yourself to the Lord God Almighty," Michael demanded.

Calliope crossed her arms, studying Michael. Glancing at the dozen angels around her, she asked, "What happens if I do not do as you request?"

"You will be terminated…with extreme prejudice."

Turning to Korax, she snickered, and then asked, "Does he know how old I am? Does he understand just how many men I have taken from *his Lord*?" she asked, snidely emphasizing the last two words. "He is no Lord of mine! I do not care what He thinks."

Korax did his best to feign confidence. He envied Calliope's ability to do this in the face of deadly circumstances. Fear is how he was ruled. Fear was his instant response.

"Korax, you have nothing left. Do *you* surrender?" Michael asked, as the angels all took a couple steps toward the pair, blocking any form of escape.

Angel moved her hand to the knife on her hip, and pulled it from its sheath. Positioning it correctly in her hand, she kept an eye on Korax. That would be her target. Fighting the visions that wanted to take over, Angel stood firm in her position.

Narrowing his eyes at Angel and Michael, Korax looked from Angel and Michael, to Calliope.

When Korax looked at her, Calliope rolled her eyes. "Seriously?" Calliope asked. "Are you really going to bend to his demands, or better yet, that of his little pet?"

"She is of no concern to you," Michael said, on edge, as he kept his sword in a position to fight if one of them tried to jump at him.

With her back to Michael's, so they wouldn't get taken by surprise, Angel said, "I am most certainly of concern."

"Let me handle this, Angel. Stand your ground."

"Yes, sir," she said, keeping her knife up, not letting Korax out of her sight.

"Do you surrender?" Michael asked Korax.

Shifting to his demon form, he grew in size as well. Korax's scales were no longer blackish-red, but reddish-black. "I have taken over Cassisusssss's position," he hissed, looking at the new color. Transfixed, he turned his hands in front of his eyes. "I have been given his power too!"

"Do you surrender?" Michael asked more assertively.

Looking up at Michael, a low growl started from the center of Korax, boiling up, until Korax let out a yell. Bat-like wings fanned out, as it drew its talons, and jumped toward Angel, shouting, "Never!"

Michael swung his sword, blocking Korax from Angel. As soon as his sword struck Korax, Korax looked down. He dropped to the ground between Michael and Angel. Grabbing his mid-section with one hand, Korax looked up at Angel, and lunged toward her.

Angel looked at it wide-eyed for a brief moment, before her training instinct kicked into gear. As it landed on top of her, talons dug into her shoulders while it pushed her to the ground, Angel jammed her knife into the side of Korax's neck. Black blood immediately cascaded from the wound like a small waterfall, and it dropped onto Angel. Angel kicked it off, just in time to see it burst into flames. As the fire consumed Korax's body, ash rained down through the metal, creating a pile on the ground two stories below.

Angel and Michael both looked to Calliope, to see her back several steps away, watching them intently. For the first time, Angel saw actual fear on Calliope's face.

"Not so cocky anymore?" Angel observed.

Glancing down at the pile of ash for a moment, Calliope's resolve took over, and she stood straighter. If she was going to go down, she would go down fighting. "I am going nowhere!"

Nodding toward one of the other angels, a smile slowly formed on Michael's face. Drawing his sword back up, he inched toward Calliope.

Calliope suspiciously narrowed her eyes. "Why are *you* suddenly so happy?"

For every step he took toward her, she took a step back. The heavenly angels kept her cornered, but allowed her to move back. "You have been a worthy adversary. You are cunning. You are sneaky. You have powers that have led many the wrong way. But, your time is at an end," Michael warned her.

Stopping, Calliope crossed her arms in defiance. Glaring at Michael, she asked, "What makes you think you will beat me?"

"For one, I serve the Lord God Almighty. He does not need me to do this battle, but He is allowing me the honor of winning for Him."

"For Him? Oh, that sounds about right. You do not do anything for yourself. You have always followed Him, and did as you were told."

"Yes. I know my place."

"Your place is to do His bidding?"

"Yes. I choose to follow Him."

"You think this is a wise choice? With all of your strength, skill, and power, you could be in a much higher position."

"I am the archangel of the Lord God Almighty. He is the Omniscient, Omnipresent, Omnipotent, Creator of all. Without Him, there is no one and nothing. He is *the* I Am. There is no better position to be, than in His service." Glancing at the roof, Michael then took one more step forward.

When he did, Calliope mirrored his step, and backed away again, with her hands at the ready. "What are you up to?" she demanded. "You are too calm. And, why are you smiling again?"

"Patience is a skill I have sharpened over the years. In doing so, I have been able to successfully defeat many an opponent. I am smiling, because you did just as I hoped you would. There are very few ways to kill a muse, but I do know one," he said, eyes twinkling. As he did, he looked toward the ceiling again.

Calliope looked up, just in time to see a liquid get released above her head when the angel pressed the button. It stung instantly when it touched her skin. She felt the piercing pain, while the liquid nitrogen immediately coated her, freezing her body. She let out a scream, which only hastened the chemical penetrating her inner core as it poured down her throat, freezing her from the inside out.

Once she was frozen solid, Michael swung his sword around, with all his might, toward the frozen Calliope. As soon as his sword touch her, she shattered into trillions of little pieces all over the ground.

As Angel stared at the pieces of Calliope, Michael ordered, "Spread the pieces throughout the world. I do not want one piece touching another. I do not want to see her on this planet ever again."

"Yes, sir," came from any number of heavenly angels as they picked up multiple pieces, and then streaked off into the early morning dawn. Continuously popping in and out until the job was completed, the heavenly angels made sure there was not one piece touching another while they scattered them throughout the world.

Meanwhile, Angel went over to Michael and touched his arm. Exhausted, he leaned on the sword as he looked at her. "Yes, my little A.N.G.E.L., what can I do for you?"

"I just wanted to thank you," she said. Moving in front of him, she explained, "I know I can be a pain in the behind. And, I also know I sometimes forget, since you have such a gracious heart and *such* an immense amount of patience, just how powerful you really are as an archangel of the Lord. Thank you for protecting me. Thank you for being hard on me. Thank you most of all, for allowing me to continue to be one of the A.N.G.E.L.s."

"You are most welcome. Thank you for answering the call."

"Michael? May I call you Michael?"

He nodded. "Michael, or archangel, will suffice."

"Okay, Michael, I just want to say that I am content to just be one of the A.N.G.E.L.s. The others are right. I don't know that I am leadership material. Rachel is *so* much better at that than I am. The only thing I keep proving is just how selfish I can be. To be on the team is more than enough for me. Thank you."

"Thank *you*," Michael said, relieved. "You have finally learned your most valuable lesson. You have set your pride aside, and are willing to be a team player. I will be adjusting the structure of the units. I will explain this once the teams are brought back together."

"Fair enough," Angel said. Turning to see the angels pick up the last pieces of Calliope, Angel said, "I'm just glad it's over. Well, at least this part is over."

"Me too. Cassius, Korax, and Calliope are gone. Jacki is gone. Who knows who the next one will be?"

"Yikes. That *is* the question," Angel agreed.

"Until then, we have some rebuilding to do," Michael continued. "Both boxes are now in our possession. The balance of power has finally shifted in our direction. As we clean up, the other side will continue to build their forces as well. Right now, there is a power vacuum. We will have to wait and see who steps up from that side. Until then, we will praise the Lord in the peace."

Angel smiled. "Amen!"

"Sir!" an angel shouted, as it streaked into the warehouse, landing next to Michael. "Sir! There is a situation you need to be aware of."

"What is that?" Michael asked Ariel.

"I have been sent to tell you about one of the A.N.G.E.L.s. Her name is Rachel."

Angel gasped, as the color drained from her face. "This can't be good."

"I am afraid there are some side effects to the injuries she sustained. Also, her brother is in crisis mode. The Lord stabilized him, but he is struggling. The Lord would like you to speak with him regarding this matter."

"And, Jesse? What's his status?" Angel asked.

"He is currently awake. Our bigger concern is Rachel, sir," the angel said, turning back to Michael. "You must go there right away."

Sighing, Michael grabbed Angel's hand, and they disappeared into the morning light, only to reappear behind the hospital, out of any camera view.

Reappearing in street clothing and a coat, Michael and Angel made their way into the hospital, up to Rachel's room. Seeing Joe still hanging out outside the room, Michael asked, "Why are you not in the room?"

Looking up at him with tears in his eyes, Joe explained, "Because I just witnessed her having a seizure. She used to be strong and confident. Now she has scattered memories, minimal use of her limbs, limited use of her voice, and now has seizures added to the list." An overwhelming feeling of anger suddenly erupted from Joe, as he asked, "Why would God let this happen?"

Michael took a deep breath. He expected this from Josh, but not from Joe.

"Seriously! As His A.N.G.E.L.s, I would expect a certain level of protection. We can't do our jobs if we are potentially going to get killed or disabled every single time we leave the Haven. Well, what's *left* of the Haven anyway," Joe snapped.

"What do you mean by what's left of the Haven?" Angel asked. "I thought the heavenly angels stopped anyone from being harmed?"

"They are not harmed beyond repair," Michael corrected. "Neither is the home." Looking back to Joe, Michael's heart broke. Joe looked beat up on the inside. Michael knew he would need to tread carefully. "Joe, you have a tender heart," Michael started.

"This is *not* answering my questions," Joe said, wiping the tears off his cheeks. "I also hate that I cry when I'm angry!"

Leaning on the wall next to Joe, Michael shoved his hands in his pockets. Obviously, Joe was too angry to listen, so Michael would let him yell until he was ready to hear the Lord's voice.

Angel, on the other hand, wasn't having it. "Joe, you shouldn't be yelling at him," she said.

"That's *rich* coming from you!" Joe shot, wiping the tears from his face. "You yell at him *and* Raphael all the time!"

Glancing at Michael before she looked back to Joe, she said, "You're right. I was wrong. I was reminded today of Whom we serve, and where our loyalties should be. I understand so much more through all of this."

"I applaud your revelations, but some of us are still upset," Josh said, coming out of the room, leaving the nurse in the room with Rachel. Closing the door as he moved out into the hall, Josh said, "I assume you were sent partially because of me?"

"Mostly because of Rachel. I am aware of the temperament of the group as well," Michael acknowledged.

"How is she going to lead in the shape she is in?" Josh demanded. "She can't pull the skin off a custard! How's she supposed to work in the field?"

"She will remain at the Haven until she is strong enough."

"*If* she gets strong enough," Josh corrected. "She is in *really* bad shape! You haven't seen her. Jesse still needs to see her as well. He's barely awake himself."

"I am fully aware of the mental and physical state of my A.N.G.E.L.s. Raphael is on his way to the station right now, with some fellow angels, to protect the station. Ariel is taking a group to the hospital to be with those from the Haven. I am here with you all to look after and protect you, while we work some things out."

"I appreciate that. How about you do the little thing you do, and make her all better now? *That* is the *only* way you will work things out with us. While you do that," Josh said, "make sure to fix Jesse while you're at it. Hey, why not have your buddy, Raphael, fix Jon since he'll be right there? That *is* what you do, right? You fix things?"

"My patience is running thin," Michael warned. "I have had an extremely rough day. Please be more respectful to whom you speak."

"Josh, you *really* need to not talk to him that way," Angel said. "You don't understand what all he's done today."

"All I know is the position my sister and your brothers are in," Josh said, all the emotions finally catching up with him. Holding back the tears, he explained, "All I know, is that my sister is half the woman she was before that mountain blew pretty much in her face. All I know is that Jesse's status is complicated, and that before she passed out, Rachel saved Jon's life. And the kicker?" Josh chuckled, before he fought the tears back again, "The best part of that is that she doesn't even remember! She can't remember half of what happened to her since that day! I don't even *want* to know what the Haven crew went through today! We are spread so thin, covering way too many assignments, while having those multiple assignments occur halfway across the world from each other. We're breaking, dude!" Josh said. "Hate to break it to you, but us…here…we're human!"

"I understand that," Michael said calmly. "I also understand your concern and fear for your sister and Jesse. You have to understand all that we did to protect those at the Haven."

"Not to mention taking out Korax and Calliope today," Angel jumped in. "That was intense! And, they face this every day. He, Raphael, and two other angels basically stood in the center of that blast, protecting me, my dad, and Liliya. That was no small feat! Seeing the shape the Haven was in, knowing we were at the center of the blast, I am honestly just grateful to be standing here in front of you right now."

"That's the thing," Josh said. Leaning near her, he explained, "Rachel can't walk right now." When he said that, she looked at him, stunned. "She can barely lift her hands and arms. She just had a major seizure. She can't remember a lot of her past. You have no idea what's on the other side of that door. That woman who helped you at your most dire, is in need herself. She won't ask for any help. She knows you are all needed elsewhere. She'll push through, because that's who Rachel is. She is strong mentally, but at this point, I don't know how much more she can go through. Oh! And, get this!" Josh said to Angel. "This is *all* going on, while my mom has been in the hospital for over a week as well. Her body was shutting down. She was in the critical care unit for several of those days. She's still in the intensive care, but they are going to let her continue her treatment. They're still keeping her in the hospital, though, because they're not sure if she can handle it."

"She will recover in time," Michael said confidently.

"You want us to *not* worry about our mother?" Josh asked. "Honestly?"

"You have much more on your mind," Michael said. "Leave your mother to the Lord."

"We've left *everything* to Him!" Josh snapped. "He calmed me down earlier, but your attitude is not helping me push past it. How about a hand here?"

"I am not to take this away from her. The Lord will not take it from her either. This is a battle she must face. She will get stronger with time."

"The Lord has all this power, and yet He refuses to help one of His A.N.G.E.L.s?" Josh asked, shocked. "Really?"

"This is a lesson for her. He has a plan."

Turning to Angel, Josh said, "Now I understand why you used to get so infuriated with this one!"

"I'm not anymore," Angel explained. "I told him that just before we came here. I realized the lessons God was teaching me through him. Look, I've been in your position."

"Stop right there, cupcake!" Josh said, pointing a finger at her. "You have *never* had a sibling face what she's facing, while your mother is facing death. You have *never* had all this go on, while one of your best friends is lying unconscious in a bed for over a week. You've *never* had all *that* go on, while you knew the rest of your team was about to get blown sky-high!"

"Well, technically most of that is inaccurate. I *do* have a brother who was unconscious for over a week, while the other one had to have his life saved in the field. I *do* have an amazing friend, battling just to function normally. I *did* have my entire family almost blown sky-high! Oh, and I *did* almost have *myself* blown sky-high *with* them. The only thing on that list that isn't directly related to me is the fact that Kit is not my mother. She is family at heart, though. And, that counts! We are *all* in this together, Josh. We are *all* facing the same thing! And, just like you all banded together to help me and Liliya, we will all band together to help Jesse and Rachel…for as long as it takes. We are battered and bruised, but we are God's. We are still alive. We are *still* His A.N.G.E.L.s, and that means something! We'll get through this…together."

"I can't even right now," Josh said, and walked out of the hospital.

"I'll go…" Angel's voice faded, as she pointed to Josh. When Michael nodded, Angel followed Josh out of the hospital, leaving Joe and Michael.

After an awkward moment, Joe looked over at Michael. Then he looked at his back, and asked, "How do you hide your wings? I *know* how big those things are."

Michael watched as Joe went from crying, to chuckling. Cocking his head to the side, Michael asked, "Are you okay?"

Shaking his head, Joe admitted, "I'm losing it. I know. It's been a *very* long week. I honestly don't know whether to laugh or cry."

"I understand," Michael said. "It *has* been a *very* long week!"

Looking back to Michael, Joe asked, "Did you really kill Korax and Calliope?"

"Yes."

"And, Cassius and his minions are all dead?"

"Yes."

"So, we can breathe for a bit while we all recover?"

"No."

"No?" Joe asked, stunned. "Why not?"

"Did you forget, young one, what Ephesians 6:12 has taught you?" Michael asked, surprised.

"No. It says, *'For our struggle is not against flesh and blood, but against the rulers, against the authorities, against the powers of this dark world, and against the spiritual forces of evil in the heavenly realms.'*"

"Exactly! If you let your guard down, even for a minute, that is where you will fall. Your main adversary is not Cassius, Korax, or Calliope…it is Lucifer. Lucifer has had many years to study you. He is a cunning adversary, who knows precisely where to strike. Do not think for a moment, just because *you* want a break, that he will give you one. There is no 'time out' with this enemy. You must put on the *full* armor of God each day, my young friend. Now, I *will* do my best to help in any way I can, but I am unable to do everything and be everywhere.

That is only the Lord's ability. He also has a plan. Trust Him. No matter what this looks like…trust Him."

"Yes, sir," Joe said.

Resting his hands on Joe's shoulders, as he stood in front of him, Michael said, "Joseph, you have been through so much in your young life. You have a family in the A.N.G.E.L.s. They are a stable family in the Lord. They will protect and fight for you, just as you will for them. This is not the end of the battles, only the beginning. You will be able to rest when you get to Heaven. As you have seen today, there have been many battles won, many chains broken. Kit has broken free of that which tried to kill her from the inside. Angel has finally broken free of the chains of pride, selfishness, and learned humility in the process. Liliya and Angel have been broken free from the chains that Calliope bound them with when she had them. You are *all* strong leaders. You have already helped so many in your short time. Know that you will help many more before you will be called home to Heaven. Until then, fight to free those from the chains of this world. Fight to bring glory to His name. Fight for your family."

Chapter 17
Two Years Later

Rachel sat down at her desk, and pulled her journal from the drawer. Here, in the office the A.N.G.E.L.s built for her off the cyber cave in the basement, is where she found her peace and quiet. Resting her hand on her pregnant belly, she knew it wouldn't be too much longer where she would have peace. Soon, her days will be filled with the chaos of the A.N.G.E.L.s at the Haven, and in the field, as Overwatch, and her and Jesse's newest charge, their little one.

"Won't be long now, little Charles Nicolas," Rachel said rubbing her belly as the baby kicked, and then stretched, sticking a foot in her rib, as he pushed on her diaphragm. "Could you take it a little easy on your Mum?"

Once he settled, she opened her journal to the next available page, and started writing about her memories from the past few years. There was so much change, she wanted to document it all. She periodically did this in order to never forget what the years taught her.

Rachel and Jesse got married a year after the mountain blew. It was a beautiful ceremony at Serenity Wells Station that took place just as the sun rose. To Rachel and Jesse, while it signified a new day, in their lives, it would also signify their new life together. All of the clansmen and their families were in attendance. All of the current A.N.G.E.L.s, along with those who were now retired showed up. Even some of the Heavenly angels, along with Michael and Raphael were joined in attendance by the three stations. And, as the icing on the cake, Leah was able to be Rachel's matron of honor – even though she was almost six months pregnant herself! The bride's maids were Angel, Delaney, Cori, Hiro, Katia, and Liliya, with Allie and Callie as the flower girls. Meanwhile, Jon, of course, was Jesse's best man, with Sasha, Jacob, Josh, Joe, Jerrod, and Kai as groomsmen. The rings were brought up by Allie and Callie. Each girl had one ring.

The three stations enjoyed a peaceful morning ceremony, and then they celebrated way into the night! There were many reasons to celebrate. The wedding was, of course, first and foremost. There was also, Kit. She was finally starting to grow stronger, to the point that while she took it easy, she didn't take a nap on that day. Rachel was thrilled to learn that about five months after her mother went into the hospital, her cancer was in remission. She would have to test each year, but at that point, it hadn't come back yet. Angel was the pleasant surprise of celebration as well. While her initial track record wasn't encouraging, after her day with Michael, she made changes in how she viewed her duties and how she fit within the team. Later that night, Rachel, along with Michael, had the honor of telling Angel that she was promoted back to lead over her team.

There were a few relationships over the past few years that stunned the groups, but somehow seemed to work. There were also some that were solid from the beginning. Angel and Sasha formally started their relationship a month or so after Angel's talk with Michael, and have been growing closer each day.

Meanwhile, Cori and Jacob, and Joe and Delaney continued their relationships as well. Those sets of couples secure from the beginning, were still growing strong. The first surprise relationship, to Rachel, was Josh and Zahra. They looked completely opposite in looks, but shared many interests. They progressively discovered these over the course of the first nine months after the mountain blew, and he finally asked her out a few months ago, and they have been inseparable since. Rachel was excited to finally see her brother happily in love. She didn't think he would ever settle down. Val and Katia were another pair that surprised her. It seems, with their time together on the Station, they bonded. They got closer as the days passed. To Rachel, they were an odd pair. Val was a pacifist, but Katia was a fighter. Val was into holistic medicine, and Katia just refused to take any…unless she was in severe pain and agony. They were an odd pair, but would often be seen laughing at some inside joke between them. Akio and Hiro were a pair that didn't surprise Rachel at all. They were so much alike, it surprised Rachel more that it took them over four months to get together. She figured they would be like Jesse and Rachel – magnets. The last pair surprised everyone! When Liliya turned eighteen, she sparked an interest in Kai. At first, Kai resisted, since there were three years between them, but after Katia gave him her blessing, he finally asked her out. Kai was so quiet, yet Liliya turned into an outgoing, spontaneous young lady! She went into the medical field, and only has one more year to finish her nursing degree. Once through, she would work at a local hospital in Reno, but would also be 'on staff' at the Haven for any medical issues. With Rachel as her tutor, she was passing all of her classes with flying colors!

Then there was Rachel. She and Jesse both had a long haul after the day the mountain blew. She went through vigorous physical therapy, which strengthened her each week, until she was mostly healed. She still struggled with the occasional seizure, or loss of thought, but she was holding her own.

Once she was back to strength, Michael sat the entire group down for a meeting. The meeting was to explain the new structure of the teams. He made Rachel in charge of both teams, as Overwatch, for both field and the cyber cave. She would be stationed at the Haven. Out in the field, Jesse was in charge of the group Rachel was originally in charge of, and Angel was in charge of the other one. Meanwhile, Cori and Kai were both in charge of the cyber cave groups. All of them reported to Rachel, who in turn, would report to Michael. Jerrod was the second in command if Rachel was not available. With her health issues, there were still days where she just didn't have the strength, and needed help. Jerrod had enough experience to fill this slot, and Michael agreed.

Spiritual gifts appeared in those who didn't have any after the mountain blew. As a complete unit, the A.N.G.E.L.s took the time to sharpen those gifts given to them by the Spirit, as well as their physical skills. Missions were either directly given to Rachel via Michael, or through those with gifts. Joe was usually the one to come to Rachel with a mission after he received a vision. She would then send out the teams necessary to complete the mission.

Then there was the Haven. It was a disaster after the explosion in the desert, but the framework was still salvageable. When they rebuilt it, they added an extra wing with rooms for those who had been doubling, and at some points, tripling-up, in rooms. This alleviated some of the arguments and space issues. The other addition was a gym, complete with an area with mats for hand-to-hand training. There was also a gun range, an archery range, and a knife-throwing area segmented off, so as not to bother anyone else in the house when someone wanted to train in those areas. The cyber cave had multiple areas as well. There was the main computer area, which was upgraded. Then there was the area for documents, an area for Spencer to have a lab, and Rachel's office. This allowed everyone to be close, yet have their own space. Having all the gym, lab, and computer areas indoors, allowed for more training opportunity, since weather was no longer a factor. The improvements allowed more flexibility in the functionality of the A.N.G.E.L. units.

Allie and Callie were growing into two beautiful, strong little girls. They finally started their schooling in a private school a few months ago. They agreed to wait until things settled, and Liliya was in college, before going into their school. In their spare time, they convinced Mark to start their training. He works with them at various times through the week. When he is too tired, he has either Jesse, Jon, or Josh teach them. They will be formidable opponents once they reach of age for the Lord! Rachel knew this was why the devil was after them when they were little. He knew they would be strong for the Lord, and would be A.N.G.E.L.s when they got old enough. This was confirmed with the list.

The list. Both boxes were secured within the graves of Katie MacKenna and Nick Locke. They would remain there until the one-hundred-year mark, keeping them sealed, safe, and sound. The A.N.G.E.L.s all knew where they were located, but the list, until the time needed, was held in Mark's safe in his office. Rachel, Jerrod, Mark, Derek, and Michael all had the combination to the safe for when the list would be needed next. Until then, the team would operate with those currently within their ranks.

Finally, last, but certainly not least, was an event that broke Rachel's heart about two months earlier. Charlie was with his clan out in the Outback, when he went hunting one afternoon. Australia is known for having nine of the ten most poisonous snakes in the world…and one of them found Charlie. This was another event that brought the clan and the three stations together in mourning. Pete, since he was married to Victoria, became Chief. He left Serenity Wells to move him and his family with the clan. This opened a spot for the doctor at the station. Pete's son, Joey, had since taken over this position. Pete raised him on learning the family 'recipes' since he was five years old. Since he was only seventeen, Caleb has him stay in the main house. When he turns eighteen, he will have the option of moving into Pete and Victoria's house on the station.

Charlie had such a desire to live life to the fullest. From the point that he first poked his head around the tree at the camp with the Australian and American A.N.G.E.L.s when Casey was attacked, the innocent childlike grin never ceased! His zest for life, was only matched by his passion for God, Jesus, and the Spirit. He didn't just talk the talk, he walked the walk. He taught many, helped even more, and never complained once about the amount of work his duties required. They lost many over the years, but losing Danny Hawke was the one that hit him the hardest. Rachel took solace in the fact that the best friends were together once again, reunited in Heaven. The two strongest Christian influences in her life were her dad and

Charlie. That's why she and Jesse wanted to honor them both in naming their firstborn after them.

All in all, even with the ups and downs, Rachel was proud and excited to be a part of the A.N.G.E.L.s. Never once had she regretted the choice answer the call when it was put before her. It was a wild ride, but one she was grateful to have taken. After all, it led her to her husband.

"Knock-knock," Jesse said, tapping the door as he poked his head in the office.

"C'mon in," Rachel said, finishing up her writing.

Jesse came in, and wrapped his arms around her midsection, resting his hands on her belly. After he kissed her cheek from behind, he asked, "How's the momma-to-be doing today?"

"Good. Charlie's a bit restless today, though."

"Oh, I'm sure it's just because he wants out. Once he does," Jesse said, shifting to the chair next to Rachel's, "he'll have more aunts and uncles than he'll know what to do with."

"Both in blood and in family," Rachel said with a smile. Closing her journal, leaving the pen to mark her place, she turned to Jesse. Tapping her belly, she said, "Only three more weeks!"

"I have to admit that while I'm thrilled he's a healthy little guy, kind of surprised he's not a twin," Jesse said. "Not saying I would trade him for anything in the world! I'm just saying with all the twins around here, I thought sure he would be one as well."

"Who knows? Maybe there'll be a set further down the line." Rachel shrugged. "Until then, we'll love any little one the Lord graces us with, with all our hearts."

Kneeling in front of her, Jesse rested his head on her stomach. "Hello, Charlie. Are you being nice to Mommy today?"

"That's 'Mummy'," Rachel corrected him.

"Well, he may not have that gorgeous accent of yours," Jesse pointed out, as he leaned up, giving Rachel a kiss.

"No, but that doesn't mean he won't learn the ways of the Aussie's," Rachel said, with a twinkle in her eyes.

"Oh, he'll learn a myriad of ways," Jesse chuckled. "We've pretty much got just about every continent, and multitude of cultures represented between the teams. He'll grow up in a unique environment for sure!"

"But, it's an environment that I wouldn't trade for anything," Rachel said on a sigh. Sitting back in her chair, as Jesse leaned against the desk remaining on the floor, Rachel said, "Some of the groups represented in the A.N.G.E.L. units here, and around the world, are filled with people whose countrymen are sworn enemies. However, the bond of the Lord brings us all together. Sometimes that amazes me beyond words!"

"Tell me about it!" Jesse chuckled. "I'm grateful for each one of them, though! I can't believe the people we have helped and run across over the years. And then, there are the accidental A.N.G.E.L.s."

"Accidental A.N.G.E.L.s? Is there such a thing?"

"Well, neither Jacob, nor Jerrod are on the original list. We just acquired them."

"This is true," Rachel said, thinking about it. "I'm glad they stepped up. The chain of events that brought them to us was unique to say the least. They are both brilliant in their own right. Just don't tell Jerrod," she said with a wink, "I like to keep him humble."

Jesse burst out in laughter. "That goes for Jacob, too!"

"I am glad they stepped up, though. There is a lot of work out there for us to do."

"There is, but as a family in Christ, we know that we're never alone, and that someone *will* step up when needed. We all have our own gifts. Even those prayer warriors out there are on Team A.N.G.E.L. without knowing it."

"What do you mean?"

"How many people have prayed for us over the years, without knowing why? Those people prayed us to safety. Just like the various gifts we have, along with the various personalities and skill sets that are on these teams, the Christians of the world are also a part of this, but on a bigger scale. If they knew the true power they held, there could very well be a wave of Christianity that would circle the globe! All of those fellow Christians, whether they know it or not, are on Team A.N.G.E.L. wherever they are located. There are U.S. A.N.G.E.L.s, Canadian A.N.G.E.L.s, Russian A.N.G.E.L.s, English A.N.G.E.L.s, Irish A.N.G.E.L.s, Cuban A.N.G.E.L.s…and the list goes on. They are all A.N.G.E.L.s in their own right."

"This is true. I pray they discover this sooner, rather than later. They will reap vast blessings when they decide to join the team for the Lord."

"Crazy when you think about how we're all linked!"

"No matter where they're from, if they are a brother or sister in Christ, they are a part of the family…*and* the team."

"Totally agree!"

Just then, there was a knock on the door. "C'mon in!" Rachel called out.

Opening the door, Joe only poked his head in, and said, "Rachel, God just gave me an assignment for us."

After Joe explained the assignment, Rachel got the two teams together in the cyber cave so everyone could be present. Once seated, Rachel leaned against Cori's desk as she said, "Guys, we have a big assignment. This will require all of you to use the strengths and skills God gave you. Part of this will take place in Jerusalem, a portion in Egypt, and another portion in Somalia. While I realize those are distinctly different areas, they are all connected. I also realize they aren't the safest of areas at the moment. This will be a volunteer mission," she declared. "While I *could* use all of you, I am making this one optional. You all have a choice to make. And, as I recite the words once said to me by a strong man of God, I ask you to consider your decision. You see, when we took over the A.N.G.E.L.s, Mark English sent us out with a commission. I am going to repeat that commission to you. He said, 'You were all called for a reason. You were called to fight the good fight for the Kingdom. This is not a position that will land you with fame and fortune. You'll never be on television, nor will you be a startling success in the eyes of the world. You will not lead a normal life in this job. You will operate in the shadows, but you will receive blessings beyond measure for what you do. There's a new army rising up all over this world – The Lord's Army. You are all a part of this. Your job is to bring those into this to help others. The Spirit has given you an assignment. You are to free those who are bound in spiritual chains. You will help provide what is needed for those who are His. You will fight some literal battles, as well as spiritual ones. You will literally take on the gates of Hell. I will caution you in this, and I pray you heed my warning. Do *not* underestimate the other side. Don't think for a moment that the mountain was a victory. We may have woken a sleeping giant when we blew up that mountain so long ago. The other side will be waiting around every corner. They will do their best to stop whatever it is that the Lord God Almighty wants you to do. This will be a race for lives, while trying to stay alive yourselves. The rewards will be great, but the cost will be tremendous. There have been many who have paid a portion of the price over the years. There will be many people you will meet along the way. Sometimes you will get there in time to help. Sometimes you will not. Know whatever you choose on this day, there will be no turning back. If you choose to go, you are potentially volunteering for your death. You *will* be marked. Satan would like nothing better than to take you out. He has had a lot of time to study you. He knows you better than you know yourself. Having said all of that, I feel each of you are here for a purpose. I feel you were each brought here for such a time as this. The Kingdom needs you. They need your training and expertise. You have been called. What is your answer?'" Rachel asked the teams.

In unison, without hesitation, all the members of both teams stood, and said, "Here I am, send me."

Luke 10: 2 – "The harvest is plentiful, but the workers are few. Ask the Lord of the harvest, therefore, to send out workers into His harvest field."

Ephesians 6:12 – "For our struggle is not against flesh and blood, but against the rulers, against the authorities, against the powers of this dark world and against the spiritual forces of evil in the heavenly realms."

The books in the Divine Legacy Series –

Connect with CJ – *CJPetersonWrites.com*

9 781952 041198